That'll Teach You!

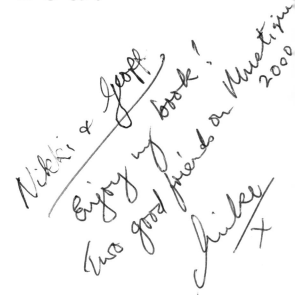

Nikki & Geoff.

Enjoy my book!

Two good friends on Menetime 2000

[signature] x

Michael James

Copyright © Michael James 1999

First published in 1999

Published by Recognition Publishing
PO Box 243, East Molesey, Surrey KT8 0YE

A catalogue record for this title is available from
the British Library

ISBN 0 9537373 0 6

Graphic design and typesetting by
Stuart Nichols Graphic Design

Printed and bound by St Edmundbury Press
Bury St Edmunds, Suffolk IP33 3TU

Dedicated to all family
and friends who stood by me,
and in loving memory
of my brother, Terry.

Chapter 1

His bowed head stuck on the cool, steel door. Sticky hands were pressed against it in a vain attempt to test its permanence.

'Fuck the police'.

It was in his face, etched in the grey paint of the door that he leaned his forehead on. There were others. *'All coppers are arseholes'. 'Death to the pigs'.* Some he read and others he felt from the deep scratches with his tracing forefinger.

For a numb package of time that didn't register, like porridge in his brain, he rocked against the barricade door that had been softly but securely closed on his dazed face and his nagging guts. Finally he pushed himself away and reversed until the backs of his knees were met by the digging edge of a low bench that served as both seat and bed. A necessarily uncomfortable bed for Saturday night inebriates. Fœtal drunks huddled amidst the puddled vomit and the seeping piss.

When he eventually lowered his clutching hands from his face he surveyed the cell with only marginal interest. Behind him natural light managed to penetrate the ice cube wall of translucent glass blocks. It was a bare room, nowhere to hang yourself, but plenty of corners to slash in. However, provided by the Wokingham Constabulary, was a toilet bowl protruding from the wall - no cistern to conceal drugs or other secreted contraband. He used it. Just because it was there, or maybe it was to make a statement. The paper was coarse and he wished he hadn't bothered. His arse was stinging. He hated that. Resuming his pathetic position on the bench he sunk back, deep in thought. The singing of the door hinges bounced him back alert.

'Mr. Stephens, your solicitor's here,' the brusque police officer announced, still swinging on his keys. 'A Mr. Manning. He's right along here.' He motioned, waving a hand at the door of a cell. Inside was a grey-suited, bespectacled man in his thirties, that Mark Stephens knew well on the phone but whose appearance was a little disorientating. No one ever looks like the picture you conjure from their wired voice.

'Mark,' he greeted, rising from his seat and pulling his glasses from his face.

'Robert Manning?'

'Yes. Eventually we meet. Unfortunate circumstances I'm sure you'll agree.' He acknowledged in quick succession as he grabbed Mark's hand with a limp grasp, and promptly sat back down. 'How are you?' he asked without lifting his head and shuffling through a pile of papers on the formica-topped table. 'Been treated okay?' Mark wasn't convinced that the fidgeting man cared. 'You look a bit frail.'

Mark wasn't feeling at all strong. In fact he was fucked, absolutely fucked - and he felt like telling everybody in earshot. 'They came at seven this morning. All of us were still in bed. Couldn't believe they would go through everything; my study, car, kitchen, shed. Took away some papers, Filofax and things. There's a list I signed.'

'Yes. Okay Mark, this is usual.' A little too cold. Mark need-ed more.

'Five of them. Going through all my private stuff.' Mark buried his face in his hands again.

Robert Manning ignored the fragile state of his client. He knew the procedure, knew how to handle everything. He looked around the sterile cell and especially at the doorway and the door wide open. That had to be closed. He checked the corridor outside and pulled the heavy door as tightly closed as he could without the ignominy of locking it.

'Walls have ears,' he whispered into Mark's ear as he sat.

'It's not bloody Russia,' Mark pointed out.

'I know, but you'd be surprised how many police officers are 'just passing' the door when a client is being interviewed by his lawyer. Now, getting down to business. We will be going to an interview room shortly. There will be two officers, probably that awful bitch Baxter, and you and me. We don't know what the charges will be, but we can bet they are based on the allegations the headmaster has. Is there anything else we can expect?'

'What do you mean?'

'Well... do you think they are going to surprise us with any new claims?' Robert Manning tried to be as diplomatic as he could.

Mark fell to the table, elbows first. His hands clasped his swirling head. 'I can't manage this. Don't you realise that only weeks ago I was minding my own business doing my job as best I could, and now... now I'm here with this shit being thrown at me!'

Robert dared a hand on Mark's shoulder. 'Remember this... and don't take it the wrong way. They think that Mark Stephens is a bloody pervert. Yes, a ghoul of a teacher who has been preying on young schoolgirls. Indecent assault, Mark. That's what they want to get you on. They don't see anything else. You may consider them blinkered morons who would believe the Pope was a rapist, but they see themselves as bloody crusaders. They want you to go down for this - guilty or not!' Robert Manning was letting some of his prejudices filter through. 'You may feel you were the best school teacher in the world, whitest of white. All they can see is a damn pædophile.' Robert laid his hand on Mark's head which had now slumped on to his collapsed arms.

It was some minutes before Mark looked up. His eyes were red and the bags under them tinged with purple. 'I think I'm going mad!'

'You ready yet?' WPC Jean Baxter, leaned a smirking head through the door she had silently pushed open.

'No. We need five more minutes,' Robert Manning sharply retorted. She retreated with the wave of an acknowledging hand.

'I'm not sure I can cope with this,' Mark muttered.

'You'll do fine. Just remember there is no answer to any question. You supply your personal details. The rest is a response of 'no comment'. Understood?'

Mark barked back. 'What, you mean I can't defend myself? We both know this is all a load of shit. Let's get it sorted out now. We finish it and I can go home.'

'I'm sorry, but no; definitely no,' urged Robert Manning. 'Don't you realise, we have no idea as to the exact nature of the charges. No way of knowing what line they are going to follow, or what they are about to ask you. We are in the dark. Honestly, I know what you must do, and what you must do is say nothing... for the moment.'

'I foolishly assumed,' Mark began, 'that once you'd arrived we could set about clearing this up, and I could be out of here... and back to school.'

'That, I am afraid, is cloud cuckoo land, old chap,' Robert concluded, pulling his paperwork together and heading for the door. 'Come on let's go. Remember, you make no comment. I'll be there by your side all the time. Chin up.' He dragged at Mark's shoulder and held it against his side, and eased him along the corridor.

The interview room was cramped, rather like a large stock room. WPC Baxter and a dumpy, balding Sergeant Mills sat opposite Mark and Robert as if at a restaurant, in one of those cosy cubicles along the wall. On the black-topped table sat a recording device with room for two tapes. Once everyone was seated WPC Baxter spoke into the machine to explain who was present and what was taking place. Mark was asked to confirm who he was, where he lived and his occupation. Of course they knew all of these. He did, however, verify these details. It all reminded him of a market research session, and he waited for them to ask him what washing powder he used. It was unreal.

WPC Baxter was pleasant enough through this innocuous part of the interview, but Mark could see she was waiting to pounce. 'As Head of English at Thomas Graham School did you know Susan Bennett and Pauline Green?' Jean Baxter spat the question across the table. Mark felt the venom splatter and burn his cheek. Mark knew the girls. Of course he would, they were pupils at this small boarding school. He saw no reason to deny this and was ready to acknowledge they were students there. And he knew what they had said he had done and he held it tight in his stomach. The urge to shout out his innocence was overwhelming and he wanted so much to get to his feet and point his finger and yell into their accusing faces. He gritted his teeth. Robert cut him with his stare, with his hardened eyes and his clenched lips.

Mark was cornered. 'No comment,' he spluttered, choking on the bitter script.

WPC Baxter and the puffing Sergeant Mills swapped snarling glances and then went back to their lines. 'Have you ever kissed or touched, in a sexual manner, either or both these girls?' Their collective gaze stabbed Mark.

If he hadn't heard this before he would have been completely floored by the question. He wanted to hoist a flag above his head which read NO! NO! NO! But he had to sheepishly choke on his denial and merely bleat, 'No comment'.

'Were you having a sexual relationship with Susan Bennett?'

'No comment.'

'Did you touch Susan Bennett in a sexual manner in the Cairo House staff accommodation on March 2nd this year? And both her and Pauline Green on April 20th at the school?'

'No comment.'

'Did you meet Susan Bennett in Wokingham and from there return to her parent's house and kiss and fondle her there? The date was 6th April of this year.'

'No comment.'

Baxter and Mills were struggling to maintain their cool. Mark was displaying all the body language of a gagged hostage. Mills read this. He reached for the recording device and announced the commencement of a short break into the grill at the front and turned it angrily off, muttering something about the time. He ran his forefinger round the inside of his tight collar and loosened his tie. 'Now Mark,' he started, the slime oozing from every word, 'let's be sensible. I can see from your expression that you want to tell us the truth. Clear it all up and go home. Go home to your wife and family. Now that would be best for us all. Wouldn't it, eh? Your solicitor here, wisely or unwisely, has obviously advised you to save your explanation for later. Think on this. We could avoid courts and all the legal maze by straightening all this out, here and now. Wouldn't that be an advantage for everyone?' Sergeant Mills wiped beads of funnelling sweat from his forehead and searched Mark's face for agreement.

'It certainly would,' Mark agreed, just happy to say anything vaguely like a denial, even if it was off the record.

Robert Manning tugged at Mark's arm and closed in with his steel eyes.

'It's all right Robert, I won't say anything,' Mark assured him, allowing something resembling a grin to break his grim face. 'Sorry officer, but it would be stupid to ignore legal advice.'

Sergeant Mills quickly lost his charm and readopted his severe visage. He announced the resumption of the interview as he set the tape trundling again.

'Right Mr. Stephens,' WPC Baxter was ready to play her trump card. 'Do you recognise this envelope?' Her face was gripped with a smugness that Mark wished he could kick. Mark looked at the envelope. It was a brown A4 one that had once been sealed at the end.

'No comment,' Mark barked, showing very little interest in the piece of paper.

Jean Baxter swivelled the envelope over to display a name and address written on the other side.

Mark froze. There lying on the table was Susan Bennett's name and address. And there drilling his incredulous eyes was his handwriting.

The two police officers read his face.

Robert, thrown aware by their reaction, looked sideways at his client. He too saw Mark's dropped-open mouth and frantic eyes.

'Now, do you recognise this envelope Mr. Stephens?' Baxter quizzed; the scent of the quarry obviously filling her nostrils. 'Well do you?' Her eyes expanded as if at the kill.

Mark woke. 'Er... no... comment,' he managed before searching the words on the envelope again.

But Baxter hadn't finished. She thrust her hand into a plastic folder in front of her, and pulled out a piece of white paper. 'How about this then?' she grilled, pushing the paper towards Mark. The smug grin persisted as she told the tape recorder exactly what she had shown Mark.

Mark was still reeling from the sight of the envelope, still racking his brain. He didn't read what was on the paper. His gaze was through it and his buzzing mind on the envelope. But he could see the writing on the white paper swirled and leaned like his. It stuttered in its progress across the paper. Not his hand. And anyway why should it concern him, it was only a scratchy note. But there was his name; an attempt to print *Mark*.

'Well?' urged Baxter.

Mark was still stuck with the envelope; a loaded gun to his head. 'Pardon?' he mumbled.

'This?' She waved it in his face. 'Do you recognise this letter?'

'No!' He didn't mean to say it and was quick enough to add, 'No, no comment.'

Robert physically swayed and clutched his perspiring forehead with slapping fingers.

WPC Baxter and Sergeant Mills exchanged looks of resignation, but continued. 'Your car, it's a Fiesta I believe?' Sergeant Mills asked, without expecting a worthwhile reply. The question was thrown down like a discarded card hand.

Mark knew he had owned a Fiesta XR2, but not now. He

7

wasn't about to boast about being the driver of a V reg. Vauxhall Chevette; bright yellow at that! 'No comment.' He was back in the groove.

The two officers managed a few further questions about previous schools Mark had worked in and his relationship with the pupils, but met by the stonewall response called it a day not long after.

'Interview terminated at 12.27p.m. Suspect following a 'no comment' answer to all questions.' Jean Baxter threw the switch on the recorder, sealed one of the tapes for official use and gave Robert Manning the other copy.

'Can my client go now?' asked a hopeful Robert.

The two officers looked at each other, conferred in whispers and responded. 'No I'm afraid we are going to ask the custody officer to charge him.'

'For what reason? What are the charges?' Robert Manning was angry now. Mark shrank, demoted to a spectator of his own destiny being played out dramatically before him.

'Four charges of indecent assault,' Jean Baxter announced confidently, while stacking papers noisily by tapping their ends on the table. 'Let's go downstairs shall we.'

All four tumbled down the concrete steps led by the chuffed face of WPC Baxter. The custody officer in the charge room was shown the paperwork. He had to decide whether, in his opinion, there was sufficient reason to formally charge Mark. Robert explained every unpleasant procedure. It was, however, a formality.

'Mark Terence Stephens, you are charged that on March 2nd, April 6th and April 20th 1994 you did indecently assault Susan Carol Bennett...' Mark's head sung and his brain baked in a swimming mix of reality and dream. The words lancing his head simply mosquito buzzed and were lost in delirium. '...you did indecently assault Pauline Tania Green. Have you anything to say?

The last few words brought him back. He wanted to be angry, but all he could feel was a sickening swelling in his guts. Four counts of kissing and fondling two fifteen-year-old girls and doing some ridiculous things with his penis. The tabloids would have a field day with this. Mark tried to figure it all out, just as he had when the headmaster had summoned him to his study. How could it have gone this far?

Robert Manning broke Mark's reverie. 'Are we okay for bail?'

The duty sergeant beckoned a response from WPC Baxter. She nodded. 'Unconditional bail,' the custody officer confirmed.

'There is one thing, Mr. Manning,' Baxter started, 'I don't want your client anywhere near that school or those girls. Do you understand? If he attempts to, and we know he's already been back since he was suspended, then we pull him in. Okay?'

'Of course,' Robert concurred. The pig of a woman was getting under his skin, but he had to try to appear professional.

'When we've done the fingerprints and the photograph he can go. He will need to appear at Wokingham Magistrates Court in four weeks time.

'Fingerprints? Photograph? Court?' Mark was muttering inaudibly. They were only words in his head.

Robert sensed the despair. 'They don't have the right to take your photograph. You can refuse.'

Sergeant Mills led Mark along to a room where his fingerprints and palms were smeared with thick black ink and forced unceremoniously onto a record card. Satisfied that the imprints were clear enough, Mark, closely followed by Robert, was moved on to a room where a camera sat on a tripod. And in a corner was a large box filled with assorted letters and numbers. Sergeant Mills proceeded to slide the letters for Mark's name along the top of a metal board.

'Now if you would take a seat this won't take long,' Sergeant Mills declared in a persuasive voice, and completing a rather long number on the lower row of the board he still held.

'Hold on!' Robert interrupted. 'He doesn't have to have that taken. And you know it!' Robert's forefinger stabbed at the

Sergeant's complacent stare.

'If your client refuses to have it taken we will keep him here. Chase him around the room if necessary, until we get our shot.'

'Mark, come here,' Robert Manning summoned. A protective arm held him. 'As I said, you are not required to co-operate with the police on this.' His grip grew firmer and more insistent as he spoke.

'Christ almighty!' exclaimed Mark. 'If they are going to hold me here until they are able to get their snap they can have one of me in my birthday suit!' He could only think about getting away, out of this hell and back home to Alison and the girls. Mark thumped down in the seat facing the camera, held his identity plate against his chest and snarled into the camera that Sergeant Mills bent over in front of him.

'Got it!' Mills jubilantly informed them.

Robert was fuming. He grabbed Mark's arm and yanked him towards the door. 'If there's nothing else we're off!'

'Just a couple of signatures and you can take him away,' WPC Baxter gloated.

Robert had to get back to Rainham and was only able to drop Mark off at the motorway junction. After phoning Alison he sat at the kerbside and waited for her to collect him.

'You all right?' she asked as the car snorted through Weybridge. Of course he wasn't. She knew that, but felt she had to ask.

'Alison... why is this happening to me?' Mark spluttered.

She couldn't reply. He had handed her the story and she was still struggling through the tougher bits to swallow. She had read the headmaster's document and read painfully what the girls had said her husband had done with them. Her tears she had kept to herself. He had his own. The doubts too she protected from him. Mark knew the torment and the nagging questions. And he had heard her private weeping in the night when she thought he was sleeping.

Alison offered a gingerly laid hand to his thigh and a snap

smile. That was enough. 'Do you want to tell me what happened at the police station?'

'Not everything, yet,' he managed. But he did outline much of his experience at the hands of Wokingham police. She wouldn't ask again.

That evening he ushered her to bed early, and he sat in his wine glass trying to make sense of it all. There was no sense. It was an April Fool balloon that should have burst, but instead was inflating grotesquely before his eyes.

Chapter 2

He found it difficult to put a date on it, but he decided that it had probably started in the Summer Term of 1993. There had been a German exchange teacher working at the school. About twenty-four and a striking blond. Mark had overheard her saying she enjoyed a game of tennis, and being the flirt he was he was quick to announce his love of the sport and to offer to 'give her a knock on the school court'. There was only one court in the school grounds, wedged uncomfortably between the school canteen and the girls' boarding house. There had been several occasions when he had played with the attractive German blond, and it had become a regular spectator sport for a group of senior girls whose rooms overlooked the court. It wasn't unusual for there to be an anonymous wolf whistle or a hastily shouted comment about his muscular legs. Mark laughed this off, but stepped in to prevent any more serious mockery or suggestive taunting.

Mark's duties at Thomas Graham School extended beyond being Head of English. He was also a boarding house tutor, which meant he spent two evenings a week and the occasional weekend in a pastoral role in one of the boys' boarding houses, Cairo House. This was a two storey Victorian extension that accommodated around fifty children aged thirteen to sixteen. He was one of a team of teachers who were needed to man the boarding facilities, but he was probably one of the most popular; playing table tennis or table football with the boys whenever he could, much to the annoyance of the senior staff at the school, and in particular Cairo House's prickly housemaster, Vernon Lander. Yes, Mark Stephens wasn't your orthodox schoolmaster, there was more bite to his life, more mischief and a spilling over of enthusiasm for living. Even at forty-eight this voracious appetite for his own mortality had not diminished. A zeal that many middle-aged men hadn't even enjoyed in their teens. Truth was he related on many occasions, far too many, more to the aspirations of the children than those of the staff, and there were those members of staff at senior management level who were actively encouraging him to seek an alternative establishment to teach at. But he knew they were 'tossers' and always would be.

The first actress in the unfolding drama was Clair Hooper, a tarty and rather buxom fifth former who was screwing most of her contemporaries at school, and most of the likely lads in the village where she lived. Mark knew her well. She had been a member of the group he took white-water rafting in the Alps and on the Shakespeare weekend to Stratford-upon-Avon. Then she had been a giggly, generous child who had stuck close to the teachers, and provided valuable assistance and inside knowledge on the locations of the smoking dens.

But now Clair Hooper was out to achieve a major success before she left school in the following June. There being no eligible young male members of staff she was going to strut her stuff in front of 'Old Stephens'.

'He's a laugh, and a bit of a tease, eh? Did you see 'im with that fancy Kraut bird, Fraulein Strummer?' Clair had declared. 'I've got to see him about that fucking Macbeth piece that's a week late. I'll wear that short skirt, eh? What d'you think? Bit of fun, eh?'

The first time Clair Hooper called in at the Cairo House staff office Mark was counselling one of the boys blubbing over being homesick.

'Oh, Mr. Stephens, can I have a word about the character studies in my Macbeth file?' she cheekily asked through the crack of the half-open door.

'Oh, Clair? I'm busy as you can see. Er...' Mark looked at the boy and at his watch and tried to gauge how long it would take to settle him down and ease him back to prep. 'Perhaps if your housemistress allows you, come back in twenty minutes.'

'Right!' Clair chirped, and scuttled off.

The tearful boy was miffed. He knew his malaise had been timed and immediately exploded in a fit of bawling.

When Clair Hooper called back she still held the same cheery grin.

'Now, what can I do for you?' Mark asked, pleased to see a new and sparkling face in the office.

'Well,' she began, 'I don't seem to have understood the significance of the Porter in the play.' Clair stood close to Mark and thrust her folder onto the desk in front of him. Her head stayed near his and he felt the prickle of her flying hair on his face, and detected from such closeness the aroma of cheap perfume. Something you get at a market with nearly a famous label on it.

'Give me room, Clair,' Mark insisted, and lifted his head from the papers spread before him. She pulled back a little and he returned to the folder.

'What you really need to do,' Mark began after giving the poorly written piece a cursory examination, 'is to...' Mark faltered. Clair had now pushed her plumpish thigh against his forearm. He pulled his arm away, certain it was accidental. But when she persisted in pressing as near as possible he was forced to move his chair in a shuffling fashion sideways. Clair was not to be discouraged and followed Mark until he was pressed comically against the wall, with Clair, lips pouted, eyes half-closed and breasts set to buffet the stunned teacher.

'What on earth are you doing?' Mark was compelled to splutter as he stood to prevent her crushing advance.

'I'm sorry Mr. Stephens.' Clair Hooper collapsed against him and gave out an awful howling sound as if in distress. But she was still able to plant her agitated form against Mark. He felt the rolling movement of her supple chest pushing against him.

'That's enough.' Mark pulled away and straightened his clothing. He was in shock. 'Go back to your boarding house now, Clair. Yes, right now!'

'I couldn't help myself,' Clair uttered as she scooped up her folder. She held it flat against her upper body, her legs tight together and her head tilted to face the floor.

'I really like you, Sir,' she sheepishly explained.

'Well, you can't!' Mark replied abruptly. 'Now go!'

'Don't tell them at the house. Not Mrs. Edgerley, Sir, please.'

'Go!' Mark's finger pointed to the door. His voice was harsh and angry. His stomach knotted and his hands visibly ticking.

A rapid succession of raps on the door restarted his stiffened body. A boy's head peered round the door. 'Sir, Fielding is calling me names. Can you come?'

'What?' grunted Mark.

'Bullying it is, Sir. Fielding won't let it go. Just keeps on. Please, Sir!' There was a danger the boy was going to go the same way as most who visited Mark on duty - collapsing in tears.

'Right. I'll see to it, Bunson. Now... you go back to prep. I'll be right there.' Mark fumbled for words to fit the situation.

'You all right, Sir?' Bunson was quick to enquire. The boy had noticed his house tutor was in a state of shock.

'Yes. Please go back now.' Mark was beginning to come out of it, and analysing the nature of what had happened. It wasn't such a big thing after all. Just a silly girl. Some time ago it had happened before. Not quite like that, but they get these ridiculous crushes. He was now brushing it off as nothing important. His immediate task was to give Fielding a good telling-off and to get back to his house duties.

It was ten in the evening when he concluded his duty at Cairo House and fell into the pub near the school where other members of staff gathered. A small cluster of sociable teachers who tried to relax and forget the stress of their job. Mark enjoyed this 'watering hole' where he could unwind in convivial company before heading home to Alison and the girls. He didn't mention what had happened. How Clair Hooper had come on to him. It was a mistake. He would regret keeping it to himself.

In the morning; another school day. Mark had slept on it

and reduced it to a minor incident, and conveniently shoved it well to the back of his priorities that day. There were the termly examinations to prepare, reports to consider and an appraisal interview on the horizon.

By the time Spring Term arrived Mark could hardly recall the matter although he always kept clear of Clair. He was busy organising the school ski trip to Canada. It was only a small party as the cost had deterred many of the pupils who had been on previous trips to Europe.

It wasn't until the group returned, tanned in the thin air of the high Rockies and spilling over with tales of mighty crashes and perilous jumps, and illicit alcohol with girls they had met, that anything else happened. Mark's younger daughter had gone with them as he had negotiated a free place for her. A trouble-free excursion 'thoroughly enjoyed by all who participated' the school magazine would say.

It was a half-term expedition. A tight schedule that threw the bubbling party back to school immediately they returned. To many of the dusty boarders at the school the skiers were seen as returning crusaders. A charisma surrounded their presence in the school community. Well, at least amongst the pupils. The staff weren't as impressed by the mavericks in their midst.

Mark Stephens had led the party. He too was tanned. Not a young cavalier, but an engaging man giving off the wrong signals at the wrong time.

Susan Bennett was on the prowl. This was a deadly female who was beginning a sequence of events that was to have disastrous consequences. She was a loner at the school, except for a close black friend, Pauline Green, who she dominated in a bizarre relationship that would find them hand in hand, and huddled together in some backwater engrossed in whispered intrigue. Susan was the butt of numerous jokes and was universally disliked. Sometimes open hostility greeted her presence. The cry of 'Moose!' would often herald her arrival at a classroom. She would meet such mockery with the snarl of a cornered cat, to which the jubilant boys would respond with jeering laughter. Mark had stepped in several times to prevent the unfortunate girl from being targeted by the vicious, verbal bullies in the top year. An action that probably contributed to what was to follow over the next few weeks.

The school lunches were free to the teaching staff. Mark had the appetite of a horse. 'You going to climb that or eat it?' George in the kitchens would joke when Mark piled his plate high from the self-service hatch in the dining hall. The head-master had encouraged staff members to dine at the pupils' tables and engage in trivial discussion; a move to pursue a car-ing policy at the school. Mark had initially, but reluctantly, plonked himself down at the first convenient table, snapped a 'hello' and proceeded to gorge his immense pile of fodder. But it wasn't long before he escaped from the spilled casserole and the flicked bread, the open mouths spitting food particles near, or even in, his own food. He didn't take much pride in his own table manners, there was often an elbow resting on the table or a spoken word from a crammed mouth, but, the atrocious behaviour he had to witness when he needed to relax was too much. He sought his own sanctuary with like-minded teachers on a corner table where they press-ganged one reasonably behaved child to sit; a gesture to the head's policy. Mark wouldn't hang around to discuss his curriculum or other school matters. He ate and promptly excused himself. He fled to his room where he read, fought with the Telegraph crossword or prepared a lesson. Mostly he did the crossword.

It was just such a lunchtime when Susan Bennett first struck. Mark didn't teach her. He had done so in the past, in her earlier years at the school. Now she was in a lower set and had little to do with him at the school, except for joint excur-sions such as theatre trips.

'Hello!' Susan Bennett's head appeared at the open door of Mark's room.

'Oh, er, hello,' Mark responded, a little thrown by the intru-sion. He looked up from his crossword.

'Do you need any help?' Susan enquired.

'Help? Well I am having trouble with six down.' Mark joked.

'Sorry. I mean around the classroom. Just seeing if I can be helpful. Well us really. Pauline is coming up soon.' Susan had sauntered into the room and was leaning against some of the front row desks.

Mark demanded his own space and was somewhat annoyed at being interrupted. 'Well there isn't anything I need doing.' He regretted being impatient.

Susan appeared to ignore the angst. 'How was the skiing in Canada, Mr. Stephens? Have a lot of fun?'

'Yes; yes it was great in fact.' He replied blind, his head bent over the newspaper.

'You've certainly caught the sun, Sir,' Susan persisted.

'Yes. Now if you don't mind.' Mark stood up to usher Susan out of his classroom.

She seemed determined not to budge and remained lodged against the furniture. 'Do I have to go?'

'Yes, you do!'

Reluctantly Susan Bennett wandered out of the room. Mark heard her greet Pauline Green on the stairs, and amidst whispers and conspiring chuckles they hurried out of the doors on the floor below and spilled out onto the playground.

On the following day Susan Bennett again broke Mark's period allocated to his own amusement, and again she offered to be of assistance. He couldn't understand why she had suddenly become so helpful, but he was pleased that even if it was purely to escape the lunchtime ridicule from the other pupils, she was trying to contribute in a positive manner. He had always thought her a sour thing without an ounce of consideration. It was good to be wrong occasionally. He relented and asked her to sort out some class readers that 3B had dumped as a mountain as they broke for lunch. It was an instruction thrown out from behind his folded paper and given little thought.

Susan Bennett had a different agenda. Rejected by her peers

she desperately sought friendship from adults. And even in the beginning the fondling by her father, when her mother was out shopping, was a form of comfort.

'The girls think you've got really nice legs,' a voice announced from behind a wall of books.

'What? What did you say?' Mark heard the comment, but asked so it could be denied. It had an ominous ring. He searched for her face. She remained hidden, but her voice stung the air again.

'Your muscular legs; quite a sight on the tennis court.' A pair of wide eyes rose above the stack of books. 'You don't mind do you?' Susan's head was now fully visible.

'You girls should concentrate on your studies and not on silly things like people's legs,' Mark insisted in a schoolmasterly manner.

Yes he did have a fine pair of legs; he knew that. But he wasn't going to be told it by this sullen little girl.

Susan took forever to complete the tidying of the books. She didn't say any more, but every time Mark checked on her progress he was met by those searching spaniel eyes. When the bell rang to warn of the impending invasion for afternoon school Susan Bennett slipped from the classroom into the waiting scrum of mumbled conversation with Pauline Green; an island of conspiracy against the flood of scrambling students.

The visits became quite frequent, but Mark did not read the danger signs, didn't know her background, didn't smell the plot, didn't suspect the creeping ambush. He had jobs ready for her to do. She had become quite helpful, but also closer to him. Standing closer. Talking closer. Near to touching. When it came to trying to recall the events that led up to it, he had to really tug it all back, to arrange the succession in his head. It had been a brilliant exercise in worming. In lowering his guard. Making the visits routine. A real insidious manœuvre. And from what was a masquerade of friendship and admiration, came the deceitful dagger. And buried in his back.

When she struck he was at his most disarmed. She sidled up

to him at his desk. She knew he would be immersed in his crossword. Without looking at her he offered, from an out-stretched hand, a list of test papers she could collect and dis-tribute for him. She never moved towards the cupboard. He realised that his monitor was stationary, but only after a few clues had been tutted at and a clockface of letters daubed to untangle an anagram. Mark looked up. Susan Bennett showed him her glistening lips. They were sucked moist and moved before she spoke. Pouting movements as if ready to be furious-ly engaged in an exchange of wetness with his.

'I'm in love with you, Mr. Stephens,' Susan told him. Her face creased with what she thought was an appealing grin. She looked stupid.

Mark froze over his crossword. He wasn't going to budge. The Clair Hooper incident came punching back. He could han-dle it better now. But he wasn't ready to face Susan Bennett for the moment. He sensed her edging nearer. Forced to speak, he ordered her to leave. 'That's bloody ludicrous, Susan! You had better go.' He knew it sounded weak, but even with his com-mand of the language he was finding it difficult to be articu-late.

'But, Mr. Stephens I really do,' she pleaded.

'Out!' Mark rose from the desk and side-stepped her offered hand. 'Out!'

She ran from the room, almost running into the Head of Mathematics, Roger Bale.

'Something wrong old chap?' he enquired, seeing the dis-tressed girl flee. 'That Bennett girl's a queer bit of work isn't she? Giving you trouble?'

'No... it's all right,' Mark assured him, and stumbled back into his seat.

Mark taught all afternoon a succession of mischievous classes. He wasn't on top of it, but bumbled through. When the last straggler had collected his possessions and swung his bag out of the door, Mark slumped exhausted at his desk. Now he could think clearly about the incident at lunchtime with Susan

Bennett. What should he do? Report her actions to Jan Edgerley the housemistress? Consult with his immediate superiors? Dismiss it as nothing, a mere menacing schoolgirl out to capture the attention of a figurehead adult? The more alternatives he considered the more misty the incident. It hadn't been much. A few words uttered; sad words from a sad girl - unintentional. He cleared his things and prepared to drive home. He'd give it more thought along the M3. He didn't. There was an accident in the opposite carriageway with an appalling mangle of lorries and cars and the drone of distant sirens. Mark, like every other motorist, stared at as much carnage as he could see, and for the remainder of the journey could only revisit the haunting scenes on the motorway.

During that evening the Susan Bennett incident was only a fleeting consideration and now only occupying a fraction of his thoughts he had juggled with earlier. It was just one of those schoolgirl things. He would speak to her, manage the matter himself. That was decided. He could get on with more important things like watching the football international on the box.

The following day he was pleased to experience an undisturbed lunch break. No Susan Bennett. However, it didn't last long. She was back the next day.

'I didn't see you yesterday because we were all out. The Geography group. Some daft field-trip to Twyford with old Sankey.' She was back with a vengeance. All smiles as if nothing had occurred.

'Before you say anymore, Susan, you have to listen carefully to me.' Mark waved a finger and his face was lined with seriousness.

On too many occasions he had probably appeared frivolous and this hadn't helped. This present predicament could have in part been the result of his flighty behaviour. Perhaps children saw him as more approachable. 'Stephens is a bit of a laugh.' 'Good bloke old Stephens' etc. It wasn't difficult to appear more accessible than the crusty people that made up the rest of the staff.

'Now, Susan, about that business the other day. I want you to promise to never say that again to me. I let you help out in here.' Mark waved his arm across the room. 'I am a teacher and you are a pupil. I am a middle-aged married man with two lovely daughters and you are a young girl.' He wanted to say 'pleasant' or 'charming' but such adjectives just didn't fit Susan Bennett. 'Do you understand what I am saying, Susan?'

'Yes,' she squirmed. Her shoulders closed in forward and her mouth dropped open. She wanted and waited for him to console her. To put his powerful arms around her collapsing body, pull her in tight to him; to his warm adult body; to feel that protection, that closeness. Something different to her father's closeness and his dirty groping hands. But Mark stood far away. Going nowhere near her dangerous ambush. Susan Bennett sobbed. A strangling cry of despair. Perhaps that would drag him in. She rested her hands on a front desk and repeated the hearty blubbering. She felt her tight skirt pulling smooth around her arse and hitching up to expose more creamy flesh. Surely he couldn't resist. Her father couldn't. She showed him a tearful eye, a twinkling, please-comfort-me, enticing eye. Who wouldn't have her now?

Mark Stephens wouldn't! He waltzed past her and clutched at the door, swinging it wide open. His eyes firm and determined.

Susan Bennett had given it her best. She scurried from the classroom past a startled Roger Bale, and even past the desperate clawing arms of Pauline Green, eager for news of the latest encounter.

That felt good. Mark was pleased. He had flushed it away. No problem now. But, Susan Bennett had a trump card to play. Not yet though. She hadn't been beaten - just a battle lost. She would be quick to lick her wounds. This was a mission and she wasn't going to be deterred that easily.

Mark was astonished when she turned up smiling again the next day. She had called out to him in front of a large group of senior boys; an intimate address. Mark attempted to dilute the significance, expressing disgust to the onlookers by feigning vomiting with the introduction of a forefinger into his gaping mouth. And she had arrived as joyful as ever in his room ten minutes before afternoon school.

'I still love you, Sir. I always will. Nothing can stop me,' she declared and skipped from the classroom.

Mark was incensed. He dragged her back in. She even enjoyed the roughness of his tugging hands. 'Now listen to me!'

'Yes?' she smiled.

'Don't ever come to this class again. Do you hear?'

'Yes,' she mumbled, still smirking.

'Do you think you can understand it this time?' Mark fumed at her belligerent eyes.

'Yes.' It was an agreement, but not convincing.

Susan skipped too contented from the classroom.

Unbelievably, but true to form and recent performances, she turned up again at the door of Mark's room the next day, with her buddy Pauline Green lurking close behind. Mark was ready, hands on his hips. 'Both of you in here!' he bellowed. Pauline tried to hide beneath the stairs. It wasn't to do with her. Mark flushed her out by a further ejecting blast. 'Here, now!'

They stood side by side emitting low giggling sounds and exchanging the occasional impish glance. Mark towered over them. He wasn't tall but he had raised himself to what seemed a greater height; fury had lifted him up.

'Pauline!'

'Yes, Sir?'

'Do you know what your good friend Susan has been up to?'

'Er... what do you mean, sir?' Pauline squeaked.

'What she has been saying to me. All the nonsense about... er... loving me?' He was embarrassed saying it, but quickly regained his angst.

'Sort of,' Pauline conceded.

'And you'll agree this is not only improper, it is a rather idiotic thing to do?'

Pauline gave Susan a wicked sideways look. 'Yes, it is a silly thing for her to do.'

He'd won that one. He turned to Susan. 'Now Susan let's start this all over again.'

'How do you mean?' Susan asked.

'For a start there's no way you are going to be alone with me in this room. If you wish to help out; to genuinely be of assistance, you have to be accompanied. Do you honestly understand that?'

Susan yelped sheepishly, 'Yes, Mr. Stephens.'

'I'll make sure she does what you say,' Pauline added. She wanted this to be over. Susan had got her penned in there and she was uncomfortable being judged alongside her obsessed friend.

'I certainly hope this is crystal clear.' Mark held his chin in thought. He hoped he had covered everything. 'Right, now, get out!'

The girls bounded out of the room. He couldn't detect any disingenuous laughter as they disappeared through the doors of the Modern Languages Block. He was satisfied, sure that this had done the trick. However, he would back up his action by speaking to the deputy head, Tom Pearson.

Mark Stephens and Tom Pearson were complete opposites. The deputy head was out to bring Mark in line. The Head of English was too cavalier by half for the authoritarian regime that Tom Pearson was trying to establish, and Mark's attitude was seen by Pearson to undermine his 'zero tolerance' policy. Mark regarded Pearson as a 'right dick' at times, and always as a conniving and ruthless bastard. However, there were times like this when he had to be approached. Even the court jester has on occasions some serious business to discuss with the despotic ruler.

Mark caught up with the deputy head as he strode across the school playground. He gripped a bulging folder under his arm and was marching determinedly, head held high.

'Tom!' Mark called, to halt the striding man.

'Ah! Mr. Stephens, just the man I wish to see.' Tom Pearson rose on his toes, a broad, treacherous grin spread across his face and ignited his piercing eyes, lit with purpose.

'I need to...' Mark began, but was cut short by abrupt stabbing words from the dreadful man.

'Lateness, Mr. Stephens!' Tom Pearson enjoyed that opening. 'Yes, lateness. School, as you know, starts at eight forty-five in the morning with our service and assembly. I am well aware of your reluctance to attend this activity, but the headmaster has emphasised the necessity for all staff to be there. I have timed your arrival at about eight fifty-five at the earliest. And last Wednesday.' Pearson flipped through his personal organiser to emphasise the point. 'You nearly knocked down some of the children emerging from the school hall as you rushed past in your car.' Tom Pearson wasn't in the mood to listen, he was giving a sermon, and, even better, it was to his favourite sinner. 'This is a verbal warning Mr. Stephens. You know the disciplinary procedure. Do you wish me to list the stages involved?'

Mark was floored. He hadn't expected an onslaught like that. There needed to be a response, but he couldn't think quick enough to challenge the deputy head now. When he had previously been carpeted Mark had written a rather effective but damning letter that Tom Pearson had run to the headmaster with. Probably he would compose one later. It was a long journey and he knew he was often late. Even shaving with his electric razor and munching what was left of his breakfast as he sped down the motorway didn't save enough time. He was going to have to fight this from a brittle position, and with Pearson out for a kill there would be little pity. The headmaster had asked him to move nearer the school; but he needed the space. A sward of open country separated the drudge of school from his life with Alison and the girls. That barrier was essential.

Well?' Tom Pearson broke his reverie.

'Well, what?' Mark quizzed, unaware Tom Pearson was waiting for a reply.

'Do you wish me to spell out the disciplinary procedure? Or are you well versed in the facets of this statutory regulation?' There was humour in there somewhere, but Tom Pearson delivered it without the hint of jocularity. Mark could, however, detect an element of self-satisfaction in both tone and facial expression.

'No!' Mark was resigned to tackling the deputy head later.

'There was something you wanted to discuss with me?'

Mark had forgotten his original purpose in the midst of the volleys of such a bombardment. For now it didn't matter. 'Never mind,' Mark shrugged. 'Some other time.'

'Have it your own way, Mr. Stephens.' Tom Pearson set off. He beamed as he paraded back to his study. It was with immense pleasure that he had been able to admonish his pet aversion, Mark Stephens.

There were only two days before the Easter break and Mark watched the situation carefully. Susan Bennett had been kept at bay. She didn't trouble him again. In fact he didn't see hide or hair of her before he drove off to enjoy three weeks holiday from school. And certainly with all his plans for the break he was determined to give Susan Bennett no thought at all.

Mark first had an inkling that everything wasn't going smoothly when he puffed in from a game of tennis. He was giving a cold beer only a brief glimpse of his throat. There was a note sitting on the worktop in the kitchen. Alison had left it before hitting the shops in Kingston. *Jan Edgerley called from school.*

So?' Mark muttered. He wasn't eager to phone back. He could see no reason why he should be bothered. It was his holiday. A break. He wouldn't return the call.

'Did you see the note?' Alison chirped when she arrived back with half of Kingston packed into a scrummage of plastic bags that she banged down on the table.

'Yes. What did she want?' Mark enquired, but without real interest.

'Didn't say. Sounded a bit odd.' Alison informed him as she hung clothes from displaying hands to the dismay or displeasure of her two daughters Jayne and Anna.

'Odd?'

'Well, I don't know. Just phone her.' Alison didn't much care for most of the staff at the school and indicated so by her short reply and disinterest.

'It's my damned holiday. Why should I be pestered by her? I need to relax.' Mark huffed. He relented and grabbed at the phone and pulled out a sheet containing a list of school numbers.

Mark hung on, listening to the anonymous ringing and still sighing. After a reasonable time he plunged the receiver back down. 'No answer,' he mumbled crossly, and grabbed at the remote control for the television. 'Now where's the golf?' he asked himself, and tapped out some hopeful numbers on the control. He had attempted the call and Jan Edgerley was obviously out. He wasn't going to try again. 'If it's that urgent she can ring back.' He continued his conversation with himself.

She did ring back. Another call from Jan Edgerley. Mark missed this one also. Jayne left a further note.

'Shit! What does she want?' Mark wasn't happy. It was an intrusion. And she was insistent. Determined to conclude the matter he returned the call immediately. It was a copy of his first call and he was forced to listen to the pleading buzzing of his unanswered enquiry. There was something wrong. The absence of a response triggered his memory. 'I'm sure Jan was off to France this holiday,' he muttered. His finger searched the staff list for a helpful name. Of course, Dave. Dave Patterson, roused from a nap, confirmed his suspicions. Jan Edgerley was out of the country. She had driven off to the Loire Valley; a walking trip with her husband and daughter.

Alarm bells rang. Mark asked Jayne about the call. Apparently the caller was abrupt and unhelpful. She had asked for Mark, and was a little disconcerted by the request for her name. 'She sounded young,' Jayne added. That did it. The next day Mark hung around the house pretending to be busy with some bogus decorating. Every phone call sent him lunging for the telephone. Eventually it came. Alison had just gone out, a forage to Waitrose.

'Hello. Who is it?' Mark demanded. No one spoke. 'Hello? I said hello!'

He was about to slam the receiver down when a mouse of a voice whimpered down the line. Mark froze.

'Hello, Mark. It's me, Susan... Susan Bennett.'

'What! What the hell do you think you are doing? Where did you get this number from? You can't phone me here... you can't phone me! Not at all! Never!'

The diluted voice refused to listen. She was through to him. Speaking to her Mark. 'You don't know how I feel about you. I really want you. I can make you want me.' It was a sickly script from a Mills and Boon novel.

'Stop that now!' Mark banged the receiver down, and stood there hissing through his clenched teeth.

Tom Pearson wasn't in when he tried his number. It was serious now and he needed to report this. All the school numbers he tried rang to an empty house or were mechanically answered by the distorted voices of the residents who had fled the campus in search of some sanity. There was no one to tell. At school it was easy to cope with, but now it had ventured into his nest. His sanctuary where he had his private space with Alison, Jayne and Anna. It shouldn't be there, shouldn't intrude on this confidential part of him. He was public property at work, but in his home he wasn't to be touched. The girl had spoken to his wife. To his daughter. She had called him Mark. What gall! He was still rummaging through the audacity of this invasion and the deviousness of the girl. The phone began ringing at the fringe of his thoughts. He instinctively grabbed at its urgency. To stop it butting in on his churning speculation.

'I love you.' The sickly voice of Susan Bennett slid like slime down the handset. 'Really, I do!' she emphasised.

Mark took hold of it. 'Stop this right now!'

Deaf ears again. 'I want you so much. I want to see you now. Come and see me, please.' She was obsessed. 'I have your address.'

'My address? How?' he blurted. Not his home. How dare she.

'Please?' She had a different script and he was getting nowhere.

'Now... now, Susan, this really has to stop.' Mark knew it needed persuasion. He would have to reason with her. She was a real threat.

'Why?' Susan quizzed. It said more. 'Why should I when I need you, and why not let's get together?' She only understood her desperate emotions. Something driving her to want only him. 'We would be good for each other.' She had read that in a crummy woman's magazine. She wanted it to sound sincere. It didn't.

'I assume your parents are aware of your calls to me?' Mark suggested. Some shock tactics were necessary.

Susan gulped. She hadn't reckoned on that. Her Mark shouldn't have mentioned them. They were out. They were always out. She was usually locked away at boarding school and even when she came back for holidays she was left alone. It wasn't so bad when her mother insisted her father went too. But when her mother went on her own she knew what would happen. Her grip on the handset slipped with perspiration. She could feel his filthy caressing hand on her neck and the snaking hand searching for her breasts, and his tobacco breath against her cheeks, and his short urgent breathing, his thrusting pelvis and his fat fingers peeling up her skirt.

'They don't care!' She exploded down the phone.

'Nonsense,' Mark replied, unaware of the significance of his question.

'Look, I can find your house. I could come over.' Susan

locked on to her original plan.

'You look here,' Mark began, 'you come anywhere near here and you're dead!' He realised he was losing it. 'Look, Susan, you have to understand...' Mark was about to say the same things again. He had repeated it so many times.

'I must see you,' she began the plea again.

'Okay, okay. I will see you.' A dreadful error. 'I want to clear this up for good. How about me coming over to see you and your parents? Discuss the best way to deal with your...' He wanted to say *stupid fucking obsession*. 'To deal with the problem.'

'No... they won't be here. No way!' She was adamant.

'This needs flushing out and away. Where is it you live?'

'Why?'

'I'll come over to somewhere, high profile, a high street in a town. Something like that.' It was a foolish thing to do. Mark didn't give it as much rational thought as he should have.

'Wokingham. That's where I live. Well nearby.'

'Right, Susan, I will em... meet you outside, em...' He was thinking wildly. Giddy, irrational notions. 'Outside Lloyds Bank. There is one is there?'

'I suppose. Why outside there?'

'Well I don't know the place, but I can find a bank. Bound to be in the high street. Remember this is to clear this up for good. Do you understand?'

'Yeah. I reckon I do,' Susan conceded, but she hadn't really given up. He was coming to meet her. This was an opportunity to impress him and she was planning and plotting already.

'I'll have to look it up on the map. Let's say one o'clock outside the bank then. Are you clear on this, Susan?' Mark was trying to detect the pitfalls as he went through the arrangements. He thought he had made the only decision possible. He would have to be hard and cruel to get this girl off his back. It had to be done now. Mark recognised the value of prompt punishment in education. Immediate action was needed here. Any delay meant a deeper and more permanent entrenchment.

Alison was out. He had to play tennis; his mate Norman at four. From the road atlas he reckoned on a forty-five minute journey. He threw all his kit in the car. His only thought was getting this straight with the bloody Bennett girl.

Mark visibly jumped when a voice pleaded in his ear. 'Couldn't give me a lift to Gary's, Dad; could you?' Anna had seen him load the racquets but was giving it the desperate voice. 'I missed the train. There isn't one for over an hour.'

'No!' Mark curtly retorted.

'Okay, only asked,' Anna whimpered.

'Sorry, love, I've got to go somewhere first and then I'm playing tennis.'

'It's only to Shepperton. Wouldn't take more than twenty minutes. Go on!' She showed her sorrowful eyes and pulled at his arm.

'Not possible. I'm going well out of your way.'

'Where? Where are you going?' Anna quizzed.

'Wokingham. Probably never heard of it.' Mark was sure she would reluctantly accept and leave it at that. He plonked himself down in the driver's seat.

But Anna hadn't given up. 'Why are you going there?'

Mark was forced to think quickly. 'Sorry?' The old stalling method. 'I didn't catch your question.' But of course his mind was racing. Anna didn't need to ask again. 'Business... school business.' It should be enough, he thought.

'Look, I'm going to save the fare if you can drop me off. Up the A3 and just over the river and left. Go on, Dad.' Anna was insistent.

Mark gave his watch a quick glance. Gone twelve already. 'I'm sorry dear, I have to be there for one.'

There was only one option left. 'How long are you going to be doing this... er... business?'

'Only about twenty minutes, half an hour. Why?' Mark was nervously checking his watch every few seconds. If only Anna knew what I have to do, she'd let me go, he thought.

Suddenly Anna was at his side. She had jumped into the

passenger seat. 'Right, let's go. I'll come along. You go and do your business and I'll wait in the car for you. You can drop me off on the way back. How about that?'

Negotiations had gone on too long. Anna smiled at her victory, however marginal.

It would be all right. He was running it through his head. Anna would stay in the car. He'd park in an out of the way car park and walk. She wouldn't need to know his business with Susan Bennett.

He would regret not cuddling up to Anna and taking her with him to see Susan Bennett. Should have shown the acid tart that he had a daughter only a year or two older. An attractive, vivacious girl who was his pride and joy. That would have been the best policy. The drab Miss Bennett would have seen some of what she was attempting to destroy. But no, Anna would have wanted to kill her.

Mark didn't have to resort to the atlas that was open ready on the back seat. The road signs were pretty good. And a large welcome notice greeted him as he entered the outskirts of Wokingham. Well not exactly him, as it clearly said *careful drivers*. Car parks were plentiful but he wanted to ensure that his car and Anna were well hidden in an anonymous multi-storey facility.

'Are you going to be okay?' he asked Anna as he opened his door.

'Yeah. But leave the keys, Dad. I want something to listen to.' Anna implored.

Mark had parked on level six of a typically concrete structure near the town centre, and Anna was looking at a solid wall telling her she had been marooned in parking bay 6D.

'Could you direct me to Lloyds Bank?' Mark asked a woman moving slowly behind a wheeled, wicker shopping basket.

'Now which one would you be wanting?' she replied, knowing that the news that there were two would be a further puzzlement.

Mark examined his watch. Five minutes after one. 'Isn't

there one in the centre of town, in the main street perhaps?' he enquired.

'Oh, yes. If you were wanting that one, sir, then you'd need to turn right at them there traffic lights, and it be on your left, down a touch.' She was pleased to talk and pleased to help. One hand gripped tightly on the supporting trolley as she gestured the route with a scrolling hand for Mark.

Susan Bennett was leaning against the wall outside the high street branch of Lloyds Bank. Mark needed a second look to recognise her. The greasy dark hair that was always tied back and smarmed down at school bounced on her shoulders; bare shoulders. A strapless top, possibly borrowed from mother's wardrobe was worn over a short, squeezing skirt. Her blubbery thighs were forced together and threatened to erupt outwards and split the garment. But the striking difference was her face. A sullen, scowling visage had been transformed. Make-up had been applied as if with a trowel and by an unskilled hand. She had slapped it on and sculpted it, to successfully resemble something mid way between a tart and a clown. Her eyes were black and her lips glistened as if varnished; a deep red that stained her cheeks and teeth as well. She waddled up to him on precarious platform shoes. He was overpowered by the stench of cheap perfume.

'You came,' she managed through a sudden bout of embarrassment. Here was the man she wanted. A man of her father's age, without the guilt. She could relate to a man like that.

'I came all right, you silly girl. What I should have done was to turn up with the headmaster and Mr. Pearson, and perhaps Mrs. Edgerley. That would have put paid to your game.' Mark spoke through clenched teeth. Spitting out all his wrath. There were too many tuned-in ears parading the pavement outside the bank. He felt conspicuous. Every eye was on him. Why was that man with the painted schoolgirl? Talking closely? Intimately? He marched her along the street. He was careful not to touch her as he coaxed her forward.

Susan Bennett didn't speak for a while; she was too intent

on searching his face and smiling into his eyes; a comic grin from the puffed, buffoon face lit scarlet by the cracking bow of her lips.

'I have sacrificed a large portion of my holiday, Susan, to stem this ridiculous crush. Believe me, I am not happy about this inconvenience. And those stupid, bloody phone calls.' Mark kept it strict. 'Look at yourself. Don't you feel ludicrous trying to get off with a middle-aged man. Dolling yourself up like a cheap hooker.' His attack was merciless, bombarding her, tearing it all down.

It was turning sour. Not as she had imagined it. He was being so cruel. 'I can't help my feelings,' she muttered, her confidence melting. She smoothed her skirt which was riding up as her strapped thighs struggled to keep up with Mark's longer strides. They were passing shops in a pedestrian precinct. And in the reflecting dark windows Mark was happy that they looked like father and delinquent daughter having the usual domestic disagreement whilst out shopping.

'Your parents would be horrified it they knew what you were up to. What do you think your father would do if he found out? If I told him? Eh?'

Susan's face screwed up. Mark read it as a realisation of a pending disaster. Parents told and the harsh repercussions from this senseless obsession. But it wasn't that. It was the pain of a cold mother, and a father whose only love came as ugly mauling in the dark, airless bedroom. And she cringed at the thought of his clawing hands and the shame of her abused body when her mother returned full of her own day, unaware of the violation; of her pleading face repeatedly slapped into the dribble on her Minnie Mouse pillow as he demonstrated such fatherly affection.

'Now, Susan, when school restarts we change everything. You never, never come near my room on your own. Is that clear? Never on your own!'

They had reached the end of the coarsely cobbled precinct and Mark was lecturing a now dejected girl. A girl festering within. She had planned to win him over. Have him for herself. She imagined such fantasies. Blown apart. He wasn't going to go with her; touch her; pull her to him and hold her firmly against his body, his lips seeking hers and meeting in a lifetime suction exchange. The dream was over. He had talked about her father. She hated her father. He could have protected her from that. Given her the real love she desperately needed. Not the disgusting love of her father, her loving father, her fucking old Dad.

'I asked you if you understood?' Mark repeated to the bowed head of Susan Bennett.

She nodded from down there. He took this as agreement, but she was barging through an alternative itinerary.

Mark left her there.

He felt elated as he turned to retreat to the car. He was triumphal when he arrived back at the car park and Anna, feet up on the dashboard.

'About time,' she huffed.

'Sorry. Didn't think I was long.'

'Perhaps not. I'm just keen to get to Gary's, Dad.'

Mark jumped into the driver's seat, beamed at Anna, turned down the thumping music Anna had tuned into and announced a rapid journey to Shepperton and her love-struck boyfriend. A glimpse at his watch showed that he had only taken about thirty-five minutes to bring order back to his life, and to eradicate a virulent obsession. He could now forget the matter. Susan Bennett had been jettisoned - abandoned and heartbroken.

'Thanks Dad,' Anna shouted as she fled from the car at Gary's house in Shepperton. Gary was such a dick. Mark couldn't understand why she was so excited.

Mark reached the tennis club at about four. Even his game showed some improvement, which was commented on over a quick pint with his old adversary, Norman.

Alison complained about his late arrival for dinner and there was some grumbling about him always playing tennis, but it couldn't shadow his buoyant mood. He even forgot at times why he felt so good.

There was one ominous phone call that perhaps could have been blamed on Susan Bennett, but Mark dismissed it as a wrong number. Nothing else untoward occurred and as usual his holiday dwindled wastefully away. He never managed to finish the bedroom that he promised Alison faithfully he would. The gutter still leaked, the grass never got its second cut, the garage remained a tip and the cars were never relieved of their winter filth.

Summer Term was always the best of a bad bunch. Year Eleven had their GCSE exams and weren't in class much, and Mark had the opportunity to escape the classroom drudge; running out with the children and taking a variety of sports, especially tennis. But if he had known what lay in store Mark would not have been so eager about this particular Summer Term.

It came as a surprise when Susan Bennett and Pauline Green entered his classroom during the first lunchtime. However, they came in bright and boisterous. He liked that. There were smiles and more offers of help. Full of fun. Mark was relieved. The stupid schoolgirl crush thing had been flushed out. He had completed the crossword very quickly. That also pleased him. He spent a few minutes chatting to them before they disappeared to lessons. It was encouraging that he could now resume a routine relationship with the girls and in particular with Susan Bennett whose infatuation was obviously as fickle as her school work.

Most lunch breaks, if he was there, and occasionally when Mark was on duty in the boarding house at a weekend the two girls would pop in and gossip. Mark wasn't averse to a session of tittle-tattle and rumour concerning senior management, as it was a mutual area of despair and hatred for both Mark and the pupils. Mark had a good relationship with most of the kids. He knew that recently this had thrown up some ugly manifestations, but generally he kept the right distance and the children knew the line; kept their side. The two infringements had now been relocated on course. Mark was confident he could manage the border, maintain the boundaries and deal with any incursions. How fragile the gossamer curtain, how delicate the dialogue, as he was soon to discover. He was proud of his achievement in Wokingham during the holiday. Maybe he could do more counselling, perhaps a 'Head of Year' post at another school. But standing alone was perilous. He had chosen not to involve anyone else. Tom Pearson was unapproachable and Jan Edgerley would have escalated it into a major crisis. So he had kept it to himself. Well, seeing how successful he'd been why ever not.

Registration was a chaotic ten minutes every morning. That morning, April 24th, was no exception. There were prep books being scattered and bodies roving around engaging in spontaneous but trivial activity associated with the previous evening's television programmes. Mark was at his desk listening to a woeful tale about a lost textbook when the door exploded open. Even the random groups deep in futile banter were flung aware. Susan Bennett burrowed into the classroom, her head seemingly some distance in front of her whirring legs and trailing body. A cartoon image homing in. She was on him like a swooping harpy before Mark could raise his eyes to her. Susan Bennett spat out all the bottled resentment and venom-fluxed blend of her anger and retribution.

'You are for it! I've really stitched you up!' Her words were bricks chucked violently at his incredulous face. She stood, legs astride, waving her short arms in the air and peering through laser eyes at the teacher. She hadn't finished. 'Wouldn't touch me. Not good enough, eh? But you do it with fucking Clair fucking Hooper, eh? Well now you've had it. Mrs. Edgerley has heard everything!' Her eyes narrowed, her head jerked and her finger stabbed.

'What have you done?' Mark meekly asked. His voice came out thin, and from somewhere in the dazed dome of his sizzling head. But it was too late to reach Susan Bennett. She had turned and bolted. She was out on the landing, hands on hips. And alongside her, with equally menacing eyes, was Pauline Green. And in the background barely daring to look in his direction was the stooping form of Clair Hooper.

The class dismissed itself. Mark was left stranded. There was an extraordinary heat rising through his chest and a numbness encompassing his head.

His first class flooded in and swirled around his foundered body. Even their twittering and fidgeting that usually sparked a raised voice and a gesture to quell the din, went uncontrolled. Mark moved to rest on the radiator by the window. He wasn't conscious of any of his own movements. Outside he saw Jan Edgerley in busy conversation with the Head of PE and erstwhile Geography teacher, Simon Sankey. The pupils choked with bewilderment as Mark leapt out the door, and some even watched from the window as he burst in on the cosy discussion below.

'Jan. I've just had Susan Bennett in my room. You should have seen her. Crazy. It seems that she spoke to you. Something about telling you everything.' Mark was speaking but his drumming voice seemed detached from his mouth. 'What is the *everything* that she told you? What exactly has this girl said?'

Jan Edgerley stared at him as if confronted by the Slime Monster emerging from the Black Lagoon. She took a step back. 'Mark, I can't tell you what has been said.'

'Why not?' Mark enquired, his wild eyes pleading the same question.

Jan Edgerley looked to Simon Sankey for support. 'This matter is, as you are aware, delicate. I am speaking to the headmaster in a few minutes.'

'Aware? I am not aware of anything. All manner of possibilities are haunting me here, Jan. That vicious little girl is up to something. Now tell me what she has said.' Mark was insistent.

Simon Sankey, not really wishing to be involved, reluctantly tried to intervene. 'Come on Mark, leave Jan alone. It's just her job, old chap.'

'You can go fuck yourself!' Mark's frantic eyes met Simon's. Simon Sankey shrivelled back in to his tracksuit.

'Are you trying to get me hanged?' Mark turned to Jan Edgerley and pleaded for a response.

'I'm not telling you anything. The headmaster is the only person I'm speaking to.' Jan Edgerley stormed off.

Mark retreated to his now disorderly classroom. Not that he noticed. Not that he cared. For the rest of the morning he simply went through the motions. Children have a radar for this sort of thing. They all, or at least enough of them, recognised his distress, and busied themselves with what they considered to be useful work. It was about as useful as they would get. Their teacher was a husk of his usual energetic self. Something was very wrong and it was going to detonate. They knew it and buckled up; waiting for the impact.

When the rather heavy form of Mrs. Roberts, Tom Pearson's secretary, lumbered into the room projecting a thunderous face, Mark knew it was time to learn the details of Susan Bennett's dreadful threat. All manner of fiends thrashed through his head.

'The headmaster wishes to see you, Mr. Stephens. He advises you to take along a friend. Apparently that is the procedure.' Mrs. Roberts proclaimed.

In front of him the silent class raised only their eyes. They sparkled. He read their 'good lucks'. They sensed trouble for their favourite teacher, but they were mere pupils and whatever was happening at the teacher level was happening in a different world.

Mark found his buddy, Dave Patterson, behind a pile of exercise books. 'You look like shit, Mark. What's the matter?' Dave peered over his glasses and prodded the space between them with his red biro.

Mark was short of words. 'Dave I need you to come with me.'

'What? Where to?'

'Headmaster's study.'

'It's got that bad has it?' Dave smirked. 'Old Pearson nailed you for being late has he? You really rub that bastard up the wrong way.' Dave found this confrontation amusing and was quick to grab his jacket from the back of the chair.

'Wish it was only that, mate,' Mark managed to utter.

'What? It's not about your punctuality? What on earth have you done now?' Dave was expecting some mischievous misdemeanour.

'I don't know. All I do know is it's bloody awful.'

Dave Patterson finally detected the seriousness of the impending interview.

The headmaster's office was cramped. Mainly because he had tried to accommodate a suite of lounge furniture to promote a more casual atmosphere to his grilling sessions with the staff. It was dingy. On oak-panelled walls morbid 19th Century prints hung alongside a rogues' gallery of previous headmasters, who Mark always imagined were sneering at him. In the room, already positioned, were Tom Pearson fingering his signet ring, the headmaster's secretary, a bulldog of a woman and Ted Frith, headmaster of Thomas Graham G.M. School. Ted Frith sat behind his protective oak desk: a small man with a sour face and reeking with the stench of furtive cigarette smoking. He had tried to quit. But the stress of his job ensured a packet of Benson and Hedges sat permanently in his top drawer, alongside a petite, stained ashtray and leather-clad lighter. An arrangement not dissimilar to an opium den.

'Come on in and take a seat, Mr. Stephens. I see that you have brought Mr. Dennis with you.' The language was quasi-friendly with a hint of apology. The headmaster greeted the two men from a standing position behind his desk. There was no disguising the lingering smoke from his last cigarette. 'Mr. Pearson is here in case I am called away, and he can continue the interview if necessary. Mrs. Peters will take a record of proceedings. Mr. Dennis is here as a friend and to make sure you understand everything that takes place. Is all this clear?'

'Yes.' Mark could manage that. He had never felt so trapped. Even breathing was difficult. He fought to keep his head clear.

'I believe you know why you are here.' Ted Frith didn't give him time to answer. 'Certain girl pupils have made allegations. They concern you. I have to investigate this. The accusations are of a sexual nature and extremely serious, and constitute gross misconduct. I can't give you any more details than that. As a matter of course you are suspended. Hopefully, Mark, this will be for a short while and you'll be back at work within the week.' A smile creased his marble face. Tom Pearson sat unmoved. Mark was sure he was grinning wildly inside his head. 'Do you wish to say anything?' Ted Frith stacked some papers.

Mark was in shock. His whole world was caving in. He sat immobile. Held by the spongy sofa, with the office walls bouncing in on him.

'Have you any questions, Mark?' the headmaster persisted.

Dave Patterson nudged Mark's arm.

'I really can't think at the moment.' Mark rubbed his eyes. 'I'll go home then... you'll contact me when I can return... sorted it out... can't possibly tell Alison. Sorry this is not making sense. Nothing makes sense any more.'

'Mr. Dennis, take Mr. Stephens and escort him off the premises, will you,' the headmaster concluded.

Dave Patterson tugged Mark's arm and lifted him off the couch. He held him until he was sure Mark wouldn't fall. And both men walked off across the playground and towards Dave Patterson' school house. And straight into Dave's whisky bottle.

Dave was trying to deal with his own version of shock and could only prod Mark with a few probing questions. 'What the hell's going on, mate? You were right, it's bloody awful.' He didn't ask the question that was at the top of his choking throat. But both men knew it was lurking.

Mark had to break his groaning silence. 'No! no Dave I

haven't. Not my style. Haven't touched the bloody girls. Fool and jester at times I may be, but I'm not a fucking idiot.'

'Yeah, of course. I knew it. You're not that stupid.' Dave was relieved by Mark's proclamation. With all the tension he was glad that that one had been trodden on and crushed into the dirt.

It was a couple of hours before Mark was ready to leave the house. He'd finished coming to terms with the situation as well as finishing the bottle of scotch.

He drove home unsteadily and painfully played out a normal evening. He'd be back at school very shortly so there was no reason to put Alison through any of the agony.

He was uncomfortable with the charade when he stumbled out of bed at seven forty-five the next morning. It was a wonderful opportunity to sleep in, to stay in that stifling warmth with Alison, a buried head against the daylight and the noise of busying people. There was no real plan. He was dressed as a teacher with no where to teach. When he drove off he had no destination in mind. But he was soon heading for Paul's house. Paul Robertson was a soul-mate. They both shared a wicked sense of humour and blatant disregard for convention, and Mark needed some anarchy desperately.

He opened up at Paul's and everything he had wanted to tell Alison he shared. There were tears that embarrassed both men. There was also laughter and some positive planning.

'What exactly does the school say you have done?' Paul enquired.

'I just don't know as yet. No details were given when I saw the headmaster. Seems he is seeing the girls again and then contacting me.'

'Could be they're going to say you shagged them. Eh?' Paul suggested. 'You didn't, did you?' Paul's eyes lit up with a mixture of mischief and excitement.

'Bollocks!' Mark retorted. 'I know you would! If it wasn't such a serious matter I would be joking about that too.' Mark wasn't able to treat his predicament as lightly as Paul. It would have been fair game for ribald humour normally, but now, for Mark, it was strictly taboo. Despite these moments the day was a great therapy for Mark and by the time he could safely leave Paul's he had decided he could no longer keep Alison in the dark.

He found her in front of the dressing-table mirror giving her mascara a refreshing lick. She always tried to look good. He liked her that way. She smelled of perfume and cream and he stood behind her and stroked her hair. In the mirror his reflection looked at her closing eyes. She sensed the tension from his touch. And his eyes in the mirror were glazed by spilling tears. Mark couldn't hold them back.

'Alison!' That's all he could say. Despairingly loud. His head fell to her shoulder and he wet her clothes. She held him with a firm hand and her eyes widened. It was something serious and she waited. Her mind conjured up all manner of disasters, but not the one that was about to unfold.

'What is it?' She spoke through the sound of him sobbing. Impatient for the reason she pulled him gently off her shoulder and pushed her face in his. 'What on earth is the matter, Mark?' She was reading too many horrors into his hopeless crying. 'Tell me!'

'At school... I haven't been today... I'm suspended.' It came clattering out in no real order. He had so many things to tell her, but all he could manage was a random dip into this mire.

'Why on earth have you been suspended? And what does it mean?' Alison was staggering under the weight her desperate husband had just dropped on her. 'I can't understand what's going on, Mark. What have you done?'

'I've *done* nothing! Apparently some girls have made allegations about me.' Mark knew he had to be stronger. Alison was reeling from all this.

'Girls? Allegations? What sort of allegations?' Alison asked.

'I don't know exactly, but I can imagine the type of thing. Anyway, you don't need to worry. I'm pretty sure this will all be cleared up in no time. It's just some ridiculous tomfoolery that's gone haywire.'

Alison went quiet. She was trying to put it all in order. Find a compartment for it. But it wasn't fitting. Mark was no angel and she had had her doubts in the past about his fidelity in their twenty-six year old relationship. However, he didn't fool about with young girls. He was no pervert. They had two lovely daughters whose friends visited, stayed. There was never any hint of her husband being a threat to them. He was no beast. He wasn't going to suddenly start messing about with his pupils after twenty-five years teaching. It was coming clearer. The mist was clearing. Alison looked up at Mark. She smiled and threw her arms round him.

He knew she was going to be his best ally. They held and fed off each other's warm body and sobbed for a long time. Until Jayne and Anna, looking for them, found their parents clung together. It wasn't so difficult telling them. They were angry but didn't take it seriously. Of course they cuddled him and mumbled their support. It was just some silly misunderstanding and they were certain there was nothing to worry about.

But there was!

Four days later the postman's heavy thud on the door announced the arrival of a plastic bound document sent 'recorded delivery' from the school. It was a rushed copy of the gross misconduct procedure that Mark would have to face and the nature of the allegations against him in the form of interviews conducted by the headmaster with the girls; Susan Bennett, Pauline Green and Clair Hooper. Mark hurried through the laborious records of the interviews. It was like reading a badly written play. Alison heard Mark reading it. She heard the bursts of derisory laughter and she heard the long periods of silence as he read with disbelief what these girls had said. What they had invented in a cul-de-sac of envy. A night when two girls were thrown into a diabolical ambush that would initiate such an inertia, posse supported, that would soar perilously out of control.

Chapter 3

Jan Edgerley's boarding house for girls was quaintly named Octavia House, and it was full of girl noises and activity. The younger ones would run and scream, giggle and whisper, and squeal at the sight of a boy. Whereas the older ones, sufficiently stocked with hormones, huddled in conspiratorial groups showing solemn or threatening faces, and giving sneering, leering peeks from the safety of pow-wow bands at the loitering boy.

Girls in the lower years were herded into long and spartan dormitories, and as they progressed through the school and demanded greater privacy their accommodation became more homely, until in their final year they were housed in quite smart rooms occupied by only a couple of girls. And these rooms shared a common room where they often slobbed around, fingered through trashy magazines or dosed themselves up on television soaps. All manner of gossip was examined over cups of coffee and the occasionally smuggled-in alcohol in this cushion-strewn room. A stale, reeking den.

On that evening before Mark's suspension there was an intense session underway. It involved the brash girls of the boarding house. The girls who had boyfriends, were sexually active and ruled the roost in the boarding house. There was no greater prestigious achievement in Octavia House than to have lost your virginity long ago and to be well practised in bed; and to talk at length about it.

Six girls were relating how to satisfy the sexual demands of their respective boyfriends. They should have been busy completing GCSE course work, but this delicious subject was far too fascinating to be missed. Most were statements of bravado and fiction woven from newspaper articles and sisters' tales.

Fate sent Susan Bennett scuttling down the corridor from the room she shared with Pauline Green to collect some shared science data. She pushed at the common room door. The girls, caught in discussion by the swinging door, jumped to find excuses and fumble with magazines. When they realised that the intrusion wasn't Mrs. Edgerley patrolling the accommodation but merely that weird creature Susan Bennett bursting in on their private discourse, the abuse was hurled.

'Fuck off, you moose!' led Clair Hooper. The rest of the group erupted in laughter. And reoccupied their original seats. Susan Bennett waited by the door. 'Get out you ugly old witch!' Clair Hooper added.

'Hop it. This is girl's talk.' Another voice chipped in.

'Yes.' Clair Hooper stood and rounded on Susan. 'We are talking about sex.' She pushed her face at Susan's. 'You know, something you've never had. Because you are so fucking ugly no one is going to want to fuck you, are they?' There was more sneering and laughter.

'That's right, Bennett. Boys don't want to fuck a hairy moose like you!' This was accompanied by further barked insults.

Clair Hooper held the door to usher Susan Bennett out. Her face was alight. She expected a rapid evacuation. Susan Bennett didn't move. Clair tried a push. It was met with determined resistance.

'Fuck off!' Clair tried again.

Susan Bennett turned her head slowly and faced Clair Hooper with a spreading smile. A smile of defiance. She'd had enough. A seed had been sown and a deadly weed was about to shoot.

'I don't trouble with boys when I've got a man!' announced Susan. 'There's nothing like being fucked by a real man!' She was showing her teeth.

'Yeah! Of course,' Clair Hooper retaliated. Her voice was less self-assured and not quite as dismissive as it should have been. 'Right! Tell us about it then, Bennett!' she challenged.

Susan Bennett had been fucked by a man. That was true. And she could tell all those eager, but despising eyes that faced her, what it was like. She could tell them of the repugnant stench of his alcohol breath, of his ivory white skin that hung loose and stained, and his forcing hands and his violent entry. Of the pain when she was younger, of his lies and promises - just once more, it won't happen again, it's because I love you, it happens in other families, your mother wouldn't understand, just between you and me, you'll be grateful one day.

'Come on then, bitch!' Clair Hooper broke Susan's nightmare recall.

'What do you want to know?' she asked. She could feel the chance for some respect.

'Ha! So which man has had the courage to fuck you then?'

'Yeah! You're just making this up,' another scowling voice resounded.

'There's one I've just finished with,' Susan started.

'Oh, yeah!' the girls echoed, clawing the air in front of them.

'And I'm now seeing a new man.' Susan quickly responded to quell the hostility. 'He's gorgeous.'

'What's his name? Where d'you meet him?' Clair enquired, more interested than the others.

'Mark,' replied Susan, giving a knowing beam.

Clair sensed something. She started digging for more answers. 'Mark? Eh?'

'Yes, Mark.' Susan was conjuring up her phantom man. And any pleasant sensation that had crept in to her father's use of her body was being transferred to her fanciful lover.

'Mark who?' Clair was chasing this answer.

'Mark... er... Stephens.' Susan's eyes dropped. It was out.

Every girl searched for another's widened eyes. They laid their hands across their gaping mouths and their saucer eyes ignited.

'You fucking liar!' Clair Hooper charged. 'You haven't been with Mr. Stephens! I know that!'

'Oh, yeah. How do you know that?' Susan frowned.

'He wouldn't go with a fucking ugly cow like you!' Clair stormed. The memory of her own rejection was etched on her ego.

'When has all this happened?' enquired a girl independent of the two in gladiatorial combat and eager to learn of this illicit affair. In fact the rest of the girls were rubbing their hands in anticipation of some vivid details.

Susan Bennett knew she to had make it good. 'Well... er... we kiss whenever we meet and there is no one around. It's so good to feel his strong arms pulling me to him. Up in his room and other places. He can't leave me alone.'

'Yes! And what else?' Came the enthusiastic request.

Susan had a catalogue of fantasy episodes spent with Mark Stephens to call on. 'We've spent hours together at Cairo House. Where he's stripped me and worshipped my body.'

'Ugh!' Responded Clair Hooper, still simmering at boiling point.

'And there's been an orgy with Pauline there.' Susan was getting excited. Pauline could confirm it. They'd believe it then. The other girls were listening to her, their mouths agape. She was the centre of it all. For once, Susan Bennett, the frumpy moose, had their attention. It was an immense buzz for her. 'Yes he wanted us both there, wanted Pauline to watch. He's so sexy. You wouldn't believe what we do.'

'That's crap! You're lying, you bitch!' Clair interrupted.

'Shut up, Clair,' came the unison comment. The other girls had turned against her. This was too juicy to miss any part of it. 'Carry on, Susan.'

Susan's eyes were aglow. This was her moment of celebrity. 'Yes, and out of school. In the Easter holidays. He came to see me. Took me out. We went back to my house and did it.' Susan was enjoying herself now. Mark's face was on her father's shoulders. And in her mind and through her words she transferred the crushing weight of her father as he slammed into her, forced down on the bed. It became the gentle, loving caresses of her spectral lover. 'He's so good.'

'Wow!' echoed through the room, and a scrum of girls, like battling hens, began twittering. They didn't see Clair Hooper slip away and run crying towards the office of Jan Edgerley.

Clair stopped at the door. She had to get this right. She rubbed her eyes. The mascara smeared and she daubed some of it on her cheeks.

Jan Edgerley was talking compassionately to a younger girl who sat opposite her cluttered desk. Clair Hooper burst in, collapsed in tears on the nearest couch and sobbed inconsolably. Jan ushered the girl unceremoniously out of her office and rushed round her desk to the distraught Clair Hooper.

'What on earth is wrong, Clair?' Jan asked, resting a comforting hand on Clair's shoulder.

'I... I thought it was only me,' Clair started, but the rest was blotted out by heavy sobbing.

'Calm down and explain,' Jan coaxed.

Clair Hooper sucked in an audible gulp of air. 'I thought Mr. Stephens had only tried it on with me. I could manage that. But he's been at it with Susan Bennett.' Clair waited. She barely looked at the housemistress. Only a quick glance as she wiped a rolling tear from her cheek. Just to gauge the response. She knew she had dropped a bomb and was enjoying seeing the effects of the blast.

Jan Edgerley rocked visibly. 'Say that again, Clair.'

'Mr. Stephens touched me once. Tried to kiss me. Wanted to start something. It was when I went over to Cairo House about my work.' Clair had stopped crying and was gladly feeding the story to her shocked housemistress.

'Where does Susan Bennett come in? What has she to do with this?' Jan Edgerley queried, now realising the seriousness of what was surfacing.

'The bastard! Sorry Miss. He has been doing things with Bennett. She's been telling us all, in the house. Telling all the girls in the common room. I had to come to you. It's sick isn't it?' Clair was performing well; she could sense that. This would stop Bennett's game.

'Yes, yes. Of course.' Jan Edgerley was attempting to run this through the mist in her head. Now scarcely acknowledging Clair Hooper, who was sitting examining her fingernails. Mark Stephens was a cavalier teacher, unorthodox, bit of a ladies' man maybe. But this? It didn't make sense. But she couldn't ignore it. 'Send Susan to me, please.'

Clair Hooper left the office, now a little afraid of what she had started. Still, she really wasn't to blame. It was bloody Bennett who had been fooling around with a teacher. Let her take the flack. And as for Stephens. It served him right. Fucking dirty old man. Didn't want her, but went with that ugly moose Bennett.

Clair found Susan deep in confab with Pauline Green, a conspiratorial discussion, intense in nature. 'Edgerley wants to see you.'

'What? Why does she want me? What's it all about?' Susan was puzzled.

Clair shrugged her shoulders and walked away.

Susan ran after her and pulled at her arm. 'What have you done, you bitch?'

'Me? You're the one! Now you'll see what fucking about with Mr. Stephens has got you into. You sad, fucking moose!' And with a Judas sneer she left Susan Bennett, as she always had been, standing alone with only her pathetic longings, her grubby family and trouble.

'Come in, Susan.' Jan Edgerley waved Susan Bennett into the room. 'Take a seat.' Jan moved to behind her desk where she had a notebook ready. It would be best to take notes, she thought. 'As you may be aware, Clair Hooper has been to see me. She has told me of your apparent involvement with one of the teachers.' Jan Edgerley pulled off her glasses. 'Please tell me what is happening, or has happened.'

Susan Bennett could feel her feet being pulled from beneath her. She dropped onto a chair and covered her face with her hands. What was happening here? She was losing the grip on her own reality on one hand, yet a demon reality was thrusting its dangerous head into her fantasy world. 'It's not really true,' she whispered.

'Sorry? What did you say?' Jan questioned.

'Not really true,' Susan mumbled.

'I see,' Jan started, 'so you have not had any involvement with Mr. Stephens, and what you told the girls in the common room was just nonsense. Do you understand what a despicable thing this is you have done? Such lies will only enhance your reputation as a sour and wicked girl. I do not envy you, Susan.' Jan Edgerley gave her a brutal dressing down.

Susan could picture it all. Life was bad enough without this. Only minutes ago she had risen to a new level of respect. It had felt good. She couldn't sacrifice that. 'Oh! Mrs. Edgerley, what I said was true. Mr. Stephens is my lover.' That was better.

'Are you sure of what you are saying now?'

'Yes. I was trying to protect him. We couldn't help our feelings. It won't have to go any further will it?'

Jan Edgerley had thought she was going to get away lightly. But no. 'I'm afraid this is far too serious, Susan. I can't believe what you're telling me. I will have to report what you and Clair have told me to the headmaster. And I cannot emphasise too strongly how serious this is for Mr. Stephens. If what I have heard about his participation in sexual encounters with both you and Clair are true then he is in deep trouble.'

'With Clair?' Susan shook.

'Yes. Clair has claimed that she was approached by Mr. Stephens. Didn't you know about this?'

'No. I... I thought it was only me. So he was hot on her. That tart!' Susan hadn't reckoned on that. She thought he was genuine in his disinterest in her advances, in his plea to her that he was not interested in the schoolgirl thing. But, no, he was a fucking, lying bastard, like the rest.

'Now, if you just tell me what's been going on between you and Mr. Stephens, perhaps we can get to bed.' It was getting late and Jan Edgerley knew that the next morning all hell would be let loose.

Susan Bennett ran through a similar account to the one she had boasted to the girls about. And when she was short of ideas, the spectre of her father's milky skin and his sickly words as he lay with her, came back to bolster her story. She knew that detail only too well.

At about one in the morning Susan was allowed back to her room. Pauline hadn't slept and was anxiously awaiting her return.

'What did she say?' Pauline's eager voice ambushed Susan from somewhere in the dark.

Susan was in a confused state; seething over the Clair Hooper revelations and agitated by the stories she had told Mrs. Edgerley. 'Look we have got to get this right!'

'What?' Pauline was confused by her friend's opener.

'I've told Edgerley that I've been having it off with Stephens.'

'Wow! I bet she flipped over that.' Pauline was getting excited. At last something to liven up school life.

'Yeah, okay, calm down. You haven't heard the worst bit.' Susan was about to spell out Pauline's part in her tales.

'I'm all ears.' Pauline stated eagerly.

'On Sunday, when we went to see Old Stephens in his office at Cairo House.'

'Yes?'

'Well... I've told Edgerley that we both went up to the staff quarters and did things with him.'

'What things?' Pauline was getting concerned.

'I've told her that we went up there and he got his dick out, and we tossed him off all afternoon. Okay?'

'You did what? Where did you dream that one up from?' Pauline Green was angry now.

'I've done it so many times for my old man, it was easy.' Susan was matter-of-fact about it. She had confided in Pauline some of the horrors of her father's abuse.

'Yeah! But why drag me in on it?' Pauline snorted.

'Look, I need some back up. May not believe just me. Anyway I need to nail him now. The bastard has been trying to screw that fucking bag Hooper. Did you know?'

'I didn't.' Pauline answered robotically. She was still puzzling through her supposed involvement.

'Well he has! Look, you better not let me down on this. I didn't mean to say all these things. But I have. All you have to do is just say you were there. Saw him with me. You can say he made you grab his cock. Okay?' Susan looked glumly at Pauline. 'You know how much I wanted him. And all the time he was trying to get his leg over fucking Hooper! I'll be in deep shit if you don't stand by me. Okay?' She desperately sought that assurance.

Pauline expelled an audible puff of air through her nose, and her shoulders sank. 'You fucking kill me. I don't believe the shit I have to suffer because of you.'

'Are you my friend or aren't you?' Susan was Pauline's only friend and Pauline would do what Susan asked. There was no one else to turn to. Pauline wasn't going to risk complete isolation in the hostile environment of Thomas Graham School, where verbal abuse stung her even more than the knuckles of physical violence.

When Susan saw Mark Stephens the following morning she was filled with a vile cocktail of jealousy and vengeance. And she was in her element spitting it at him with the words of hatred and betrayal. He had dared to spurn her advances yet succumb to the barge arse, the school dog, the whore Clair Hooper. Now she saw her purpose. A resentment, born of years of defilement by a beast of a father, was aimed at this unsuspecting teacher, who dared fend off her clawing demands.

Jan Edgerley went straight from her confrontation with Mark to the headmaster's study.

'This is a most distressing business. From what you told me earlier on the phone we have a major crisis here.' Ted Frith was already getting to grips with the situation as he lead Jan to her chair. 'Tell me what you know so far. No. Hold it a moment. I think I had better have Mrs. Peters take some notes.' Ted Frith was beginning to witness the complexities and the dangers. He hurried to the door to summon his secretary.

Doreen Peters shuffled in and pulled out a hard chair. She looked over her glasses at the other two and waited for them to begin. Her shorthand pad hung open, ready to accuse.

Jan Edgerley recalled the arrival of Clair Hooper at her office the previous evening, the accusations she had made and Jan's subsequent interview with Susan Bennett. Doreen Peters impassively noted every word. It was quite a scandal and she loved every minute of it.

Ted Frith envisaged an ugly state of affairs. He was right. After consultation with Tom Pearson and a phone call to the Chairman of Governors, Ted Frith had the backing to get Mark off the campus as quickly as he could. Then it was imperative to interview the girls. There must be no delay there.

Following the late morning announcement of Mark's suspension Ted Frith began the gruesome task of learning what his Head of English had been doing with his fifteen-year-old pupils.

Clair Hooper was brought to the headmaster's study by Jan Edgerley. An apologetic figure who sat with her head bowed throughout the session. It was easier for her to invent her retaliatory experience. There was little detail, and when she was quizzed for more information she would shrink into her school jumper and splutter some tears. Ted Frith was a sucker for the girl in distress. According to her account she was unable to put a date or even a month to the incident. All she could tell was of a teacher who, during a visit to his boarding house for assistance with her GCSE work, moved uncomfortably close to her and laid a searching hand on her thigh, pulled her towards him and attempted to kiss her, asked her to meet him out of school and clutched at her breasts. How simple. Just review how she wished it had occurred. Remember the day he pulled away from her crude attempts at winning his affections. It was enough for the headmaster and all the charitable faces that she could look up at with her watering, spaniel eyes.

The same kid gloves approach was adopted for the interview with Susan Bennett. Hers was a complex story with numerous encounters on several days. Of lunchtimes in the arms of her teacher lover, of four-hour long lovemaking sessions while Mark was on duty in his boarding house, and their romantic meeting during the Easter holidays.

When he thought it necessary, or in such shock at the revelation, the headmaster probed further.

'Mr. Stephens is a married man and in his forties. What on earth were you doing having a relationship with him?'

'He made me feel wanted. Sort of mature. An adult, like,' Susan sheepishly replied, secretly enjoying this notoriety. She hadn't realised how she could milk this falsehood. Susan Bennett would be the talk of the school. At every playground scrum and during those talkative times in lessons there would be salacious gossip about her and Mr. Stephens. And all those who hurled stinging names in her face would stop her in corridors or outside classroom doors and plead for the sordid details. She could live off that for a long time.

'I understand from Mrs. Edgerley that Pauline Green is somehow involved. Is that correct?' Ted Frith broke into her daydream.

'Pauline? Oh, yes.' She now wished she hadn't thought up this one. It didn't quite fit in.

'Can you tell us about it,' the headmaster urged.

'Well, he gave us wine and took us up to where he sleeps in the boarding house. It must have been for hours. We got his...' Susan was not sure which word for penis to use. 'He got his thing out,' That would do. There was little imagination necessary. She had a nightmare gallery of mucky images to call upon.

'His thing?' Asked the headmaster.

Susan started to snigger at the headmaster's question. 'You know what I mean.'

'Yes, yes,' agreed Ted Frith, embarrassed by his initial query.

'When was this?'

'Last Sunday,' confirmed Susan. 'We wanked him off,' she added with glee. And then thought it unwise to treat the matter with such mirth. Susan had forgotten momentarily who she was spinning this yarn to.

'Well, yes, thank you, Susan. You may go. And I must emphasise that you discuss this with no one. Is that understood?'

'Yes.' Susan confirmed. But there was no chance of that. She couldn't wait to enhance even the most lurid accounts that were circulating round the school. She was queen bee now.

By the time Pauline Green was trundled in it seemed that there was overwhelming indication that the school's most troublesome teacher was on his way out. Three girls now. All ready to supply information about the depraved activities of Mark Stephens.

'We understand that you have been involved with Mr. Stephens, Pauline. Is this true?' Ted Frith began.

'No!' Pauline Green snapped.

'Susan Bennett has said you have been,' the headmaster added.

'Well... sort of,' Pauline grunted. Far from keen to follow Susan's directions.

'Tell me what happened,' insisted the head.

'It... it's just like Susan told you,' Pauline mumbled.

'What do you mean? How do you know what was said?' Ted Frith queried.

'Er... well we were there together weren't we. It's going to be the same isn't it?' Pauline was sounding irritated.

'Okay. But we must hear it from you. We must be fair to everyone here. What you have to say is important. It is the only collaboration, I mean corroboration of these events.' Ted Frith didn't realise how prophetic his slip had been.

'Sorry,' Pauline intervened, 'I'm lost here. What does corrob... corrob... that word, mean?'

'Corroboration,' the head helped. 'It means that you are able to confirm what happened to Susan, and, of course, she can support what you tell us.'

'Yeah... I suppose so,' Pauline nervously agreed.

'So, now tell us everything.' Ted Frith was getting impatient.

'We went to the staff bedroom and he made us touch his...' Pauline was stuck at the word.

'Penis?' Ted Frith assisted.

'Yes,' Pauline tensely accepted.

'In the staff accommodation, you say? How long were you there with Mr. Stephens and Susan?'

Shit, thought Pauline, that hadn't been on the agenda that she could recall. 'Not long... I think. It was a shock, you see.'

'Susan said... er.' Ted turned to his secretary. 'Mrs. Peters could you read from her statement.'

'Let me see, headmaster. Ah, yes, here it is. *Stayed for hours.* That's what she said.'

'Well, Pauline?' The headmaster quizzed.

'Probably,' Pauline added, throwing up a decoy of deep sobs.

Jan Edgerley hurried to console her, and gave Ted Frith a complaining look from her stooped position over the tearful Pauline Green.

'No more questions, then.' The headmaster was resigned to leaving it at that.

Ted Frith was still reeling from the girls submissions when he was asked to speak to a boy, Michael Spear, who claimed he had seen Clair Hooper hurrying, from Mark Stephens' office in Cairo House.

The chubby boy was led in.

'As you know, Michael, there are many rumours spreading round the school, and it is important to all involved that I get to the truth quickly. Now, I believe, you have something you wish to say to me. Something that concerns Mr. Stephens and Clair Hooper?'

'Yes, sir!' Michael was raring to go. He could see his part in this inquisition.

'Go ahead.'

'Well, sir, it was one evening. Can't remember the exact day. I was returning from Christian Fellowship with Russell, when Clair Hooper came running out of Mr. Stephens' office. She was really disturbed and crying, and muttering something about Mr. Stephens.' Michael had finished giving his evidence and a ridiculous look of pride was stuck on his face.

'Did you speak to her? Did you see anything that you would regard as improper behaviour by Mr. Stephens?'

'Er... no, I don't think so.' Michael still held on to his smirk, but wasn't prepared for trick questions like that.

'Have you observed any other girls coming to the house and seeing Mr. Stephens?'

'Occasionally they're there,' Michael confirmed.

'And when they come to the house, what do they do?' quizzed the head.

'He, Mr. Stephens, is usually chatting and making jokes. Like he takes the micky out of some of the other teachers. Makes us laugh. The girls like that.'

'But, have you seen him touch the girls. Touch in a manner that you think isn't the way a teacher should?' Ted Frith was trying to make it sound like a minor infringement rather than a serious crime.

'I'm not sure. Sometimes the door is shut when he's in his office with pupils,' Michael added.

'But you haven't seen anything you can tell me about?' The headmaster could see this was going nowhere fast and he was now trying to wrap it up.

'I don't think so.' Michael was still hanging on. He hoped he could really help the enquiries, but his thread of evidence, was getting more frayed and he wasn't managing to produce anything juicy enough to tempt the headmaster.

When the day was over Ted Frith wished he wasn't a headmaster at all. This was a dreadful mess, and he knew it would dominate his valuable time for many weeks ahead. He had the statements from the girls, Jan Edgerley and Michael Spear.

Mrs. Peters was typing them up. His packet of Bensons was now lying on his desk and his office reeked of smoke. He needed his cigarettes now. Had Mark Stephens done all this? Twelve years he had been at the school. Did he? How could he? Why? It was all too much to juggle with that evening. He was shattered.

First thing the next morning the Bursar was at Ted's office. He had the staff disciplinary procedure manual under his arm and was revelling in its implementation in this case.

Bursar Colonel James Hall was a washed-up army officer who strutted around the school treating pupils and staff like mindless recruits. A small man with a small mind, and the temperament of a wasp. He despised teachers, and in particular ones who recognised him as the tosspot he was. Mark Stephens couldn't stand the man. Colonel James Hall was a self-opinionated, vile individual - a nasty little git. And the Colonel knew of Mark's sentiments. So it was with immense glee that he arrived at the head's office and began detailing the process aimed at nailing this renegade teacher. The recipe began with a select committee of Governors, a date for a hearing, a list of witnesses and details of the allegations that the school thought constituted gross misconduct. In Mark's absence the school was incurring the additional expense of employing a temporary supply teacher, and Colonel Hall, answerable to the Governors for expenditure, was adamant that financial considerations were top of the agenda.

'Of course the little shit did it!' he barked at the headmaster.

'You may be right,' the headmaster pondered.

'Now, here is what we need to do. Decide on the date for the hearing and send all this off to him.' He pointed to the completed statements that Doreen Peters had piled on the head's desk. 'He'll most likely get his union involved. That may drag it along for a bit.'

'We'll get it in the post today.' Ted Frith shouted at the door. 'Doreen, make sure there are no errors in this, and send copies of everything to Mr. Stephens, recorded delivery, today.'

'Yes, sir,' agreed a voice from beyond the partially open door.

Chapter 4

Charles Cornwall mopped his brow as he held the telephone between his shoulder and his ear, and scribbled on the pad in front of him. He was a heavy man who sweated a lot. Often ruddy-faced and flustered.

'We need to meet as soon as possible. Just let me examine my dates. Hold on.' Charles Cornwall screwed up his eyes and then sprung them open, and looked heavenwards, throwing up despairing hands. This was the last thing he needed. 'Look, Mark, I can see you on Thursday. I reckon I can be there at about two. Okay? Are you all right? Good.' Charles replaced the receiver. It glistened black and wet from his perspiration. 'Bugger!' His secretary next door heard the expletive and knew it meant trouble.

Mark had phoned his NAS/UWT representative following the arrival of the documents from the school. He wasn't a great union man and had never needed to contact them before. In fact he'd only recently joined. It had been prompted after another run-in with Tom Pearson.

Charles Cornwall arrived early on Thursday afternoon. He was red-faced, and sweat stained the armpits of his shirt. He carried his jacket and puffed a 'Hello' as he stumbled in.

'Made good time on the motorway,' Charles muttered as he lay down his jacket and parked his briefcase alongside the sofa. 'Nice house you have here,' he continued as he delved into the case and pulled out a pink folder. Mark's name had been scribbled on the front. 'Now, I have to leave in time to avoid the traffic down to Eastbourne. So we need to get started. Let me see what the school have sent you, and then you can tell me what exactly has happened here.'

Mark pushed the envelope towards Charles and flopped

back in his chair. It took the union representative a considerable time to read through the documents. He sighed and chuckled at intervals. Finally he placed it down beside him, held his lips firmly together and gazed intently at Mark.

'Even I can see some blatant discrepancies, and I haven't heard from you yet, Mark. But what's here constitutes some serious allegations. There is a good possibility the police are going to be called in.'

'What?' Mark hadn't even given that a second thought. 'Why?'

'These girls are fifteen, Mark. What they have claimed happened would be a criminal offence. You'll need to speak to Elizabeth Burns who is the solicitor who normally deals with this type of case. She's the Union's solicitor. But I expect she'll hand it on to Robert Manning, a new recruit in her department; can be a little brash at times but a thorough type. You'll need that.'

Charles pulled a grey handkerchief out of his trouser pocket and wiped his forehead. He glistened but he didn't smell. 'Now Mark,' Charles began again, 'let's hear it from the horse's mouth.'

Mark summoned the words to overwhelm the knot in his stomach; to keep it precise; to avoid the parts that dragged clumsy and difficult through thoughts of Alison, Jayne and Anna. Charles listened through the whole history of these schoolgirls, Mark's actions in dealing with it and the horror of the day of his suspension.

Charles made notes. When Mark had finished he traced the points with his finger. 'Why didn't you inform senior management at the school when you were approached by these girls?' Charles looked over his glasses. A hawk waiting for a reply.

'Well I... er tried.' He felt uncomfortable with the question. He knew Charles had homed in on the major problem. It stood out like a beacon. It was a procedure that should have been followed. Mark felt unwell. He attempted to explain it away. 'On one occasion I was on the verge, and the deputy head turned on me about something else. And then on the occasions during the holiday there was no one about. I suppose I should have persisted. I don't get on with Pearson.' Mark was examining his own feeble excuses as he recounted them. He knew Charles had found a flaw in his reaction to this problem. Despite his discomfort it gave him some faith in the union representative.

'Pearson? Oh! Yes, Tom Pearson. He's a real bastard isn't he?' Charles was recalling the man. 'And this trip to Wokingham. It doesn't look good. A rather unnecessary and dangerous mission.' Charles made more notes. 'They're rushing this disciplinary hearing. It's only three and a half weeks away. We need to see where we can challenge them and which witnesses we need to speak to. Have you had any thoughts?'

Mark was seeing the holes. Even the truth wasn't watertight.

The phone rang in the hall. Only a few rings. Alison would have picked it up, he thought.

Mark held the statements open on his palms as if reading a Sunday School lesson. 'On this day I wasn't at school. You can't be absent from duty for several hours. There is no way a person could smuggle girls up past all the boys to the staff accommodation. On this day I know I was watching TV with several of the boys, Aston Villa in the cup. There are so many, Charles.'

'Slow down. Let's get this in some sort of order.' Charles Cornwall wasn't a stranger to this type of incident and had in the past dealt with cases where he either felt the teacher was guilty of the offences or even where the offender admitted guilt. Usually spluttered through a flood of tears. And there was the Davidson case, of course, where suicide had followed. That haunted him. Charles had left Clifford Davidson at his door and within four hours the teacher accused of stroking the bottoms of primary school girls had hanged himself from the rafters in his garage. He wouldn't mention that one to Mark. 'I'm with you all the way. This isn't my first case,' he assured

Mark. 'Now, who do we need to talk to at the school?'

By the time Charles Cornwall had left Mark's house he had definitely avoided the rush hour traffic. That had reached its height several hours earlier. It was now night and the roads comparatively empty. Mark had been left with the task of drawing up a list of potential witnesses, and Charles was going to contact the school to arrange for them to be interviewed to see if they would be suitable to give evidence at the disciplinary hearing.

When Mark sent off the names he had listed eighteen; a mix of pupils and staff. He was quite enthusiastic for once.

'I forgot to tell you, Ann Bull from the school phoned twice when you were in with the sweaty union man,' Alison announced at about ten in the evening.

'What did she want?'

'Didn't say. But, the first was a message on the answerphone. I've left it on there for you.'

It hadn't recorded well. Didn't sound like Ann at all. Mark chanced a return call. Ann was a night bird and didn't retire early. She taught PE, but her lifestyle didn't reflect the ethos expounded at college.

'Hello Ann.' Mark's nervous voice croaked down the phone. She was up as predicted.

'Mark...? How are you?' A rocky reply. 'What a shocking business. I was going to phone.' She meandered through embarrassed phrases. It was a plastic conversation.

'You phoned. What was it?' Mark enquired.

'Phoned? Sorry, I didn't phone. Are you sure you've got it right?' Ann was startled. She hadn't phoned. Mark Stephens was suspended. He had been touching up girls at the school. Why should she speak to him? The filthy bastard! She got rid of him as quickly as possible.

Two things threw Mark. Ann's attitude and the mystery calls. He was more concerned about the former. Why should she be so short with him. They were always great pals at school. In the staff room there was risqué banter and kidding around.

'Dad!' He was jolted from his thoughts.

'Yes?'

'Phone for you!' Came the call from upstairs where Anna had taken it.

'Who is it?' Mark didn't feel like taking any calls. He was still coming to grips with the tone of the conversation with Ann Bull.

'Ann something from school,' his daughter shouted.

She's rung back to clear the air; apologise for her attitude, Mark supposed. He picked up the phone in the hall. 'Hello, Ann. That was quick.' Mark was bouncing again, pleased that he had mistaken the nature of her reaction to his call.

There was a wooden silence. No one spoke. Mark mouthed another greeting. Still chirpy. 'Hello, Ann, you there?'

And then, crawling down the line, came the recognisable voice of Susan Bennett. 'Hello, Mark,' the diseased tongue dribbled.

'What on earth!' I don't believe you have the gall to contact me. Do you know what you've done?'

'It wasn't my fault. I'm sorry about the lies. I've sent you a letter. I was angry. It's Pauline's fault. The thought of you with Hooper.' Susan Bennett wasn't making sense. She was spilling out random statements that went straight through Mark. All he knew was, that here talking to him was the girl who had invented an incredible story. Had damned him.

'Why the hell are you phoning me? Now go! Go away and tell the truth to someone!' Mark couldn't listen to her voice again. He slung down the handset. His head swam. He grabbed at the phone. Dialling tone. Good. He smacked in the number.

'Hello Jan. It's Mark Stephens here.'

Jan Edgerley rocked. 'What do you want?' It was a robotic enquiry. A metal voice.

'Look I've just had Susan Bennett phone me. Is she in the boarding house? She must be phoning from there at this time of night. She's just apologised for lying. Go and see her right away. She'll tell you the truth now! I'm sure!' Mark's language was urgent. He could see this all being solved. A naïve idea.

Jan Edgerley heard him raving. She was alarmed by his call. Not only was it late. But she was a witness against him. She had been told of his behaviour. His foul deeds. She was scared of him now. He had become a monster. 'I'll go and see. Goodbye.' She was able to get rid of him. He allowed her to go, assuming she was the cavalry. But it was a ghostly bugle call. She didn't bother to seek out Susan Bennett. Instead she phoned Ted Frith, to tell him of the pervert's call and her fears.

Mark sent off the witness list to Charles Cornwall first thing in the morning. He didn't hear from Jan Edgerley, but thought it unwise to ring again. The mail arrived about nine thirty. Mark was suddenly more interested in the post. Perhaps something from the school. Some more information. Even the come back it was all a mistake letter. He was still in shock over the phone call but he hadn't thought any more about her rambling message until, in the midst of the beige envelopes and plastic wrapped junk mail, he saw a small white envelope addressed by a child's hand. He was used to reading such handwriting - some bloody awful essays usually. Mark snatched it from the floor. Alison was watching from the kitchen.

'What's that, Mark?' Alison had become equally more eager to examine the post.

It came flooding back. The Bennett girl had said she'd written. Said she was angry. 'Looks like those tickets I sent for.' Mark's imagination wasn't up to producing a better lie. He took the small envelope into the downstairs toilet. Deep down he hoped it was a full confession or even enough in it to confirm his account of her pestering.

It was worse than he could have dreaded. The back of his neck stuck with sweat and he steamed with anger as he read. It was an evil letter. One she had written as if to her father. Mark was nearly sick when he had only finished a few lines. Without thinking he snarled deeply like a beast from within a dismal cavern - and tore the letter into ever-decreasing sized squares.

It was almost confetti when he flushed it away from him and his family. Down, down to the sewer where it belonged. Mark sat on the seat above, re-reading from inside his sizzling head what she had written. She shouldn't have written that. Not that!

'Mark!' Alison called from the other side of the door.

'Yes, just coming.' Mark shuffled around inside and ran some taps. When he crept from the door Alison was waiting for him. He still clutched the envelope in his hand.

'Well? What was that?' Alison sensed the importance of the small envelope.

Mark wanted to maintain the lie. Alison must never know what was in the letter. But he saw her determined face and knew he was bound to tell her that Susan Bennett had written. 'It was from her. A letter. So revolting.'

Alison could read his face. 'Where is it?' She needed to read it. To make her move. Her anger had a purpose and was seeking an avenue.

'It's gone. I flushed it down the bog.' Mark wanted her to know that it had been defused, floated harmlessly away. Where it wouldn't hurt her or the girls. Especially the girls.

'What? Why did you do that?' Her anger drilled her husband. 'You bloody fool! Don't you realise that could have been the deciding evidence. I can't believe you did that.' Alison collapsed in tears. That hurt him more than anything. But he knew that he'd destroyed more than just a letter. He had exorcised a blood-curdling phantom.

'What did it say?' Alison mumbled from behind her smothering hands.

Mark didn't reply. He cried. Not in competition. Not to seek her sympathy. He cried because he could only store the haunting contents of the letter. He couldn't share that with Alison. 'I can't tell you,' he spluttered. 'I won't ever tell you that... not that!'

Charles Cornwall phoned the next day to let Mark know that the school was co-operating and that a date had been fixed for him and Mark to interview potential witnesses. Only two staff members had refused to attend. Mark busied himself with details of how these witnesses could help his case. It was an exercise with two objectives - to prove that these allegations were all lies, and to keep him sane. To curb the gnawing agony of the whole thing. He was excited by the prospect of holding some solid evidence of his innocence. Of confronting these girls and making them admit these falsehoods in front of the hearing. For him to stand up and thump his chest and admonish all those who dared accuse him or even have the faintest doubt about his innocence. He wanted that moment so badly.

'Charles Cornwall from the Union,' Alison informed Mark, holding out the phone to him in the breakfast room.

'Yes, Charles.' Mark opened, as he clutched at the phone. 'What? Why is that? Do you think so? Okay. Let me know. It's all going pear-shaped isn't it?' The new found self-assurance quickly evaporated.

'What is it?' Alison was quick to ask. The jumbled responses from one end of the conversation had made very little sense.

'The bloody school has cancelled the interviews and the disciplinary hearing has been postponed. Charles thinks the police have had a word and put everything on hold. This is really pissing me off.' Mark was despondent.

Charles had interpreted the situation accurately. Ted Frith had studied the guidelines issued with the Child Protection Act and informed the local police a few days after Mark's suspension. A note of the headmaster's call had eventually arrived on the desk of WPC Jean Baxter working with the Child Protection Group at Wokingham Police Station. She would be in charge of the investigation under the guidance of Sergeant Bernard Mills, and in conjunction with some anoraks at Social Services. At their first conference they planned how to trap Mark Stephens, how to bring him to justice, how to remove to a safe place this menace to society. They were never to consider his innocence. There were the girls to question. The skeletons of Stephens' past? Did he have a record? Other crimes? His other schools? Local police knowledge? They needed a pro-file of this villain. Jean Baxter was getting her teeth into this one. She was enjoying herself.

The school provided Mark's employment background. Schools where he had worked and where Jean Baxter hoped to discover he had preyed on young girls in an evil quest for his male sexual satisfaction. Men had such brutal sex drives. She hated their perpetual demands on women. But this camouflaged the fact that none had ever demanded anything like sex from her.

At the schools Mark had worked at in his first few years of teaching there was no one who knew him, his record was clean of disciplinary action, although there were notes observing his poor punctuality. And the school he had left to take up the Head of English post at Thomas Graham School were adamant about him being an ordinary chap, a regular fellow. There was a lateness problem, but no hint of an unhealthy interest in girl pupils.

Sure he would be the first to acknowledge the attractive-ness of new female staff or even the potential of some of the mothers, but he was no 'baby snatcher'.

Jean Baxter wasn't happy that this line of enquiry had evaporated. But it was only a minor setback. There were the girls to interview. She had seen the statements made to the headmaster. It didn't follow procedures to do that. However, there seemed to be damning evidence there all right. She couldn't wait to get some of that on to official police statement stationery. Once it was there they could start closing the net on that revolting creature who had been abusing innocent young girls.

WPC Baxter first called to see Jan Edgerley. She made sure she befriended the housemistress. Cemented a relationship. That was an important move.

'We have to tackle this carefully,' Baxter started. 'It's a deli-cate matter, and no action must be taken that could be seen as insensitive, Jan. I'm sure you understand.'

'Of course. These are my girls and I feel responsible. This has been a terrible ordeal for them. My first consideration is for their welfare.' Jan Edgerley was sincere in her concern.

'However, we do need every detail if we are going to successfully prosecute Mr. Stephens.' She wanted to say foul predator. She didn't. Take it from me, there are a lot of other girls at risk if we don't get him put away for this.' Jean Baxter steamed. 'Now there are three girls to interview. Are there any others we need to talk to? Witnesses?'

'I don't think so. No one has come forward.' Jan Edgerley was mulling over some possibilities.

'There must be someone who can support what the girls are going to tell me,' the policewoman insisted.

'I have had a word. Given them the opportunity to do so. Not one of the three involved has suggested any likely names. Of course, Pauline and Susan can support each other's testimony on the one occasion.'

'Is that all?' WPC Baxter sounded disappointed. 'We'll see when we have more information. It will take a while to get the statements from the girls. I suggest we see Susan Bennett first. It appears she is at the centre of this. Then we will talk to Pauline, and then Clair. Can you keep them apart as best you can. I'm a little concerned about their proximity in the house.' Jean Baxter wanted this leak-proof.

The next morning Susan Bennett was guided in to Jan Edgerley's office. It was an environment she knew. Not frightening like the police station. Somewhere she could feel comfortable, relaxed enough to tell it as it was.

'Come in Susan. Have a seat.' There was no uniform and Jean Baxter was in her good fairy mode. 'You know why you're here, don't you?'

'Yes,' came the timid reply.

'I want you to tell me what exactly has happened to you. This will be an official police statement. You must tell me the truth. If you don't you will be liable to be prosecuted. Wasting police time is a very serious business. What you say I will write down. At the end I will read it through to you. You can read it also. If you agree it is an accurate record I will ask you to sign the document. Do you understand? Are there any questions?' Even the good fairy had to use harsh words here.

'Yes,' Susan replied, 'I understand.' She didn't really. She hadn't listened. It was all just a jumble of words. She knew only that this was where she got her own back, but she didn't comprehend the consequences of what she was going to say. Everything she ever wanted to reveal that made her feel so dirty she was ready to tell, and she didn't mind at that moment that Mark Stephens was the sacrifice.

'Give your full name, your age and date of birth,' Baxter stated. An encouraging smile spread strangely across her face. 'If you want to stop at anytime just say. Don't feel there is any pressure on you. As you know, Susan, we are only searching for the truth here.' Baxter had it off pat. This was her benevolent face that served to promote her as the caring policewoman.

Susan Bennett gave her full name, her age, fifteen, and her date of birth. She would be sixteen in two months time. She felt comfortable with that. There were no lies yet.

'Now, Susan, tell us about you and Mr. Mark Stephens,' WPC Baxter encouraged.

'Mr. Stephens is a teacher at the school.'

Susan paused as if that was all she had to say.

'Yes?' Baxter goaded.

'We have been seeing each other.'

A further pause.

'What does that mean?' Baxter was edgy.

'He's my lover,' Susan boasted, and gripped her chair and swung her head.

'So, you and Mr. Stephens have been having a relationship?' Baxter continued.

'That's right.'

'When have you seen him?' Baxter prodded.

'At lunchtimes in his room. We kiss and cuddle.' Susan had to imagine the harsh, horny hands of her father to conjure up that one. 'And he has taken me up to his room in Cairo House on two occasions. And he has met me in Wokingham. We went back to my house where we...' Susan stumbled.

Her bedroom loomed up. A huge screen display. Every cupboard and surface, every drape and poster. A little girl's room with little girl things... and him. Him slipping in when the coast was clear, through the yellow lit gap of the half open door. A bulky form. The door closing and in the darkness that awful waiting for the delving hand, pawing at her chubby body, at her developing breasts and the forcing fingers between her legs.

'You were telling us about the events at your house.' Jean Baxter watched Susan's eyes stuck on the far wall, nightmare thoughts running through her head. That Stephens was a bloody monster to do this to her. A terrified child.

'Yes... er... well. He...' It was now fresh in her memory and the detail stark and vivid. 'He took off my clothes and he caressed my tits, and put his fingers in my vagina. That's what he always did.'

She retreated back to the black bedroom and the clawing hands, and the heavy body resting on her; the reek of his breath. The coarse hairs on his chest pushed against her puppy-fat skin and the impatient jabbing of his aroused penis.

'Always did?' quizzed Baxter.

Susan had to think fast. She was still screaming inside for him to stop. For her mother to come in. Just for it to be over. And the guilt of her own wetness. That was the worst thing.

'Yeah... whenever we were alone.'

'You mean in the Cairo House accommodation? The times up there?'

'Yeah.' Susan was drifting back to the office now.

'Tell me about the time you went up to that room with Pauline, will you, Susan.' Baxter wasn't sure about some of this. 'Take your time.' She could see that Susan wasn't finding it easy with the details. But they were important. Could be vital.

'He was on duty in the house. We went to see him. He was eating his lunch, drinking some wine. He gave us some and asked if we wanted to go up to the room where he sometimes slept.' Susan stopped. This was a difficult part that needed some thought. The bits that were merely the precursory to the graphic accounts of sexual activity sapped even her devious mind. 'We agreed... yes... we agreed to go up there.' She faltered again. 'He got out his penis.' Susan was back to familiar territory.

It had looked so huge when she was younger. The first time he forced her hands around it she could hardly keep hold. She looked with amusement at the thing when he started doing it. But soon she was thrown into terror every time she saw him touching himself, and then, holding the top of his trousers with one hand, run the zip of his fly down, and reaching in bring the sprung-rubber organ to face her.

'Carry on, Susan,' urged WPC Baxter. 'What happened after that?'

'The usual.' Susan hadn't meant to say that, but she could fit it in to her narrative.

'What does that mean?' asked Baxter, still a little unsettled by the girl's statement.

'I had to hold it and jerk him off. Well we did. Pauline did it as well.'

'Just like that? What was said?' Jean Baxter wanted more detail.

Said? Her father said things. Stupid, drunken things. Promised it was just that time. Not to worry. Not to tell. And all the other sounds that could have been words but were blocked out as she pumped until her wrist hurt. And the groaning from his wetted lips, and that stupid look on his face when she dared peep.

'Said? Oh... he said things like he wanted us to put it in our mouths and wanted sex.'

The phantoms reared up and shrieked in her head again.

She wondered why on that occasion he had pulled her hands away from his penis. He hadn't done that before. And why he tugged her gently from the back of her neck until she felt the elastic skin of his cock on her cheek. She hadn't known what to do. He'd bent his head forward and whispered what he wanted in her ear. You didn't do things like that! It wasn't clean! He'd been so concerned about her cleanliness when she was younger. His whispers became urgent. There was anger creeping in when she did nothing. She could remember the stale smell of it and the small amount of glistening dampness at the end. But most of all she recalled the putrid taste as he pressed her down on his wart-ridden dick. And how she had vomited when he filled her mouth, thick and warm; his linked hands on the back of her head stopping her wrenching away.

'Susan! Is that all that was said?' Jean Baxter could see her subject drifting in and out of the session. She was concerned it was trauma. Very often recollecting a shocking experience brought it on.

'Yes. I can't remember the exact words. But he wanted it all right.' Susan was ready to condemn. He had really done those things to her. It had happened.

'We'll break for a drink,' announced Baxter, unsure about the success of this first period. She would have to go over each incident separately and in detail. At the moment she was getting a crazy stew; nothing concrete.

Susan Bennett performed better after a coffee and was firm in her resolve to denounce her former teacher. He deserved it.

Pauline Green didn't have the reservoir of squalid experiences that Susan could call upon. Her father, a West Indian immigrant, had 'disappeared' when she was two, and her mother had worked at anything and everything to bring her up. She was sitting facing WPC Jean Baxter simply because her only friend was a vindictive, screwed-up, little bitch. It was only the one incident. Just enough to back up her story. It didn't really matter. No big deal.

'So, Pauline. Full name, age and date of birth please,' requested Jean Baxter, a fresh plastic smile for a fresh face.

Formalities completed Pauline was asked to state what she knew about Mr. Mark Stephens. She couldn't tell them much. She outlined the supposed relationship with her friend Susan Bennett, but admitted it was what she had been told.

'Never saw 'em together, doing any of those things,' she informed the quizzing policewoman.

'Never?'

'Oh. Except that once.' Pauline's repair job didn't go smoothly.

'You knew it was taking place at other times?' Baxter asked.

'Yeah.'

'How?'

'Susan told me when she was going to see him. Saw her leave his room. Said he kissed her and things.' Pauline was very vague. Baxter didn't like it. It wasn't material that she could use in court.

'Tell me about the Sunday you went to see Mr. Stephens at his boarding house with Susan. You remember that don't you?'

'Yeah. He gave us some of his drink and wanted to play a game upstairs in the house. We went up and he got his willy out. We rubbed it for him. Up and down like.' Pauline imitated the motion for WPC Baxter.

'What else?' Baxter continued.

'What d'yer mean?' replied Pauline, a little puzzled by the question.

'Did anything else happen, or was anything said?'

Pauline had to remember quickly what Susan had told her. They had spent many hours after prep going through it. Susan had to explain to Pauline some of the words, describe what was done and could add some vivid mental pictures. Sex education had been completed at home, but not in a manner recommended by the education authority. Susan could tell Pauline some of the things her father forced her to do. Sometimes it helped and other times it opened a wound, and tore at that deep and grievous lesion, leaving her shaking with startled, frightened eyes. There were things that she didn't tell. Things he'd done to her that she would never tell anyone, and that she would never let a man do to her again. And of the times when she hated herself for some fleeting moments of pleasure.

'He wanted,' Pauline started up again, 'to do it to us. Have sex.' She stopped and looked at the floor. It was a silly lie. And she couldn't face the people she told it to.

Jean Baxter needed her to mention the oral sex bit. She hadn't so far, but if she initiated it then the value of Pauline's testimony would have been considerably depreciated.

'Is that all?' Jean Baxter asked.

Pauline surveyed the ceiling. She had tried to cover all that Susan had asked her to. She strained to recall it all.

Baxter could see Pauline was agitated. She could see that this would all blow up in her face if it wasn't alluded to now. Baxter stepped in. Gingerly enough she thought to maintain the merit of the evidence.

'Susan has told us that something else was suggested by Mr. Stephens when you were in that room together.'

Pauline cringed. What was it? She struggled. Then it dawned. 'Oh! Yeah that. Wanted us to put it in our mouths, sort of kiss it.' She smiled as would a young child at such imagery. Pauline hadn't the knowledge, hadn't been coerced to suck a man's cock, half suffocated by rough, encouraging, clammy hands; snorting through her nose for air. So it was a naïve description of events. 'Disgusting aint it?' she added.

The faces of the two women required that. Pauline knew Susan had done it. She had told her in the darkness of their room. Anonymous. When she couldn't see her face. Safe under the covers of a bed where she hadn't been abused. Pauline had been shocked. What a thing to do. They piss through it don't they. For goodness sake, her father? Must be an animal, she had thought.

'Thank you, Pauline. I understand how distressing this must be for you.' Baxter had to be satisfied with that. When it came to giving evidence Pauline Green would know her lines a lot better. WPC Baxter showed her out of the room. Her mother had arrived while the interview was in session, and greeted her daughter as she came out. She vainly attempted to put a hand on Pauline's shoulder, but Pauline threw it off and stormed away, her mother in pursuit.

'Jan, I think we have time to start the Clair Hooper interview before lunch. What do you think? Got the stomach for it?'

'I would like to get it over with. For my sake and the girls'. No one wants them hanging around getting worried about this.'

'Fine. Let's go.'

Clair Hooper was fetched by Jan Edgerley. She was a reluctant figure who followed the walls of the room without looking at either Jan Edgerley or WPC Baxter. Clair didn't acknowledge the supercilious smile spread especially for her by Jean Baxter, but hung her head even when she was seated.

'Hello Clair.' Jean Baxter cheerfully greeted the shrunken form of Clair Hooper. There was no response. 'Now, Clair, I want you to tell me your full name, age and date of birth, and then I want you to tell me about your encounter with Mr. Stephens.'

Clair Hooper said nothing. Her rounded back was like a smoothed erratic boulder stuck in the centre of a lake of green carpet.

'Clair. Are you ready?' Baxter prompted.

Jan Edgerley approached and curved an arm around Clair's back and tapped her shoulder gently. 'Are you okay, Clair?' she asked quietly.

Clair Hooper exploded in tears and sobbed for several minutes. Jean Baxter cursed to herself. This wasn't going to be an easy one and she wished she had waited until after a bite to eat.

'Now,' Baxter started, once Clair's tears were dried on her sleeve, 'just tell us in your own time.'

'Not me... it wasn't me. I wasn't involved,' Clair spluttered.

'What do you mean?' Baxter was launched backwards, her

vulture eyes popping.

'It was her. Bennett. Not me!' Clair added.

'You told Mrs. Edgerley and the headmaster that you were involved. That Mr. Stephens touched you, and made other suggestions.' Jean Baxter wasn't able to retain her charm. She was livid.

'Well I wasn't. Nothing to do with me,' persisted Clair. Her head was still down and she spoke to the floor.

'So you lied?' Jean Baxter questioned. Her eyes resembling a vicious laser weapon.

'Sort of,' Clair replied. The clarity of her response suffocated by her hanging head.

'What does that mean? You were the first to rush and speak to Mrs. Edgerley here, weren't you?' Jan Edgerley nodded to Baxter to confirm that.

'Yeah. But it was a mistake.' Clair shrugged.

'Mistake!' Baxter exclaimed in disbelief. 'So what you told Mrs. Edgerley and the headmaster didn't happen? Is that it?'

'Yeah.'

Jan Edgerley and Jean Baxter traded exasperated expressions.

'Now; are you sure? This will be your last chance to change your mind. I hope you aren't concealing anything from us.' Jean Baxter stacked her papers and stood up. With no response from the crouched form of Clair Hooper she motioned to Jan Edgerley to escort Clair out of the room.

Outside in the corridor Colonel Hall was waiting, impatiently shuffling about like an irascible gerbil. 'Ah! Policewoman Baxter,' he twittered as he saw she was free, 'could I have a word. Most important matter. Need to clear a point.' He spoke in shrunken sentences and clicking phrases. An old army condition.

'Yes, okay.' WPC Baxter spoke automatically. Her thoughts remained with the new turn of events that still had her knocked sideways.

'Stephens, via his damn union, has asked to interview

potential witnesses. For the disciplinary hearing, business. We have made arrangements. A room over the road by the playing fields. Doesn't need to come on the premises. All right with you lot?' Clipped the irritable little man.

'No, no!' Baxter was back with the programme. 'He must not speak to anyone. He must not come near the school. Is that understood?' There were two choleric people now.

'What?' the squat Colonel questioned. 'This hearing has to take place. Soon as possible. Paying for a temporary replacement. Costs a lot.'

'I don't care! If you want me to make this official I can!' The policewoman was giving her adversary the full Baxter stare.

Colonel James Hall, Bursar of Thomas Graham School, stormed off. This was going to cost the school dear, and he was answerable to the Governors. It would be murder approaching him for the rest of that day.

Chapter 5

The Magistrates Court in Wokingham sits alongside the Waitrose car park and is no more than a compact village hall with some austere oak furniture. It buzzes with petty male offenders and their painted girlfriends, and the occasional elderly shoplifter. Young or inarticulate solicitors unable to attract more lucrative business cluck amidst the chaos, looking for clients barely known.

Mark arrived there with his friend Paul. They met Robert Manning outside. Crowded and barged by smokers and the tattoo-necked house breakers and TDA merchants, Robert explained the procedure. It was a new style committal hearing and Robert told Mark that this would merely be a decision-making process whereby his case could be sent to Crown Court, or, but there was not evidence of it as yet, that the girls retracted their allegations. Robert listed the advantages of using this route. It would ensure the girls could be cross-examined, would give Mark's exoneration a more public stage and, important to him, time to prepare the case properly.

'Surely I'm not going in there?' Mark queried. He saw the stained oak benches and the green leather backs of the magistrates' high chairs. 'This is ludicrous. It should be over by now!' He was panicking. He had been all right; a strong and positive attitude, but now some cracks were reappearing.

'Take it easy,' urged Paul.

'Yes.' Robert added. 'You've got to keep your head here. I've just seen that evil cow Baxter. She's supposed to hand me all the documents. She's leaving it a bit late.'

Jean Baxter caught sight of Mark's group and strutted over. The sickly smile was aimed at Mark as she approached. 'Ah! Mr. Manning, here you are.' She pushed a thick pile of loose-leaf papers at the solicitor and strode off.

'Shit! I'll have to try and flick through these as quick as possible. I'm going to lock myself in there for as long as I can.' Robert Manning pointed to a consultation room that had just been vacated by a shaven-headed yob and his spotty counsel.

Mark and Paul walked outside. The waiting area was cramped, and stunk of stale and hovering tobacco smoke. At the kerbside Paul put a consoling arm around Mark and stuck his knuckles playfully under his chin. 'Got to stay strong, mate. We're depending on you.'

'Yeah,' Mark managed.

'Mr. Stephens? Mr. Mark Stephens?' A shrill voice enquired to Mark's left. 'Mr. Mark Stephens, teacher at Thomas Graham School?' the enquirer continued.

Mark turned to see an acne-faced young man in a grey suit clutching a writing pad, its leaves fluttering as he made the last few steps towards him. Behind this urgent person, half running to keep up with the questioning man, was what seemed to be a photographer. He held a camera in one hand and was clinging to his flapping jacket with the other.

It took a few seconds for it to dawn on Mark. And then it hit him with a hammer blow. The Press! He should have known. Robert should have prepared him. Mark didn't respond to the question. His fissure mouth and shaking head confirmed it enough for the local reporter hot on the tail of the teacher facing indecent assault accusations.

'Only a few questions, Mr. Stephens; if you don't mind. What have you to say about these charges?'

Paul stepped in. 'Why don't you leave him alone.' He threw his back against the reporter and shielded Mark, who was still blank faced, taking it all in.

The eager reporter dodged around to confront Mark again. 'Come on Mr. Stephens. You can have your say. Tell the people the story from your side. The truth, eh?'

Paul was seething and frantically turning Mark away from the insistent journalist. He was almost waltzing him up and down the pavement. All the time the panting photographer was one step behind, waiting for the opportunity to snap the man being swirled around in the protective arms of his friend.

Mark had caught some of the words of the pursuing reporter and was spluttering from the smothering, hugging arms of Paul. 'It's all lies!... All damn lies!' That was all that Mark could squeeze out before he was delivered from the melée by the clutching hands of Robert Manning. He dragged Mark through the doors of the court. Paul scrambled after, shielding the two men from the hailing hands of the scrawny reporter and the lumbering cameraman.

The antics outside and the subsequent rescue had not gone unnoticed by the audience of petty criminals and their respective young lawyers.

When Mark had recovered from his impromptu dancing lesson Robert was able to deliver some good news. 'Listen Mark. One of the girls has come clean,' he announced. His face was beaming to encourage Mark to do the same.

'Great!' Mark's delight was evident. 'They should all crumble now. Who is it?'

'It would appear that Clair Hooper has admitted that she wasn't involved. It was all a mistake she now reckons.'

'Pity it wasn't the Bennett girl. Well anyway it's a start and should undermine the rest of the pile of lies. I feel better.' And he looked it.

'That's good,' Robert added, 'you need something to get you through this session.'

'Oh!' Mark was brought down to earth.

'Mark Stephens! Mark Stephens!' His name was being chanted again. But this time by an elderly man wearing a frayed black gown, rather like that worn by a church sexton. The court attendant was summoning him.

'Now, I won't be able to sit with you,' Robert whispered as they were shown into the hushed court. He touched Mark's arm in reassurance as he peeled off and entered a pew running parallel to the bench. Mark, like the rabid dog, was separated off and penned in a long dock. Paul stayed outside on the pretext of watching out for more preying newsmen, when in fact he'd spotted a rather tasty young lawyer dressed in his favourite black. He enjoyed a pursuit like that.

Three severe hang-dog faces sat raised above the general chaos of the bustling courtroom. Magistrates administering the law. Puppets operated by a bustling clerk who sat flustered beneath these grave notaries.

'Yes, Mr. Clayton, we can begin,' the central owl commanded.

Mark was asked only to identify himself. He never spoke again.

Clayton was counsel for the Crown Prosecution Service. He stood to address the court, shuffling papers and tugging on his jacket. It would seem he didn't know the case well.

'Excuse me madam. I wish to make the argument for referral of this case to the Crown Court. There are four separate charges, all of indecent assault against girls under the age of sixteen.' Clayton paused, and pulled at the papers in front of him. 'There are... um, where is it?... er... three. No sorry, two. Yes, two girls. The charges are serious and the accused here is said to have touched one of the girls' breasts and performed digital penetration of the vagina. The defendant has been accused of making the girls touch his penis and perform masturbation.'

Mark was unsure whether he should be horrified, or collapse laughing. It sounded unreal. It was a rag week prank. Or one of those frightening dreams where you try to shout through locked jaws, or attempt to run but are riveted to the spot, or your raucous laughter is silent and running in slow motion.

He was the only one. The rest of the court had taken it seriously. On the bench they were cemented in concentration. What a list of sordid acts. What a pervert this man was. It was great stuff.

'I think you will agree that this court is not in a position to deal with a case of this gravity. I believe Mr. Manning here, representing the defendant, is in agreement.' Clayton half turned and threw a hand out in a gesture to identify the man sitting next to him.

'Is that right, Mr. Manning?' The Chairwoman lowered her spectacles and jabbed the question in Robert's direction. Her voice was of glass; pointed shards of splintered glass.

Robert nodded and muttered a brief response. 'That's so, Madam Chairwoman.'

There was a short conference between the three Justices of the Peace using blinkering hands and leaning heads. After which the Chairwoman's scything voice sanctioned the CPS request. She then turned to Mark, who was still bewildered and clutching the dock's restricting rail. 'Mr. Stephens, do you understand what we have decided here? Well it is my duty to explain this to you.' It seemed she had made this statement several times before.

Despite her cutting tongue Mark detected a tone of concern as she explained their decision.

'We have made provision for your case to be dealt with at the Crown Court. It is obvious to us that there are serious matters of witness testimony and evidence. We here are not in a position to provide the facilities or the expertise involved. For the sake of both sides we have committed this case to a higher court. You will remain on bail under the same conditions, and you will receive notice of your appearance at the Crown Court.' She raised her chubby form from the throne-like seat and leaned forward to speak with the clerk. 'I assume this will be Guildford?'

The clerk gripped his lips together and concurred with a nod.

'Guildford Crown Court most probably Mr. Stephens.' She turned to the other magistrates to see if there were further questions. The shaking of heads signalled that there were none. 'Thank you Mr. Clayton, Mr. Manning.'

Mark was led by the court usher from the dock and left

alongside his solicitor who fed him his comforting arms. 'All right, Mark?' Robert enquired, concerned by the vacant expression still displayed in his client's eyes.

Paul met them outside. The flighty young woman lawyer had been swallowed up by another court. He had talked briefly to her, but she had seen through his usual chat-up line. Ten out of ten for effort, he would have joked with Mark at a better time.

'How'd it go?' Paul was eager to know the outcome.

Robert answered for Mark who wasn't speaking yet. 'Just a formality. All done. It goes to Crown Court. No dates as yet. Now I suggest you bring the car round to get him home. There are probably more news hounds waiting outside.'

Paul hurried out. There were more reporters hanging around. Some recent arrivals were quick to question Paul, believing him to be Mark Stephens, but a brisk shake of the head by the pimply one who had accosted Mark earlier pushed them back into their ambush positions. However, they watched Paul's progress towards the car park and expected an escape was being initiated. When he brought the car outside and sat on the double-yellow line with the engine running their suspicions were confirmed.

'Let's go!' Robert commanded, and dragged at Mark's arm. They rushed through some moaning youths who were nudged aside by the fleeing men. Robert literally chucked Mark into the passenger seat of Paul's car. Paul wasn't an experienced getaway driver. There was no screeching of tyres, but he did make a rapid exit and prevented any worthwhile photographs being taken.

Alison wanted to know everything that had happened. She couldn't have gone with him. To see him as some kind of freak; the subject of people's base curiosity, even hatred. She waited until he was ready. There wasn't that much to tell. He made light of the procedure and even joked a little about the magistrates. Alison was delighted when he told her that Clair Hooper had come clean.

'That's great. The other two must follow soon. I am so pleased for you, Mark.' She gave him a gentle but encouraging hug.

She was less enthusiastic about the newsmen. She didn't realise the significance of this initial press interest.

The next day brought it home with a vengeance. An innocuous ring of the bell sent Mark, still dressed in his old T-shirt he slept in, to the front door. There, standing peculiarly to one side, was a skinny young man wearing a light-grey suit, buttoned uncomfortably tight.

'Mr. Mark Stephens?' he questioned through a broad grin, and in a South London accent.

Mark didn't know why, but he retorted a crisp, 'No!' Perhaps it was a defensive instinct. The caller was dubious and his doorstep manner strange.

'Oh. I understood this is where he lived.' He held his chin and looked out towards the road. 'Right. I'll have to check this. Thank you.'

Mark shut the door thoughtfully. He wandered into the lounge to watch the man's departure from the lounge window. At the roadside the lean man rendezvoused with a heavily-set colleague, hanging on to a swinging camera, who had been positioned beside one of the trees in the front garden.

'Shit!' Mark exclaimed, and rushed to warn Alison.

Within five or ten minutes the doorbell sounded again. Mark and Alison crept to the window. It was the press back for more. They didn't answer the door. They weren't going to answer the door. The bell rang once more. And again. Mark and Alison Stephens were huddled on the floor. The wagons had been circled and they were besieged. But there was no cavalry to rescue this couple.

A clicking noise from the hall heralded a new ploy. 'Mr. Stephens! Phil Pascal from the *News of the World*. Can I have a word?' The slimy journalist was speaking through the letter box, to the empty hall and hopefully to the imprisoned teacher whose recent court appearance had alerted the national press.

And this sort of story was as attractive to the sensationalist press as the *Vicar and his Choirboys* expose that he had already filed for next Sunday's edition.

Mark and Alison remained in hiding. Not speaking, but swapping anxious expressions.

'Come on Mr. Stephens. The opportunity to tell your story. Let the readers know the other side. We could write it just on the bits from yesterday's court hearing if you want. Much better for you to give it some balance. It's to your advantage.' The mouth at the letter box was persuasive. He had probably performed this manner of negotiation before. It was a wonder he didn't carry knee pads with him.

Yet again the doorbell. And again the strained voice spluttering through the letter box. 'Come on Mr. Stephens. Just a few minutes of your time. Then we'll go. Leave you alone. Come on. Your story. Tell the readers what's happened.'

After forty minutes or so he hadn't gone. Mark gave Alison a look of resignation and lifted himself up to arrange his surrender. As he approached the swinging flap on the door he could make out the tunnel eyes of Phil Pascal.

'Ah! Mr. Stephens.' Pascal continued, now by habit, to talk through the narrow slit in the door. It wasn't until Mark opened it wide that the reporter rose from his knees. 'Thank you. Now tell me your side of this terrible business. Must be a shock for you and your family. Such awful accusations.' Phil Pascal was well-practised in sounding sincere, getting on the side of even the foulest creatures just for a story, being their buddy, taking a confession, joining his camp, arguing along with him, agreeing that there was an injustice - a tricky, slippery slime-ball. But that was what he was paid to be, and he was damn good at it.

Behind the sycophantic smile of Phil Pascal lurked, half-hidden in the neighbours bushes, the burly cameraman Mark had seen earlier. 'Oh, yeah Mr. Stephens; just a few shots. Looks better. You understand.' The shutter stuttered as the eager photographer caught Mark Stephens looking like shit.

Mark found it difficult to talk at first. His mouth started up several times without success. Everything was out of order. In a jumble.

He attempted to put the pack straight but it was still awry when he dealt it to the scratching pen of Phil Pascal.

'It's... all... lies. For some reason these... girls are bloody lying. I haven't done these things. Couldn't have. At least one girl has admitted it wasn't true.'

'Which girl is that?' Pascal interrupted.

'Oh. Not one mentioned yesterday. There were three. It was Clair Hooper who has told the truth now. Print that. Susan Bennett and Pauline Green are maintaining these inventions but I do believe it's all breaking down, and it will dissipate really soon.' Mark's tone was hopeful.

'It's not easy. I can't use everything.' Pascal continued. 'The bloody beaks have put a restriction on mentioning the girls' names. And I'm expecting them to do the same with the name of the school. Only you we can name. Bit of a bastard isn't it? Is there a particular reason why these girls should have made such scandalous allegations, Mr. Stephens? It does seem an unusually brutal thing to do to you. Did they dislike you? Had you punished them at school? You must have upset them, eh?'

'They approached me improperly - that is Clair Hooper and Susan Bennett. On separate occasions. I dealt with the matter. Put them straight. Sorted it out.'

'I see,' Pascal pondered. His mind worked quickly. Exploring every seedy angle. 'Perhaps they were sort of competing. Making this up. Their separate stories to outdo each other. Been with a teacher. Impress their mates, eh?'

Mark gave that some thought. He recalled Susan Bennett mentioning the Hooper girl when she burst into his classroom and again on the phone. Of course. What a dimwit he had been. 'You may have something there. Yes, that could well be it.'

Pascal jotted more notes. 'We'll suggest that. It'll be a good angle. Maybe our piece will do you more favours than the one in The Times, eh?'

'Times?' Mark snapped.

'Yeah. Haven't you seen it? In there today. And in a few others. Shame, would have gone better as an exclusive. Well, thanks a lot Mr. Stephens. This should be in Sunday's paper. Bye.' With that Phil Pascal collected his cameraman from the undergrowth and they climbed in his car.

Mark was frozen on the doorstep. He had no idea. In the national papers? Everyone reading his name. Thinking he'd done those things. Not all his friends knew and hardly any of his family other than close relations had been told. He was always confident that it would be a short term problem. Solved promptly and back at school without having to broadcast that he had been accused of such smutty deeds.

Now there was his ageing mother to deal with. She would see the papers, or one of the scatty old dears at the Friendship Club would be ready to broadcast it. He would break it to her gently. Make out it wasn't as serious as it sounded. Getting Anna and Jayne involved would help. Granddaughters have a great influence. Or he might enlist his God-squad brother to tackle her from a spiritual angle. He was certainly a master of charm and patience.

Mark hovered over the piles of papers in the small newsagents, run, as most appear to be, by the Patel family. His nostrils were filled with the porridge odour of newsprint as he crouched down to examine the front pages of every tabloid and broadsheet. It was no good. He would have to buy a copy of each one. Flicking through all the pages of every paper would be a mistake and draw attention to him. He was already certain he had been recognised. Besides Mr. Patel would consider it bad form and tut continuously from behind the high racks of chewing gum. Mark collected one paper from each stack and handed the bundle over to the puzzled grandmother of the Patel family. She hated adding all that up.

Alison helped him hunt through every column of every newspaper. 'Page two in The Times,' she announced from behind the flapping mainsail of the extended broadsheet.

'Tell me the worst.' Mark braced himself.

'Teacher on Sex Charges.' Alison declared. She announced the headlines of a four inch story, trying to control a volatile mixture of distress and anger. She didn't read any more aloud. And her strained expression stuck to her face throughout. When she had finished she handed him the paper. She searched through the pile for more accounts, fearing what she might find in some of the seedier tabloids.

The report that Mark now read and re-read had his full name, his address, all but the number of the house, named the school and the position he held there. It wasn't explicit about the charges except the sexual nature of them. There was a brief history of the school and Mark's experience there. No one could be in any doubt the identity of this dastardly offender.

There were a couple of shorter reports in the other papers with a summary of the same information. They were in corners near adverts and fillers; diluted stories to allow for other scandals and photographs. There was no witch hunt.

He knew it would happen. The first one came at lunchtime. The bell rang right through him.

'Ah! Mark. Stuart here. How are you?'

'Fine.' Mark waited for it.

'Hope you don't mind the call, but I was just flicking through *The Times* in the office and saw...'

Mark stopped him there. 'Flicking through eh? Well, yes, it's me.'

'Oh! Dear. I hoped it was a mistake. My God! What's happened?'

'Well it's a long story. A load of rubbish. Basically a couple of girls competing, we think, with fantasies about relationships with me. I should think it will collapse pretty soon.' Mark spluttered out a condensed version of the terrible business. Stuart was from the tennis club. And Mark was glad Stuart could be a messenger. Convey his innocence. Prevent any fanciful accounts being spread round the members. They liked a juicy scandal.

There were more calls from concerned or curious people. Mark spoke to them all. He wouldn't delegate that. He had to assure the persistent questioners that these were girls nearly sixteen and not much younger. Despite their insistence that they were behind Mark wholeheartedly and could never believe he would do such a thing, they had to be sure he wasn't going to touch their pre-pubescent daughters. They tried to hide the real reason behind their enquiry. But he knew, and it hurt.

Charles Cornwall phoned the next morning. He had read the reports. 'Sorry it got into the papers, Mark.'

'Yeah. A bit of a bugger that.' Mark was resigned to the notoriety. As long as it didn't escalate.

'I've just received a call from the school,' Charles continued. 'There's a new date for the hearing. You'll probably get something in the post today or tomorrow. They want to go ahead on July 6th. I've spoken to that dick of a bursar Hall and informed him, in no mean terms, that he can't possibly continue while the police are still pursuing a criminal enquiry. Robert Manning has backed me on this. And Robert is particularly resolute that you should not say anything that you may have to mention should this come to trial. Colonel Hall says he has spoken to the Chairman of Governors, Alexander Darlington, and he is adamant that they should proceed with the disciplinary hearing.'

'Shit!' Mark was not prepared for a further kick in the groin. 'So we have to go in there without any witnesses because they won't let us interview, and a defence we can't even present. Sitting duck I think sums it up! Do you mean to say that we face those Governors, sat as dummies, and just accept my dismissal without uttering a word?'

'No.' Charles was quick to step in. 'I will address the panel of Governors. Ask them to adjourn. Tell them it is impossible to expose your explanation in view of the criminal proceedings. They've got to realise they are out of order to decide your fate under these conditions. Assure them that as soon as the case is dropped we will fight these bogus allegations. Then of course there is always the appeal procedure. If the worst happens and they go through with the gross misconduct charges and you're fired, then we can immediately appeal. The police business should be history by then.'

'Are they going to listen to you?'

'I have a feeling that that little shit, Colonel Hall, is running the entire show. It's a financial thing. He wants you out of there to save the money. Most of the Governors are his stooges. Particularly that Darlington goon. It could look better.'

'Why is it, Charles, that every time I climb back up I am smashed down again? It's so frustrating; so unfair.'

'I know.' Charles could only offer sympathy. 'I'm working at everything, exploring all the options. They'd be making a massive mistake if they went ahead with the hearing. I have spoken to the Union head office and they are looking at other cases. I'm getting a letter from Robert outlining the prejudice situation. You can go through the headmaster's statements and see if there is anything new you can think of.'

'Seems a wasteful exercise if we can't even present a case.' Mark was disconsolate now.

'We have to be prepared. If the girls tell the truth or are unwilling to repeat their allegations we might get the go ahead to defend these charges at the hearing. It is important we keep on our toes.' Charles attempted to keep Mark focused.

'I suppose you're right, Charles.' Mark conceded.

❧

The weeks passed rapidly and nothing changed. There was no word that the girls had confessed. Robert Manning had no new information and as far as Charles was concerned the hearing would take place as planned.

And it did.

Chapter 6

It was the first time he had worn his suit since the day of his suspension. Alison had pressed the trousers and even run the iron over his tie. He couldn't eat much. A twisted stomach and not much time to spare. Even for this event he was cutting it fine. Alison didn't go. He needed to be alone on the journey; to think things through. He didn't want Alison associated with it. She was his rock at home. That's where he needed her.

Charles Cornwall met him on the playing fields car park. He had arrived forty minutes before Mark. There was a shaking of hands and 'tough-it-out' smiles, but not long to exchange news. They were interrupted by the attention-seeking cough of Captain Donald Cutter, assistant bursar. Cutter was an ugly man. Mark reckoned that some gruesome pitbull had chewed the head off a cadaver and that had been sewn on the body of Toad from *Wind in the Willows* to produce the form of Captain Cutter. He was an Ulsterman and he was riddled with all the bigotry and prejudice that went with it. Not only was he physically unattractive. His voice dragged coarse and rasping, faltering and contaminating. He had condemned Mark Stephens already. Cutter's brain had been allocated reduced thinking capacity whilst serving in the army, and there was little anyone could do to restore a degree of reason.

'You're to follow me. This way, the two of you,' he fussed. He didn't look Mark in the eye. He had known him for four years yet he couldn't acknowledge his presence.

Neither Mark nor Charles wanted to speak to him, so merely followed behind his waddling gait, occasionally swapping calming glances.

The school had never conducted a disciplinary hearing on this scale before, and Colonel Hall had been forced to read carefully and follow his own code to the letter. A special panel of Governors had been selected and assembled. The five members of the panel had read the statements published by the headmaster prior to the hearing. It was clear that this teacher was really a depraved monster who had committed the most appalling assaults on these poor girls.

The bursar's secretary escorted Mark and Charles into the staff social room where the trial was to take place. Mark could hear the buzz of children in lessons and hoped he would spot some of the pupils. They would have yelled their support if they were aware of what he was facing.

Inside the claustrophobic room sat three male Governors and two female, and at one end of the long table that they sat at was the fidgety form of Colonel James Hall, Clerk to the Governors, orchestrating it all. In the centre, and spokesman for the panel, propped up with cushions, was Alexander Darlington, seeming to be wearing the black cloth on his head, and determined to sentence Mark Stephens to a horrible execution.

'It is my responsibility to introduce everyone here. Isn't that correct Colonel Hall?' Darlington mumbled, unsure of his purpose at the hearing, but certain of its outcome.

James Hall jumped up. 'That's the procedure Mr. Darlington.'

'Thank you.' There was a pause. Then the five people recruited from the main governing body were introduced. A full list of names that Darlington had been provided with sat in front of him to prevent his usual trick of forgetting the names of even his closest colleagues. He concluded with his own name. Not that he would forget who he was, but Colonel Hall wasn't going to chance that. He watched the Chairman of Governors like a hawk. This had to go smoothly. The man was a fool and couldn't be trusted to perform properly without the twitching little Colonel behind him. James Hall, however, needed a senile dolt like that. Easy to twist around his fiddling little fingers. Total control of every aspect of the school at the tips of his fund-diving digits. Yes, it would be murder to have someone with intellect or common sense in that position. So there was no greater supporter (in more ways than one) of the Chairman of the Governors than Colonel James Hall.

Mark and Charles introduced themselves despite there being no reason to think Mark Stephens was anybody other than the despicable fiend they were there to try.

Darlington was hoisted to his feet by the signalling hand of his puppeteer, James Hall.

'Now, what will happen at this disciplinary hearing will be that the headmaster, Mr. Frith, will put the case of gross misconduct against Mr. Stephens on behalf of the school and produce any witnesses...' Darlington faltered. 'That's it isn't it Colonel?' Colonel Hall, embarrassed by the consultation quickly nodded agreement, but also waved a hand in the direction of Charles and Mark. 'Oh, yes. And Mr. Cornwall will reply on Mr. Stephens' behalf. Is that clear?' He wasn't certain it was clear to himself and stood pondering, hand on chin. The Colonel's scorching eyes hauled him down.

Charles Cornwall stood up. The panel targeted and challenged him with their aiming eyes.

'If I could address the panel. I have a statement to make.' Charles announced.

'This is out of order. Can't you make your statement when you present Mr. Stephens' case?' Darlington questioned.

'No. I believe it is important that I am heard now, as what I have to say is critical. The nature of this hearing depends on it. I wish to present arguments for the adjournment of this hearing,' Charles insisted.

Colonel Hall puffed and tightened his lips. The panel clucked like hens, and heads nodded and jerked. Alexander Darlington was fed a slip of paper by the vexatious bursar. He climbed out of his seat again. 'If you and Mr. Stephens would leave the room. We wish to confer on this request.'

Charles and Mark left the twittering panel. Old or middle-aged people out of their depth, left to be guided or misguided in their quarantine by the ticking Colonel. It took only a couple of minutes before Mark and Charles were ushered back into the hearing.

'We have decided to hear your statement Mr. Cornwall. To hear what you have to say. Although we are most definitely against any adjournment or delay.'

'Thank you.' Charles held the floor. 'Members of this disciplinary panel, I ask you to adjourn the hearing for the following reasons. First, the member of my Union, who I represent, Mark Stephens, is unable to defend himself here today against the charges that the headmaster will put. He cannot make known any aspect of his absolute refutation of the allegations that have been made. I have here a letter from Mr. Robert Manning, Mr. Stephens' solicitor, to confirm what I have said.' Charles Cornwall waved the paper to demonstrate its availability. 'Should the hearing continue to take place my client is forced to say nothing. Secondly we have not been allowed the opportunity to interview potential witnesses. An arrangement was made but was subsequently cancelled. Thirdly, a police investigation of these matters continues and what is said here could easily prejudice this inquiry. Fourthly, I understand that the girls who have made these allegations will not be present for me to cross-examine. That process is only fair and just, and is essential to our case. These statements that the headmaster obtained are riddled with contradictions and inconsistencies. In fact they are a total fabrication. Finally, we understand that one of the girls, Clair Hooper, has admitted to the police that her account of what happened was a complete lie. I therefore ask you to adjourn this hearing for the sake of justice. There can be no justice if you judge Mark Stephens on only evidence from one source.' Charles Cornwall plonked himself down and waited. It was a sound delivery without unnecessarily emotive phrases.

Nonplussed faces scoured the room. The panel, thrown together to solely process this affair, were now dealing with complications. They hadn't been told. It was to be so simple.

They had clear statements about this teacher's misbehaviour, about his sexual assaults on these poor young girls. But now this. Doubt? Surely there was not doubt! Colonel Hall and the headmaster received their confused glare. Darlington was totally lost. Hall scrambled to reach the ear of the Chairman of Governors.

After a few agonising minutes Darlington spoke. 'Well. I am informed that we must consider this request. To do so we require Mr. Cornwall and Mr. Stephens to vacate the room once more.'

Charles and Mark stood, shook their heads in frustration, and made for the headmaster's office where they were to wait.

Inside, where the panel still sat, the bursar set to work. It would be a disaster if there was an adjournment. There was no idea whether it would go to court, or when. The school would be paying Stephens for ever. He had to be vanquished now.

'Look, this is an open and shut case.' Hall herded them in. He had to keep them on track. 'You've all read the statements made by the girls. He did it. The man's a monster. Surely there's enough evidence to prove a charge of gross misconduct here!' The Colonel's eyes were blazing.

At least one governor was troubled. A lone voice. 'But, there were some sound points put forward by Mr. Cornwall. If all we are going to hear is the one side it can't possibly be fair. Can it?' Mrs. Veronica Jenkins, a parent governor, showed the only concern. She could see it was a cry from an uninhabited wilderness and said no more.

'It's only a stalling exercise. They want him to get paid while we wait around for some decision by the police or CPS. He has the opportunity to appeal. So there's his avenue should he need it. But, from what I hear, unofficially of course, he's a prime candidate for prosecution, and it's more than likely that he'll get a prison sentence for this.' Colonel Hall had more than Darlington on the end of his tugging strings. 'You will need to vote on the proposal to adjourn as requested by Mr. Cornwall.'

Darlington proposed the rejection of Mr. Cornwall's suggestion. All five waved a limp arm to signal their agreement. Even Mrs. Jenkins was with them. Too concerned about being seen as a renegade.

Colonel Hall sighed inwardly. A relieved man.

When Mark and Charles were invited back in they sensed from the stony faces that their plea had been a waste of time. And an announcement to that effect by Alexander Darlington confirmed it.

'If that is your decision I must inform you that Mr. Stephens and myself will take no further part in these proceedings. We will, however, remain in the room, but merely as observers. I would like that noted.' Charles Cornwall was pissed off. Another fucking panel of school governors who didn't care about justice and fair play.

So they kicked off. Only one team on the field. A farce.

The headmaster gave an account of Jan Edgerley's call and her report about what the girls had told her. The suspension of his Head of English. How he had taken the statements the afternoon of the day Mark Stephens was suspended. The statements were not read out and no one was called as a witness. Not even Jan Edgerley. A few of the Governors asked naïve questions out of a duty to appear interested in fair play. Mrs. Jenkins, still uncomfortable about the lack of defence and guilty about her Judas vote, attempted to question in a manner she thought Mr. Cornwall might have approached it. She was nowhere near as aggressive as he would have been.

'Excuse me headmaster,' Mrs. Jenkins began. 'Did you try to find some children who had seen something, some corroboration of these accounts? It does seem strange that there are no other pupils, other than the girls involved, who can confirm some of these events. And, Mr. Stephens has been a teacher at the school for over twelve years, I believe. Surely it comes as a shock to you that he should do these things?' She was crossing tracks in her effort to chase out areas where she saw some investigation was necessary.

Clumsy as it was, Mark hung on to what Veronica Jenkins

was asking. It was his only lifeline.

Ted Frith stood to answer. 'It would appear that we only have support from Pauline Green and Susan Bennett. They can verify each other's story. You are correct in your observation. I couldn't find anybody who could support these allegations other than, as you have read, Michael Speer who saw Clair Hooper upset outside Cairo House. And, yes it did come as a shock to me that Mr. Stephens would do such things. He is perhaps not the most conformist teacher at the school but I would never have dreamt of him having sexual relationships with the pupils.'

An empty silence followed. Veronica Jenkins struggled to find another question. She knew there had to be a way through these accusations. She could read the urgency on Mark Stephen's face. There was something wrong here but it was such a maze to her. She could feel the other governors eyes fixed on her.

The prickly Colonel was baffled by her enquiries. Why was she bothering? Whenever she looked his way he cut her down with a sickle stare.

She fought on. 'Do you believe these girls, headmaster? Is there any chance that they have fabricated these versions? Mr. Cornwall has told us that Clair Hooper has admitted her account was untrue. What of that?'

'As far as I'm concerned I must treat what these girls have told me as the truth. I know of no reason why they should lie. I have not been told of any development with regard to Clair Hooper's statement.'

Have you even bloody looked into it? Are these statements etched in stone? Mark shouted from the silence of his clenched teeth and urging eyes.

Mrs. Jenkins asked no further questions. She was alone and knew a brick wall when she ran into one.

Seeing her flag Alexander Darlington stepped in. 'Are there any more questions?' He could recognise there were none and was determined the hearing should make a decision as soon as possible. He turned to Mark. And lashed out a final request. 'Now, Mr. Stephens here is your opportunity. Won't you rethink your approach and defend yourself against these charges.' He knew Mark wouldn't break his silence. He could afford this generous invitation.

But Mark did. An escape from the gagging fury. He hadn't intended to. It just exploded from his frustration and flew from his mouth.

'I didn't do it! I did not do it! You sit there in judgement. You know I can't give you details. Show how it was impossible. Don't you think I am ready to boil? Struck dumb while you all decide my future. It's a bloody nightmare. Take it from me I could demonstrate that all this is a complete nonsense. But I can't. I have been hounded by the press, treated like a damn criminal and now I'm about to lose my job. You haven't the decency to wait until I can clear my name. You're going to condemn me without a fair hearing. As I said; a bloody nightmare.' Mark shook his head in despair.

Charles managed to claw Mark down and back to his seat.

'Okay, Mark, okay. Take it easy. We'll get them at the appeal.' Charles was making highly visible attempts at calming him. There was purpose in that.

'Yes. Thank you.' Darlington wished he hadn't made the gesture. 'If you gentlemen would retire once more, we will consider our decision.'

Mark and Charles were glad to escape. They didn't talk much as they waited to be recalled. It was a forgone conclusion. Both men knew it. Mark felt sick. Charles felt awkward. He didn't have the words he needed now.

Doreen Peters summoned them. The panel was ready. They had spent only a matter of minutes deliberating. Darlington had been well prepared by the scheming Colonel. There was nothing really to discuss. How could there be when they had heard nothing from the man they were about to sack for gross misconduct. It was a sham.

When Mark and Charles entered the room they could feel

the weight of the panel's combined guilt. They understood what they had done. Expediency designed by the strutting, poisoned-dwarf of a Colonel. But Mark Stephens wasn't going to forgive them for this.

'The decision of the panel will be given verbally now and also confirmed in writing.' Darlington's last prepared speech. 'This hearing finds the charge of gross misconduct by Mr. Stephens proven to the panel's satisfaction and Mr. Stephens is hereby dismissed, subject to any appeal, from this date.'

Mark sucked his lip. Charles touched his arm and managed a grin of comfort through his own dejected eyes. Both men grunted in disgust and left. They left Darlington standing at the table struggling with some of the details of Mark's departure from Thomas Graham School.

'Fucking hell!' Mark said it several times as the two men crossed the road to where their cars were parked. Donald Cutter scampered behind them insisting they were to be escorted from the premises by an official of the school. Mark turned round to confront the jabbering Captain. Cutter stopped in his tracks. He recognised a man who could kill. Mark Stephens was ready to tear the hideous man apart. Donald Cutter only restarted his herding role after Mark had been yanked back by Charles' attending hand.

'Keep in line. Stop that Phillips! No mud throwing!' The strained voice of Simon Sankey broke the edible silence of the retreating men and chasing toad. Sankey was escorting a snaking group of Year Nine athletes to practise for the school sports. As usual he struggled to hold their attention and to make any impression on their disruptive behaviour.

Wailing in space. Sankey's voice was no longer shrieking above the wild yells and squabbling disobedience of the chaotic group. He was heard alone. Above the sudden switched-on silence. For several seconds he ripped the air with his piercing pleas that demanded order and respect. And when he realised all was calm and there was no disruption, no insolence, no disorder; he sucked on his lip to his register surprise; to smother his stupidity. All the children who had been swarming uncontrollably to their lesson were struck dumb by the sight of Mark. Of course there had been talk, all sorts of gossip about why he had left. They knew it involved Susan Bennett. And they knew, even the young ones, what a bloody stupid moose she was.

They lined up to talk but said nothing. The line grew longer as they all wrestled for the front row. A boy with a bubble growing white and wet at his nose spluttered first. 'You coming back, Sir?'

'Yeah. When are you going to be teaching us again, Mr. Stephens?' Another boy added.

'Yeah!' Came the chorus.

'That fool of a woman doesn't know what she's on about. The one they got in for you,' the first speaker continued.

'Yeah!' came the responding refrain from the assembled athletes.

Mark couldn't reply. These weren't kids he particularly knew well, or in fact had noticed much. But it seemed they knew him enough. Liked him.

Charles watched Mark's face and the faces of his new supporters. He was ready to speak for him but gave Mark a chance to pull the strings together.

'You lot get out of here!' Donald Cutter made a scooping movement with his curving arms as he waddled along the row of children. 'Mr. Sankey get them onto the field and about their business, would you.'

'Yes, Captain Cutter.' Sankey spoke like a timid girl, and made enticing gestures at the children. 'Come on now, let's get going.'

They ignored him. Their faces growled at the prancing master coaxing them with swishing arms. They searched the face of their teacher. The disgraced one; Mark Stephens, still clutching the car door.

'You coming back or what, Sir?' The first boy insisted. He closed in on Mark, and the others followed. They surrounded him. Charles eased away. Cutter and Sankey muttered and cursed in the background. 'Get back here Sir. Go on. We miss you.' It was hard for the boy to say and he spoke as if to a pal just to ease his embarrassment. He had his street cred to consider. Couldn't usually be seen to be soft. But there was no barracking. Truth was, they all wanted to say the same thing. A general murmur of support rumbled around him. The boy felt safer now about what he had said.

Mark summoned some painful words. It was difficult and they emerged accompanied by a great deal of swallowing and biting of lips.

'Nice of you... to say so. Miss being at the place. Miss teaching you rowdy lot.' Mark smiled. It had to be a bit of humour; it was the only way. 'You know it's not true, don't you?' There was no reaction. He felt a little unsettled. 'You know I wouldn't do anything like they have said. It's that Susan Bennett. You wouldn't believe what I am supposed to have done.' Mark looked into their dazed eyes. Perhaps they didn't understand.

They certainly found it uncomfortable to respond.

'She's a moose!' A girl at the back shouted. All the heads turned to identify the speaker and then rotated back to Mark.

'That's right. She aint going to be believed. Right liar her!' A flood of support for Mark followed.

Charles eased him into the car. It couldn't go too far. There were legal implications here. Some of the kids were potential witnesses. Mark turned to smile as he was persuaded through the car door.

There were more yells of support and ugly and vulgar condemnation of Susan Bennett, which continued even when Simon Sankey and Donald Cutter managed to lead the straggling group of protesters away from the marooned cars.

Mark drove home a numbed man. He had been sacked. They had all believed the lies. There wasn't the anger he hoped would fill and even overspill. There was only the deep and lingering sickness swelling in his stomach.

Alison didn't need to be told. His face broadcast all she

needed to know.

'Those little bastards. Mark, why are they doing it? Surely they should have told the truth by now? What are we going to do? Mark? How are we going to get through this?' Alison had lost it. She was raving. Mark hadn't seen her like this before.

He wrapped up her lashing arms; encircled them in his restraining hug, and spoke soothingly in her ear. Now it was his time to show some strength. It was a fucking mess but he wasn't going to let her hear that.

'It'll be all right. Now just calm down.' Inside his securing grasp she gripped her mouth shut with forcing lips and glowed scarlet at the cheeks. 'I'm on full pay. There's an appeal. The girls could easily break down before that. It's not as bad as you imagine.'

Of course it was. It was probably worse. If it went all the way and there was a court case then there would be the same scenario at the appeal, and he'd lose it. Lose his job permanently, lose his salary; probably lose the house. And perhaps lose her. He rocked her within his clenched arms. The warm tears tumbled off her cheeks and on to his shoulder, wetting his shirt. She eventually fell limp but he still gently swung her loose form on the spot and whispered comforting words as if coaxing a baby to sleep.

When he let her slip from his grip she dropped to the sofa and curled up. She sobbed a little more. Anna and Jayne sat either side and continued where their father had left off.

Later that evening, when they could talk through the despair, Alison opened another wound. 'I'm appalled at the lack of support you've received from the other staff at that bloody school. No one has phoned. You'd expect them to be contacting you regularly. I know you would if it was someone else. It isn't fair. It's not fair at all.' She was slipping back. It was hurting.

He spread a grin and tilted his head with a shrug. 'There are some I would have expected to call. There are others who never would. And there are those, probably in the majority, who don't know what to do. Not being sexist, but this is mainly the women. According to Dave the headmaster has spoken to the staff. Told them the seriousness of the matter and not to discuss it. There have, most likely, been some scurrilous comments from certain members of senior management maligning me. Overhearing malicious rumour and supposition. It is safer for them to sink their heads in the sand and ignore the presence of this affair. Or, they have been warned to keep clear of the unclean; the leper syndrome.' Mark fell silent at his last observation. Mud has the knack of sticking no matter who has thrown it, or at whom it has been thrown.

It was Alison's turn to extend a comforting hand. She touched his elbow to show him her smile. 'Forget those ostriches. Remember this; all your friends, all our friends, our families; they know you, know the truth. And furthermore they have said so. There has never been one person confronting us with doubt. That's where we must build our strength from, wield our retaliation from.' She showed her fist and pumped it firmly in the air. She was strong once again.

Chapter 7

Every delivery of post and every ring of the phone stung Mark and Alison. A peculiar mixture of hope and fear sent them to intercept the falling mail and to tug the receiver off the hailing telephone. A twitching alertness. A gnawing impatience.

Robert Manning had delayed until the school hearing was over. Mark had enough on his plate so he worked at what he could without disturbing him and moving the focus. Now he needed to work fast. It was no good assuming that these girls were going to alter their stories. He knew how the police would be handling them and there was little chance of a change of mind. It was going to court, to the Crown Court, and all his plans had to have that firmly etched in them.

'You have to make a formal statement to me, Mark,' Robert announced over the phone.

Mark was still shaking after pouncing on the receiver immediately he had heard the first ring.

'Now, it will help me out if you could come over here to Essex. Do you think you could manage that? We need to get this down as soon as possible.'

'Yes, I suppose so.' Mark was disoriented by the call. He couldn't quite respond with more than staccato sentences. 'Where are you exactly? When shall I come?'

Robert explained the location of the office and the route he personally preferred, but left the final route planning to Mark. 'Ten in the morning, on Tuesday, okay? See you then.' Robert signed off. He had more to attend to. It wasn't going to be an easy case; he could feel that. He hurried in to another office; a partner who knew the best barristers for this type of charge. It was a delicate matter and not just any lawyer would do. He would have a name for Mark when he saw him on Tuesday.

Robert contacted Charles Cornwall with details of progress so far. The Union were paying for all this and the costs were going to rise considerably once counsel was engaged.

Mark set off early Tuesday morning. He had decided he wouldn't follow Robert's route that took him through Blackwall Tunnel. Instead he bravely followed the M25 through Surrey and Kent and under the Thames at the Dartford Tunnel. A hell of a journey during the rush hour and only marginally better either side of it. Mark went with the flow. His head was full of his statement and the recent conversation he had had with Cameron Rudley, a barrister friend. Cameron had flicked through the papers amidst groans and other noises expressing concern. It wasn't encouraging but Mark was pleased to have an independent appraisal.

'You'll need someone good for this,' Cameron had said, 'someone who has dealt with cases like this before. I'm not happy with some of this.' He had rustled through the statements, stopped and pointed out areas where it would be difficult to defend, sucked his lips, expelled air audibly and moved on. He knew he wasn't up to it. 'There is a girl at our chambers. Bright thing. Does some of the sordid stuff. You may have read that case involving the woman who enticed young boys in off the streets. It was in the tabloids a few weeks back, and even in the Telegraph if I'm not mistaken. Well, she didn't exactly win the case, but everyone reckons she put up a great performance. She's done others. Can't remember all of them. I can get some details for you and your solicitor if you like.' Cameron was always a bit vague and this probably was the reason he was only a jobbing counsel taking on a variety of cases without a specialism. He never seemed to get the big ones and stake a claim on the honeypot that came with notoriety around Lincoln's Inn. 'Margaret Cullen; you'll like her. Pleasant girl, sense of humour and a real worker.'

The offices of Gilbert Johnson and Partners were housed in a hideous monstrosity that some cravated seventies architect had once boasted was the structure of the future, but which was one of thousands of ugly monoliths that punctuated the inner and outer suburbs of London. This jumbled corner of south-east Essex was no exception; in fact it had more than its fair share. Anyway, some people had already written off this twilight zone of multicultural muddle and sprawling hinterland.

Robert Manning's office was one of several that led off a crazy typing pool, where all manner of legal documents, some ridiculously huge, were being handled by a bevy of clattering women. A stocky woman who had managed to force her ample frame into an extremely tight skirt ushered Mark in. He watched her arse straining at the seams as she led him to Robert's empty desk. 'He'll be back in a minute, luv.' A real Essex girl, Mark thought, such unmistakable cheerfulness and unique plastic cockney lilt.

'Ah, Mark, sorry to keep you waiting.' Robert gave his apology as he rounded his desk to sit in front of Mark. 'You wouldn't believe it but I have other cases to deal with; you're not the only poor devil being hounded by the law.' He was in good spirits. Max Hulton, the senior partner had managed to secure the services of Gordon Crichton a pushy young barrister who he thought ideal for Mark's case. This would be Robert's good news for Mark. 'Now we must get this statement down. The way we will tackle this is that I will be your scribe. You just tell me everything. Don't leave out even the most minute speck of detail. I will read back to you what I have written and you can alter it here and now. Alternatively, when Mandy has typed it all up you will be sent a couple of copies. Read these thoroughly. Make any changes and initial them. Return the top copy signed. You keep the other copy. Is all this clear, Mark?'

'I think so.' Mark was a little flabbergasted. Robert's sudden efficiency threw him.

'Right let's start. I imagine it's going to take a long time. I am not the fastest writer so don't go too quickly.'

Mark took a deep breath. He had told this many times to many people. This was the most crucial account, the watertight one. However, he knew this wasn't going to be as straightforward as other renderings. He was clearly aware of one deep and deadly bear pit waiting for him.

He ran agonisingly through the advances by Clair Hooper and Susan Bennett, his managing of Susan Bennett's obsession, the visits to the classroom, the bogus phone calls, his meeting in Wokingham, the vicious approach at registration time, his interview with Ted Frith, his suspension, the vile letter. He cemented all this with other observations that he initiated or that Robert prompted.

When he thought he had covered everything Robert spoiled the party. 'At the police station they showed you an envelope and a letter. You haven't mentioned them in this statement.'

Mark tingled from his feet to the hairs on his neck and he could feel his face inflate, scarlet. He had shut it out. Now it came thundering back. Wokingham Police Station and the cell. Baxter and Mills throwing him questions and his repetitive 'no comment' response. And that envelope! And now the fatal mistake.

'Nothing to say. Never seen them before.' It was curt and dismissive. Cold and uncomfortable. Both men felt it.

Robert wasn't that easily fooled. 'Now, are you certain, Mark? This is bloody important. It seemed to throw you at the police station and now you still don't look at ease with it.'

'I have never sent that little tart a letter. The letter they showed me at the station was not written by me!' Mark snapped at Robert.

It was out of character and stunned the solicitor. But still the envelope and his handwriting was the phantom he wasn't willing to share. He couldn't tell Robert. It would go away. It wasn't important. Bloody hell, he was the victim here. He hadn't got to explain or justify anything.

'Okay, Mark. I'm only asking for your own good. It's a piece of material evidence they reckon they've got and we need to be prepared for whatever they are going to chuck at you. You understand, don't you?'

'Sure. I'm sorry I threw a wobbly. It must be getting to me. But truly I didn't write the bitch a letter.' Mark endeavoured to explain; pleaded to be believed. It was the truth, but it was a watery effort between guilty gulps of air.

'It's all right, Mark.' Robert knew there was a sore but he couldn't pursue it. He was troubled by Mark's attitude. He'd tried to unpack it but Mark had closed in and wouldn't budge. Robert just prayed it wouldn't be the huge time bomb that his intuition shouted was ticking away in there. 'Finally, Mark, I have some good news.'

Mark was all ears. He needed something other than the microscopic analysis of his account. He was on trial already.

'We have managed to secure the services of one of the most prestigious barristers in this field; Gordon Crichton. You have probably heard of him.' Robert's face was lit with satisfaction, for the first time that afternoon.

'No, I haven't.' Mark wasn't ready to join in the elation.

'Well, never mind. I can assure you of his pedigree.' Robert gathered up the thick pile of notes and tapped them straight.

Mark felt a little embarrassed in challenging Robert's commitment to Crichton. 'Robert, don't you think this needs a woman? Surely if this runs on and ends up in court it would be better for a woman to handle these girls.'

'I'm not sure that I see the value in that.' He was shaken by what he saw as Mark's ungratefulness.

'Well, I have been speaking to a barrister friend who has recommended a woman in his chambers; a Margaret Cullen. Do you know her?'

'I can't say I do.' Robert was severely put out. 'Crichton is my man. He will do the job well. I have never had my judgement questioned like this, and never, ever received a nomination from a client.'

'It's my arse on the line, Robert. Please consider it.' Mark had faith in Margaret Cullen even though he had never met her. Cameron had been genuine in his suggestion and Mark was not going to lose any advantage.

'I'll have to think this through. We'll talk tomorrow. I think that's it. We can both go home.' Robert was seething and wanted to pursue the matter but didn't have the patience. He had taken the statement. Both men had their own reasons for calling it a day.

When Mark left Robert's office the typing pool was silent. Only the buffing sound of the cleaner's duster and her monotone humming accompanied his exit from the offices of GilbertJohnson and Partners. He wouldn't visit the offices again.

Within three days the two copies of his statement had arrived. Mark meticulously went through the first few pages, but was less exact as he ploughed through the senseless recounting of what he considered were quite irrelevant details. His was a tale of partial mismanagement of events, innocently undertaken. He had done his best to deal with these girls, had made every effort to be a good teacher and judge. What was being alleged was make-believe and nothing to do with the real incidents. He couldn't understand why there were still people believing the Disney version. Mark signed the top copy as instructed after making a few alterations. He was glad to get it in the post and away from the house.

༺❀༻

Charles didn't phone very often over the next few months. He knew the real action was in Robert's corner and was well aware of the impotence of the school disciplinary appeal hearing as long as the criminal charges were unresolved. However, being a veteran of such cases he had made initial enquiries about the possibility of an Industrial Tribunal hearing if things went sour for Mark at the appeal.

Robert phoned as soon as he had received Mark's signed statement. There was to be a preliminary hearing at Guildford Crown Court.

'What does that mean?' Mark asked, not yet accustomed to what he saw as the maze of legal channels.

'It's only to hear your plea and to set an approximate date for the next stage,' Robert assured him.

'The next stage?' Mark was quick to respond.

Robert had attempted to camouflage it. To soften the blow. 'The court case,' he was forced to admit. 'Didn't like to smack you in the face with it. Wasn't very subtle was I?'

'I see. Time's running out isn't it, Robert? I assume there's still no word from the other side. Have the CPS spoken to you at all?'

'We have talked, but there's no meat in it. Procedure and dates; that's about as much as I get. Sorry.'

'It's all right. I still live in hope. Wish I had some of my brother's faith and felt that a prayer would set it all straight. Well there we are.' Mark was low. He'd been lower.

'About that matter we didn't conclude up here; your representation in court. I've given it some thought, made enquiries about your lady and discussed it with some of my colleagues. I go with my first feelings. Gordon Crichton has the experience and the expertise. He is likely to become Queen's Counsel very soon. We are very fortunate to get him.' Robert tried to cajole Mark into accepting his better judgement. He was of course the solicitor; the adviser with the trained legal background. What did a teacher charged with indecent assault know about selecting a barrister.

'I'm not convinced.' Mark was firm. 'The more I think about it the more I see the benefits of having Margaret Cullen. Cameron has also informed me that Margaret was a teacher before she went into the law. Ideal credentials don't you think?'

'I can see you're not going to budge.' Robert huffed. His client was bloody obstinate. He thought for a moment. 'If we do go with her then I need to meet her and come to my own conclusion. Give me her details and I'll fix it up.'

Mark could feel Robert's suppressed anger at his stubbornness. 'I'm sorry to be awkward. You know my feelings on this.'

'Yes, yes. Now give me Margaret Cullen's address and

phone number.'

'Right.' Mark read from a scruffy note that Cameron had given him.

'Thanks. I'll be in touch about the preliminary hearing as soon as we get a date. I expect it will be at the end of the month.' Robert rang off abruptly. He was pissed off with Mark Stephens. This would be a further inconvenience, checking on this bloody woman Mark was banking on to be his saviour.

It was the 29th August when Mark met Robert in the car park of Guildford Crown Court. The buildings that made up the complex were located near the centre of the town, but the drivers in hissing cars that swept past on the wet roads and the tripping pedestrians took no notice of the two men. There were no reporters lurking outside the courthouse. Mark felt more at ease.

'Morning, Mark.' Robert had forgotten his resentment over the selection of counsel. He had been to see Margaret Cullen at her chambers and had been impressed by her. He wasn't going to give Mark the satisfaction of 'I told you so'. He had grudgingly agreed to his request, repeated his faith in Gordon Crichton and expressed regret at Mark's lack of confidence. But now he didn't have any doubts about Margaret Cullen's ability to fight the charges expertly and diligently. She was a formidable woman. Even at the first meeting she had suggested avenues of enquiry that he hadn't considered.

'Morning, Robert.' Mark was remarkably cheerful considering the prospects awaiting him in the Crown Court.

They walked together through the entrance of the building housing the four separate courtrooms; both grey-suited and lugging briefcases. Mark carried an assortment of relevant documents and Robert as much of his case library as he could manage.

'Remember, all we are going to do here is allow the court to hear your formal plea. However, Margaret Cullen has instructed her junior counsel, who is sitting in on this, to request a change of venue for your case. This is too local, and with the coverage in the provincial press she feels you wouldn't get the best crack of the whip. We will be asking for a London court, perhaps the Central Criminal Courts at the Old Bailey.'

'Impressive. But won't that encourage media interest?'

'We will have to live with that. You must have the best opportunity, and I agree with Margaret, we need to move it from Guildford.' Robert didn't want to say that; to build Margaret up.

'Fine. I'll go along with the experts,' Mark concurred, content to recognise Robert's low-key acceptance of his choice of defence attorney.

There were very few people bustling round the courtroom when Mark and Robert shuffled in; black-gowned, stooping people collecting and clearing documents. They took no notice of the pervert teacher and his solicitor. The door squealed contemptuously to announce the arrival of the two barristers deep in far-too-close conference for Mark's liking. They swooped in, their gowns bat-winging and their arms clutching slipping papers. Close behind and near enough to prevent the door wheezing again strutted WPC Jean Baxter. She acknowledged Robert Manning and smiled audaciously at Mark.

Time was short and the court usher, under orders from the clerk, hurried everyone to their positions. Mark was shown the dock, the star performer, and the remainder inserted into their respective slots along the wooden benches allocated to prosecution and defence. Once in position a nod from the clerk sent the usher to summon the judge. Obviously he was waiting behind the door, as the usher was forced to retreat smartly in reverse after only a cursory rap.

Mark, unaware of the protocol, sat firmly in his seat, whilst the rest of those assembled snapped to attention with a bowing of their heads. By the time he realised he should also be on his feet he suffered the indignation of being on the ascent when the rest were sinking back into their seats. Robert should have told him, he thought, as he slumped back down, to the apparent displeasure of the austere, cardinal-robed judge.

'Regina versus Stephens,' the clerk announced. 'Would the defendant please rise.'

It didn't register immediately. *The defendant?* Who was that? Mark sat and waited. It wasn't for long, but when he did realise, thrown awake to it by the turned heads and the urging eyes, it seemed an embarrassing lifetime. He stumbled to his feet. The heads returned, nodding forwards. Mark swayed a little. So he wasn't Mark Stephens any longer. He was the defendant. They had stolen his identity as well. Patrick McGoohan, The Prisoner, shouted out from his television memory: **I am not a number!**

'Are you Mark Terence Stephens of thirty-eight Middleton Road, East Horsley?'

'Yes?' Mark was still dazed. Questioning their reason to know.

Robert turned. He could tell this wasn't going well. His client's head darted in several directions, like a startled bird.

'You are charged that you did indecently assault, on three occasions between the dates of March 1st and April 20th 1994, Susan Carol Bennett and that on one occasion did indecently assault Pauline Tania Green.' The clerk's voice was in a tin-walled room and tinkled like ice fragments against the metal floor and resonated inside Mark's muddled head. 'How do you plea?'

There was a lengthy pause. Mr. Justice Cromer snorted loudly and stared over his half-glasses at the junior barrister sent in haste by Margaret Cullen, who was away in Watford concluding a murder trial. The young man gritted his teeth and shrugged his shoulders and held on to his lapels tightly with both hands.

Robert swung round to Mark. His wide eyes yelled at him to answer. It was enough.

'Er... not guilty.' Mark choked on his reply.

The courtroom gave a collective sigh and the players took up their positions once more.

'So gentlemen, we need to set a date for this case. Are there any restrictions I need to know about? How is your diary Mr. Lambert? I assume you will conducting the prosecution.' Mr. Justice Cromer was eager to complete this. He had a bugger of a backlog to deal with in Court Four.

'I assume so, also, your honour.' Lambert replied smiling. Lambert was well aware that you just never knew what they had planned for you at the Crown Prosecution Service.

'And how does Mrs. Cullen stand? I trust she has indicated her commitments to you er... Mr. Dawson.' Cromer searched his papers for the young man's name.

Lambert stood to speak. 'I was asking Mr. Dawson. Mr. Lambert, would you kindly wait?'

'I'm sorry your honour. Only I have spoken with Mr. Dawson and we have compared availability in advance. To save court time.'

'Most commendable, Mr. Lambert. Then go ahead.'

'Both Mrs. Cullen and myself have no dates booked for January and February next year.'

'That helps, but only a little. The clerk tells me that this case should go to court before that and he has a slot at the end of November where we could be accommodated. How does that suit you?'

'Sir, do you mind?' Lambert indicated a brief discussion was needed with Dawson and Manning.'

'Certainly.' Cromer gasped. This was taking far too long. He could see the Court Four usher hovering outside.

They whispered in a huddled group, eager not to upset the testy Judge. Mr. Lambert turned as soon as he had the picture clear. 'Your honour, neither side will be ready by November.'

'Why not?' asked the Judge, a redness tingeing his cheeks.

Dawson rose to meet this one. 'I am informed by Mr. Manning, Mr. Stephens' solicitor, that they still have not had access to the girl's files at the school and that the school were not even allowing them to interview potential witnesses. We can not possibly be ready by November.'

'Is this so. Mr. Lambert?' Cromer howled.

'Excuse me one moment.' He turned abruptly to face Jean Baxter. There was whispered intercourse and a variety of facial expressions exchanged. 'WPC Baxter, who is in charge of the investigation, has informed me that she is at present making every effort to persuade the school to allow the access required by Mr. Manning and Mrs. Cullen. She confirms that the school bursar, a Colonel Hall, has not been very co-operative.'

'Well, if this Colonel prevents a proper discovery of evidence I will have him before me for contempt of court. Is that understood?' Justice Cromer was showing his frustration. 'So we can forget November. What else is there?' The Judge was leaning over his bench and consulting with the clerk, who frantically turned the pages of a heavily-fingered double spreadsheet.

'Perhaps, your honour,' suggested Mr. Dawson, now on his feet, 'a request I have to make will prevent the need to make a decision at this time?'

'And what may that be?' quizzed the Judge.

'The defence would like this case moved away from Guildford.'

'What? What reason?' stormed Cromer.

Dawson pulled some newspaper cuttings from a folder in front of him. 'Your honour, there have been numerous reports in the local press that could influence a jury recruited from this area and so jeopardise a fair trial.' Dawson handed the cuttings to an attending usher who promptly passed them on to the Judge. 'We are too near to the school and there is a real danger that it will be identified, and with that the identity of the girls. Mr. Lambert concurs and has no objections to this request.'

Lambert nodded in response.

'I see.' Justice Cromer flicked through the newspaper reports. He didn't look up. 'So where are you asking for this to be placed?'

'Mrs. Cullen has asked for it to be sent up to the Central Criminal Court in London.' Mr. Dawson was pleased to declare.

'Um...' The Judge considered the request. 'I believe you do

have a point. It will be one less here and get it out of my hair. Yes, I will send it up. But you do realise there is no guarantee where it will end up on that circuit. Good luck gentlemen.' He rose without waiting for the formal upstanding from the assemblage and hurried from the court; his attendant scrambling behind him.

Robert walked over to the 'caged-up' defendant. 'It's only a door that we can open.' Robert pulled at the low wooden gate and gestured Mark through it. 'Well, that wasn't too bad was it?'

'I suppose not. I seem to go to jelly every time I enter these pens. And when I'm called the bloody defendant I lose it. I'm sorry if I'm an embarrassment.' Mark was a little lost boy.

'Don't worry. Well, we've secured the change of venue, that's good isn't it? That will be to our advantage.' Robert was a happy soul. Mark still somewhat perplexed. 'You get on home and I'll speak to you in the next couple of days about the conference with Margaret. And chin up!'

Mark sucked in some diesel air on the courthouse steps and waved a limp goodbye.

Margaret Cullen was one of five barristers working in the chambers of Dorothy Mayers QC, a prominent attorney based in a small cul-de-sac bordering Lincoln's Inn Fields. Most of the lawyers were recently qualified except for Cameron Rudley who was only really working out his last few years before retirement. Margaret had trained as a teacher at Sheffield University but only lasted eight years in that profession. When she had enough capital she swept through a law degree at Surrey and went on to complete her studies at the Law School at Southampton. Why she specialised in criminal law was not clear, although she did have a morbid interest in some of the more sordid crimes that filled the tabloids and this was a natural extension of that fascination.

Mark had been told by Robert that he should be at the chambers at 3pm. Margaret Cullen was in court that day but was expecting an early conclusion to her participation in the case. When Mark reached the third floor offices his solicitor was already drinking coffee in the clerk's reception.

'Mr. Stephens, hello.' A cup of coffee was offered before he sat down. As in all legal practices the clerk is the real boss. He runs the show. This was no exception.

'Thank you.' Mark sank back into a seat next to a photocopier being fed a volley of sheets by a sombrely dressed young woman. A junior had to perform the mundane jobs, even after a long day in court.

'Good journey?' Robert asked. One of those innocuous questions to make a client feel at ease.

'Not bad. And you?'

'Fine, except for a cancelled train at South Woodford.'

Fortunately this inane exchange was interrupted by the entrance of Margaret Cullen. Her toothy smile preceded her tacking eyes. She wanted a first impression of Mark Stephens. That was important to her. Was he an honest man struggling to prove his innocence, or really a conniving liar, a sex offender using her to camouflage the truth, and for him to assault again, under licence from her. This wasn't a moral question ever asked openly, but Margaret Cullen needed to know for her own sake.

'Hello Mark!' She bellowed her welcome even while her scanning eyes were still drawing the picture. 'It's good to meet you.' She shook his hand firmly. It was part of the analysis. 'Come through to the...' She turned to her clerk. 'Where can we hold this conference, Peter?'

'You'll have to use Dorothy's room; it's the only spare one.'

'Right. Follow me.' Margaret beckoned with a plump forearm.

Mark and Robert trailed behind the swaying posterior that waddled ahead of them. Margaret Cullen was a squat woman bulging at the armpits and hips and sitting on dumpy, bowing legs. What some might call a cuddly female. This did not belie her intelligence and warm personality.

They settled down at a long table. Robert and Margaret pulled out thick files. Mark sat empty-handed. 'Mark, we have a lot to do.' Margaret started. 'This isn't an easy case and you need to focus as much as possible on it. Difficult though it may be, forget how damn innocent you are, and how you are the real victim. If we have to fight this in the Crown Court we are going to have to be sharp.' Margaret Cullen wanted him to know the score. To tell him up front so there were no doubts. 'This may shock you, but it's the only way. And you won't like this part. Play it as if you were in their shoes; trying to corner you. Understand their logic. Look for ways to disprove their evidence. It's the technique I use all the time. Makes you hungry. None better. Not sure about the ethics though.' Margaret Cullen was sure of one thing. She had faith in Mark Stephens. It was down to intuition; he was a genuine guy.

Margaret dealt with the easy topics first. 'We urgently need to view the files at the school. That is the girls', including Clair Hooper's, and yours Mark. What is the present position?'

Robert was quick to reply. 'The CPS have promised to speak to the school, but at the moment we have not received permission to go there yet.'

'And the witnesses? Mark, there are two dates when Susan Bennett on her own, and then accompanied by Pauline Green, claims you committed an indecent assault. You have stated that you weren't there. Where were you? Think about it. Write down for Robert the names of any person, it may be a pupil, who can vouch for your whereabouts.'

'Yes, I'll do that.' He welcomed a chore like that; getting involved.

'I am busy getting statements from Anna Stephens, Norman Munnie and Dave Patterson. There are, as you have pointed out, quite a few possible witnesses at the school that we haven't got to. I am concerned that they won't remember anything when we do speak. It'll be nearly a year. Have we mentioned the character witnesses?' Robert asked.

From being a tennis spectator; following the words of Robert and Margaret thrown at each other and out of his reach, he was involved in the rally. 'We need from you, Mark, the names and addresses of people who can vouch for your good character. Including, if possible, parents of children you have taught, particularly the parents of young teenage girls. You get the idea. Give it some thought and send Robert a list. Although these are not material witnesses, it is essential to have this background. A jury relies on knowing more about the defendant from this type of testament. We have to let them know what a really great person you are.' There was a trickle of a smile from the plump barrister.

'I notice,' Margaret continued, 'that the police were asking about your Fiesta car when they interviewed you at Wokingham, yet you state that you drove to meet Susan Bennett in your wife's Mini. Why did you use her car and not your own?'

'The MOT certificate had run out on the Fiesta so I was unable to use it.'

'Do you have the old certificate and the new one dated at the time of the new test?' Margaret asked eagerly.

'Yes, I believe I do.'

'Excellent! Get these to Robert's office as soon as you can.' Margaret loved a bit of concrete evidence. 'It would seem the Bennett girl has said you met her in your Fiesta car. This will be a good one to use.' She penned a note alongside the entry in Mark's statement. Her planning had already started and she knew just when to hurl this one at Susan Bennett during her cross-examination.

'The phone calls made by Susan Bennett to your home? Who spoke to her?' Margaret enquired, her head poised over the words in Mark's statement.

'Er... Alison, my wife, and I think one of my daughters.'

'Would that be Anna?'

'Yes. Yes it was her.'

'We need to ask her about that when you take her statement Robert.' Margaret was turning over everything.

'Right,' confirmed Robert.

'Even better than that!' exclaimed Mark, suddenly realising he could contribute. 'We have a recording she left on our answer machine.' His face formed a huge smile and he directed it point blank at Margaret Cullen. A gruesome but ecstatic visage that made her pull back sharply.

'You have her voice on tape?' Margaret sought confirmation. Her tone tinged with disbelief.

'Yes,' Mark responded; pride seeping into *his* voice.

'What a coup!' Margaret couldn't believe her luck. She rubbed her hands. 'You must let Robert have that also.'

Margaret Cullen's smile lasted throughout the rest of her cruise through Mark's statement. But she was holding back. She knew what she had to raise and it was a bloody nuisance. This would be a rock solid case if this didn't exist. She closed the folder but held on to two pieces of paper, both photocopies.

'Mark, about this letter that Susan Bennett claims you wrote to her. I have to ask you this so that I have it straight and we can be honest with each other. Did you write to Susan Bennett?' She studied the paper again to remind her about its content. 'A note about cancelling a meeting with her and apparently signed by you?' She pinned him back with a threatening stare.

'No. I have never written to the girl.' Mark was firm and his eyes stayed on hers when he replied. He wanted her to see his truth.

'Is this your handwriting?' Margaret held the letter out. The envelope remained on the table. She thrust the letter forward, nearer to his face, further away from his accusing handwriting that shouted out from the front of the photocopied envelope.

'That is not my handwriting.' He could just say it through the tightness of his chest. But it was true. The note that she held and pushed at his face hadn't been written by him.

'Susan Bennett claims that you sent her this letter. It

appears to be an apology for not meeting her, and it is clearly signed by you. I can think of several reasons why she is maintaining that this is from you. However, we have to soundly refute this in court and provide an alternative explanation for twelve credulous but reluctant citizens press-ganged to try you. So, Mark, is the handwriting anything like yours?'

'Well... it does resemble some of the loops in my handwriting and I can see a similarity, but there isn't the smoothness. It's a faltering hand, and there isn't the pressure. It enters the word hard and slides out faltering and weak. I'm no expert.' But he was sounding like one.

The envelope was left on the table. It was now almost under Margaret Cullen's ample breasts as she leaned over towards Mark, still clutching the scorching letter. 'What we will need to do is have Henry Brolin take a look at this and get Mark down there to have his writing analysed. Send him copies of these two.' She scooped up the envelope and now held both exhibits in her hand. 'And when he's ready to conduct the test he can contact Mark directly and make an appointment.'

'Got that,' Robert confirmed.

'I don't think I have anything else.' Margaret slumped back in her chair and raised her fleshy arms high above her head. 'What about you, Robert, anything your end?'

'I don't think so. I'm sure we can have a further conference as things develop.'

'Quite so,' Margaret concurred. 'Mark, any queries? I trust this hasn't been too distressing. I intend to be thorough, so you have to live with me sometimes. I don't mean to be a witch.' She smiled and pushed herself to her feet.

'It's all right. I understand what you have to do.'

Mark and Robert left the building together, but soon split with a shake of hands. Robert headed for Fenchurch Street Station and Mark strode off towards Waterloo.

⚜

Mark was busying himself with the details of his activities whilst on boarding house duty in Cairo House on the two days he had to haul from a waste bin of a memory. He thought he would be able to recall most of what he had done on those dates, but it was a hazy muddle. He was one of those people that once a day was spent it was truly spent – slung in to the slurry that made up his history.

The phone punctured his thoughts. 'Hello Robert.' Manning phoning yet again. His guts descended every time he heard his voice now. 'What's up?'

'I've spoken to Henry Brolin. He can see you on Friday at eleven thirty. Is that okay with you? I do hope so. He is a very busy man. We mustn't lose this opportunity.'

Mark was never really busy. He was only busy waiting. Waiting for the next stage. Waiting for some news. Waiting for the day all this would be over; lifted off his shoulders. 'That will be fine. Give me the directions. I know it's another monumental journey.' Mark was determined to sound relaxed. In reality his abdomen had seized and his stomach in spasm. He couldn't sideline his concerns about the envelope.

Robert explained the location of Brolin's laboratory in Hertfordshire and wished him luck. He would need it.

Mark had four days to practice. He was a man in panic. Sitting in every folder carried by those involved in this investigation, prosecution or defence, was a copy of an envelope with his handwriting blazon in black ink. His black ink! But no one was going to pin this on him. He was innocent. In his head he cried it out once more. Those who had heard him when he proclaimed it aloud either believed him or smirked behind a concealing hand with whispers of *who's he kidding*. His writing would change. For Henry Brolin he would prepare a foreign hand that didn't belong to the telltale scribbling on the envelope. No, they weren't going to frame him with that. Alison wasn't to know. He would see Paul every day and practise. It couldn't be difficult to develop a different style.

His first attempts were only additional swirls and exaggerated introductions with a trailing lead to the first letter. Useless! Towards the end of the second day he had started to dig deep into the paper and correct his usual slant. The letters were huge compared to his normal hand and the flowing lines that entered and left each word curled like wisps of lingering smoke from a cigarette swung in a gesticulating hand. He imagined it very different to his tame handwriting. Paul was not that convinced. Time was running out.

On the third day he wrote reams, copied from a multiplicity of publications. It wasn't like changing a computer chip. He was forced to block out all the old messages his brain was used to sending. He was now the owner of a lavish hand that dented the page and had to be written to the brutal tempo of the 1812. Gone were the limp swinging loops of Susan Bennett's name and address on that fucking envelope.

Mark didn't write in his new style on the Thursday. He stayed at home and only when Alison wasn't around did he scrawl on an old A4 pad he kept deep in his desk in the study. When he was asked to prepare a shopping list he was thrown. It would be a disaster to revert back to the recognisable Mark Stephen's scribble but he couldn't let Alison see this quite ridiculous indentation and the colossal letters that made even a packet of biscuits look like a newspaper headline. The list was delegated to Jayne, who begrudgingly scratched it out to his repeated calls from inside echoing cupboards and gagging fridge.

Henry Brolin's laboratory wasn't easy to find. It was hidden in a corner of a mucky industrial estate cosmetically concealed behind a grand entrance and a totally inappropriate sign welcoming visitors to a business park. Mark had to climb a linoleum-covered staircase that smelled of disinfectant to reach the lab reception; a glorified window. He was met by an oriental woman; young and attractive and a body well worth a gormless stare, which Mark readily provided.

'Ah, Mr. Stephens.' Henry Brolin skirted round his assistant who had shown Mark in. Henry was a bespectacled boffin who dashed around swinging his white lab coat like a nerd super-hero or a lunatic scientist ready to provide 007 with a new device to eliminate an evil foe. 'No trouble finding HQ eh?'

'No. Just the last mile.'

'Of course. Not well signposted is it? Now if you'd come this way.'

Brolin didn't want the small talk and smartly led Mark to a small office where he was asked to sit at a metal desk. The dishy oriental brought paper and some printed material. He was given a choice of pens. Well, a choice of ballpoints. He had been using fibre-tips during his preparation. If he wasn't care-ful his heavy hand armed with a biro would cut through the paper like a craft knife.

'All I need you to do is to copy out these sheets. Do them one at a time and don't start the next one until one of us tells you. Is that okay Mr. Stephens?' Henry Brolin smiled.

He smiled at them all. The guilty and the innocent. The ones that had forged. The ones that had sent the filth through the post. The writers of the ransom notes. The unfaithful. The killers. The fiends. Mark Stephens was to be treated just like the rest.

'Zenuo or I will be watching you as you write. I trust it won't disturb you. So go ahead. Write as relaxed as possible in your usual style.' He took a step back, still in possession of the same enchanting grin.

Mark raised his pen. A blue Bic.

Brolin jabbed a stopwatch.

He could feel the eyes on him. They wanted to see how nat-ural he was. It wouldn't be the first time someone had tried this. They weren't stupid. The sheets were separate; thin on the hard surface. He had developed his new style on a pad that sank with the force of his pen, soft and absorbing, creating a deep channel for his driving pen. Now he was scratching on the surface, sliding along out of control. It was a bad start. He needed the cushioning for the rhythm. He panicked. A letter from his real hand formed in front of him. He scribbled it out.

Smothered and hidden. They would look at that under a micro-scope or something. He scored the paper again. Calm. He knew he had to calm down. He breathed deeply within himself. They mustn't see him trying to pull it together. Half way down the page he began to get into his stride as if he was at Paul's copy-ing page after page of senseless text.

Mark looked up as he completed the first sheet. Zenuo, the oriental beauty, was already on him, pushing the next piece of paper under his writing hand. They swapped smiles. Her smile plastic and a trained courtesy; his, the thanking smile of a sad guinea pig in a laboratory experiment.

His writing was mechanical. They couldn't shunt him off course now. But, as he copied words from Brolin's sheet he recognised, standing out of the ordinary, the occasional entrapping word. There were phrases from the note that Susan Bennett had said he had written. Carefully positioned and strategically attached to ensnare him, a bear pit, for him to topple and fall into. He negotiated his way through the hunters' deliberately laid ambush.

Henry Brolin provided the final manuscript for him to repli-cate. He slid it into the path of Mark's tracking eyes as soon as he had completed the previous one. With the stealth and preci-sion of a cat stalking a mouse, the scientist tailed his prey. The traps were still there, even more shrouded, to trip the unwary counterfeiter. Mark's hold on the pen changed to a death-grip when he encountered fragments of the words on the envelope. He could picture how he had formed those letters in his old script and he dug deep into the furrows of his current tech-nique to provide, for their analysis, a different picture. Not his writing at all.

And when it was all over he leaned back. Both Zenuo and Brolin faced him and beamed, a grin that oozed satisfaction. Had they already found some similarity, tied him in with the envelope?

'Do you have an example of your handwriting with you; a credit card with your signature or something like that?' Zenuo enquired.

Mark had such evidence in the car, but he wasn't going to let on. 'No, I don't think I do. Why do you need that?'

'Just... a procedure. We should have warned you.' She looked hard at Henry Brolin. What should she do now?

'I think we can work without it, Zenuo. Don't worry Mr. Stephens now.' Brolin showed him the door. He wanted to see something from the past. The heavy hand he had watched was not as fluid as he would have liked. Too forcing and rigid. He had his doubts.

Mark's departure was quick. Brolin's keenness to get at Mark's handwriting prompted a brief goodbye and the crisp closing of the solid front door behind him.

Motoring home he couldn't decide whether he had done enough to fool the eminent graphologist and his tantalising assistant. At the beginning there was that stupid mistake. Other than that he'd held on. He had ground away, carving out fresh characters. He wondered if he would ever regain his original style. Not that it was much to desire.

Three days later the report from Henry Brolin was on Robert Manning's desk, and a copy waiting for Margaret Cullen to study. Robert was quick to confer with the barrister. Robert got on to Mark as soon as he could.

'I have Mr. Brolin's assessment in front of me, Mark,' Robert announced over the phone. 'It's not bad, but I'm afraid it's not conclusive.'

Mark sucked in hard and filled his lungs. 'What does that mean?'

'There are similarities, but there are also many areas where there is no match. He can't definitely say you didn't write this stuff. That's the down side. However, he certainly can't say you did. He points out that your display at his laboratory, to quote, *exhibited a lack of fluidity typical of a writer uneasy with a subsequently adopted method of writing.* I have spoken to Margaret. She wants this sorted out immediately. We need to go back to Brolin and ask him to change this report if we are to use him as an expert witness. She wants you to provide evidence that this is your normal hand. Have you such things as birthday cards written by you to members of your family that they have kept. Some solid evidence that you aren't supplying a falsified style.'

Mark gulped. 'Maybe I have the cards.'

He should have come clean. He hadn't done anything wrong. Now was the time. It was closing in. Instead he prolonged the deceit.

'Well, you must let me have them right away. Margaret is insistent.' Robert declared firmly.

Mark agreed to send the cards. While he remained convinced he could escape the truth he grabbed a couple of unused ones from the stack that Alison kept in case she forgot a birthday. It wasn't hard to score out his new hand, wishing Alison a happy birthday and many happy returns to Anna. He made sure the ink wouldn't run. Even rubbed his smearing finger to add some age to the forgery. Then pushed them into an envelope and rushed them to the post-box. He swallowed hard. It shouldn't have been necessary for him to act like a furtive trickster? It was his only guilt.

Chapter 8

Following the interviews with the police the three girls reached celebrity status at Thomas Graham School. But from the hanging heads and shuffling steps of two of them it wasn't a notoriety they were enjoying.

Mark Stephens was suspended and dumped by the school. He was in dead trouble.

Clair Hooper was torn between the status she had achieved by supposedly being involved with a schoolmaster, and a sickening remorse for conjuring up the story. She had made amends in part. Told that cow of a policewoman. But she had to keep to the original with her peers. There would be hell to pay if she didn't maintain the collateral earned from this incident. She could fend off questions about her and Mr. Stephens from packs of Year Seven pupils who squealed childish enquiries about what she and the teacher had done. And she added little more information to even her close associates who crowded her, back in the boarding house, with constant demands for the sordid details. *Mrs. Edgerley had told her not to say any more*, was the story, and that would be her safeguard for now.

Pauline Green didn't enjoy her role. School was shit now. She had thought about breaking friends with Susan but was stifled by the suffocating attention her friend gave her. Then, who would be a friend at that hole? There was only Susan Bennett, and she had to face that until she left in July. It wasn't that she was black that made her an outcast. It was her vile mate that tarnished her. The nearest she got to a new acquaintance was some curious decoy sent searching for some dirt. A volunteer from a gang wanting the scandal first hand. Of course Susan Bennett was blabbing every opportunity she got.

Somehow she could live off, even prosper from the lie. Pauline wanted it shoved away. She said the things. Now it needed to be forgotten.

Susan Bennett felt liberated. She had channelled all her shame. The man who wouldn't fall in line; be her lover, was saddled with all the responsibility for her violated body. And along with that she had picked up this new infamy that was just as good as renown at Thomas Graham School, where celebrity came from misdeed and crossing the divide between leaders and led. Her account to Ted Frith and WPC Baxter bore no recognition to the fables she composed whenever quizzed about her rampant affair with the Head of English. What embroidered her official version was an injection of romance. Susan kept clamouring crowds mesmerised with dripping accounts of Mr. Stephen taking her in his arms and pressing his hungry lips onto hers. Of the lingering embrace and knowing eyes. Their days clinging together unable to bear parting. His promises to leave his wife and carry her away; to live together. And of their passionate correspondence. It was salvation from her hollow life.

What her father had done to her was committed in cold lust. Woken from sleep or ambushed in her room, her mind stepped out of the flesh he preyed on, and that with tugging, greasy hands he eased towards his urgent body already self-primed for the assault. Often only lasting minutes he slunk from her pliant form muttering excuses about his inadequacies and the same old *last time* promises. And when she was sure from the viscous and stale plastic fluid spilling from her that he had come and he wouldn't be back, she filled the bath until she heard the gushing of the overflow. And flushed out, with thrashing, swilling water, his *fucking* semen, and scrubbed with a brutal nail brush his loathsome smell from her skin, until she was sore.

Now Susan could piece it all together to make some sense of it. But it was a cardboard jigsaw, a sad dummy of a real relationship. A mixture of twin fantasies. There was the physical sex that her mind was detaching from the ogre manhandling of her own father being graced by the fanciful association, embodying tender love, with Mark Stephens. In its own way it brought some satisfaction, however Frankenstein the concept.

Susan held Pauline close to her with greater determination now. The statements had been taken. Clair Hooper was still the enemy. Neither Susan nor Pauline spoke to her. They were unaware that she had lied, and equally unaware that she had admitted it to the Child Protection Unit officer, Jean Baxter.

Jan Edgerley was supposed to ensure that the subject was not discussed. But it was impossible to control every aspect of these girls' lives and Susan would talk to the early hours with Pauline. It was during one of these late night sessions that Susan first showed it to Pauline. She pulled from an anonymous page in one of her classwork files.

'Do you remember these?' Susan whispered. Not because of the lateness of their meeting. It was a secret; an unkind plot.

'No, I don't,' Pauline answered, looking puzzled at the envelope that Susan had carefully drawn from deep in the files of her GCSE English coursework.

'Last year. About eighteen months ago. You know. When Stephens took us to the bloody stupid play at that round theatre in London. Remember those boys from another school smoking, and us getting a puff? It was a bit of fun all right. With those blokes. Not the play or anything.'

'Oh, yeah. I know the one. Only bit of a laugh we've had on an outing.' Pauline picked at her nails and giggled to herself. They had been black schoolboys. She liked that. There weren't many at the school. It had been like being back in Tottenham.

'Well? Don't you remember?' Susan continued.

'What?'

'This!' She held the brown envelope in both hands. Hanging it from the top corners. Susan Bennett's name and address was scrawled across it. Every detail including the postcode. And in the corner, smudged by a smeared black postmark, a bright red first class stamp.

'No!' Pauline shrugged her shoulders.

'Mr. Stephens asked if we wanted him to forward the programmes we couldn't get on the night. So they could be included in the work we had to do in the holidays. There were about eight of us who wanted them. Recall it now?'

'Vaguely.' Pauline was bored with the subject.

'Well, he didn't manage to get them from the theatre during the holidays, and we collected them about a week after we got back. I took my envelope off his desk. They'd been left lying there for weeks. You know what a mess his desk always was. And I kept it.'

'So?' Pauline asked, only half interested.

'Those cows in Year Ten have been having a go. Saying I've been lying about all this.'

'Well, you have,' Pauline chipped in; a hint of a smile beginning at the corner of her mouth.

'Okay. Shut it! I'm only telling you. So keep mum. See, the date's not clear. I posted it home in March I think, a bit before I'm telling them about Stephens and me, but I can say it was an even more intense relationship. It had that filthy poem in it that we found in Tabby's magazine. You know. To stop old Edgerley finding it. Well now it has another purpose. This'll stop those fucking girls thinking I've been lying.' Susan dived back into her folder and pulled out a sheet of white paper.

Pauline surveyed it. 'What's this?'

'It's going to be a note from my lover Mark Stephens; *to me*. Pete Black in my art class reckons he can copy anyone's handwriting. All those study notes Stephens sends round are done by him so he says it's a doddle. And with this envelope no one is ever going to doubt me again.' She curled her lips, lifted her chin, concealed the papers once more and headed for bed.

Pauline hauled her back. 'Let it go! Don't do anymore. We've done enough. Black will tell on you.'

'He won't know what it's for, you see. And anyway I've

promised him a blow job for it.' Susan continued through the door waving her folder at Pauline.

'Fuck me. She's fucking mad.' Pauline shook her head. Susan was losing it.

⁂

Jean Baxter hadn't put the Stephens case to bed, hadn't finished with the girls. Jan Edgerley was feeding back alarming developments. There were fresh events reported to the housemistress that none of the girls had spoken about in their previous statements and she would have to let the CPS see everything soon. She arranged to meet the girls once more before she finalised her investigations. She would have one more go at Clair Hooper. The girl was definitely involved. Jean Baxter needed her testimony. She had tried the friendly approach despite hating being so nice, and it had failed. Now she was going to show her the sharp edge of WPC Baxter.

Jan Edgerley greeted Jean Baxter. Their relationship was strong. Not that Baxter liked her, she needed her. It was a deliberate ploy by the policewoman. Having someone at the school who could keep a close eye on the girls and an ear to the ground was a bonus. She would continue to nurture this *friendship* until Stephens was convicted.

'Good morning, Jean,' Jan Edgerley was warm. She accepted the fellowship without any pretensions, knowing nothing of the bogus nature of the policewoman's association.

'Morning, Jan. Good to see you.' It seemed friendly enough.

'How do you want to do this? The head has given me the time off from class so I am at your disposal.'

'Let's have Clair Hooper in first this time.'

'But she's told you it didn't happen. I thought you were finished with her?'

'Jan, I'm not entirely happy about the first interview. I want to try again. She's involved all right. That basta... That man touched her. Of that I am certain.' Jean Baxter couldn't quite contain it. Mark Stephens was more than the quarry. He was the male target in her sights. He had to go down.

'She's a different girl since this happened. You should see her moping around the school.'

'Probably because she can't live with it eh? Knows she should have shopped him. Misguided loyalty for a child molester. Could be we can help her. Get her to confess. Tell us about her ordeal.' Baxter was full of it. Her hunger for Mark's hide shone in her haunting eyes.

Clair Hooper crept into the office in Octavia House. Her head was dropped. Gone was the carefree, flirty countenance that she had previously displayed. She liked Mr. Stephens. She knew she shouldn't have tried it on. Now he was suspended from school; was going to face a disciplinary hearing. Why had he touched that little rat Susan Bennett? She couldn't forget that. It was all too complicated. A fucking mess all right. So was she.

'Ah! Clair. How are you?'

'All right.' Clair spoke with her chin almost on her chest.

'You can remember when we spoke before, can't you Clair?' Jean Baxter leaned forward to get nearer to Clair's bowed head. To almost climb under her cowl of long hair that had curtained forward to surround her face.

'Yep.' Clair snapped her reply.

'You told me that you had made up the account you gave to the headmaster. Remember that?'

'Yep.' The head remained down and the same clipped response came from behind the waterfall hair.

'I want you to seriously reconsider what you have said. I'll tell you why.' WPC Baxter shuffled even closer. 'If this man did the things you told Mr. Frith about, then something needs to be done. There are a lot of girls in danger from him. You know what Susan Bennett told you, and there is what Pauline has said. This man is a menace. No child is safe.' Baxter pulled back and huffed. 'Can you live with that?'

The bent head didn't reply immediately. Clair stroked and

tugged at her hair, exposing one side of her pale face.

'Well if he's done it with Bennett you don't need me to tell you anything, do you?' Her eyes caught Baxter's. They were steel-grey and mad.

'If you can tell us what happened it will help. The more evidence the better.' Jean Baxter had stirred something and was eager to winkle out her truth. 'Just because we have the statements of the other two it doesn't mean he can worm out of what he has done to you. What would happen if one of the others, Pauline for example, was to decide that she should withdraw her statement?' Baxter wished she hadn't said that. It was what she was thinking about. What she feared. 'Now, Clair, you can tell us. Don't be afraid.'

Clair Hooper fizzled behind her hands like the spluttering ignition of a firework fuse. 'I've told you!' She exploded. 'I've told you! Just leave me alone. I've told you.' Clair subsided in an even lower huddle and wept uncontrollably between long rattling breaths.

Jan Edgerley tightened her lips and gave Jean Baxter a stern look. That was enough. Clair Hooper was saying nothing more. Jan lifted Clair up and escorted her out of the door and down to her room. The girl was still wheezing in distress when she left her on the bed.

Jean Baxter was rummaging through her papers when Jan returned. 'It really pisses me off that the bloody girl won't say anything. She's scared or something.'

Jan Edgerley had never heard the policewoman speak like that before.

'Get Susan Bennett in.' It sounded like an order, and she realised it. 'I'm sorry Jan. Would you mind?' Jean Baxter's veneer was wearing thin.

In contrast Susan Bennett strolled into the room full of confidence, and greeted WPC Baxter with a tilt of the head and a spirited grin. How good it was to have a witness like this girl, she thought. If only Hooper could be so firm. She blanked out what she should have been reasoning. If what this girl has said is true why did she have a sexual relationship with a man old enough to be her father? The girl must be a real slut. If she was to be believed there were a catalogue of discrepancies to be considered. Jean Baxter wasn't going to delve any further in that direction. She was travelling away from that. Mark Stephens had abused his position. Had taken to using these girls for his pleasure. There was only one diseased monster to be tackled.

'How are you Susan?' Jan Edgerley recognised Baxter's return to pleasant mode. 'Take a seat. We need to talk a little more about this matter. Are you okay with that?'

'Fine.' Susan was chirpy and the ideal co-operator.

Jean Baxter slid in a fresh tape. She would dump the one that Clair Hooper had cried into. 'Now, is there anything else you need to add to your statement that I took when we first talked? The one you've been shown and signed? I assume you have read through it closely.'

Susan hadn't bothered. 'No, don't think there's anything else.' She had done it all. Susan just wanted to sit back and enjoy her fame. Although the rest of the school knew where she was and it would be a further endorsement of her reputation, she was mildly annoyed at having to talk to the 'Baxter woman' again.

'Are you sure?' Baxter retorted.

'Yeah.'

'Mrs. Edgerley has overheard some of the other girls talking, discussing you and this business. As you know they shouldn't know anything about it. However, without prompting you to say any more, these girls were relating among other things how you had shown them a letter sent to you by Mr. Stephens. You never mentioned this before. Is this something you should have told us, Susan?' Baxter was drooling.

Susan was thrown. This wasn't going to be as easy as she imagined. 'Letter?' She tried to stall.

'Yes, a letter. It appears you were exhibiting it to quite a large group of the girls a few days ago.'

'Er... yes.'

'So there is a letter?' Jean licked her lips.

'Yes.' Susan was reduced to the single response.

'Can you show me?' Baxter ventured, treading very carefully. She had to discover this evidence according to the book.

Susan scrambled to her feet.

'Wait a minute!' Jan Edgerley insisted. It was the middle of a police interview. She couldn't just turn tail and leave.

'Are you going to fetch the letter?' Jean Baxter asked into the microphone. A dual purpose.

'Yeah.' Susan confirmed.

'Then I will accompany you. Wait a second.' Baxter told the machine the exact nature of the excursion and switched it off. 'Lead on.' She was excited now. A letter. A letter from that shit to his tart schoolgirl lover. It was more than she had hoped for.

In Susan Bennett's room that smelled of stale clothes and cheap scent Jean Baxter and Jan Edgerley stood watching Susan pull a long brown envelope from a battered school folder and hand it out behind her without looking. A trailing hand offering a rare delicacy to the beaming policewoman.

The three of them tramped back to the office. Baxter started the machine and announced their return and what their voyage had discovered. She described the envelope and the black, hand-written address, and then, pulling the white folded sheet from inside explained to the dumb, whirring tape-recorder the nature of the note that she opened with such obvious glee.

29/3/94

Susan,
I am sorry I can't see you as planned. I really wanted to meet. I will phone you.

Mark

She read it aloud. It was disappointingly little. Yet she was sure it was enough. She didn't question its purpose. Something easily sent over the phone. An incriminating correspondence. A note her parents could readily have intercepted.

'When did you receive this?' Jean Baxter asked.

'Dunno.' Susan muttered.

'It's dated twenty-ninth of March. Perhaps it came the day after. It has been sent first class.'

'Yeah. Probably did.' Susan was ready to confirm anything. Anything would do to stop further questions.

'Why did he write this to you?' Baxter continued.

The ugly policewoman seemed to say, 'Why would he write to you, you little slut?'

Susan wasn't pleased. For a long period she assembled it in her head. 'It was like when we met before... in the town. This time he couldn't make it. He really wanted to. He told me. Wanted to be with me. So... he sent this. Always sending me letters.' Susan realised what she had said and went in to damage limitation. 'The others I never kept. Never kept those.'

Baxter fumed. 'Others?'

'Yeah. We wrote to each other a lot. It was that type of relationship. The others were long letters; how he felt about me. They were lovely letters. Him being an English teacher. Not like this one.' Susan wanted to rub Baxter's face in it.

'What did you do with them?' Baxter quizzed; her eyes scorching and angry. 'When did you get rid of them and where?'

'Can't remember. Not sure exactly. Probably the bin at home.' Susan struggled to picture their disposal. Where she would dump such things. She had never really had the need to.

'Did you show these other letters to anyone? Pauline perhaps?' Baxter wanted those letters. She was clutching at threads to revive their existence. A second-hand witness. Anybody.

Susan was eager to keep it running. Wanted to tell someone about him. Her teacher lover. It would be a desperate thing to do. Perhaps if she said Pauline had seen them. Just that. But

Pauline hadn't been prepared. Couldn't embellish the story. She hadn't better. The signals weren't good. 'No... I did bring them in to school but never got to show them round. Too dangerous at the time.'

'Shit!' grunted Baxter.

It wouldn't be the first time an officer had expressed disappointment in such a way during a recorded interview, but Jean Baxter wasn't pleased that she had lost her cool. She stood and smoothed her clothing. Running the palms of her hands down her crumpled skirt. It was an effort to restore her dignity. And she tried to convince herself that the one letter would be enough. Damning evidence. And, perhaps, as Stephens wouldn't know the other mail had been destroyed, a decent CPS barrister could get him to admit the exchange of correspondence. And wildly she imagined finding one of Susan's letters in his possession.

'Now, Susan, let's get this straight. There were a lot of letters both ways, yes? You sent him some?'

'Yeah.' Susan blinked and wondered where this was leading.

'Where did you send these letters?'

'Well...' Susan began, still trying to establish a credible explanation. 'I left some on his desk.'

'On his desk?' interjected the baffled policewoman.

'Yeah, and some I posted to him.'

'You had his address?' Baxter asked briskly. 'How?'

Susan Bennett did have Mark Stephens address, did have his phone number. This was easy to answer. She had got it from a staff list prominently displayed on the Octavia House tutors' notice-board.

'He was my boyfriend. Couples swap things like that. He wanted me to write. We were lovers.' It sounded good to hear but even Susan Bennett felt it stick in her throat. Even *she* nearly choked on that lie. Susan guessed at Jean Baxter's lack of success with men or lack of interest in them and wanted to make sure this was delivered with spite.

Jean Baxter was beginning to dislike Susan Bennett

immensely. She wouldn't continue the interview any longer than was necessary. If she had given the matter more thought, avoided the distorted and venomous pursuit of Mark Stephens, she may have seen the situation clearer; questioned and delved and uncovered the festering obsession and the terrible defilement that had manufactured this senseless treachery.

'Okay Susan. So what we have is this. There is one surviving letter. This one.' Baxter waved it in Susan Bennett's face. 'All the other letters you destroyed. You wrote letters to Mr. Stephens, some of which you delivered by hand. Left them on his desk. And the rest you posted to him at his home. Is that it?'

'Yeah.' Susan realised this nonsense was being wound up.

'There were some further but minor matters, but I don't think we need investigate those. They appear to revolve round your readiness to discuss your relationship with Mr. Stephens with the rest of the school. I must warn you now that we will be seeing Mr. Stephens and this whole police investigation will be *sub judice*, which means you could be in serious trouble if you speak about the matter. In other words, say no more. Don't mention any of the subjects you have told me about. Is that understood?' Jean Baxter launched one of her worst *you fucking dare* expressions at the self-satisfied face of Susan Bennett and reached for the tape-recorder switch. With a snort that spoke of both frustration and relief she waved Susan Bennett from the room.

At Wokingham Police Station the small conference room on the third floor filled slowly. Smokers were filtering in from the fire door at the end of the corridor, and a succession of muffled flushes confirmed the last minute ablutions of those destined for the strategy meeting called by DS Mills.

It was a tight fit. There were six plain clothes police constables, mostly middle-aged, Jean Baxter and the head of the

Child Protection Unit at Wokingham, Detective Sergeant Bernard Mills.

'The suspect is a teacher at Thomas Graham School, name of Mark Stephens. He has been indecently assaulting some of the girls. We will be going in tomorrow morning. The address is 38, Middleton Road, East Horsley. The local force is aware and there's no problem. It'll be plain clothes and should be a soft call. Early of course. We will rendezvous at 5am. Sorry!' Sergeant Mills smirked at the sour faces that met his final announcement. 'Jean will give you the details. Listen up.'

'Yes, I'm sorry about the unearthly hour, but as you know we need to catch him off guard. He's apparently a plausible character and lives in a pleasant enough area with his wife and two teenage daughters. I won't go into the exact nature of the charges we are considering, but it is safe to assume these are serious sexual offences. The girls he has been involved with are under age. He has abused his position.' Jean Baxter nearly gave away her inner rage. 'I'm looking for any material linking him with children. Other than, of course, genuine teaching stuff. I think we have a serious pædophile here. There must be some pornography, magazines or tapes. I want to see anything. Show me the slightest suspicious item. I will confirm its relevance.

'I'm also looking for envelopes like this.' Jean Baxter held up the long brown envelope held in a clear plastic folder. 'We need to check all mail. There may be, if we are lucky, a hidden batch of letters from one of the girls. I don't need to tell you your job. We've done enough of these. But there are certain items I'm particularly interested in. So locate his diary or organiser, notebook, slips of paper with names and addresses, phone numbers. Writing paper; that's another special one. The piece of paper I've got hasn't any watermarks and might be difficult to match, but I'm no scientist. Some boffin might be able to square it.

As Bernard has said, this is expected to be a soft call. He shouldn't be any trouble. I'll caution him at the door and then call the rest of you in once he realises we are going through his drum. Then he'll be hauled down to the nick for questioning.' WPC Baxter tickled her papers and ran her forefinger down a list in front of her. 'I don't think I have anything else. Any questions?' There were only blank faces. She turned to DS Mills. 'Bernard; anything to add?' Sergeant Mills shook his head. 'Right. See you in the early hours lads.' She was pleased with her briefing, and now verging on humour. She had the bastard in her sights and was going to enjoy tomorrow.

That evening Jean Baxter telephoned Jan Edgerley to inform her of the progress of the investigation and felt sufficiently happy with their relationship to inform her of the pending operation. She reiterated the necessity to isolate the girls as much as possible. These little sluts were her case. They were as much guilty as Stephens, but they would put him away, so they had to be cocooned and only accessible to her.

The housemistress was shocked when Jean Baxter began to lecture in a grim voice. It was a far from friendly instruction that she was to relay to the girls. They had signed statements with the knowledge of their parents or guardians. It was necessary to warn them emphatically that if they were to consider altering any of the basic content it could lead to criminal charges being made for wasting police time. WPC Baxter didn't want them following Clair Hooper's example. There mustn't be any turncoats in the camp.

'Is that necessary?' questioned Jan.

'This is a damn serious business, Jan. They need to be aware of the consequences should they want to retract anything. There will be pressure from many sources and I want to ensure these are resisted at all costs. I don't want this thing collapsing now. Tomorrow we will be half way there. Jan, help me hold this together. For both our sakes let's not put the skids under this case. He has to be stopped. You know that.'

'If that's how it has to be done.' Jan reluctantly agreed.

'Cheer up, Jan, there are a couple of bonus points for our darling witnesses.' Baxter was smart enough not to order harsh tactics without softening it with some positive news. 'There's a good chance, according to reliable sources at the exam boards, that the girls can receive special consideration for their GCSE examinations as they are victims of crime. This has been an ordeal and it's only fair they get some help. Wouldn't you agree?' Jean Baxter enjoyed offering this sweetener. 'And, of course, there's the counselling. There's no knowing what damage this sod has done. Marissa Caldwell at Social Services will be contacting you to arrange sessions for the girls if they feel they need them.'

'They appear okay, but then I'm no expert,' admitted Jan Edgerley. 'It might be a good move. Does this include Clair Hooper?'

'Er... why not. It might stir something helpful to us,' Jean Baxter concluded.

It was early June. A sun-spilling morning. Mark Stephens was sleeping fretfully. The night had been warm and an evening drinking wine had turned up the volume on his snorting and snoring. He had been suspended for over a month from his post as Head of English at Thomas Graham School and falsely accused of sexually molesting children. Alison, his shock-absorbing wife, slept equally shallowly. She should have elbowed Mark as he spluttered and dribbled in his fidgeting slumber. Her night's sleep would have improved. Anna and Jayne were sound sleepers. But when the Child Protection Unit based at Wokingham rapped at the front door all the household was thrown rudely awake. Mark stumbled downstairs with frog-like gait and shoved the yapping Jack Russell, DJ, into the lounge. He groped at the mortice lock and clicked the Yale open. Jean Baxter peered through the tightly held gap protecting the early morning Mark Stephens from critical eyes.

'Mr. Stephens?' she prodded through the narrow opening. A sickly smile seeping in with the question.

Mark had been prepared. He was warned of the tactics. Not

that he had anything to hide. There were some sordid magazines that Norman had asked him to store. He had got rid of
those. But that was all. They could tear the place apart. They
would find nothing.

'Yes, I'm Mark Stephens,' he admitted.

'WPC Baxter, Wokingham Constabulary. And this is
Detective Sergeant Mills. Do you understand why we are here?'

'I have a good idea,' Mark responded. He needed the toilet
badly.

So here he was. In person. Baxter tried to briefly imagine
him with Susan Bennett just to revitalise the demon. 'Mark
Terence Stephens I must caution you that I am arresting you
on suspicion of indecent assault. You do not have to say anything unless you wish to do so, but what you do say may be
taken down and given in evidence. Do you understand?'
Baxter reeled it off without flinching, and with a great deal of
satisfaction.

Mark fell back into the hallway. Bernard Mills followed.

Jean Baxter summoned the other officers from their smoke-
filled cars. Even in plain clothes their manner yelled police.
You couldn't hide a pig inside a purple bomber jacket.

'Where shall we start?' asked one of the constables as he
skated on the door mat.

'If Mr. Stephens would show us to his office or study we
will begin there. I trust that won't be inconvenient.' Jean
Baxter turned to Mark and served up another gruesome grin.
She didn't care a damn about the inconvenience. She hated
having to be nice to this monster. 'Is there a table we can use?'

Mark guided the line of police officers to the breakfast
room. He cleared the strewn newspapers and other assorted
junk that littered it from the night before. Four of the police
constables sat at the table while the other two, along with
Baxter, began rummaging through his study. Sergeant Mills
stood talking to Mark. What appeared to be a frightfully polite
conversation prompted by the grinning sergeant was designed
to keep the suspect occupied; to keep a close eye on him. Stop

him heading for hills. High-tailing it out of there. Mark was going nowhere. He didn't trust the people handling his property. Poking around in his drawers and prying into every file and folder, every book and scrap of paper. He made them coffee. He didn't know why.

It wasn't until the kettle had boiled and while he was watching them reading through his personal documents that he remembered to call Robert Manning. How stupid of him to forget that. The moment they invaded his home he should have been on the phone. He rushed to the telephone. DS Mills, alerted by his sudden movement, flew after him.

'What are you doing, sir?' He was agitated and naturally suspicious. However, he remained outwardly polite.

'Phoning my solicitor,' Mark retorted. Surely they couldn't stop him. He'd seen it in the films or on TV. You can always make one phone call. You phone your solicitor. He comes rushing to bail you out. That's got to be right. Mark was panicking a little.

'Who would that be?' Mills asked.

'Er... Robert Manning. He's my solicitor. Appointed by the Union.' Mark endeavoured to explain as he listened to the metal voice of the answer machine in Robert's office.

'Okay.' Mills stood nearby to monitor that end of the call.

'Damn! There's no one there. Of course it's so bloody early.' Mark left a garbled message on the clicking machine. And immediately regretted even trying to sound sensible.

Alison stayed in the bedroom. She knew strangers were touching their things. It was like being robbed. Her house was being soiled. A band of ridiculous men were looking at every photograph of every holiday to see whether her husband had been over zealous with the snapping of his daughters. Were there naked shots? Was he naked with them? Could they find neighbours' children frolicking in the paddling pool? What innocent snapshot were they going to turn into the craft of the preying pervert?

Anna and Jayne prepared to go out, there were lectures at

college to attend. As long as the brutes stayed downstairs they weren't that put out by their presence. They gave Mark a comforting hug in front of the snooping policemen and the bloodhound policewoman. Giving razor stares to any who looked, and whispered encouragement. Anna was unsure whether she should leave, fearing that Mark was going to be taken away and locked up. A few tears bubbled and trickled down her cheeks. She wiped them away before the oafs at the table could see.

'Go on, it's all right,' Mark assured her.

Baxter watched him. He was vile enough to prey on his own daughters. She knew the type. She hunted their body languages for the signs. Mark caught her and knew her intentions. He despised her for that.

They examined every drawer and file in his study, every minute scrap of paper; and even the empty desk was treated to an inspection of its skeletal frame. It took nearly an hour, maybe longer. He tried to keep track but he was bursting for a shit and in desperate need of a shower. Once the study had been thoroughly searched there were the other rooms. There was less enthusiasm for those where documents were scarce. The dining room, lounge and kitchen were given very little attention. These were areas where Alison ruled and where he wouldn't have kept anything incriminating. More eagerly they asked Mark to show them his garage and garden shed. That's where he would have wanked over pictures of children and kept the details of his network of other child molesters. A sordid ring of depraved teachers feeding their fantasies of sex with young girls.

So they stomped through his cluttered garage and examined every sheet of sandpaper and DIY catalogue. They emptied pots of old screws and delved into the cobwebs of the cat box. And in the shed they trundled over his mower and strimmer, and peeped into the half-empty compost bags where his disgusting literature would be hidden. Almost comically they demanded he opened up the old yellow Chevette that he had resorted to driving, and they flicked through the musty MOT certificates and greasy maintenance manual.

And when they had nowhere left they went upstairs where Alison had remained and dared them to invade. Jean Baxter knocked on her door and tried to exhibit a caring visage. Alison fumed. There was a quick fumble through his bedside cabinet followed by a hasty retreat. Equally brief was the inspection of the girls' rooms. They were, as usual, a mess. No one was going to apologise to these marauders for that.

Even in her early morning blandness and the haunted red eyes of distress, Alison looked good. She had always been a looker. And Mark was the first to admit it was purely physical in the beginning. WPC Jean Baxter could recognise this woman's glamour, however uncomfortable the feeling, but only momentarily considered why, with such a ravishing wife, Mark had found a squat, rubbery schoolgirl attractive.

Mr. Nice Guy, Sergeant Mills, took Mark aside and explained that there were certain items that they would be taking away and that a list was being prepared so that he could verify their confiscation and eventual return. He also informed the suspect that he would be taken to the police station for questioning. A normal procedure.

'Surely this is going too far?' Mark meekly protested. 'This is so bloody stupid.' As if to make a point he insisted on the shower. His desire to shit had long been overtaken by stronger emotions. However, once alone in the bathroom he accomplished both activities at an alarmingly speedy pace. He didn't like to leave the team of idiots roaming round his home unattended for long. When he emerged the six officers, the muscle, had crept back into their car and were waiting. Mark was to have the dubious honour of being carted to Wokingham Police Station by the harpy Baxter and the grinning plod Mills.

Mark climbed the stairs to say goodbye to Alison. His legs were strangely heavy. Usually he bounded up each step. Alison was sitting on the edge of the bed. On the edge of her sanity. She kept the tears back until after he had gone.

'Where are you going? Where are they taking you?' The sniffles were there. She knew where he was heading. She pulled him to her and held on.

'I've got to go to the police station at Wokingham. I don't think I will be long.' He was near to weeping himself. 'You going to be all right? Do you need someone here? Shall I call Marion?'

'No. Go on. I'll be okay. How will you get back? Will they bring you?' These were smoke-screen questions.

'I don't know. Perhaps Robert Manning will drop me off.' Mark reached for the bedroom phone. He had to try Robert's office once more. He wasn't sure his recorded words had made sense.

'Gilbert Johnson and Partners.' A woman's sleepy voice answered. Not the anonymous mechanical one he stuttered an SOS to, pleading for the cavalry in the form of Robert Manning.

'Is Robert Manning there?' Mark appealed.

'Sorry, sir, Mr. Manning has not arrived yet.'

'Oh shit! Look I need to leave him an urgent message.' Mark waited for her to grab a pad and pencil and gave her the details of the morning raid and his imminent departure for Wokingham Police Station.

He gave Alison one more kiss and a reassuring squeeze, and plodded downstairs where Baxter and Mills were eager to escort him to the car.

In the cell waiting for Robert to arrive his bowed head stuck on the cool, steel door...

In the office of Octavia House Marissa Caldwell waited for Clair Hooper to arrive. Marissa was a counsellor with Ransdown Forest Social Services. In preparation for the girls' arrival she had rearranged the furniture to soften the look. An attempt to promote an environment where the girls she was going to see would feel at ease. She sat in one corner so as not to dominate the room, not behind a desk and not raised above the girl. Ms Caldwell deliberately sank down. She was a big woman who tried hard to camouflage a jelly body inside a maroon, patterned tent. A dress that she carefully organised in her lowered position so that the now bubbling rolls of fat were well veiled.

'Come on in and take a seat.' Marissa Caldwell greeted Clair Hooper who had walked in through the open door. A door purposely left wide. It was part of the approach.

Clair had recovered some of her old self-assurance. Her head was held higher and she strode confidently into the office. The whole grubby business was fading away. She had now escaped the attention. Susan Bennett and Pauline Green were being given the special treatment. The old bag of a policewoman was always calling in to see how they were. It made her sick to see Baxter in the boarding house being all chummy with that vile tart Bennett. Clair had only agreed to see the counsellor because it took her out of double science with that lecherous half-wit, Mr. Shelley.

'How are you, Clair?' Marissa Caldwell automatically asked. It wasn't a special technique. 'Mrs. Edgerley has told you who I am and why I'm here I presume?'

'Yes she has. And I'm fine.' Clair replied cheerfully. There wasn't the reticence she had displayed when she was last in that room being interrogated by Jean Baxter.

'This has been a trying time for you hasn't it? How are you coping with everything?'

'I'm fine. I'm not involved. Did you know? It's only that dozy moose Bennett and her little buddy Green. It's them you need to see.'

'Why them and not you?' Quizzed Marissa.

'I've just told you. Bennett was having it off with Mr. Stephens. She needs to have her head examined not me. He didn't want me.' Clair let it slip out. She hoped it wouldn't be picked up by this fat crumbly asking the questions.

'I'm not here to examine heads. I'm not a shrink, Clair,' Marissa was ready to assure her. 'Let's not discuss the other girls. I am only interested in you.' She cracked a huge benevolent smile. She was good at those. 'So you haven't been upset by what has happened? So you don't need me? You're quite chipper, eh?'

'Yes, I'm all right. Just as I told you.' Clair gave her the wide eyes and the tilted head. 'Can I go now?'

'Well I don't seem to be able to help you.' Marissa shuffled through her documents and pulled one out like a conjuror easing out the chosen playing card. 'Now let me see.' She lifted on her reading glasses, scanned the page, peered over the spectacles and prepared to confront Clair. The girl wasn't ready for this trap. 'I have a copy of correspondence from the Southern Examination Group confirming special consideration being offered to you because of the trauma you suffered.' Marissa raised her eyebrows and her face questioned the blank face of Clair Hooper.

Clair gritted her teeth and creased her nose. Shit! She'd forgotten that. The old bat was giving her daggers. She had to think quickly. 'Yeah... Well I'm all right in myself. Where it affected me was... the whole investigation of Mr. Stephens. And me getting confused.' Still the woman's face questioned. This would hurt, but she was looking for an escape. 'And my friends Susan and Pauline. What happened to them really upset me. They're in the House. We're close.' Ugh! The thought of it. 'Quite difficult to get down to work, to concentrate, like.' Clair's eyes searched the counsellor's for sympathy. She knew this was a desperate effort to repair her credibility.

'I'm not sure I believe all you're saying, Clair. You don't have to lie to me. All this is in strict confidence.' Marissa Caldwell was worried about some of the cracks now appearing.

'Well, that's how it is,' Clair declared. She rose from her seat and made for the door.

'Is there anything you want to disclose? I'm here to share it with you. Don't leave here with it still troubling you. Friend to friend?'

Clair stared at the dumpy woman. Friend? She wasn't going to tell her anything. Not a word about how she had tried it on with Mr. Stephens and then boasted of his advances. Not to her. And certainly not how that all went wrong. She was nearly clear of that. Soon she would leave the fucking school and could forget it.

'No, that's all.' Clair disappeared out the door.

Marissa Caldwell sat rubbing her chin. She was still trying to fathom out where Clair Hooper actually fitted into all this, when Jan Edgerley sauntered in.

'Has Clair gone?' Jan enquired, a little surprised by the briefness of the session.

'Yes. Not much I could do there.'

Marissa stopped thinking about Clair and prepared herself for the next girl.

'Pauline will be along in few minutes. I'll get her released from her science class,' Jan informed the social worker.

Marissa Caldwell pulled a new file from her briefcase. She was reading some of the black girl's background when Pauline crept into the office. She entered more sheepish than the brazen Clair Hooper.

It was a difficult one for Pauline to read. She was supposed to be a bit player in all this. Just helping her trusty friend out. But she had been lifted to equal status with Susan Bennett who had supposedly been seduced by the errant teacher, and who had openly admitted to a flourishing relationship with Mark Stephens. She was still bemused. She really couldn't understand why she had agreed to say she'd done that.

'Hello Pauline. It's nice to meet you.' Marissa wanted this to go well. Pauline Green was a definite victim. She had been identified by the police as being subjected to a serious sexual assault by Mark Stephens and an important collaboratory witness in the case against him. 'Sorry to drag you out of lessons.'

'It's all right. Only old Shelley's lesson. Don't do much there anyway. As long as it's quiet he don't trouble us.' Pauline examined her fingernails. She didn't look at the social worker. Just at dirt she was going to scrape from her thumb.

'This going to take long?' Pauline had no interest in discussing anything with this porky woman.

Marissa Caldwell was beginning to worry about her role. There wasn't much call for counselling so far.

'As long as you need me,' she assured Pauline. 'Tell me how you are feeling. How this has affected you. You don't have to do anything special. I can just listen if you wish.'

There was an edible silence that expanded the space in the room. Pauline's slightest movement seemed to resound in the auditorium office with its high Victorian ceiling and bare walls.

'You know what he did, don't you,' Pauline began. 'Well it weren't with me really. He done it with Susan. I was only there for just a bit, like. Not really his girlfriend like Susan. Not much I can say.'

It was an awkward explanation that had Marissa Caldwell puzzled. 'Do you feel different to how you felt before this happened?'

She did. Now life was complicated. She had all the secrets stashed. Pauline Green knew that Susan Bennett's lies were in the hands of the police. That Stephens would be in serious trouble. And she knew that her only friend at the school was relying on her to support an episode where a senior teacher at the school had reputedly pulled out his penis and made the two of them jerk him off. It was something she would readily do for a boy. She had done it a few times. Quite enjoyed it. But for a teacher? Anyhow it was only a few weeks before they left. Susan insisted she kept to the story. And now there was the threat. Mrs. Edgerley had warned her about going back on what she had claimed; police charges and worse.

'I suppose I'm on edge. Sort of not myself. You know; can't relax.' It was Pauline's only manifestation of guilt.

'Would you like to talk me through it? Go through the details? It may help.' Marissa was keen to hear it.

'There's no more to tell. I'll be all right after I've left. End of June and I'm gone.' Pauline was picturing the release. She could take her crime with her. There wouldn't be the constant reminder. There would be some space between her and Susan.

As careful as she could, but with an impish motive Marissa dropped in on Pauline's thoughts. 'You understand that in all likelihood there will be a trial. Mr. Stephens will have to go to court. You and Susan are only fifteen.' She hoped this would initiate further elements coming to the surface. 'And more importantly you will have to give evidence in that court. Have you thought that through?'

Pauline hadn't. Now she was. Christ! She thought it wouldn't go this far. Susan had assured her it would all end when Stephens was thrown out. It wasn't going to be like this. Even Jean Baxter had been telling her that it was unlikely she would be needed again. That the case against Stephens was enough. He'd have to plead guilty to this and Pauline could slip away from it all. She had not really understood the seriousness. People always seemed to be acting it out for her. She knew she was slow. Didn't pick things up easily.

'It's Susan you want to see. It's not me. I aint going to court. Not me. Fucking Susan Bennett!' Pauline was breaking up and Marissa could see a purpose to her session.

'Slow down, Pauline. I seem to have sparked off something. Let me get you a drink. Coffee maybe?' Marissa had to steady the girl.

'No! I don't want anything.' Pauline slumped in her seat and screwed up her face. 'Look I can't tell you. There's no point in this.'

'What can't you tell me? There certainly does seem a point to it. Look at you. You've dissolved into a real mess. This event is locked deeper down than you thought. It's now coming to the surface. Seen it before. Not all at once, but short, sharp eruptions of it. A classic case of repressed anxiety.' Marissa Caldwell was as precise as she could be. She was slightly thrown by the sudden surge. 'Now we're lancing the boil, so to speak, let's keep going.' Marissa was excited by the unexpected progress.

'I said no!' Pauline stood and shouted at the plump woman who was now leaning forward eagerly on her flabby forearms. 'You talk to Susan. Get her to see sense. That'll be the best for everyone.'

Pauline was out of the door before Marissa could stand. She wasn't having a successful day.

Jan Edgerley had seen Pauline fly past the window and was back to the office at pace. 'Wow! Pauline shot out of here,' she exclaimed to Marissa Caldwell who stood dabbing her brow with a floral handkerchief. 'Everything all right?'

'I'm not sure. Neither of these girls has been a good subject for the counselling we're offering. I thought I had Pauline opening up. But it ended in another explosion. I seem to be detonating my subjects today.' Marissa tried to make light of her lack of achievement.

If she thought her day had been bad so far she hadn't reckoned with her third customer. Susan Bennett had been summoned as soon as Pauline Green was seen to return to her form. The disruptive pupils fooling around in the physics lab had coordinated to strike up a chorus of there's a moose loose as she was called out of class by the headmaster's secretary.

Marissa Caldwell was slouched back in her embedded berth when Susan Bennett blew through the door. It took Susan a few seconds to locate the reclining social worker. She sat down in a chair near the centre of the room, a hard chair. There was no eye contact. Susan Bennett sat rigid, smoothing her skirt round her chumpy thighs and fixing her gaze on the wall above Marissa Caldwell.

'Hello, Susan.' It was a warm and jolly greeting.

'Hi,' responded Susan with less enthusiasm. Demonstrating about the same interest as the two previous candidates.

Marissa dispensed with apology for taking her out of class. It would seem from the other girls' reactions that this was in no way an inconvenience or damaging to their education. The science lesson sounded chaotic.

'I have been informed, as you will obviously know, about what has happened to you, exactly how it developed and the outcome of your liaison with Mr. Stephens. I am not here to sit in judgement. I'm only here to help you. That's if you need it. How are you feeling, Susan?'

'I'm okay,' Susan was quick to convince her.

'Would you like to talk through any problems you are having as a result of all this. It must be a difficult and confusing time for you. You are probably battling with some strong and contradictory emotions. These can produce a volatile cocktail threatening to manifest itself in many troublesome ways.' Marissa Caldwell was in part fascinated by Susan Bennett's relationship with Mark Stephens, but also disgusted by some of the aspects. Her tender coaxing was an attempt to extract more detail, and to a lesser degree to track down any adverse affects.

'So you know about me and Mr. Stephens.' Susan now fixed her eyes on the frump stuck in the soft chair. What an old trout. How would she know jack shit about what I've been through. Susan was in urgent need of counselling, but it was doubtful that Marissa Caldwell, grinning from her prone nest, would be able to deal with the stored horrors this girl carried around. 'What d'you think then? A teacher my lover, eh? Bet you think I'm a right whore. Don't you?'

'No judgement, Susan, as I said. I make no moral judgement. I'm here only to help you manage this ordeal.' Marissa continued. She thought the schoolgirl was a real slag but she would never tell her. Hypocrisy was an essential element in the social workers' liberal approach.

Susan felt alone in the centre of the spartan office. Her natural reaction was to fill the space with extravagant bragging about her affair with Mr. Stephens. Only, when she tried to outline the complete and fulfilling nature of this emotional and physical relationship the old ghosts swept back to haunt her. Taunting phantoms that wouldn't let go; that nagged and jabbed and threw up big-screen video replays of her dark childhood and guilt-ridden adolescence. Of him. Of that fucking old man who had stolen all the magic and excitement, and left a testimony of shame and fear. Unexpectedly and out of character her eyes welled, and the cold and stony girl sobbed hysterically.

Absolutely! thought Marissa. Here we go. She struggled free of the deep chair and waddled up to Susan's side. She offered a fist of tissues. Susan grabbed at them, eager to stem the embarrassing flow.

'Just let it out. Tell me. It will help.' Marissa was ready for Susan to purge herself. Empty it all out for her to sift through. Marissa searched for massaging words.

'The bastard! The fucking bastard!' Susan spluttered from behind the shielding hands she held tight against her face. Then she fell silent.

'Go on,' urged Marissa. She wasn't shocked by the language and would have side-stepped that anyway. This was getting superbly intense. 'You can open up to me. Just allow it to pour naturally. It's the only way to expel it.'

Susan didn't speak, but Marissa could hear a medley of low and angry sounds. Susan was simmering. Marissa had lit a low flame and was happy to sit back until her subject boiled.

Cutting through the silence, like a stalking big cat who is abruptly confronted by an intruder, a deep growling. 'He used me. Used me until I was sore. For so long. Is that how he showed his love?'

Susan pulled back behind her hands and wept some more. She was back in the hell of one of those black days when he had been drinking. Probably when he started. When she was seven or eight. Susan spoke to herself. Marissa listened.

'Ugh! That breath. His sickly breath. And his hands pulling, tearing at my clothes. The clutching hand between my legs and his shallow breathing and stupid words. The bastard!'

Marissa laid a hand on Susan's shoulder. Susan shuddered and pulled her face from her damp palms. Her cheeks were stained and she whimpered.

'Take it easy, Susan.' Marissa's arm surrounded Susan's quivering broad shoulders. 'Try not to upset yourself so. I didn't realise what had happened. He must have been a beast to you. How on earth could a teacher do that?'

'A teacher?' murmured Susan. 'A teacher?' She wasn't back with the programme yet.

'Mr. Stephens. I just can't fathom why he would be so brutal. So evil.' Marissa looked puzzled. It wasn't at all what she had expected to hear.

Susan needed to tell how it was, how it had been. 'Mr. Stephens. Yes, Mr. Stephens.' She repeated the name, but she was only conscious of the habitual incest she was logged on to. 'So many times! I hated it at first when it hurt. Couldn't understand why he wanted me to suffer. And then... then there were times when I could see it happening, make out it was someone else. Looked at the flashing pink flesh squeezing inside and pulling out long and firm. When I didn't mind. When I wanted to keep watching... time when I sort of enjoyed it.' That was Susan's real pain.

Marissa was shocked by the graphics. She could detect the conflict and the agony. But all wasn't clear. The girl seemed to be strangely affected by what was a mutual association. It didn't add up. Marissa was uncomfortable on more than one count.

'But now,' Susan persisted, 'when it happens. Not as often... I lie there with his warm fluid spilled on me and soaking into the sheets, and my clothes still pushed round my neck and my hair stuck to the pillow. I hear his change rattle as he pulls on his trousers and the whipping sound of his swinging tie as he puts himself back together again, as if he hadn't done it. Refits the jig-saw of his life. And I'm left in pieces, mapping out the darting, crazy cracks in the ceiling plaster and know what a prostitute feels like.'

Marissa's mouth stuck open. Frozen. She could have swallowed the room.

Susan saw Marissa's statue frame and her incredulous face.

She wanted to continue. Tell some truths. It helped.

'And sometimes when I have cleaned myself up and made the room my sanctuary once more he'd come back. When I was sleeping. And probe again with those stubby fingers, burrowing inside my knickers, feeling for the shameful wetness. And with his legs across me, pull off my clothes that I had locked tight in defence. That stupid grin and his hard cock straining in his cheap suit trousers. And I... knew. So many times I lay there with his thumping frame smacking into me. And his rolling, lolling head trying to reach my lips.

'I can still smell his stale saliva that oozed onto my pillow. And I can still feel the coldness of my dumped naked body that I daren't touch until morning. And how long it took for his stench to leave me alone.'

'My God, Susan. You have been through it.'

Marissa couldn't digest it all. She wiped the dribble from her chin and tried to build a picture of how and what Stephens had done to her. There was too much. There was no equation.

'You poor child. And Mr. Stephens did all this to you? I must have got it wrong. I understood there were only two or three encounters. You obviously haven't told anyone about all this. Poor girl.'

Marissa hunted through her papers. What a day! She wasn't at all in control of this session. 'Here. Yes, that's what I thought. You have told the school and the police that there were these three separate incidents, two when you were alone with Mr. Stephens and one when Pauline was with you.'

Susan was still escaping from her dreadful bedroom and the pale spectre of her father's lust. She gave Marissa Caldwell a penetrating stare from red and haunted eyes. The stare of a devil. Susan's teeth bared and she hissed as if clearing the taste of a middle-aged man's stinking penis. Fuck there being three fucking separate fucking occasions, Susan steamed in her head. There had been at least three hundred despicable acts of fatherly love. He had always touched her, always preyed on her body. Somebody had to pay for that. Mark Stephens had crossed her and he would do. Yes, my darling Mark, he'd be the ideal sacrifice. She could admit to all those acts with him, her loving school teacher.

'Susan, Susan.' Marissa called gently as if waking her from precious slumber. 'I hear your agony, but I can't help you a lot on this one visit. Without doubt I need to see you again. If not on a regular basis. You are lugging some heavy baggage there, and it will take quite a few sessions to unload it.' Marissa resorted to camouflaging metaphors to cover her retreat. 'I'll fix it up with Mrs. Edgerley.'

Marissa began collecting her papers and loading her briefcase. She stuffed the unused tissues in her handbag. 'Now I need to be going.' Marissa's cooling-tower dress was still sticking to her rubbery, ribbed belly, and there was an uncomfortable glueyness inside her 15 denier tights that had collected during her time wallowing in the cushioning furniture.

Susan Bennett didn't move. She was wet too. Beads of sweat met the trickling tears that bubbled from her glazed eyes. She was still marooned in the middle of the room when Marissa Caldwell edged past her. There was a hand placed on her bent head and an embarrassed farewell.

'Until next time. Goodbye.' Marissa clutched at her throat and her chest pumped. She could only breathe properly once she was out of that room.

Susan Bennett would never agree to see her again.

Chapter 9

September 6th 1994 saw the appeal hearing at the school.

Mark was on unconditional bail and there had been no word from the police that the girls had changed their story. Charles Cornwall had little to prepare and could offer no change in tactics. It looked like a foregone conclusion. Margaret Cullen and Robert Manning were adamant that Mark was not to speak in his own defence and Charles was warned against giving any details of the case. After much persuasion and firm promises the legal double act allowed him to question the girls' evidence at the hearing, but that was all. It was the only concession. It would be a good opportunity to test their statements. Have a go at the inconsistencies. Challenge the lies. However, Margaret was pretty sure that the girls wouldn't be there.

Charles was to make a further speech asking for an adjournment in view of the possible court case. He would take a letter from Margaret Cullen outlining the legal implications of divulging the defence case and the confidentiality aspect of the material heard at such a hearing. Urging a postponement.

It was *déjà vu*. The panel was different. Yet it was the same. A row of puppets. And the puppeteer, Colonel James Hall, still pulling the strings. The school had already employed a replacement for Mark, according to Dave Patterson. Talk about a sure thing.

Mark relived the original hearing. The same emotions. Another encounter with Captain Donald Cutter and the long walk with Charles Cornwall to the staff club room where the line of limp, geriatric governors presided. Ridiculously austere on a long blanket-covered table. Again there were the introductions. Such a pleasant formality!

And Charles stood to seek the adjournment, ask for a reasonable response to his request, for them to take into account the letter explaining the sensible route to be taken. He included some further information, such as a petition to the education minister to call a halt to this ludicrous hearing. Really only straw clutching. He emphasised the injustice of making a decision without Mark being able to defend himself.

And they sat with the content of Susan Bennett's statement stuck in their heads and the vile acts like murals on the walls of a long corridor. At the end of which stood Mark Stephens. Words slung either way could not erase the indelible images that had been imprinted by the vicious lies, that they held on to as being the only truth. Still attached was the already discredited statement by Clair Hooper. There was nothing that the tiny despot, James Hall, wouldn't try.

The chairman of the panel, not too dissimilar to Alexander Darlington, a Captain Robb, called the obligatory temporary suspension of proceedings merely as a sop to the union representative. Colonel Hall had forewarned them that this would be Cornwall's ploy, and instructed them how best to react.

'You know. Damn union people. Pull the team out. Consider what he's said. Wouldn't budge though. Don't give in to that sort. Need to resolve this on the day. School could suffer. Understand?' The expeditious little Hitler wasn't going to allow Mark Stephens even one more day as an employee of Thomas Graham School.

There were two frightened starlings on the panel of governors who cringed at the thought of making a decision based on only one side of the case being heard, but not wanting to appear wet remained silent, joining in the nodding at the right time. There was some manufactured emotion involving *our duty to the children* and a plea to get the school back on track with a full complement of staff. But no word for the silent one, the gagged and impotent teacher who could only ask for their patience and fairness with his begging eyes.

So when the panel returned, nursing dour expressions, they

could only announce that they weren't prepared to agree to the adjournment, and based on the evidence they had in front of them, they dismissed the appeal and confirmed Mr. Stephen's sacking.

'But you have listened to no witnesses. I haven't been given the opportunity to question any of the evidence. All you have is this joke of a document! How on earth can you decide like that?'

Charles could hold back no longer. He brandished the statements above his head and shouted at each of the panel in turn.

'You are going to throw out this teacher. One who's been here over twelve years, on the flimsy fantasies of two little liars.'

With his raised and punching fists Charles reminded Mark of an old picture of Lenin at a rally in Red Square.

'This is not justice! And you know it!' Charles collected up his papers and pulled Mark up by the elbow. 'Let's get out of here.'

Mark had become used to being shot at point blank range. He shook his head at the absurd individuals who had made a mockery of justice. There was no manifestation of shock. In fact there was an astonishing calm, perhaps more attributable to numbness than serenity.

Charles and Mark stormed from the room. Charles was still seething. Donald Cutter was stationed outside and had reckoned on a difficult escorting task, but when he saw the barbarous eyes of the two men escaping from the hearing he stepped back and turned away. Even Charles Cornwall was game for fisticuffs at that moment. Mark had too many that he wanted to murder. In his great plan though, he'd start with that little bitch Susan Bennett. Boy, had he a fitting end for her.

By the time they had reached the cars Charles' pressure-cooker head had cooled a little and his crimson face was toning down.

'My doctor would have kittens.' Charles reached into his waistcoat pocket and pulled out some pills. 'The old ticker needs these now.' He threw them into his mouth and swallowed quickly. 'Blood pressure. A damn curse!'

'You should take it easy. Don't kill yourself for me.' Mark was concerned more about Charles than the tragedy of his own dismissal.

'Not just for you, young man,' gushed Charles, still smarting. 'It's for all the other Mark Stephens who could well face a panel of bloody idiots like those, who will continue to administer a distorted version of justice, either because they have a perverted loyalty to their school or because they are the ignorant pawns in the hands of unscrupulous managers like that moron midget, Hall.' Mark could almost see Charles' hypertension measurement hitting the bell.

'What now?' Mark leaned on the bonnet of his ugly yellow car.

Charles expelled air as if it were the remains of his tirade. 'We have the Industrial Tribunal of course. I will make an application as soon as I get into the office tomorrow morning. I won't get back in time tonight. But, Mark, we can go so far. Everything rests on the criminal side now. As soon as that's over we can plough ahead.' Charles' tone never questioned the result of that phase. Mark was walking away, either before it got to court or with complete exoneration at the Crown Court. He preferred the latter option. If it all evaporated before it could be tested in court there would always be a question mark, and with the burden of proof being less in an Industrial Tribunal it was a head start to take a *not guilty* verdict into the employment arena. 'You will probably not hear from me for a while. I know you haven't got a date yet, but I will take a back seat until Margaret and Robert have finished with you.' He slapped Mark on the thigh and shook Mark's hand with both of his. It was a good luck gesture. Unspoken but deeply sincere.

Alison didn't hold it up to his face, didn't blatantly question Mark about their financial future, but it was linked to most of their discussions after the appeal hearing.

'You'll have to sign on,' was her first reaction. 'Do they pay the mortgage? Can I work?' Neither knew the exact nature of living on benefit. They were to soon find out.

Mark was loath to go to the Job Centre the next day and put it off. He didn't receive the official letter from the school until late on the 7th September. He was secretly and romantically imagining that the cavalry was on its way, and that there was going to be a sudden realisation that he wasn't the filthy pervert teacher and he had been cruelly and unjustly fired from his job. He was, however, an early caller the following day at the Job Centre that posed as a harmless shop in the high street.

First he sauntered past the window masquerading as a disinterested pedestrian. A window full of postcards on red fabric display boards. He was unsure what to do. He slowed down at the window on his return journey. The cards carried details of dull and mundane jobs paid by the hour. Mainly cleaners, cooks and labourers. Inside there were rows of desks occupied by cream-coloured computer monitors, and behind each screen sat a bespectacled schoolboy or spotty girl. And milling around looking at other cards inside, or thumbing through benefit pamphlets, was a motley crew of shuffling creatures going through the motions of looking for a job. A decoy. They were waiting to register their attendance and eligibility for the unemployment payment.

Mark checked that no one he knew was watching and slipped in the door. He was conspicuous. No tattoo and complete absence of stale tobacco smoke. There was no obvious reception. He didn't expect a formal and generous greeting but he did feel awkward searching for the appropriate desk. No one looked up from their paperwork and still the scuffling bodies hunted through the maze of free-standing displays. Mark was abandoned in unfamiliar territory. He caught hold of one of the drifting customers and asked directions. He was pointed towards a freckled woman, spinster-dressed, in her late twenties; peering fiercely through hawk glasses.

'Yes?' She hated the unemployed, that was for sure.

Mark was uncomfortable from the start. 'I'm... well... out of a job. I need to *sign on.*' He was clumsy and the austere frown did nothing to put him at ease.

Aggressively she grabbed a thick booklet from a drawer. 'Usually we ask you to come back for your interview. Fortunately someone has just cancelled his, and I can deal with you.' She slapped the paper on the table in front of Mark. 'You'll need to fill this in. All of it. Sit here and do it.' It was a concession; he could feel it. Perhaps she realised he wasn't a usual candidate for the dole.

Mark waded through typical questions; name, age, address and employment history, followed by education and other qualifications, and finally his expectations as to the type of job and wage required. It was where Mark wanted to put Prime Minister or rock star and slap down a million pounds as an annual salary.

'There we are.' Mark handed it back. The freckly girl was surprised by his speed.

She plodded through the completed document making notes alongside some the entries and giving him a quizzical look when she encountered his previous employer and his impressive list of qualifications. She could smell a rat. 'Are you available for work?' Something like a smile was hoisted from behind her glasses. She wanted to see his reaction.

'I suppose I am. Only I'm not sure I feel ready to do so.'

'You must be available for work, Mr. Stephens. It is a pre-requisite. You haven't indicated that you have a disability. So, can I assume there is no medical problem that could prevent your immediate employment?' She prodded again for his story. 'I see you intend looking in the newspapers for vacancies and other professional journals.'

'Yes.' Mark was aware how close she was and how close she wanted to get.

'I'm not up with the recruitment situation in teaching. What are your chances?' She persisted. Radiating an entrapping grin.

'To be honest... not good.'

She'd got him. 'Oh, I see.' It was like sympathy, but only

just.

Mark couldn't hold on to it any longer. 'Look. It is very unlikely I will be wanted by any school. I have just been thrown out of my school accused of indecent assault. These are totally false allegations, but as yet this hasn't been proven.' Mark looked hard into the woman's eyes.

She pulled back. It came as a shock. She hadn't dreamt of that. It took a while for her to compose herself. He was a different man now and she had lost her edge. 'I see.' She managed. But she didn't. She had no idea. She hurried to feed him his documents. Her tight superiority had gone slack and she was content to dispose of him.

'Here is your book that you need to bring every time you are required to sign on. Your day and time are shown on the reverse. Do you need help with your mortgage and will you be claiming council tax relief?' She tried to flush him through the system with a greased delivery.

Mark nodded. Of course he fucking did! He needed every damned penny he could get. He'd paid enough in twenty-five years of teaching. Surely he deserved something now.

She threw down a massive wad of paper. 'This is the Income Support form you need to complete. Send it to the address on the back when you have done so. There's also one for the council tax.' She added to the pile with a slapping down of the extra paper.

Mark was left to lift the heap. She had turned her head. He was dismissed. It was time to restore the dragon in her. She couldn't scare anyone the way she felt now. She watched Mark leave and summoned a snarl of disapproval aimed at the closing door.

There wasn't much money offered. No unemployment benefit immediately because he had been sacked, and only partial help with the mortgage. Mark tried to find odd jobs to supplement this meagre charity.

Margaret Cullen and Robert had several meetings without Mark. But everything seemed to be at a standstill until they could get access to the school records and interview potential witnesses there. In the meantime Robert had taken witness statements from Dave Patterson, Norman Munnie and Anna. He had also requested written testimony from the many character witnesses. It was a slow and methodical preparation. Mark hoped that none of it would be needed. He nursed the gnawing frustration of an innocent man well, but there were times when he felt like vomiting from the sickening despair of this bizarre situation. Like a mute trying to deliver erudite philosophy imprisoned in his head.

It came as a real shock when the pace hotted up, especially when, in the middle of November, Robert phoned to announce that a trial date had been set, 27th February. The venue was Snaresbrook Crown Court, not the Old Bailey, but a London satellite. Margaret apparently approved. She had seen success there many times. It would be good to play at home.

It wasn't until January that Margaret and Robert were allowed to study files at the school and obtain the home addresses of the witnesses.

Their arrival at Thomas Graham School was greeted with the same enthusiasm as Mark's attendance at the two disciplinary hearings. Donald Cutter met them on the back fields where they were asked to park. Only desirables were honoured by being allowed to enter the main gate. Although they were respected professionals that Cutter would have normally admired and grovelled around, these two were tainted. They belonged to 'that arsehole Stephens'. He was abrupt and overtly rude.

'This way.' Cutter gestured with his flipper arm.

Margaret had arrived separately from Robert and there were preliminary matters to discuss. 'We are not ready just yet.' Margaret could recognise the reptilian Captain as an imbecile. She pulled Robert away and spoke in a low voice. 'Have you the list we agreed on?' Robert confirmed with a nod. 'You realise that we will have to study these documents in the presence of some nosy police officer, so we must be careful what we say to each other and not draw attention to any major finds. If there is anything significant we will withdraw and speak privately. The documents can be copied but the originals have to stay put.'

Donald Cutter reminded them of his presence with a lame attempt at a cough. Coincidentally, but aptly, it sounded like the croak of an irritable toad.

'We're ready,' Margaret declared.

The two lawyers strolled behind the waddling plod of the ugly man. He showed them to a small office in the administration area of the school. Cramped enough with two people and the spread documents, but blatantly overcrowded when they were joined by WPC Jean Baxter.

'Good morning!' Baxter greeted them with a beaming superiority. 'My, it is a tight fit.' She plonked herself down across the table from Robert and Margaret. They could feel her breath. And her head hung over the bare surface where the papers would lie. 'You understand why I'm here I'm sure. Don't let me get in your way.' Of course she was delighted to get in the way of the scum who were attempting to jemmy Stephens out of this mess. 'Just let me know what you wish to see and I will arrange for it to be brought to you,' she explained. It sounded patronising. It was meant to.

Robert pulled out his initial list. 'First we require the house and school records of Susan Bennett, Pauline Green and Clair Hooper.' He sank back in his chair and held his hands as if in prayer and waited.

Jean Baxter struggled out from her wedged position and headed off to complete the errand. It was approximately twenty minutes before she returned. The folders were slammed down. Smacking the table. Baxter tucked herself back into her position of surveillance.

Self-consciously Margaret opened Susan Bennett's school file. She hoped it hadn't been doctored and that the school wasn't attempting to conceal anything that embarrassed them. They could well have done so, but what was left was ample ammunition for the astute barrister. Susan had been suspended from school on two occasions and reprimanded several other times. Almost every incident involved Pauline Green. There were copies of letters sent by the headmaster to her parents detailing the offences. Margaret and Robert read them together. Looking straight into each other's eyes when there were highly relevant aspects. They both took notes and thrust in sticky yellow markers to indicate the documents they needed photocopied.

Jean Baxter was ordered off to arrange it. Robert and Margaret blew out air in relief when she left. They quickly turned to the house discipline file for Susan Bennett, and were encouraged by even more misdemeanours that involved lying and some of a sexual nature. These too were thrust into the returning Baxter's arms for her to process. And on every trip to the secretary, who was frantically photocopying, she picked through the markers to see the relevance of what these two smarmy lawyers had found.

Pauline Green's history at the school was a perfect shadow of her mentor's record. Usually a minor or supporting part, but still a leading player. Prior to Susan Bennett's arrival at the school there was no evidence of Pauline having gone astray.

Clair Hooper's files were filled with relatively minor offences that broke school rules. Mostly there were boys involved, and the recorder recognised her tarty traits. There was little helpful here, but Margaret was eager to send Baxter off for copies just to mislead her, and encourage her to believe the defence thought that there was life in Clair Hooper's story.

They took a break after a couple of hours, and sat, heavily wrapped on a bench overlooking the playground, clutching mugs of steaming coffee. Margaret was pleased with what they had found so far. She spoke enthusiastically about some of the details they had discovered.

Deep inside one of the school buildings they heard the dull

ringing of a bell, and within seconds children streamed out of several swinging doors. There wouldn't be Susan Bennett or Pauline Green. They were long gone. Frightening phantoms. But there were girls Margaret could think of as these two malevolent bitches. That helped. They met in magnetic groups; arriving from all directions. All speaking at once. Margaret strained to hear them. She was certain they spoke of salacious things and the incredibly luscious topic of boys. The jerking glances of several of the scrum told of juicy secrets and exaggerated boasts. She sensed the ghosts of Susan Bennett and Pauline Green.

Some of the younger pupils, like inquisitive chicks, approached the two strangers sat spectating in the crisp winter air. Almost to see if they were alive or sane, and definitely to know their business they gathered round.

'You new teachers?' asked a bold, red-headed youngster with more a grimace than a smile.

'No, we're not teachers,' Robert assured him with a grin.

'Good. We don't like teachers,' announced a small boy sandwiched between two towering girls. It brought some laughter that spread deep into the group.

'We are here on other business,' Margaret added, wishing to be included in the exchange. 'So you don't like the staff here, eh?' She was fishing. It was an opportunity to test the waters. She wasn't sure of the ethics or the pitfalls. 'Surely some of them are okay?'

'Well, yeah. There are a couple that are all right.' A tall spindly boy answered her. He scratched his head and looked about him for support. Who were the okay teachers?

'Yeah, Mr. Dennis is a good bloke, and... so was Mr. Stephens. He aint here no more. Took the skiing and football. Good tennis player. Bit of a laugh.' The red-head lad contributed.

There were several supporters for that view, and it initiated some discussion in the crowd. Anecdotal accounts of episodes involving Mark were swapped and there was a spreading wave of chuckles.

'You liked Mr. Stephens then?' Margaret continued. Robert looked hard at her. She couldn't maintain this line. Couldn't recruit character witnesses there. Couldn't declare who she was. Couldn't worm from these cherry-faced kids their observations of Susan Bennett, and any secrets they held about her.

'S'right. Everyone liked Mr. Stephens. He...' A swollen little girl, quite unused to speaking to a crowd, began. A little more than a whisper. All the other squeaking voices stopped and the sparrow faces listened. They admired such bottle. 'He... made us laugh. Joked and things. I miss him.' Strangely the jostling mass said nothing. Just watched her bravely summon more uncomfortable words. 'We don't know why he isn't here. No one tells us...'

Her eyes darted to her left to identify a flashing figure hurrying towards the assembly. 'Back to boarding houses! Go! Straight away!' The shooing arms of Tom Pearson fluttered before him as he descended on the startled pupils. 'Go! Go!'

Margaret and Robert retreated with their mugs back to the small office as the shepherding deputy head scattered dissidents at the 'unlawful meeting'.

Baxter was on her feet when they returned. She had caught some of the action from the window. She glared at them both. 'You shouldn't be talking to the children,' Baxter informed them.

'Why not?' snapped Margaret. She wasn't going to tolerate the policewoman's interference. 'We were merely responding to their questions and didn't discuss the reason for our visit. Satisfied?'

Jean Baxter wasn't, but she had to be.

Robert sifted through the copies that Baxter had laid on the table. Margaret studied her notes.

'Now, if you don't mind, we will continue.' It was to be officious from now on and the bloody police bitch was going to behave and do her job. Margaret didn't suffer fools, and particularly foolish policewomen, readily. 'Mark Stephens' school employment record please,' she demanded.

It threw Jean Baxter. 'What?'

'His school file please. Is that a problem?' Margaret cut Baxter with her lacerating eyes.

Baxter tumbled out of the room. Why did they want his records? She'd seen it of course, but what good was it to them? It was still puzzling her when she returned and slammed the beige folder down in front of the two lawyers. She sat opposite them, her arms tightly folded and her chin shoved forward. She pressed her lips together and held them firm. And her scouring eyes searched their every movement and every document they dwelt on.

There were notes about Mark's initial interview and numerous other events that involved him at the school. In particular there were several incidents reported concerning his punctuality, and memos from Tom Pearson to this effect. Nasty sniping missives to nudge the headmaster; prompt some disciplinary manœuvre. And there were Mark's fencing letters to counter the deputy head's attacks. Ferocious letters. He could fight with written, crafted words; they were deadly ammunition for Mark. He couldn't quite get it together face to face. He needed time.

Margaret and Robert read them with relish. They were entertained. Forgotten was their real purpose for that moment. But they were brought down to earth when they came across the report of a meeting Ted Frith had had with Mark, involving an incident observed by Tom Pearson. Apparently Mark had been seen with his arm round the young telephonist at the school back in 1984. The deputy head had reported this as an amorous encounter. It had been shrugged off by Mark as a merely playful episode. However, it was down there in black and white, and there was no doubt Baxter could use it to blacken Mark's reputation. It would suit her purpose to show him as a womaniser. Robert swapped grim glances with Margaret.

'I think I need a short break,' Margaret announced.

Baxter stood and peered through the window. The children

had returned to classes and there was no one on the netball court marked out on the playground. 'Okay, but only while those blighters are inside.'

They found a corner where they weren't overlooked or overheard. Robert waited to hear Margaret's outburst and disappointment at the report in Mark's file.

She wasn't too worried about that. Margaret had another, titanic, concern that Robert had failed to pick up. She stormed about in a small circle laying her feet down heavily.

'Did you see it? On every page that he wrote!' Margaret was steaming.

Robert hadn't got there yet, he was still fishing. 'On every page?' he quizzed.

'Yes! His bloody handwriting! Didn't you notice?'

Robert screwed up his eyes and stamped a foot. 'Of course! I was too busy with the content.'

'Have you got that report from Henry Brolin?' Margaret's head was nearly in Robert's briefcase as he fingered through the files.

He slid it out without disturbing the others either side. 'Here.'

Margaret greedily searched through it. 'See!' She thrust the paper and the heavily etched lettering into Robert's face. 'Nothing like the writing on all his bloody letters. What is he up to?'

'It's not good.' Robert hissed lowly.

'Not good! It's a damn disaster.' Margaret chewed at her knuckles and thought it through. Eventually she turned to Robert and gave a resigned sigh. 'This means they will produce an expert witness who will testify that Mark wrote the note to Susan Bennett, and we will have...' Margaret thought for a moment. 'And I will have jack shit!'

Robert was taken aback by the last remark. Margaret didn't say things like that. It took a lot to make her that mad. He felt inclined to join in, in the same vein. 'Oh! Shit,' he added in support.

Both of them crept back to the room. Baxter saw their dejection and smiled. Margaret asked for copies of all the contents just to annoy the bumptious policewoman.

When she returned Robert sent her scurrying back to retrieve the parental names and addresses of the pupils he wished to take witness statements from.

Baxter was pissed off with this yo-yo activity, and visibly relieved when her latest mission concluded with Robert and Margaret packing away their document cases. They left the tiny room without a word to Jean Baxter or even the hint of acknowledgement.

Mark was hauled to Margaret Cullen's chambers eight days later. This was to be an important conference. She and Robert had a lot to deal with. There weren't going to be any kid gloves; they were gunning for their client, Mark Stephens.

Mark could feel the ice when he entered Margaret's room. And Robert's face had trouble in capital letters cut deep into the furrows of his brow. They both exchanged smiles with Mark. They were painfully given. It would be their only concession. Their pricking eyes would spend the rest of the session aimed at him and his statement.

Margaret was stern and her words deliberately sharpened. 'Hello Mark. How are you?' She wasn't particularly interested. It's just what she always asked.

'I'm okay.' He was getting some black vibrations. 'But I have the distinct feeling I'm not going to be soon. What's wrong? What happened at the school? Didn't you find anything useful?' Mark was straining to reach the reason for the obvious dejection.

Robert began. 'We visited the school last week as you know. The Susan Bennett file was most useful. Less so those of Pauline Green and Clair Hooper. There were two suspensions and several incidents that Margaret deemed helpful. These involved episodes of lying, and some misdemeanours involving boys. She is shown as being no saint, which is what we hoped to achieve.'

Margaret sat resting her elbows on the table. She waited for Robert to complete the necessarily mundane part before she entered the stage and the drama really began. She had high hopes in this case before being bushwhacked by Mark's indelible hand. She was pig sick.

'Your file,' Robert began, 'was a little distressing.'

'What?' Mark interrupted, shocked that there would be a problem. He hadn't even considered they would be prying into his school record.

'There was your war, for want of a better word, with Tom Pearson about your punctuality. Not that this really sheds any light on the allegations, but we would have liked you to have been spotless.'

'Sorry.' Mark for once regretted his poor timekeeping. But surely they weren't going to give him stick for that?

'And,' continued Robert, getting into the real meat of his disappointment, 'there was that incident with the young telephonist.'

'Oh! Shit. That was nothing. Just me larking about. Pearson, the prat, took it all too seriously. I can't believe that would be in there. That was about ten years ago. Surely they can't use that?'

'They'll use anything. If they think it will score points. It's all ammo for them. You'll have to explain yourself to the court. Margaret can help you through this.' Robert sucked in his lips. 'Of more concern to us both, Mark, is something considerably more grave than any playful flirting way back in your history.'

Mark swallowed heavily. He hoped no one noticed. The game was up. He felt his stomach trying to reach up and grab his throat.

Margaret stood, and as if cable-connected like a funicular railway, Robert plonked himself down. She was orchestrating the show now.

'This is pivotal, Mark. I cannot overstate the importance of what we have had to discover for ourselves. Without your help, I might add.' Her spitting her words were almost sparking.

'Your handwriting in those letters on file at the school. It was nothing like the sample you gave Henry Brolin, and what you led us all to believe was your natural hand. You have stupidly deceived us.' Margaret stopped to hiss audibly. 'What have you to say?'

Mark's head thumped and burned hot. Robert and Margaret stripped him of his dignity with their leering eyes. 'I didn't write that note.' He could afford to be adamant.

Margaret shook her head. She couldn't go any further. She wouldn't call him a liar and demand her truth.

'I can see it looks bad. I know what you are thinking. Believe me. I did not write a note to Susan Bennett. That isn't my writing.'

'They are going to crucify us in court if they have had it analysed. And they would be quite inept if they haven't. I would have done it immediately.' Margaret screwed up her face and tried to consider the options. Mark's response hadn't been what she had expected. She was certain he would have admitted something. Yet she dreaded what that might be.

'I did a stupid thing,' Mark began again. He spoke from a bowed head. Confession time.

'What was that?' Robert was quick to enquire.

'The handwriting on that letter to Susan Bennett was very similar to mine. I could see that. It threw me at first. But I knew it wasn't me who had written it. I suppose I panicked a bit. I thought it would look better if I diverted everyone away from any comparison by adopting this other style. Desperately difficult to cut a new groove with your handwriting. What a fool. So bloody short-sighted. Never thought Baxter would compare it with some past stuff. Hadn't even thought about that existing.' Mark shrugged his shoulders and flashed Robert and Margaret a doleful, resigned countenance.

There was a clumsy silence. Mark looked for absolution in their eyes. Robert broke the heavy hush with an introductory cough.

'Don't get me wrong. Misinterpret my intention. This is

only for clarification, Mark. To clear the way for future strategies. And as your solicitor I must make this enquiry.' He tip-
toed around the edge of a deep and icy pool, unsure of his
footing and summoning the courage to jump in.

'What? What's going on?' Mark quizzed. He could see
Robert fighting to proceed. It was something heavy he was carrying.

'Well...' It was now or never. 'Your plea?'

'Yes?' Mark was alert to the menace afoot.

'Do you want to change it?' Robert was relieved he had
managed to ask.

'Why should I?' Mark roared. He was a lion that had been
prodded through the bars of his cage and was ready to lash out
at the cowardly offender. 'What a question!' he growled. He
fought to find the words. He wasn't good at sounding angry
and wanted to convince this Judas.

'Now, take it easy, Mark.' Margaret rushed across to initiate
a rescue. 'Robert had to ask.'

'After all this! Now you want to tear me apart as well. You
think I bloody did it, don't you?' Unleashed rage that neither
had witnessed before.

'No! We don't, Mark. Robert would be negligent in his duty
if he didn't give you that option.' Margaret used reassuring
words and calming signals. But they needed to know. After the
blow with the handwriting evidence it would be a rugged route
ahead. Margaret had numerous briefs demanding her attention.
Especially a singularly delicious murder case at the Bailey. She
could do without a heroic battle with little chance of success.

Mark sat stunned. He shook his head slowly from side to
side.

Robert took the opportunity to assure him of his genuine
purpose. 'No doubt intended. Just doing my job.'

Margaret stepped in to distract Mark. 'We need to plan from
here. Now, Mark, we have the names and addresses we needed
from the school and Robert is arranging to interview the children. Hopefully we will get lucky there and have some more

weapons to take in with us.' She leaned across and put her hand on Mark's shoulder. 'You should have heard what some of the pupils at the school said about you. You've got some friends there. They were singing your praises. Weren't they, Robert?'

'Most certainly. A favourite with the kids, all right.' Robert was quick to respond and repair the damage.

'Well, at least someone is on my side.' Mark was licking his wounds. 'The staff are nowhere to be seen. They obviously think I'm some sort of demon.'

'Now, Mark,' Margaret massaged, 'what I need you to do is go away and think long and hard again about those dates when Susan Bennett reckons you were with her for several hours. What were you doing? Who did you see or speak to? We may have missed something. It's vital we get it right before we get in there.'

It was a fine exhibition. Her real purpose was to keep him busy. Not to contemplate what he had to face. She stood and held out his briefcase to signal the conference was over. Mark left Robert and Margaret in conspiratorial discussion and lumbered to Waterloo Station and home.

Throughout February Alison and Mark continued to live for the sound of the letterbox and the drilling ring of the phone. Each mail delivery and every call should have brought an end to this hell. There should have been a releasing letter or a saviour voice to break the spell. It never came. Right up to the eve of the trial they chased the tipping post and the hailing medley of bells. Red herrings and wild goose chases. Round and round in circles and up dead end alleyways.

Margaret called a concluding conference on the 26th February to discuss the final arrangements and last minute strategies. Mark trundled up to her chambers. A gentle off-peak excursion by rail.

It was a mad idea and something he shouldn't have tried. But he did. Susan Bennett's address and telephone number had been inadvertently left on unused prosecution documents and

Mark had copies. He took them with him. Giving himself an extra hour to waste in town he toured tourist London hoping to find an inconspicuous phone box. There weren't any. He chose one of several crowded together and the haunt of scurrying Japanese visitors, near Charing Cross Station.

The bloody girl had to see sense. It couldn't go this far. He would talk to her. He knew he shouldn't. It was totally out of order. Desperate and cornered he fed the coin box. The muffled traffic edged past and oriental faces scampered round, peering in on his frantic call. The dropping money echoed around the grimy kiosk. His damp fingers tapped out Susan Bennett's telephone number. It rang. He wished it hadn't. He held on.

'Hello?'

It wasn't her. He hadn't been prepared for the man questioning his call. It was a mousy, defensive voice. Mark gripped the handset tight. His sweat diluted the dirt staining the grey plastic, and it trickled in rivulets down the receiver.

'Is... Susan Bennett there?' A voice from somewhere in the booth asked. It was his voice, but it seemed detached and from a separate source.

'Er... she isn't home. Who's calling?' The man at the other end was as nervous as Mark.

Mark was forced to improvise. 'The school... Thomas Graham School... Director of Studies.'

'What's it about?' the thin voice enquired.

How could he tell him. It was probably her father. Mark ran out of ideas and guts. 'It doesn't matter.' It was limp and pathetic.

The man at the other end was equally satisfied to end this strained conversation.

Mark stumbled from the phone box through a curtain of Japanese faces. What a damn fool. It was a ridiculous thing to attempt. That was her father. Perhaps he should have approached him? Called for some sanity? A reasonable person would have understood. Mark's brain hurtled wildly. But, then again what sort of a monster was he in her parent's eyes. It was a messy business that he should never have started. Margaret and Robert would crucify him if they knew. Mark hurried away from his embarrassment and tried to shake off the cloud of guilt before he reached the conference. Margaret was intuitive. She might recognise the albatross round his neck.

The atmosphere at Margaret Cullen's chambers wasn't pleasant, but thankfully it lacked the brittle tension of the last conference. It was businesslike and serious.

Quite a few of the children interviewed by Robert had provided good information. Some could even remember what Mark was doing on the days he was supposed to be with Susan Bennett, and at the times the alleged assaults were said to have taken place. Margaret was happier. She had some anchorage now.

'I don't like the fragments in this case,' she informed Mark. 'We have a solid defence, but it's bitty and not tightly packaged. We hold contradictory evidence to every charge. Even alibi support. But it's just like scrambling to return a tennis ball that is always being smashed in your direction. It would be pleasant to be serving for a change. As you know their main shot will be the handwriting. If only we could call an expert witness, we would have it game, set and match.' Margaret hadn't meant to slip into the sporting metaphors, but it summed up her feelings about the case. Margaret bit her lip. She hated to have to play left-handed, and that's how it felt without Henry Brolin to call on.

'The estimation is that the trial will take a week to ten days. Mr. Justice Chalden will preside. Margaret says he has a reputation for being fair. However, we could have done better with the prosecution counsel.' Robert wanted Mark to have all the information, even the unpleasant parts. 'It's not going to be Dawson as we thought. Name of Piers Mallett. They call him 'pitbull'. A rugged character who chases everything down. Teamed up with that Baxter woman it will be quite a contest. Not that we aren't a formidable opposition.' Robert smiled across at Margaret.

Margaret responded. 'We have to stay alert throughout, Mark. Especially you. There may be some surprises, though I'm sure we've covered everything. You'll have to think on your feet. We will have to communicate with notes. Robert will convey anything you want me to have from the dock. I might be wrong-footed and need information quickly. I'll be relying on you.' Margaret was setting up her stall. 'I can't think of anything more. Now, Mark, get a good sleep and we'll see you at nine in the morning inside the court building. Hopefully there won't be any press about. We should kick off at ten. Dress smartly and try not to worry. We are all gunning for you.' Margaret moved towards Mark and gripped his arm. 'I know all this is easy for us to say. It's your future on the line. And it hasn't escaped this legal machine that a lot depends on me tomorrow and over the next few days, or weeks. And I'll fight tooth and nail for you.'

Margaret surprised him. She was warm and caring. She didn't show that side often.

Mark managed a thankful grin and dragged himself outside. He knew there was no criticism of all that Margaret and Robert had done. He couldn't believe, however, that he was really and truly going on trial the next day for a crime that had never, ever taken place. It was an even more difficult task. An exercise in chasing shadows. In truth it should have exploded in a cloud of dust, leaving a leering painted clown dancing through the settling mist and giggling into his own goofy face. And Mark Stephens should have woken from that ridiculous, hair-raising dream.

Mark was wrong about nothing having taken place. There had been crimes. Years of crime. A sickening history of violation that was now loaded into the most deadly weapon, a malignant and destructive girl, set on her own revenge. An insidious arsenal of vengeance.

Susan Bennett spent the evening at home. She sat on the sofa in a tasteless living room. Her father avoided her. Her mother smiled when they passed, but little was said. It was a confusing time for a mother. Her daughter had gloated over having a consensual sexual relationship with a teacher; a middle-aged man. And now she was the chief prosecution witness in the Crown Court trial of her despicable lover.

Jean Baxter phoned at seven to make certain the family were aware of the arrangements for the following day. Mrs. Bennett was quick to assure her. Mr. Bennett sat in the kitchen, at a Formica breakfast bar. He was fighting his own battle. It was a conflict fought at three levels. As an outraged father, a jealous lover and shameful offender. He couldn't quite come to grips with the tugging emotions of the contesting positions. It was hypocrisy to condemn Mark Stephens, yet he had to appear to harbour disgust and anger verging on violence. Not to Susan. He couldn't face her with his ire. She would see through such counterfeit passion. But essentially to his dough-nut of a wife.

To think Susan wanted this man, and willingly let him touch her body, his possession. Feeling the smoothness of her young skin. The curving milky buttocks. Susan's tight and squeezing vagina. How could she? It was for him. She should have saved it. Only for him. He'd shown her all his love. It tor-tured him to picture this fucking teacher scrambling through her clothes, peeling off her clinging underwear and visiting all those soft, wet and warm places that were meant only for his probing hands and his urgent penis.

But, on his shoulder, left over from his nagging moral his-tory, prodding him with a digging finger, was an angel or demon of sorts to remind him. Usually during that sagging aftermath, when he had left her trembling from his assault and he turned his back to dress, he heard from his conscience that what he did to his daughter was so wrong. He was a shambles.

His wife blamed that ogre, Mark Stephens, for her hus-band's gloom. A convenient myopia.

Mr. Bennett would escort his daughter to court. Linda Bennett insisted. But he wouldn't hear her give evidence. On too many fronts that would be painful.

Susan knew he couldn't touch her for now. She shuffled to bed. Her mother listened for once for the light switch to click and later for the soft murmur of her daughter's slumber.

Chapter 10

As methodical as dressing for work Mark prepared himself for trial. For some reason he had conflicting feelings about that day. He was scared stiff of what was going to happen, yet somewhat intrigued by the whole theatre of his ordeal.

Alison was still in her dressing gown when he was leaving. She held him close and pressed her lips against his; soft and honest. Her grip was firm. It told him of her resolve, her faith in him and it urged justice as if it was spiritual and something she could transfer with her touch. There wasn't any talk of luck. She would be at the court for the start of it all at ten.

Mark felt like the other commuters on the train. Suit creasing at the knees, plastic briefcase and folded paper. Not one of those harassed businessmen clinging to the rocking carriage and their flapping newspaper could have guessed at his destination or his dilemma.

Mark walked from the station. The Crown Court was only a couple of streets away. He peered at all the people hurrying in the same direction; eager to spot a familiar face. Perhaps he would see Susan Bennett and persuade her to stop this bloody nonsense, or, perhaps, kill the fucking, little bitch. That plan hadn't escaped his moments of dark imagination.

The courthouse wasn't as he pictured it; yellow sandstone and a wall of tinted glass, stuck in a Victorian industrial back-water. Mark was sure it would be a granite monstrosity like the Old Bailey.

At the entrance he was scanned and his case searched, just like the airport. He'd arrived before either Robert or Margaret. So as not to draw attention to his infamy he paced around the corridors amidst the darting, gown-clutching barristers and confused hoodlums. It was difficult searching for the court whilst trying to look like the casual visitor. Eventually, by process of elimination he found the place. Court six. Alongside the door a notice announced *'Regina v Stephens'*.

'Fuck me!' It simply slipped out. Not loud. Not overheard. He had encountered it before, at Guildford, but brought home this time by the thought of the Queen actually prosecuting him. He was still looking at his name, mesmerised, when he was pulled by the shoulder.

'Morning, Mark.' Robert greeted him. 'Have you seen Margaret yet?'

'No,' Mark panicked.

'Don't worry. She has a long journey. She'd have phoned if there was a problem.' Robert gripped his arm. 'Now, come on. How are you? Good ride in?' Robert made a dismal attempt at making Mark feel at ease.

'Are they here?' Mark ignored Robert's question. He needed to know. 'Are those girls going through with this?'

Robert broke it to him. 'I'm afraid I've just seen WPC Baxter, and she was pleased to inform me that Susan Bennett and Pauline Green were at court. She drove them up with Susan Bennett's father this morning. She's gloating in the witness restroom at this moment.'

Margaret arrived just before Mark was going to slip away from Robert and wander towards the witness sanctuary to catch a glimpse of the two harlots.

'Hello there. Sorry I'm late. Let's pop in here for a few minutes.' Margaret gestured towards a row of three conference rooms allocated to lawyers and their clients. She was in a different gear. It went with this territory. Busy and bossy. It was necessary for the sake of efficiency. Dressed in her black robe and grey wig she really was another woman.

She bundled them into the room. 'So, the girls are here.' Margaret gave a smile of resignation to Mark. 'Sorry. I had hoped, as I'm sure you did, that they wouldn't have attended.' She tipped out some papers. 'It goes ahead!' She declared. 'And we must always believe that it will go all the way. If we don't we start weakening our resolution. We play until we hear the final whistle.' Margaret was doing a good job coaching the team. 'I don't think we'll get much done this morning. Judge Chalden has a few matters to deal with in open court and jury selection will take some time.

'Now, Mark, you have the right to object to any of the jurors, but I suggest you don't. Unless there appears to be an obvious reason just stick with the first twelve they bring on. We need to keep in Bernard Chalden's good books. He hates any fussing about jury members. They should be a relatively good bunch.'

But really it was a lottery and you could be faced by an awful assortment. Margaret had experienced incredibly odd collections. Some, so bloody terrible she'd nearly torn the hair out of her wig at their stupidity. She would be playing to this jury, a dramatic performance. It made all the difference if they were an alert audience. She couldn't afford to allow them to miss strategic points. She wouldn't tell Mark any of her horror stories now.

A rap on the glass sent Margaret pushing a fan of documents back into her case and handing a pile of thick legal references for Robert to carry.

'We're about to start,' announced the woman usher hanging on to the door.

It was like passing through an airlock to reach the courtroom. Two doors had to be negotiated with a small lobby between them. Inside, Mark was strangely disappointed to find it wasn't a dusty place with dark wood furniture and a throne of a chair for the judge, and a dock decorated with long metal spikes like it was out of an Ealing Comedy with Alistair Sim presiding. Instead there was a carefully fitted, bright arrangement of purpose-built light wood furnishings. He could recognise the raised area for the judge, a centrally placed witness box, where he would spend a whole day, two rows of seats in a rectangular compartment for the jury and a long dock right at the back with room for a football team of defendants.

'You can stay here with me until we get going,' Margaret told Mark, seeing him contemplating his home for the duration of the trial. 'You don't want to be in there any longer than necessary.'

The room was filling up. Ushers flitted about. Some set out the judge's desk. A recording clerk was setting up equipment. Margaret and Robert were laying out documents and setting out legal text.

Piers Mallett entered with Jean Baxter. He acknowledged Margaret and at a half turn threw a sneer at Mark. It was evident the show would be on the road very soon. The senior usher signalled to both barristers, and Margaret in turn nodded to Mark. He climbed through the heavy, waist-high door and was met by a security officer.

'Would you mind stepping this way.' The man was courteous. Mark was shown through a door to a small anteroom. 'Could you raise your arms, please,' asked the officer.

'Why?' Mark hadn't twigged.

'I have to search you,' insisted the officer, forthright but civil.

Mark wasn't prepared for that. He held his arms up in surrender. He was patted and stroked briefly to ensure he carried no offensive weapons.

'Fine! Thank you, sir.' Mark was led back into the dock.

Checking beforehand that all parties were ready, the woman usher knocked on a door where the judge was obviously waiting to be beckoned.

He strode out. A little annoyed at having been kept waiting. With a nod of his head he motioned for everyone to be seated. Chalden was a solemn man dressed in a stiff red gown cut diagonally by blue band, and balanced on his head sat a small, neat wig. The clerk reached up to present a series of papers that he briefly examined and then signed. Mark didn't understand the procedure. It involved other petitions and other anonymous cases. Eventually Judge Chalden was able to address the court. He welcomed the battling barristers and signalled for the jury to be shown in. Mark was not acknowledged. The Judge sat immediately opposite the accused but did not look in his direction.

A door near to the jury corral opened and a motley crew tugged from the electoral register paraded into the twelve spaces allocated. Mark watched their every move and their disorientated faces. Scooped up from a reluctant pool of coffee-swillers they had been led, unprepared, into a fully-fitted courtroom. Everyone in place. Waiting to begin. They were the only element missing. And when they were seated they trawled, with glazed eyes the stage and its props thrust before them.

There he was. The one they had to try. What had he done? What sort of case was this? It was juicier than they dared imagine. Caged in the dock he appeared half guilty already. Mark could feel that. Why couldn't he sit alongside his attorneys like in the States? Even the wildest, most vicious killers are dressed in flattering suits and sit as equals with their lawyers. Innocent until proven guilty.

The twelve recruits studied Mark from the corner of their scanning eyes, careful not to exchange glances. Some were more interested than others. While there were several who remained bland and difficult to pigeon-hole. Mark had the rest immediately assessed. He was instantly drawn to a small, drably dressed, young woman in the front row. Not a great intellect and harbouring no vanity he recognised her as an honest and reliable adjudicator. He needed her. He thought he could detect a smile.

Also in front was a young lad, already slipping down in his seat. No more than about twenty-one. It was clear he was there reluctantly. He had *pissed-off* written across his face. Behind him sat two middle-aged men. One was frail with a pasty face; lean and sickly. Very insecure and uneasy about his part. The other, a spiteful looking individual enjoying himself and his new importance. A chance to put a villain away for a stretch. Mark felt uncomfortable with him on the jury. He was going to be the troublesome red-neck out to send this poncy bloke down. Mark would have to wait to determine the pedigree of the other jurors.

His assessment was halted abruptly by Judge Chalden addressing them. A well-rehearsed blend of condescension and pomposity. He explained how they were to decide their verdict, of their obligations to both parties, the need for discretion and a warning about inappropriate discussion of the case. They would, of course, tell all their friends and relations the spicy bits. Those who promised not to tell. Each one was sworn in individually after a brief charade where both barristers made intrusive personal enquiries of a few members which resulted in no objections to the chosen twelve. A couple of the jurors where English was their second language had problems, and the pale man was shown to be far from literate and had to be assisted in reading the card held aloft by the usher. Immediately this was over the whole lot were led out, in order that points of law could be discussed.

Mark found progress frustratingly slow. Margaret was admonished by the Judge for late notice of alibi witnesses and the CPS equally scolded for the delay in making evidence available to the defence. It was resembling something between a chess game and poker. Mark saw that there would be less emphasis on the evidence produced in his trial than on the performance of the two gladiatorial lawyers. It was now in their hands. So Mark Stephens' fate was to be decided by the relative abilities of two jousting barristers. Near impotent he could only watch the real contestants tussle before him.

The charges were read. Four separate counts of indecent assault. Mark found himself miming his disgust at the allegations to the vacant faces of the jury. They had to be told somehow that he was no pervert. He was determined that his 'not guilty' response was firm and bold.

'Mr. Mallett.' Judge Chalden peered over his reading glasses and fired the starter's pistol.

Piers Mallett rose. He carried a ridiculous smile that he presented to the jury. Tugging his gown and looking occasionally to the ceiling he began his greasy introduction. Fawning and befriending he squirmed his way into their favours.

'Ladies and gentlemen of the jury.' His face cracked again with a further enticing grin. He spoke gently. Even a right bastard has to win friends. It would be folly not to. 'The prosecution will show you that the accused, Mr. Mark Terence Stephens, used his position as teacher of trusting children to lure an innocent schoolgirl, Susan Bennett, into a relationship, a sexual relationship, indecently assault her on three different occasions, and on one occasion assault both her and her friend, Pauline Green. We will also demonstrate how the accused met Susan Bennett alone in his classroom where they kissed and embraced, how he arranged to see her in Wokingham and went back to Susan's house and indecently assaulted her there while her parents were at work.

'Susan Bennett and Pauline Green were only fifteen years old when Mark Stephens abused his position and committed these acts.' Mallett was finding his rhythm. Every member of the jury was given an individual smile. He was bonding nicely with the lay people.

'You will hear from Susan Bennett and Pauline Green. And there should be no doubt in your mind that what they tell you did take place. They have no reason to lie. No earthly reason to invent these crimes.' Mallett was really laying it on thick. 'Susan Bennett will tell you of many clandestine meetings and times spent with Mr. Stephens in the staff quarters of a school boarding house, and, most emphatic, his correspondence with her. Pauline Green will corroborate Susan's account of one incident and the existence of the relationship. There will be evidence presented to show beyond reasonable doubt, because that is what it must be, that Mark Stephens committed a catalogue of crimes against these girls.' Mallett looked down at his papers and then turned to Jean Baxter. 'I would like to call the prosecution's first witness, Susan Bennett.'

An usher left to bring Susan Bennett to court six. There

wasn't that repeated shouting of a name as depicted in so many courtroom dramas. WPC Baxter slipped out to accompany Susan into the hushed room. To boost her. Ensure she was comfortable with what she was about to do.

The last time that Mark had seen Susan Bennett was when she stormed into his classroom. Through the haze of the past months it remained vivid. He could still picture the blades in her eyes, and he could hear her treacherous voice. *I've really stitched you up!* It was carved deep in granite. He hadn't known what she meant. Now, by God, he knew all right.

A low hiss of the door heralded Susan Bennett's entrance. Baxter had prepared her well. Gone was the evil sneer and lunging finger, jabbed at him in a vicious tirade. She had been groomed for this appearance. Dressed to hide any curves and to emphasise her short, fleshy limbs. There was nothing recognisable. Nothing resembling the tart Mark had met in Wokingham wedged into a throttling skirt and painted like a Halloween ghoul.

The usher placed her in the witness box with the care of settling a china doll in a display cabinet.

Susan could feel Mark's eyes on her, but she wouldn't look. WPC Baxter had told her not to. That would help.

'I solemnly promise to tell the truth, the whole truth and nothing but the truth, so help me God.' Even that had been rehearsed. A sweet angelic voice trickled out, and with a tilt of the head she waited to tell the court of the awful acts committed against her.

Mark sensed an unusual and unpleasant calmness about the girl. As if drugged. Maybe they legitimately gave witnesses valium or something to soothe them during testimony.

'Hello, Susan.' Piers Mallett greeted his star witness. 'I'm going to ask you some questions and help you tell us what happened to you. Take your time and speak as clearly as you can when you answer. These people here are the jury.' He waved a hand in their direction. 'You should aim everything at them.'

A gingerly approach suited his purpose. He had to convey to the jury how frail and innocent Susan Bennett was. It was the foundation of his strategy. She was to be Little Red Riding Hood, and Mark Stephens, introduced, at the moment of her seeming most fragile, as the dastardly wolf. Big and bad.

'State your full name for the court.'

A tiny voice squeaked. 'Susan Carol Bennett.'

'You'll have to speak a little louder. My hearing, and I expect that of some of the jury isn't as good as it used to be,' encouraged the fatherly interjection by Justice Chalden. A reassuring beam accompanied it.

'Do you know the defendant, Mark Terence Stephens?'

'Yes.'

'How do you know him?' Mallett questioned further.

Mark could see a sniper lining up his target. The cross-hairs of the sight scanning.

'He was a teacher at my school.' The replies slid out effortlessly. It was safe ground.

'Has he ever been more than a teacher to you?' The sniper's itchy finger was poised on the trigger.

Susan Bennett froze. The courtroom characters were statues urging her to answer. She bit her lip. Glanced at Jean Baxter who pretended not to be aware.

'Yes.' It stumbled out.

Mark Stephens was hit.

'Can you, please, tell the court what your relationship was.' Mallett tinkered with some papers. He didn't look at Susan.

Susan sucked in the thick air. It was getting more difficult. 'We were sort of boyfriend, girlfriend. Lovers like.' Susan let the air out through her nose. In the dizzy pause that followed she stole a glimpse of Mark in the dock. Oh! Shit. She hadn't pictured him like that.

Mallett was stalling deliberately. He wanted the jurors to take it in. A man nearly fifty and this sensitive child. What a beast. The revulsion needed to percolate. Particularly the women where the disgust would ferment. When he sensed the

Judge fidget he resumed. 'And tell the court, Susan, when you began this liaison with Mr. Stephens.'

Baxter had been through the dates with her, but it would be a struggle to get it right. 'When he came back from the school skiing trip. He was on duty in Cairo House at the weekend. Asked me to come and see him in the house office on the Sunday. Took me up to the staff room upstairs and shut the door.' *Her pink bedroom door slammed tight. He stood there breathing shallowly, dribbling at the corner of his mouth and sucking it back.*

Mallett saw her treading water. 'Tell the court what happened next.' It had been an encouraging start. Now he had to work to keep Susan afloat.

'Put his arms around me.' *Pushed against me and breathed on to my face.* 'We kissed.' Susan juggled precariously with the two images; the speculative fantasy and the brutal reality. 'Ran his hands over my body and started to take my clothes off.' *Yanked my skirt up to my waist and tore at my knickers. And pushed my legs apart with his horny fingers. And as his flicking finger whipped me wet he smiled with his teeth at my blinking eyes and quivering lips.* 'He felt my breasts and he put his fingers in my vagina.' *One then two were jammed in. And he touched them with his other hand from behind just to feel how firmly he had thrust them. And he pulled the crack of my arse apart and a digging finger groped my clenching arsehole.* 'We laid on the bed. I touched his penis.' *He wrapped my hand round the smooth end of his dick. It was already seeping wet. He moved it inside my grip and urged me to rub harder.* 'He wanted to make love, but I wouldn't without a condom.' *Bent me over and filled me painfully from behind. My head was thrown about like a rag doll as he rammed me over and over again. I shuddered at every stab. He came, deep and harsh inside me. And when he pulled himself out of me I felt the thick fluid run down my leg.* 'We spent all afternoon in each other's arms.' I wanted to puke. *I had come as well. And he knew. The fucking bastard.* 'I dressed and went back to my boarding house.' Susan delivered her evidence with long breaks. Such nauseous pauses that were stuck in her past like a malignant tumour.

Piers Mallett was forced to wait patiently while she delivered her broken testimony. He could not have guessed at the gangrenous images that infected a parallel territory.

Margaret Cullen jotted notes vigorously.

Mark cringed at every word that Susan Bennett was weaving into a monstrous fairy tale.

'When did anything else happen?' Mallett asked, trying to maintain some momentum.

'Let me see.' The ghosts rested. 'We saw each other most lunchtimes.'

'What went on then?' Mallett chased.

'We just kissed and cuddled. That's all.' Susan tried to capture how that would have been.

'Did anyone see you?'

'I don't think so. Pauline knew though.'

'But she didn't see you and Mr. Stephens kissing and cuddling?'

'I'm not sure.' Perhaps Pauline could say she did once. Susan wasn't going to commit herself.

'And were there other incidents?'

'In the Easter holidays he met me in Wokingham. We walked through the town and then went back to my house.' Her house. The house of her loving family. 'Up to my room. We touched each other and kissed... passionately.' *His tie was loose and the booze was on his breath. He was jerking at his cock from outside his trousers, and his glazed eyes and pressed lips were fucking already.* 'He was gentle and tender. Kind and perfect.' *Vile and deceitful. She watched her room swim round as he pumped at her baggy torso. Her little girl's room. It seemed so long ago that she was able to be a little girl. He had ruined that. He'd stolen so many innocent years. It was hard to remember him not doing it to her. To remember when he was simply, Dad. When she was naïve about her body; liked herself.*

Before she was riddled with guilt. 'And he left to go home.' *Left her uncovered and cold. It had taken him a long time. She could smell the dampness of his sweat on her neck; feel the cool semen clinging in her silky pubic hair. Her room was still and paralysed in her arrested vision. She only saw a stairway crack on the ceiling, which she followed back and forth until she slept beneath a single sheet. She wouldn't dirty anything else.*

Piers Mallett watched Susan's swinging eyes. He wasn't happy with her evidence so far. 'What time did he leave you?'

Susan was in danger of mixing the images. 'Left me? Well... about four thirty, I think. Yes, four thirty.'

'How did you get from Wokingham back to your house, Susan?'

'Car. We went in his car.'

'What car was that?'

'His Ford XR2 of course.' She loved his car. Always wanted to go in it with him. On many occasions she and Pauline would peer inside, when it was parked at the school, and imagine the ride.

'Did you see Mr. Stephens any other time during the school holiday?'

'No.'

'Was any meeting planned?' Mallett was leading, but Margaret wasn't going to be seen as being concerned about any of this evidence.

It took Susan a while to fall in. 'Oh, yes. We were going to see each other. He couldn't make it.'

'How did he let you know that?' Mallett was going to enjoy this bit. There was nothing like the moment when you introduced a crushing piece of concrete evidence.

'He wrote me a letter.'

Mallett raised a clear plastic folder containing a small piece of white paper and a brown envelope.

'Can you look at these, Susan, and tell the court if this is the note and the envelope Mr. Stephens sent you.'

An usher took the folder and handed it to Susan Bennett. Mallett stole a glimpse of Mark. Wanted to see his face. His eyes sparkled.

'Yes. This is the letter and the envelope it came in.' Susan barely looked at it.

'Would you read it to the court.'

Susan fumbled with the folder. And felt the whole court boring into her skull. Did they know the history? Did they know her agenda?

'Er...' She gulped and sniffed. '*Susan. I am sorry I can't see you as planned. I really wanted to meet. I will phone you. Mark.*' She looked up when she had finished. She hadn't seen it for a long time. She prayed that Pete Black had kept his mouth shut.

'Thank you, Susan.'

Mark could have knocked the smugness off his face.

'Could this letter and envelope be exhibit one, your honour?'

Justice Chalden nodded his agreement. The usher took exhibit one from the witness box and handed it to the jury. Each one in turn read the words, not sure of their significance. Piers Mallett would make certain that they did.

It took some time for the twelve jurors to study exhibit one. Mark examined every perusing face. What were they thinking? How could he tell them that there was no way he wrote the note to that cow, Susan Bennett, now looking at her feet in the witness box. He hoped their eyes would stray in his direction. He could speak to those. Three or four glanced his way whilst exhibit one was being handed round elsewhere. Not long enough for Mark to demonstrate his disgust. He shook his head gently from side to side and gripped his lips tightly together. Only the small girl at the front caught his facial denial.

'And did he? Did Mr. Stephens phone you?' Piers Mallett was keen to keep this alive.

Susan was caught off guard. 'Er... yes.'

'When?' Mallett wanted to pursue this one.

'In the holidays some time. I'm not sure exactly.'

'Excuse me your honour.' Mallett turned quickly to face Jean Baxter. He whispered in her ear. Baxter shook her head in response. To take this line of questioning all the way meant he had to have some decent evidence. But Jean Baxter couldn't offer what he needed. There was no British Telecom statement showing the call. She had hunted through all the calls made from Mark's house over a three month period. Susan Bennett's number was not there. It was assumed any phone call was made from somewhere else. Mallett turned back disappointed. Not that he showed it. He had to appear confident at all times.

'What was said?' He would ride it a little longer. See if there was mileage in it.

'Said? Let me think. Just junky stuff like how he missed me. Sort of things couples say. Nothing special.' Susan wasn't eager to answer any more. Mallett was supposed to be on her side. Shouldn't be trying to catch her out.

'Where was Mr. Stephens phoning from?' Mallett chanced his arm. An attempt to lever something useful, possibly.

'From? I suppose from his home.' Susan looked puzzled. She wasn't aware of Mallett's strategy.

Piers Mallett turned a page in front of him. He was moving on. He could sense a cul-de-sac here. 'Did you see Mr. Stephens when school started after the Easter break?'

'Yes.' She was glad to change direction.

'Did you see him at lunchtimes as you told us you did before the holidays?'

'Sometimes.'

'Did you see him alone in the staff quarters at Cairo House again?' Mallett knew that this was another winning ticket. He raised the volume to alert two fading jurors.

'No. This time Pauline was there.'

'Describe to the court what happened, Susan.'

'It was the first Sunday after we got back. Me and Pauline knew he was on duty. We were waiting near his office when he shot in late. Rushed past us with his lunch in his hands. There were boys from the house hanging about. Wanting permission to go down to the village. We went in to see him when they'd gone. He was eating a sandwich and drinking some wine.' It was seamless. It was the truth. 'We asked for a sip. He gave us some. He had to go out of the office to see to a boy who was upset, and me and Pauline played about with his after-shave which was on his desk. When he returned he asked Pauline and me whether we wanted to go up to the staff quarters. We both said okay.' Now she was diving again. Into her fantasy.

'What happened then?' Mallett used Susan's pause to keep her on track. She was flowing now and he wanted that maintained.

'When we got in the room he got his penis out. He asked us to toss him off.' She needed to be quick with these bits. It sounded so matter of fact.

'Did you masturbate him?' Mallett pronounced the words carefully to accentuate the lewd nature of this event.

'I think. A bit.' Why the question? Did it matter? Susan was uneasy.

'What else happened?' Mallett was a little unsure how to treat her answer.

'Asked us to give him a blow job. Suck it for him.' It was too much like her father. Susan was quivering. She had to protect her special association. 'It wasn't like him. He was different. I couldn't understand why he wanted Pauline there.' Susan stopped. She had to tread carefully. She was swapping identities in her head. Merging sordid reality with amorous invention.

'How long were you in the room?'

'It seemed like hours.' *It always seemed like hours. Even when he had used her quickly it felt like an eternity.*

The knife was in. Mark Stephens was being torn by a jagged blade, ripped by Susan Bennett's reaping tongue. Mark sighed. Hardly audible. Susan Bennett swung round in the witness box and hit him with the old vicious eyes.

'They're all the same!' Aimed right at him for his dismissal of her affectionate advances. So much she was offering him and he had just dismissed it. It was a betrayal. A treachery. And this was payback time.

The lingering venom didn't please Piers Mallett. Susan had wanted Mark Stephens. She had some purpose. It was only natural that now she would create a monster. An erratic fusion of Casanova and a monstrous freak.

The jury were witness to a fine character demolition. They had their ogre neatly packaged.

'Did you see Mr. Stephens after that?'

'No. I didn't want to.'

'Susan, how did all this come to light?' Mallett was ready to close.

'On the Tuesday afterwards I was talking with some of the girls in the house. Clair Hooper was there. I went to see Mrs. Edgerley that evening and told her everything.'

'Mrs. Edgerley was your housemistress?'

'Yes.'

Thank you, Susan. Now Mrs. Cullen here will want to ask you a few questions.' Piers Mallett gestured towards Margaret and sat down.

Justice Chalden butted in. 'I know it's awkward, but Mr. Mallett has managed to get far too near lunchtime for you to start, Mrs. Cullen. I think we will recess now and return at one thirty.'

Chalden rose, and with him so did the whole court. He slid quickly out of the door from where he had first emerged. It was more to relieve a throbbing bladder than a keenness to dine.

Susan Bennett was collected by Jean Baxter from the witness box, where she still stood. And when she was safely out of the room, Mark was allowed to walk out of the dock. At least he had that freedom.

Margaret grabbed him and Robert and coaxed them into an interview room. She needed to discuss the morning session. To reassure Mark.

'It's always bad to start with. Prosecution revving them up.

This afternoon should be better, when I have a go at her.' Margaret seemed to be relishing the prospect. There was excitement in her voice. 'You go and get some lunch. You can't really do anything. I have to go through some things with Robert.'

'Okay,' Mark confirmed. 'It's bloody awful having to sit through that shit. Do you think the jury believed her?'

'Can't tell. They're a mixed bunch, difficult to read yet, but I'm sure that any swing that's occurred so far isn't irreversible. So chin up, Mark. Need you optimistic.' Margaret began easing him out of the small room by the arm.

'Before I forget, that answerphone recording you gave Robert, I'll probably use that tomorrow, and to prevent any playback problems I suggest you bring your own machine in. We know it plays on that.'

'Yes. I'll remember...' Mark's words trailed off.

Alison was waiting for him outside. So much had happened he hadn't registered her absence in court. It came flooding back. 'Where have you been?' His eyes pleaded more than his voice.

'Didn't Margaret Cullen tell you? She wants me to testify. It means I can't sit in. Are you disappointed?' She crushed his hand in hers.

'What can you say?' Mark was at a loss. Why on earth would Alison be a defence witness? He charged back into the interview room for an explanation.

Margaret was quick to realise Mark's mission. 'I need her. You need her. I want the jury to see her. Know she's your wife. There are some aspects she can shed light on. The car for instance. The recording. Listen, Mark. Why would you consider having a relationship with that ugly little pig when you have such an attractive wife? Believe me it makes sense to use her.' Margaret had a gift for calming people. She didn't fail with Mark.

Mark and Alison found a stainless steel wine bar and pecked at open sandwiches. Neither was very hungry.

'How did it go?' Alison ventured, prodding some rather dubious cheese around her plate.

'It wasn't good. Margaret says it never is. First morning and prosecution opening up. No defence yet. She claims it gets better. I can't believe what that fucking girl's saying. How can she stand there and invent those things?' But he had said that so many times before. There was no answer then either.

Alison leaned across and held his hand. 'I saw her, Mark. There's something sinister about that girl. A podgy thing with such evil eyes. It was peculiar. I always thought I would want to smack her in the face or worse. But she seemed lost. That Baxter woman appeared to be manipulating her. And she's got that queer looking father trailing along all the time. The whole family must be bloody odd.' She faltered. It was difficult to say. 'I know for certain you couldn't have thought she was attractive.'

Mark questioned her with his eyes. 'Have you had doubts then?'

'I didn't think I had. But I suppose there's always going to be a lurking uncertainty that you are not aware of. I needed to see her. That was all. I've been living with a picture, but it wasn't enough. Now I feel better.'

Mark was unsure whether he was comfortable with what Alison had admitted. He'd always assumed he had her one hundred percent backing. Perhaps it was too much to ask? If it was him in that position he knew there would be the nagging question.

Margaret Cullen had been a teacher before she decided she disliked most children and that there wasn't enough money in the profession. She had taught girls like Susan Bennett. Knew their behaviour and their deceit. Not that she'd come across it manifested with such malevolence. It wasn't a vendetta, but Margaret Cullen harboured a helpful resentment for girls like Susan Bennett. She was determined to break the little cow. Yet she would be forced to tread carefully. Any sign of tears or distress and the jury could be reaching for their handkerchiefs and all the compassion would descend on Susan Bennett. It was a delicate balance. Her skill here was what Cameron Rudley had recognised and why she was recommended to Mark.

Court six came to order at one thirty in the case of Regina v Stephens. Judge Bernard Chalden sat everyone down with a smart nod of his responding head.

'Mrs. Cullen.' Margaret was summoned to her feet by the Judge's keen voice.

'Susan, as Mr. Mallett has told you, I will be asking some questions. If any confuse you or you don't hear properly just ask me to explain or repeat them. Is that okay?' Margaret forced a warm grin. She had to appear harmless and far from menacing. The smile was a huge lie. Margaret Cullen was a ferocious and dangerous attorney on a devious mission; a crusade.

'Yeah.' Susan snarled. Baxter had warned her about cross-examination by this goat.

If Margaret could prompt a surly response from Susan then discrediting her would be easier. Turn the fickle jury against this girl.

'You've told Mr. Mallett that Mr. Stephens was a teacher at your school. Did he teach you?'

'When I was in the first three years he did.' That was simple. 'But I was in a different set after that.' Susan was answering confidently.

'Who decided that you should be in that set?'

'Um... I suppose Mr. Stephens did. He was head of the English department.'

Susan wasn't following the plot. It was no big trap, but a first hurdle. Margaret needed to sow the first seeds of suspicion.

'Did you resent being put down to a lower group? That's what it meant, that you had been demoted, didn't it?'

'I suppose so. I wasn't that upset about it.' Susan spotted the reason for the question and did her best to hand it off.

'Did you blame Mr. Stephens?'

'No!' There was impatience in the reply.

Margaret moved on. That was enough. She had achieved sufficient. The jury could give that some thought. Get them thinking. Get them doubting.

'Was there any other activity where you were in contact with Mr. Stephens, other than the early English lessons?'

'He took us on trips.' Susan swallowed. The envelope. She had forgotten that. 'I didn't go on many,' she added. An attempt to cover her tracks.

Margaret was oblivious. She'd missed out. Mark hadn't told anybody about his handwriting on the envelope. Hadn't dared.

'Did you get on all right with him on these trips?'

'Yes.' It was a clear but grumpy reply. Susan was going to be more careful. This woman was a right bitch.

'You liked Mr. Stephens didn't you? He was a fun teacher. Not stuffy like the others. Perhaps more than liked him. A crush eh?'

'I liked him.' She did. She couldn't deny that.

'You've told the court that he was your boyfriend. So you more than liked him, didn't you?'

Susan was cornered. 'Yeah, I suppose I did.'

Margaret now had to steer the jury. Enlighten them as to the back-bone of the defence.

'Mark Stephens was never your boyfriend, was he?' Margaret raised her voice and lanced Susan Bennett with her spearing question. A hot, provoking poker it would seem.

'Yeah. He was!' Susan threw up a rapid defence.

'Isn't the truth that you wanted him to be? Asked him to be? Made persistent advances to him? But he clearly rejected them. He wasn't interested in you, was he?'

'No. That's not it!' Susan's eyes were wide. She had to hold on here.

'Well let's examine how you say this relationship started. You told the court that Mr. Stephens asked you to come and see him in the Cairo House office on the Sunday after the school ski party returned. Where were you when he made this request?' Margaret was trying to find the flaws. Jemmy open the fissures.

Susan moved to lay down some fog. 'Not sure exactly. I think he stopped me in the corridor.'

'He just came up to you, out of the blue, and asked you to see him on the Sunday? Didn't you find that strange behaviour?'

'No.' Susan kept it simple. She wasn't going to admit anything. Margaret Cullen was too devious.

'You've told the court that Mr. Stephens took you up to the staff quarters when you went to the boarding house on that Sunday. Where on earth did you think you were going?'

'I wasn't sure.' Susan was edgy.

'Didn't you think it odd that this teacher, who didn't actually teach you, was escorting you up to a staff bedroom?'

'I didn't know what to think.'

'To get to this room upstairs in Cairo House it is necessary to go past common rooms, boys' dormitories, bathrooms and large windows. And the room is situated next to the senior boys' rooms. Did you see anybody?'

There was no one she could use. Susan was forced to admit it. 'No.'

'A boys' boarding house. A lengthy journey. And no one saw you being smuggled up to a staff bedroom? Strange.' Margaret placed a forefinger on her lips. 'Very strange.'

'Well. There weren't any around.' Susan spat out an answer. She couldn't let anyone question or distrust her account. Couldn't let anyone suspect the truth. Not now.

The jury members were in on the hunt. Some even enjoying the chase. Margaret had her cornered. Susan Bennett wasn't winning friends.

'You told Mr. Mallett that you were in the staff bedroom for several hours. During this extremely long period of time did any boy or other member of staff come looking for the duty tutor of Cairo House, Mr. Stephens?'

'No.' Susan Bennett wasn't comfortable.

'So a whole afternoon went past with no boy from Cairo House, or any other person, wanting to see Mr. Stephens; ask permission to go to the village or elsewhere? I regard that as weird.'

Susan Bennett shrugged her shoulders but said nothing.

'It didn't happen, did it, Susan?' Margaret attacked.

'Yes.' Susan Bennett parried.

'You never went upstairs in the boarding house with Mr. Stephens. He never touched you. This is all an invention isn't it, Susan?'

Margaret was premature if she expected the break down and confession now. Susan was harder than that and her resolve reinforced by the years of indignity festering below, and bubbling to the surface. She couldn't tell anyone about that. So this would do.

'It's not!' Susan trembled, and stared with scorching eyes at Margaret Cullen. 'It's all true.'

The courtroom could detect the targeted lasers. Even Mark was sitting on the edge of his seat.

'Yes, of course.' Margaret cynically accepted. She would leave it there. The schoolmistress in her was easy to spot. 'I would like to move on to these meetings you claim you had with Mr. Stephens, at lunchtimes. According to your evidence these were frequent and involved embracing and kissing. Did Mr. Stephens ever close and lock the classroom door and draw any curtains or blinds during these intense sessions?'

'No. I don't think he did. Can't remember him doing it.' Susan wasn't sure where this was leading.

'You were there, you say, so surely you can recall if he did or not.'

'No, he didn't.' Susan was back, blocking.

'As I understand it, Mr. Stephens' room was off a first floor landing shared by three other classrooms. Is that correct?'

Susan counted the doors in her head. Trying to picture the Modern Language block.

'Yeah.' She was giving little away.

'And, wasn't Mr. Stephens' room overlooked by the Science Block and another building?'

'Sort of. S'pose so.' Susan strummed her fingers on the edge of the witness box, and looked down to express her disinterest.

'And no one going to the other classes on the landing saw you and Mr. Stephens canoodling? And no one from the adjacent buildings caught a glimpse of this loving couple? Don't you think that is unusual?' Margaret pressed and emphasised. She was performing well.

Susan wrestled with her answer. 'Perhaps they weren't looking. We were always in a corner where no one could see.' She had pictures of that. It was where she wanted to do it in her original plan.

'What if someone had come in? Surely it was an extremely dangerous thing for Mr. Stephens to do? You could have been surprised by anyone coming to the classroom.' Margaret wasn't letting this one go. She could see it was hurting.

'But they didn't, did they?' Susan stormed.

'No, they didn't.' Margaret paused and spring loaded. She had to deliver this with force. 'No one saw you and Mr. Stephens together, because you never were. You have never spent any time in his arms. Never had a relationship with this man, have you?' Margaret's words were sharp and thrusting. Mark wanted to applaud.

'I did!' Susan's reply was from a girl in a playground argument. 'Oh, yes I did.'

'Yes. Yes. Isn't the truth, Susan, that you did visit Mr. Stephens some lunchtimes when he was in his room, and helped sort out books and do other chores. And you took this opportunity to approach him to tell him you were fond of him, and on occasions that you loved him, and ask him to have a relationship? And isn't it the truth that he wasn't interested and told you not to be silly and to stop it? To go away?'

Margaret was suggesting with precision what had happened. Susan recognised these events, but she had to hold on to her version. To cling to her lifeline.

'You pestered this man. You were obsessed with Mark Stephens for some reason. You couldn't stand the thought of not having him. You couldn't bear the rejection could you?' Margaret pulled back.

Susan Bennett was visibly shaking. Judge Chalden looked concerned, and Mallett was fidgeting; about to stand and object. Margaret had taken it as close as she could, for the moment.

'No, no,' Susan whimpered. She was near tears, but not there yet. Margaret had taken a chance.

'Now, Susan you have told the court that you met Mr. Stephens in Wokingham.' Margaret was on a fresh tack, satisfied that she had accrued bonus marks from the previous encounters. 'How was this meeting arranged?'

'Before I left for the holidays. He said he wanted to and we agreed where.' Susan sounded robotic.

'You didn't plan this on the phone?' Margaret was setting another trap.

'No.'

'So you didn't phone Mr. Stephens and discuss this meeting?'

'No.'

'Have you ever phoned Mr. Stephens at his house?' It was check again. But was it mate?

Susan considered her options. She had to think quickly. It was safer to say no. 'Don't think I have.' She looked around in an attempt to display increasing disinterest in these questions.

That answer was now in the bag. Margaret stored that in her treasure chest. It would be a jewel she would exhibit later.

'I put it to you, Susan, that you plagued Mr. Stephens, to such an extent during the first part of the Easter holidays that he was forced to speak to you in person. Isn't that so?'

'No... no.' Susan gulped heavily.

'You telephoned his house using false names in order to further your obsession, until finally Mr. Stephens agreed to meet you in Wokingham in a desperate bid to rid himself of your unsolicited calls. That's the truth isn't it?'

'No.' Susan was reduced to sullen monosyllabic retorts.

She had worked hard to winkle him out and rendezvous with her. How she had prepared! It took her hours to squeeze into teasing clothes and decorate her dumpy features with her mother's makeup. And all he could do was lecture her. She had really wanted him that day. He'd left her there in the town centre to waddle home, running the gauntlet of mocking building workers and passing lorry drivers. Now she had him locked up like a wretched criminal. She took some solace in that.

'During the time he spoke to you in Wokingham he made you promise to halt the madness that it had become. Explained to you how stupid it was. And threatened to take it further if you persisted. That's the truth isn't it, Susan?' Margaret still hadn't prodded her sufficiently. She needed more of a breakthrough.

'Did not!' Susan was adamant. She could be just as nasty. Waste her bloody time, would he. Spurn her affection, would he!

Margaret flicked through her notes that she had scribbled during Piers Mallett's audit of Susan's evidence-in-chief.

Mr. Justice Chalden, high up in his padded seat was prompted at this hiatus to study the wall clock and study the girl rocking in the witness box. 'I think we've done enough today. Have you much else? We could perhaps carry on if we are near a conclusion of your cross-examination, Mrs. Cullen.'

'Nowhere near, your honour.'

'I thought as much. I need to finish early today. Well, until tomorrow at ten.' He rose and lifted the flagging courtroom to its feet. Before he reached his 'escape hatch' he turned to Susan Bennett, supporting herself in the witness box. 'I'm sorry about this, Susan, but you'll need to be here in the morning. Remember that you are still under oath, and you must not speak to anyone about this case. Okay?'

Susan nodded awkwardly. She was exhausted, glad the

questions had finished but horrified that she would have to face Margaret Cullen for a further onslaught.

The jury filed out. Mark swapped glances with two in the front row. Did they want to register their support now? Had they already seen through Susan Bennett? Mark was optimistic. He had to be.

Mark and Alison walked arm in arm back to the station. It wasn't a thing they normally did. Years since they had felt that close. Not that either mentioned it. They didn't discuss their relationship. It had been rocky at times but usually it was of rock. Even on the train they touched. Subtle, sensual touching. That was enough. The communication was just that.

Mark was up on time the next day. Remarkable for him. He would maintain his good time-keeping throughout the trial. And every day Alison would travel up later, to be there for ten. Occasionally Eric Tibbs would meet her at Waterloo.

Eric was a family friend; a retired barrister. Alison appreciated the company, and with her being excluded from the courtroom Eric was an invaluable support, and conveyor and interpreter of news from within. 'Under the clock on platform 6 at nine thirty. See you in the morning.' It was Eric's parting instruction on those evenings he ran for his Guildford train. He knew when Alison needed him and made sure he attended on the difficult or pivotal days.

As well as his briefcase, Mark lugged a conspicuous plastic bag containing the answerphone from the breakfast room. The security officers at the courthouse doors were intrigued. They had detected mobile phones before, but a domestic answering machine and telephone in a Tesco bag was a surprise. 'Hope you don't get any calls on it during the trial, old Chalden'll go potty,' joked one comic.

Margaret Cullen was buoyant when she arrived. She was pleased with her cross-examination of Susan Bennett so far. She clasped her hands together and smiled.

'So, Mark, got the answerphone I see. Excellent. I'll need you to set it up in the courtroom. When I see a clerk about I'll arrange it. Let's hope this hits her hard. We may be in trouble if she denies it's her.'

Susan Bennett crept to the witness box and sat. She was installed early. The court wasn't yet in session. Mark had been through his morning search and sat back, hands in pockets, daring her to look a him. If the lawyers and other extras hadn't been there he could have gone and shaken the bitch by the neck. That would get her to tell the truth. And if she didn't he would throttle her. There was some pleasure in thinking about squeezing the life out of Susan Bennett and watching her purple face contort and yell silently in the last throes of her putrid existence.

When Margaret Cullen rose to confront the sneering witness there was a cumbersome silence. Margaret's schoolteacher tone was thrown louder by the pregnant background. Almost echo conditions.

'In your evidence, Susan, you stated that the car you were driven in by Mr. Stephens was a Ford Fiesta XR2. Can you confirm that once again for the court?'

'Yeah. That's his car.' Susan Bennett was still surly. There was no time to think about his car again. She had to keep a tight rein on her answers. That bloody woman was determined to catch her out.

'The Ford? Not any other car?' Margaret wanted the jury to remember this answer.

'I've told you. The XR2. His car.' Susan tossed her head to show her annoyance at the repetition.

'You have told the court, Susan, that Mr. Stephens wrote you a letter. You read it out. It is exhibit one.' Margaret was well aware she was treading on glass. She tried to explode it in Susan Bennett's face. 'Didn't you in fact write this letter, Susan?'

'No!'

Margaret's glare was wild and questioning. 'Mr. Stephens never sent you a letter, did he?'

'Yes... sent me lots.'

Baxter cringed. She wasn't supposed to say that. Piers Mallett swung round and met the policewoman's tightened eyes and shrugging shoulders.

Margaret hadn't reckoned on this. She had to think quickly. 'Lots? Where are the others?' It was all she could offer as a response.

'Threw them away.' Susan could see Baxter wasn't pleased with her announcement and would try and kill the topic if she could.

'But you kept this one? This paltry note?' Margaret waved exhibit one at the witness. 'Undated. Postmark indistinct. Could be the 20th or the 26th of some month or the other.'

Margaret slapped the folder down on the table. It was an action to devalue its importance. To dismiss its legitimacy. She wouldn't ask anymore questions. Best to leave it hanging. Let the jury juggle with the dubious side of it. It was impossible to pursue this far. There was an almighty trap she needed to avoid.

'I see from your school records,' Margaret flicked through some sheets on the lectern, 'that you are a good artist. Is that so?'

'Yeah. I suppose so.' Susan was relieved the cow had got off the subject of letters. Little did she know the plunger of the detonator was just about to be pulled up and Margaret Cullen was going to thrust it down with two hands and cause the biggest explosion yet in court six.

'Mr. Stephens never rang you did he?' Margaret swayed on her toes. Ready for the kill.

'Yes, he did.' Susan was cautious. There were some hidden obstacles and she was determined she wasn't tripping over them.

'It was you that phoned Mr. Stephens, wasn't it?' She was nearly hooked.

'No.' Susan shook her head to emphasise her answer.

'Objection your honour. The witness has already told the court that she didn't phone the accused.' Piers Mallett had put his foot in it. Margaret couldn't have planned it better herself. Now it was really highlighted.

'Mrs. Cullen, you are quite aware that this has already been answered' Chalden was grouchy. 'What is your purpose in asking it again?'

'If you bear with me, your honour, I believe you will understand the significance of my question. Why I wanted it to be crystal clear for the jury.'

Judge Chalden gave a limp shrug. 'Okay, proceed.'

'You phoned Mr. Stephen's home on at least two occasions, pretending to be a member of the teaching staff, didn't you?'

Susan shuddered. 'No. Not me.'

'On one occasion you said you were Jan Edgerley and on the other you made out you were Ann Bull. Isn't that so?' Margaret hammered the words at Susan Bennett.

'No.' There was no confidence in her reply.

Margaret signalled to Robert Manning who was standing in a back corner of the courtroom. Robert bent down and sent Mark's answerphone buzzing. There was limited volume capacity in the small unit, and everyone strained to hear.

Hello Mark. Ann from school here. I will phone again.

Susan Bennett's slightly distorted but trilling voice sprung from the small speaker.

Margaret grinned. Nothing like an open goal. 'Now, Susan. I'll ask you again. Did you phone Mr. Stephens at his home?'

Piers Mallett's face went taut. The skin almost splitting. Jean Baxter was stung motionless. And both appeared to mouth shit! through raging teeth.

Susan didn't answer. She was trapped.

Margaret prompted again. 'That is your voice isn't it, Susan?'

Still silence.

'You phoned Mr. Stephens at his house didn't you?'

'Er... yes.' Susan mumbled her reply. She couldn't look at any of the searchlight faces that were aimed at her.

Margaret's face lit with triumph.

Mark sank back from the edge of his seat. Got her!

'You pestered and pestered this poor man. Tormented him and made his life a misery. You were obsessed with him. But you couldn't have him. Could you?' Margaret twisted the knife.

Susan Bennett sucked her bottom lip and looked at some distant point on the floor. She had no intention of replying.

From the bench Judge Chalden raised his eyebrows. Suddenly he was caught in the after-shock of the revelation and the bruising attack now being launched by defence counsel.

'Mrs. Cullen, I think this would be a good opportunity to break for lunch.'

It wasn't. Margaret was in full flow. It took time to reach that head of steam. But she had to concede. 'If you say so, your honour.'

Robert and Margaret slid off together. Margaret needed to keep her target in her sights.

Mark, Alison and Eric found a friendly wine bar under the railway viaduct; in one of the converted industrial arches. Creeping gentrification had reached even this humble area. Mark felt good about the morning session and Eric was oozing confidence. In part to infect his two friends. Alison listened as they ran through the events. Particularly the tape recording which was as good as a hat-trick of trophies. They anticipated Margaret's strategy for the afternoon action. And spoke excitedly in the wake of the morning's success.

When they reassembled Margaret had held on to the leash and was ready to bring the dog to heel.

'And, Susan, when you couldn't succeed in winning this teacher's affection you made up this preposterous story. Didn't you, Susan?'

Susan's head swam. Hissing and throbbing. She struggled to hold on to the fabric of her fantasy. If she let go now she would fizzle like water droplets on hot metal, and disappear in searing steam and be no more. Be nothing. Just like she was before. Just the ugly moose, ostracised and abused. No. She needed to clutch and protect her celebrity. It was all she had left.

Margaret waited. Susan Bennett's silence was useful. The jury was watching her sweeping head and her vacant eyes. Hopefully she would spill it all now. Come clean. Let everyone go home. Let Mark Stephens live again.

Margaret urged gently. 'It was a story, wasn't it, Susan? You never had a relationship with Mr. Stephens, did you?'

'I did. I did.' Susan's denial tumbled out. She was going to survive this.

Margaret Cullen was disappointed, but far from disheartened. She moved on. It was relentless. 'I want to ask you about the incident you told Mr. Mallett about, when you and Pauline went to see Mr. Stephens at Cairo House. You stated that you drank wine there. Is that so?'

'Yeah.' Susan blew out a stream of air. Another crucial hurdle she had stumbled over.

'What sort of wine was it?' Margaret enquired.

'Some non-alcoholic stuff.' Susan was dismissive.

Susan was playing into her hands. Excellent. 'Non-alcoholic. So it had no affect on you?' Margaret wouldn't have to defend Mark on that score. The little bitch had dropped her guard there.

Susan wasn't sure what to say. It was stupid to admit that. She couldn't believe she had been so careless. She was forced to reply. 'No.'

'You said that Mr. Stephens asked you and Pauline to accompany him to the staff quarters, and that you both willingly went there. Again the three of you would have to go past many rooms where there were boys playing or relaxing, past large windows and to a room next to the senior boys' rooms. And, according to your testimony, you spent hours in that room. But no one saw you in the boarding house. No one came looking for the duty tutor, Mr. Stephens, and no one missed either of you. All afternoon? All afternoon you were in that room and there was no one who knew you were there. Isn't that strange, Susan?'

Susan could only shrug. It was a mix of bafflement and dis-missiveness.

Margaret couldn't pursue it. She knew she was seeking an opinion. 'And in that room Mr. Stephens asked your friend to masturbate him and to suck his penis. In front of his girlfriend? That's what you were, wasn't it Susan, his girlfriend?' Margaret mocked the whole notion and moved from one thrust of her offensive to another. She was well armed.

It didn't add up. No matter how long she had thought this through and papered the cracks as she went, there were some hairline flaws that were being jemmied open and expanded into giant crevasses by this fucking barrister. Susan swallowed.

'That's what happened.' She couldn't say any more. She was tottering on the edge of ravines.

'You and Pauline are good friends, aren't you?'

'Yes.' What was she going to ask now? Susan trod deliber-ately. Keeping a foothold and staying on her path. She was negotiating a minefield. Of course Pauline was a friend. Her only friend.

'Lead her on a bit, don't you? Get her into trouble?'

'No!'

'I have here your school and house records, Susan.' Margaret shook the papers at Susan Bennett. 'Makes good reading. It seems you have made it a practice to lie. Haven't you, Susan? Suspension for breaking school rules, lying about furtive activities with boys. It's that sort of thing isn't it, Susan?'

'That's old stuff,' Susan volunteered.

'And on nearly every occasion Pauline Green, your friend, has been involved. You drag her down don't you? Drag her into your sordid little escapades, don't you?'

'No.'

'This is another one isn't it? Only this is serious business. The poor man in the dock, a dedicated teacher, is there because you have lied. And you have, as usual, sought dishonest support from your weak and pathetic friend.' Margaret was pinning her rigid in the witness box.

Piers Mallett looked concerned.

Susan was brittle now. But she hadn't broken. She glanced at Baxter who was urging her on with her eyes. 'Not true.' She had been taught this response.

'I see.' Margaret was nearly finished.

She was eager to use the opportunity. As soon as Susan Bennett was discharged she would ask for the case to be dismissed. The Judge would be aware of the unreliability of this girl. The main prosecution witness.

'Susan, you recall the night you spoke to your housemistress, Mrs. Edgerley, about this alleged relationship with Mr. Stephens? Exactly what happened?'

Susan realised it was nearly over and took care to word her answer safely.

'Some of the girls were talking about boys and things. I let it out about me and Mr. Stephens. Clair Hooper went and told Mrs. Edgerley and I had to go and see her.'

'You were boasting to the girls, weren't you? They had experiences with boyfriends, and you had nothing. So you invented this fantasy to make yourself look big. Nobody liked you. It was your passport to acclaim. That's how it was, wasn't it, Susan?' Margaret didn't grasp how accurate her conjecture was.

Nothing? Margaret was wrong there. Susan had been submitted to everything. From the early surreptitious caressing that she didn't understand to the most depraved animal activity instigated by her beast of a father. She knew more about the unpredictable and aggressive demands of a sex fiend than most adults. Margaret Cullen would have been rooted speechless if Susan Bennett had spoken of the ravages of her rag-doll body from prepubescent innocence to her sexual maturity.

'I invented nothing.' Susan spoke firmly.

It was all there, stored and terrifying. Susan allowed it to swallow her for the moment. *He was on top of her. Crushing her with his thrumping carcass and blowing into her face with gushing breath and urgent groans.* 'It all happened.' *He was rolling off with a releasing slurp of suction sweat and the chill of damp skin. And of course his guilt. It was easy to find an apology and an excuse after he had filled her with his stagnant semen, and watched her pale body stuck corpse-like. And he sidled through the barest crack in the door like an escaping necrophile who had just vacated a submissive cadaver.*

'Before I finish, Susan, can you confirm to the court that you in fact wrote Mr. Stephens a letter after he had been suspended from school?'

She couldn't deny it. They'd probably got it there. 'Yes, I did.'

'And can you also confirm that this letter was extremely nasty and contained some disgusting references to Mr. Stephens' family?'

'Probably. He'd let me down and that.' Susan dribbled out an inarticulate reply.

It had been written in anger and it wouldn't look good when they heard it in court, but she reckoned she could scrape through with an excuse involving the incident with Pauline. She had no idea that Mark had flushed it away after only reading the first sentence.

Margaret had gambled successfully. Now as the *coup de grâce* she desperately wanted to bring in the Clair Hooper aspect, but she knew she didn't dare. She was sure that was the key. If only she had one of those girls from Octavia House to testify in court. Just one who had witnessed Susan Bennett's gloating accounts and Clair's reaction.

'That's all I have,' Margaret announced.

Susan Bennett snorted expelling air. Relief. It was over. She was hustled from the witness box by an usher and was soon scooped up by Jean Baxter who intercepted her before she disappeared through the puffing doors. She was led past Alison, who watched her scuttling journey back to the protective room and her abomination of a father.

Margaret was on her feet as soon as Susan Bennett had been released from the witness box. 'Your honour, would you please entertain a motion?'

'Slightly premature I would have thought Mrs. Cullen.' Judge Chalden flashed a smile of resignation and swung around to face the jurors. 'I'm sorry, members of the jury. This means you need to withdraw while we discuss this motion from defence counsel.'

They were pleased to escape the constrictions of the courtroom. There were several regular smokers who relished this break, and were fingering their fag packets as they filed out.

'Now Mrs. Cullen. Let's have it.'

Margaret wasn't optimistic. She could read the Judge's reluctance. He hadn't attempted to hide his annoyance. Too much time was being lost in courts these days by wasteful efforts to truncate trials without proper cause.

'The defence asks you, your honour, to declare no case to answer. The witness we have just heard has been shown to be unreliable, to have lied under oath and been totally discredited under cross-examination. Susan Bennett is the principal witness for the prosecution and it would, therefore, be only reasonable to conclude that this witness, having been shown as disreputable, devalues the whole of the Prosecution's assertions. Surely we are not going to hear from anyone else who can establish any credibility for Mr. Mallett's case.'

'Well, Mr. Mallett?' Chalden quizzed.

'Your honour, I have several witnesses to call.'

Mallett was flustered. He was pissed off that Susan Bennett had looked so bad on the stand and was trying to repackage the prosecution's case.

'Pauline Green will corroborate part of Susan Bennett's testimony, a home office forensic scientist, Arthur Gidden, is here to confirm the handwriting, the school's headmaster and deputy are to give evidence, Mrs. Edgerley, the housemistress will be called. And possibly others. It would be ridiculous not to hear all these willing to attest. If I thought I was relying on the word of just one girl, I wouldn't be here. There would be no case to answer, I recognise that. No, Susan Bennett did her best to tell us how it was. She wasn't perfect. Who in her position would be? But much of what she had to say can be verified by these other honourable people.' Piers Mallett was Mark Anthony pleading to keep the memory of his Cæsar alive.

Mark Stephens despised him. Surely he could see through the girl. He had no right to be an accomplice to the conspiracy. How could he be part of this fabrication? Mark agonised.

Piers Mallett and Margaret Cullen waited. Judge Chalden ran his finger down his notes and nodded his head. 'Mrs. Cullen, I'm afraid we need to let this one run. It's far too early to consider that there isn't a case to answer. I would be derelict in my duty to halt things here.'

Pauline Green was black. Not proud and brash about being black. She was daunted and uncomfortable about her blackness. When she joined Thomas Graham School she was one of only two black pupils. She hardly spoke and found few friendly faces. Pauline was driven to find solace in the precarious company of another loner, Susan Bennett. No other student was close to them, and their relationship intense and unhealthy. Susan dominated the inadequate girl from a north London broken family, who regarded Susan's pre-eminence as a protective shield against the taunts and quasi-racism inescapable at a British secondary school. And in this stifling, throttling communion she had become the unwitting collaborator in an insidious manœuvre hatched by the tormented mind of a chronically abused child.

Pauline was a worthless witness. She breezed across the mundane stepping stones that Piers Mallett laid out for her to trip through her story. She could confirm that there was a relationship between Mark and Susan Bennett, and gave a monotone account of the bizarre incident she had committed to memory when the Head of English at Thomas Graham School, out of the blue, pulled his penis from his trousers and requested a wank and a blow job. And when she had completed her delivery Pauline Green sat back with an air of achievement. Her performance over. It hadn't been too bad. She hadn't reckoned with the formidable Margaret Cullen.

As a bull, believing he is indomitable, scrapes at the dusty bullring floor, wary of those around but unsure of the assault about to be launched or the spectacle it will generate; Pauline Green watched the matador enter the fray.

'Hello, Pauline. I will ask you just a few questions.' Margaret was stroking her victim; winning her confidence. 'If you want me to repeat anything, simply ask.' The smile was insincere but necessary. 'You have told the court that you knew that Susan Bennett was having a relationship with Mr. Stephens. How did you know?'

'Everyone knew.'

'Everyone?' Margaret's retort stung. 'Who exactly knew?' Margaret enquired, fixing her eyes on Pauline's.

'The girls in the house.' Pauline was tightening up.

'But wasn't that on or after the evening that Mrs. Edgerley was told?' Margaret was urging Pauline into a funnel.

'Yeah, I s'pose it was.' Pauline was not a spontaneous liar. She had to keep to her script. This wasn't one she was prepared for.

'So, how did you know about the relationship before that evening?' Further down the narrowing neck of the funnel Margaret drove her.

'From what Susan told me, and her going to see him. That's how I knew it.' It was a feasible explanation, but it was a slippery route she was following.

Margaret was eager to take her feet away. 'So you knew about this relationship only from what Susan Bennett told you, and a presumption that Susan's visits to Mr. Stephens' classroom were trysts of lovers?'

Pauline was trapped in the restricted spout of the funnel and scrambling to climb out. 'I just knew. It was obvious,' she babbled.

'Isn't it true that you went to the classroom with Susan sev-

eral times, and that you saw no evidence of Mr. Stephens'
affection for Susan Bennett? On the contrary weren't you a
witness to a dressing down that he gave Susan about her
hounding him?'

Pauline felt a surge of supercharged heat drive up her body
and smoke her head. She spoke from the atrocious screenplay,
not the truth.

'No, I wasn't in the classroom.'

'I see.'

Mark yelled liar in his head, but Margaret couldn't shout it
for him, but she had the ability to dismiss as highly dubious a
witness's answer with the tone of her voice, and never more so
than with these two words. Pauline was still struggling in the
narrow neck of the funnel and Margaret was determined to
keep her there.

'So, it must have been puzzling for you when Mr. Stephens
asked you and Susan to accompany him to the staff quarters in
Cairo House? What did you think was planned?'

'Don't know.' Pauline was now facing her feet to hide her
tell-tale eyes.

'And when he, as you allege, pulled out his penis, you must
have been terrified. Here was Susan's boyfriend taking his
penis from his trousers and asking you to touch it and perform
sexual acts. Absolutely petrified, weren't you?'

Fuck! Pauline gulped and panicked. She was damp with
perspiration yet suddenly cool. Trembling with the icy fear. It
had all been neatly packaged for her. Everything tidy and
manageable. She hadn't been equipped for this. There was no
answer. Her head hung and swayed a little but she couldn't
speak.

Margaret feared the jury would imagine the experience was
being relived and spark some sympathy. 'It's not what a
boyfriend would do to his girlfriend's best friend. Is it,
Pauline?'

'I s'pose not.' Pauline was trying to appear disinterested. But
she couldn't stop her heart pounding in her ears and the thun-

derous smacking echo of her deep swallowing.

'Exactly,' Margaret was able to conclude. 'It didn't happen, did it Pauline? It's all made up. For some reason, which we have yet to discover, you and Susan have invented these monstrous allegations. Mark Stephens didn't do these things, did he, Pauline?'

Piers Mallett was far from impressed by his witnesses so far, and sat with his glum face clutched in his hands and prayed Pauline wouldn't crack up.

Margaret realised Pauline was again struck dumb. It was better to plough on. She was reaping more from the strangled silence than the dismissive throw-away responses. She tugged the shoulders of her robe and changed tack.

'Susan and you get on well, don't you, Pauline?'

'She's my friend.' Pauline could hear her lungs emptying. She hadn't dare breathe when Margaret Cullen was bombarding her with the brutal truth.

'A very close friend? Your only friend?'

'I have other friends!' She hadn't, but Pauline was determined to avoid anyone there thinking she was that desperate for companionship.

'Bosses you about a bit, doesn't she? Leads you on?'

'No!'

'Gets you involved. Gets you in trouble. Do you recall when you were suspended from school? Wasn't that her fault?' Margaret was once again on the offensive.

Mark was urging her on. How he wished he could applaud loudly as she pinned her quarry. And how he wanted to experience the kill.

'We both did it. Wasn't her doing.' Pauline wouldn't concede. She was weak and wretched, needed friendship, but no one was going to know. Christ! Was she weak? Why on earth had she agreed to all this? It was a nightmare.

'Are you telling the court untruths because Susan Bennett has asked you to, or threatened you? Because, if you are lying, you will be in serious trouble. Do understand the gravity of committing perjury?'

There were too many questions. Pauline was victim to a volley of penetrating theories that made her feel naked. Piers Mallett rescued her by objecting to the medley of petitions.

Margaret conceded, and sat down. She had finished with Pauline Green.

Piers Mallett wanted to re-examine, to clear up some minor matters and leave the jury with a better opinion of his witness, but thought it wiser to get her off the stand before she made any terminal errors.

Following Pauline Green came a succession of witnesses for the prosecution who did their level best to help convict Mark Stephens on four charges of indecent assault. He watched in numbed disbelief as this assortment of people, mainly from the school, condemned their former colleague.

Jean Baxter catalogued the events that led to Mark's arrest. She described the first call from the school and the interviews with the girls, and how she had followed standard procedure throughout the investigation. It was important that she was seen as squeaky clean and that there was nothing vindictive in the manner of her enquiries. It was a fine performance.

Mark hated her for what she was doing. It was beyond his comprehension that this bitch was cementing the whole fabrication in place without seeing the giant cracks and the yawning breaches.

The jury seemed duly deceived by her apparent honesty and charm; her dedication to duty. She was oily and plausible. What a fine upright custodian of the law. Margaret tried to rock her, but Baxter was far too gracious and Margaret saw no value, and a great deal of risk, in attempting to undermine this upstanding police officer.

Ted Frith, wearing a ghastly check suit, reminiscent of something Conan Doyle might have dressed Dr. Watson in, scrambled to the stand after the grinning WPC vacated it with a sickly smirk for the Judge. Frith had been only a mediocre teacher and had networked industriously to weave his way through tough vetting procedures to become a headmaster. He bumbled along at the job, enjoying the celebrity but quick to avoid or delegate the harsh realities of responsibility. He hadn't particularly disliked Mark, had been quite friendly at times, but regarded him as a nuisance, largely because Tom Pearson was forever running to him to report on Mark's punctuality and caustic memos.

Ted Frith's evidence traced the events from Jan Edgerley's first contact, through the suspension and the subsequent disciplinary action taken by the school. His role, he was quick to inform the court, was one of responsible and independent initiator of the proper action throughout this terrible business. And how he maintained fairness to both his pupils and accused teacher. It was a masterful display of stroking his own ego. He was out to protect his reputation and that of the school. Fuck anyone else. Fuck justice. Fuck Mark Stephens!

Mallett concentrated his efforts on Mark's demeanour when he was suspended. He was going to squeeze the last drop out of even the most dehydrated event.

'So you say that Mr. Stephens' reaction to the news that there were allegations made against him by two girls, was to say nothing?'

'Yes. He just sat blank-faced, even after I told him he would be suspended immediately.' Ted Frith was adding weight to Mallett's inference.

'From what you know of Mr. Stephens, is that the reaction you would expect?' Mallett persisted. He had a foothold.

'No. I would have thought he would instantly deny such a suggestion; be outraged at the accusations.'

Thanks Ted. Thanks for the help, Mark thought. Friends like Ted Frith were as welcome as the plague.

'Exactly how I would be,' confessed Mallett. 'Furious at such a charge. What did Mr. Stephens say? If anything?'

'He indicated that he couldn't tell his wife and that he would contact me to discover what was happening. I had told him that this would be dealt with by the disciplinary procedures governing gross misconduct and he would need to know the next stage in the investigation.'

'I see. He said he couldn't tell his wife.' Mallett thought aloud for the benefit of the jury. He needed them to register Mark's behaviour at this crucial time.

There were few other questions. Piers Mallett didn't want to cloud the essentials. Mark Stephens hadn't protested his innocence when first charged. Mark Stephens wasn't a person who suffered injustices lying down. He was the first to roar in demonstration of unfairness. Well at least on paper. Mallett had purloined copies of several of Mark's letters informing Tom Pearson of his displeasure. Vehement, forceful letters written by a man who didn't accept inequity with dumb concession. It would be a topic that he planned to exhume several times during the trial.

Margaret Cullen made straight for this area and initiated a repair job. 'As I understand it, Mr. Stephens was suspended as soon as news of these allegations was confirmed to you by Mrs. Edgerley. Before you had spoken to the girls. Is that so, Mr. Frith?'

'Yes, that's quite correct. I wanted to get Mr. Stephens off site as soon as possible. In the interest of both parties of course.'

Mark could see Ted Frith was covering his arse. Not that worms really had arses.

'So when you spoke to Mr. Stephens in your office you had no idea what the allegations were?'

'Not the exact nature. A rough idea.'

'You weren't able to be specific when you tackled Mr. Stephens. He had no idea what was being alleged, had he?'

'No one knew the details. Not even me.' Ted Frith admitted.

'Exactly. He didn't know, and you weren't in a position to tell him. So his reaction was not out of the ordinary. Stunned by the horror of being accused of any foul deed after teaching for nearly twenty-five years. A natural response, wouldn't you say?'

'I don't know. I suppose so.' Ted Frith was reluctant to give way.

Margaret had put out the fire for the time being, although she was well aware of it flaring up again at any time. 'The only thing Mr. Stephens said as he rambled in shock, according to your evidence, was that he couldn't tell his wife. Who could? Didn't you inform him that you might clear this up that day and that he would probably be back at work within a week?'

'Yes.' Ted Frith had been optimistic at the time. Certain that this was just a schoolgirl thing, and his Head of English would be promptly cleared. He had not reckoned on the complicity and the entrenched and driving malevolence. The woolly head-master was no match for Susan Bennett.

Margaret left it there. She managed to portray Ted Frith as a bumbling individual who had conducted the interviews incorrectly and unfairly, and manœuvre him into admitting that Susan Bennett had an unhealthy influence over Pauline Green.

Mark enjoyed the sparring, and for a very short period forgot what was at stake.

As if in descending order of senior management, Tom Pearson marched to the stand. As a CCF officer he had adopted military bearing. It suited the pompous deputy headmaster. Strutting like a clockwork soldier and taking the oath crisply at attention. Mark made a hidden fist. He could have punched the bumptious man and knocked the hideous grin off his face. He was there to tell the court what a pain in the arse Mark Stephens was, and confirm the nature of the letters he had received from the accused; who was now piercing his head with laser eyes. Tom Pearson relished the opportunity to repay him for all the grief Mark had caused him at the school. Mallett used Pearson as a mischief element to begin with, but moved on to a more sinister aspect.

'The court has been told by Susan Bennett that she met the accused at lunchtimes in his classroom. You remember the lay-out of Mr. Stephens' classroom as it was in April 1994. Would it have been possible for two people to have embraced and kissed without being observed?' Mallett knew Pearson's answer before his lips moved. Piers Mallett prepared well. Baxter had recognised the antagonism when Pearson was first questioned, and these qualities would provide further weaponry to assail the good name of Mark Stephens.

Tom Pearson was picturing Mark's classroom. His eyes surveyed the ceiling in the courtroom as he pushed everything in place. Not that he had really taken it all in when he went in the room, which wasn't often, considering the relationship he had with Stephens. And now it was March 1995 and there was a new regime working out of Mark's old room, with a different layout of furniture.

'As I recall it, there were units on two walls, windows on the others,' Pearson started off, 'and a tall cupboard near the door. Between the units, which were bookshelves and filing cabinets, there were gaps. And to answer your question, I think you could conceal a couple of people in one of these gaps.'

What a Judas! The bastard believes I did it! Mark was spitting with anger, but the rage was only manifested in his tight grip of the rail in front of him and his dagger eyes.

Tom Pearson wouldn't look at him now.

'Thank you, Mr. Pearson.' Piers Mallett gloated.

Judge Chalden intervened. He could see several of the jury were perplexed by this latest evidence. 'It would help us all if you could give us a rough sketch of the classroom Mr. Pearson.' Chalden waved a hand towards an usher. 'Fetch some paper for Mr. Pearson,' he commanded.

Tom Pearson was allowed several minutes to produce his plan. It was a further exhibit. Mark was shown it after the jury had passed it between them. It was completely wrong. Mark was astonished that this arsehole Pearson was given leave to produce his fairy-tale map. He shook his head and sent a message to Margaret to say that it was nothing like the arrangement in the classroom. Most noticeably was the absence of the computer unit, which was at least four feet wide. There were no gaps.

Tom Pearson concluded his evidence by relating an account of Mark's apparent scandalous liaison with the telephonist as if it was yesterday. And enlarging on his precipitous relationship with Mark. The scolding letters and their stormy conversations. And how he tried his hardest to control the maverick mentality of the Head of English in a most reasonable manner.

It was all horseshit. Mark knew better.

Margaret wasn't prepared to have to challenge the deputy headmaster over classroom layout. However, she needed to establish some doubt in his evidence for the jury to hang on to.

'Do you recall a computer unit in Mr. Stephens' classroom?'

Tom Pearson pondered, finger on chin. 'Could be.'

'So you aren't sure?'

'I'm trying to picture it. It's a little difficult.'

'Understandably Mr. Pearson. It was nearly a year ago when Mr. Stephens left the school. It would take a remarkably accurate memory to get everything correct. Wouldn't it?' Margaret was half way there.

'I do pride myself on having better than average recall.'

Tom Pearson lifted his head and puffed out his chest. He hated being quizzed and having his word questioned. But this was one place where he couldn't boss people around. Put the shit up pupils or harass the staff, which was his forte. He was a shark out of water here, and Mark would enjoy watching him flap about in his impotence.

'I'll ask you again, then. Was there a computer unit that was on the wall where the other units were?' Margaret pushed for a reply. Perhaps too eagerly.

'Tom Pearson was struggling. 'I think I remember a computer on a trolley, but it was at the front of the class.'

Mark huffed in disbelief. He could have jogged Pearson's memory.

Margaret left it there. It had no future. Margaret dropped exploration of that subject.

'You have explained how you and Mr. Stephens were not

the best of friends and that there was considerable friction. He found it difficult to approach you, didn't he?'

'He was the only one. I encourage staff to talk to me about problems.'

Oh! Yes, Mark thought. There was more chance of slipping a hand into an alligator's snapping jaw and not sustain injury.

'Do you recall a day in the latter part of the Spring Term last year. Mr. Stephens stopped you in the playground to talk to you? I believe you lambasted him for being late. You gave him no time to explain the problem he was having with Susan Bennett.'

'I do remember warning him about his punctuality. And... yes, it was in the playground. He made no mention of a problem with a pupil. Susan Bennett wasn't referred to.' Tom Pearson recalled the discussion. It still gave him pleasure.

'But he did wish to discuss a matter with you. And it must have been important. He kept clear of you normally. You made it impossible for him to raise it as you immediately went on the offensive.' Margaret tried to rescue something.

'Maybe. I can't remember if there was a special topic he wanted to discuss.'

Margaret had squeezed all the useful points she could out of this self-opinionated man. She thought twice about examining the incident with the telephonist. She didn't pursue it and hoped the jury had discarded that red herring already.

Tom Pearson left the witness box with the same military precision as he had entered it. And he paraded out of the courtroom having done his best to incriminate his former colleague.

Jan Edgerley appeared as the first prosecution witness of the next day. She was incredibly nervous and swapped jittery glances with Mark before she was sworn in. She described the events of that evening when she was alerted by some girls in her house. Briefly Clair Hooper was referred to, but Jan Edgerley was steered round that and Piers Mallett helped her concentrate on Susan Bennett and Pauline Green.

Her recollection of the incident when Mark approached her following the incursion into Mark's classroom by a venom-spitting Susan Bennett was slanted differently. Mark was supposed to have said that he might as well hang himself. A subtle yet useful change. But, fortunately, she could confirm Mark's desperate call to the boarding house in response to Susan Bennett phoning his home. Even though she saw no significance in it. It was unhelpful rather than malicious. She considered him a filthy beast for what she thought he had done, but she had fond memories of the many years that they had been on the staff together. A bit of a prankster; an iconoclast in the most insincere manner. But that memory was smudged by the accounts of his behaviour with three of her girls.

Jan Edgerley's parting observations were further disappointments for Mark. According to the generous but gullible housemistress, whilst the two girls were good friends and occasionally mischievous, they were not inveterate liars or capable of any despicable plot against Mark Stephens. Her girls always had the sun shining out of their arses. It wasn't possible for her to comprehend the dreadful falsehoods that Susan Bennett competently effected.

Arthur Gidden was the only witness who Mark didn't know. But he knew his purpose; knew the danger.

'Would you please confirm your name.' Piers Mallett snarled. He was playing his trump card and the euphoria was filling his flicking mouth with spittle.

'Arthur George Gidden.' The slight, bespectacled man announced in a lisping voice.

'And your occupation, Mr. Gidden?'

'Forensic officer at the Home Office Laboratories in Kew.'

'I believe your expertise is graphology; handwriting to the uninformed.' Piers Mallett's eyes sparkled and he resisted a giggle at his own attempt at humour.

Judge Chalden glowered.

'I've spent over twenty years at the laboratory, and twelve of these dealing with handwriting analysis.' He spoke as if it was a serious misdemeanour to question his pedigree in this field. You could read Civil Service emblazoned across his stern expression and his shiny suit. There would be turn-ups fraying on crumpled shoes, and fluff beneath the collar of his jacket, and Elastoplast securing his reading glasses.

'Would you please take a look at exhibit one in this case?' Mallett asked. 'And tell us if you recognise it.'

Gidden was handed the folder containing the envelope and note. He barely glanced at it. This was pure formality. These had been in his hands for several weeks. The laboratory was overworked and understaffed. It was simple to acknowledge familiarity with exhibit one. And equally he could confirm recognition of a bulky folder that Baxter had removed from Thomas Graham School. In it were letters and other notes that Mark had written in correspondence with the headmaster and Tom Pearson.

Arthur Gidden then delivered the cruellest blow, in response to Piers Mallett's gentle processing. He wanted to savour every moment of the revelation. Each word was a carefully handled delicacy, served on silver and held for every juror to take his or her fill.

'I compared writing on the note and envelope, exhibit one, given to me by WPC Baxter, with the handwriting on the letters from this folder.' Arthur Gidden waved the heavy beige file. 'I was asked to consider if they had been written by the same person, the accused.' He looked for the first time at Mark Stephens, but he felt nothing. Just another criminal. 'The headmaster had confirmed that the letters in the file were in Mr. Stephens' hand.'

Arthur Gidden had appeared at many trials, some famous ones, as an expert witness. There was no pause in his delivery. Old hat to him.

Mark swallowed silently and pushed himself forward, his sweaty palms clinging to the coarse fabric of the seat.

'Having meticulously studied the handwriting. I won't go into all the details but it includes pressure, angle of letter formation, spacing, individual characteristics et cetera.' Arthur Gidden gave Mark another stinging glance. 'I produced a comparison analysis to illustrate similarities between the two, exhibit one and Mr. Stephens' letters in the headmaster's file.'

'If it please the court.' Piers Mallett stood up clutching a pile of plastic-bound folders. 'I have copies for everyone.' He bore a jovial visage not unlike an impression of Santa Claus about to distribute gifts.

For the next ten minutes or so the jury, Judge Chalden and Margaret Cullen perused Arthur Gidden's loving work. Mark was not entitled to view the document. He could not see where his loops and erratic stems, his snowstorm dots and his tilting down-strokes were set alongside those extracted from his own hand on the brown envelope and Pete Black's Judas letter.

'As you can see.' Arthur Gidden guided his audience when he saw a majority of the jury had lifted their heads. 'There are striking similarities that I have displayed in this document.' He proceeded to set about giving twenty minutes of detail and explanation.

Piers Mallett didn't let him go on too long. Some of the jurors were flagging and it was essential the bombshell was dropped at the most effective time. 'So, Mr. Gidden, in your expert opinion how convinced are you that exhibit one was written by the accused?'

'There's very little doubt. There are so many aspects, as I have pointed out, of the two that match. This can only mean there is an extremely high percentage of probability that this is the accused's handwriting.'

Piers Mallett stiffened his jaw. His eyes shot wide and he let out a self-satisfied gush of air that hissed through his clenched teeth.

Margaret remained impassive. She knew she had been hit broadside, but she wasn't going to look like she was sinking.

Mark rocked. His worst fear realised. Around the edges of his thoughts a black border was being drawn, barricading him in.

'Thank you, Mr. Gidden.' Mallett leaned back in his seat, hands gripped tight, an irremovable smile stuck on his face.

Treading carefully and intent on getting rid of this horrid little man as quickly as possible Margaret tidied up what she could. Nothing would fit under the carpet so she was resigned to hiding or spreading some of the dirt. There was no chance of getting an expert to challenge Gidden's conclusion.

'Could a person who is a reasonable artist copy someone else's handwriting?' Margaret enquired softly.

'Possible, but highly unlikely.' Arthur Gidden wasn't eager to discuss such a suggestion.

'So it's possible. Thank you.' She pulled the plug. She wouldn't let him respond. Hopefully the jury would remember Susan Bennett's admission that she was good at art. Margaret moved on quickly. 'The analysis of handwriting, Mr. Gidden, it isn't exactly foolproof is it?'

Arthur Gidden was uneasy and annoyed. Trust a defence barrister to call into doubt his hours of toil. 'If you say so. Not like physical laws that are determined by experiment and justification by recognised values and limitations. But nevertheless it has, through rigorous testing been seen to establish a highly regarded reputation.'

'Of course Mr. Gidden. It is only natural for you to defend the existence of your particular field or profession, isn't it?' Margaret had got under his skin and now she couldn't hide the cynicism as she toyed briefly with the prickly civil servant. She wouldn't be able to pursue it any further. As it was she had been tip-toeing on quicksand or negotiating a tight-rope across a piranha-filled river.

Arthur Gidden mumbled his resentment. He hadn't been spoken to like that before. Never had his beloved career ridiculed in public. An expert witness should be afforded more respect.

The general opinion when Mark, Robert and Margaret conferred at the end of the day was that, considering the weight of the evidence the forensic scientist had lobbed at them, they had been less harmed than they had expected. Neither Robert nor Margaret pointed a finger, but Mark could feel their frustration and the burning questions caught in their throats. Begging to know why they were being hijacked by this damning evidence. Why there were these sheets of paper showing a disconcerting match between his hand and the one that wrote an intimate note to a young schoolgirl.

No further witnesses were called for the prosecution when court reconvened the next day. Margaret took centre stage. She would have to labour even harder. Despite her remarkable performance in the first round she had suffered a knock down that she was still reeling from.

Mark was let out of his pen. As he strode across the courtroom floor to take the witness stand the jury were transfixed. What had been let out? Was the silent and dreadful man to prove to be the monster the prosecution maintained?

Now he was to speak. How he performed from that box would be crucial. He was both nervous and excited. At last the opportunity to blow away the web of lies started by the evil intent of a vile girl and embroidered by the police into an insidious vendetta against a vulnerable teacher.

Mark told them how it was. He could only tell the truth no matter how improbable anyone thought it was. The court heard from an unremarkable but reasonable man.

Susan Bennett had made advances; it had happened before in his career. She had been insistent with her pestering. The phone calls to his home. He had dealt with it himself. Travelled, perhaps unwisely, to Wokingham to end her nagging annoyance. Taken his daughter. He unravelled his relationship with Tom Pearson and gave an account of his attempt at alerting the deputy headmaster about Susan Bennett. Rebuked any notion that he touched either girl and described how it would have been impossible to have had these lunchtime assignations or spend hours away from his tutorial duties. The horror of Susan Bennett's stampede into his classroom. There was the MOT on the Fiesta to mention, as well as tennis with Norman on the afternoon he was supposedly undressing Susan Bennett at her home. Even another plan of his classroom was drawn to show the elusive computer. He spoke too much. Elaborated too often. Margaret had warned him of that. But most of all he wanted to demonstrate who he was. The picture Piers Mallett had painted was a monstrous lie and he needed to scrub that out.

Margaret steered Mark as best she could. There was an opportunity to deny writing the letter. She planned to counter this with a wrenching question that Mark dreaded. Susan Bennett's letter despatched hatefully to his home. Until now no one had heard the contents. Margaret knew it would hurt. But she needed it. Mark needed it.

'Did you receive anything in the post following your suspension from school?' Margaret eased him in.

'Yes.' Mark swallowed to dislodge a lump in his throat.

'What was it?'

'A letter from... the girl, Susan Bennett.' His voice was losing its strength. Mark had delivered his account with conviction. Every aspect of Susan Bennett's obsession he had detailed with convincing authority. But now there was his Achilles heel. He could feel himself shaking.

'Please tell the court what you did with this letter.' Margaret appeared to be commanding him. Plucking the information from a failing source before all the functions closed down and expired.

'I... I flushed it down the lavatory.' It was a mouse talking.

'And why did you do that?' Margaret was near.

'It was... was an awful letter... I could never have shown anyone. I didn't want Alison to see it. And... Anna and Jayne... no.' Mark was rambling. It was torture.

Margaret tried to hold him together. When this was over he would be all right. 'Tell us what was in the letter. I realise it's upsetting.'

There was a strangled silence. Mark spluttered. 'I didn't read it all. Only the first few lines... that was enough.' He studied all their faces. They were visibly straining. It was theatre, and he was going to have to share his deep gnawing wound with them. A macabre scene. Inertia and audience expectation forced him to carry on. 'It said...' His voice almost faded completely. Tears tipped down his pale cheeks. He coughed into his fist to bring some volume back.

He heard Susan Bennett saying the words as she penned it. The savagery in her eyes. *'You should have gone with me. Now the only way you're going to have it with a young girl is to fuck...'* He wanted to vomit the script. Cleanse it. Get it over with. But he choked on the repulsive words. Words that shot him down. *'... is... is to... fuck your daughters. You probably have already.'*

That was it. His body lost its skeletal frame. There was just jelly. Mark sobbed. The courtroom waited. Baxter and Mallett sneered. Margaret apologised with her spaniel eyes as soon as Mark looked up at her. She had made him tell them for his sake. The young girl in the jury never blinked. Her eyes stuck open. Others dabbed droplets from their faces. They had shared his pain.

Margaret left his testimony there. A theatrical yet necessary finale.

Piers Mallett wasn't keen on the emotive conclusion to Mark's evidence and was determined to dismiss the make-believe that Mark had conjured up to cover his slimy tracks. He needed to take aim thoughtfully, there had been a stirring of the sympathy vote. Mark Stephens had committed some disgusting acts and he wasn't going to let him acquire sainthood status in this court.

'So, Mr. Stephens, you like being a teacher, do you?' A smirk clung to Mallett's face.

'Yes.' Mark tightened up. He had to be vigilant. The 'Pitbull' was ready to bare his teeth.

'Prefer the girls to the boys, eh?' Mallett's direction was blatant.

'Not really.' Some of the girls were a real pain. Mark more

often than not took greater interest in the boys. Playing table-tennis, skiing and other physical pursuits. He was still a lad at heart.

'You have told the court that none of the events described by Susan Bennett and Pauline Green took place. That they are all fabrication and collusion. What a fantastic story these girls have made up. For what reason Mr. Stephens? For what reason?'

'I don't know exactly. God! I wish I did. It probably is centred on my rejection of Susan Bennett's advances.' Mark had been warned off introducing the Clair Hooper angle.

'Her advances? Of course.' Mallett held his chin and stiffened his lips. 'A girl of fifteen tells you she fancies you, even loves you. These are wild and unnerving declarations aren't they?'

'Yes. Very disconcerting.' Mark recalled the incidents vividly.

'Surely a matter for higher ranked personnel? No disrespect to you, of course, Mr. Stephens. Wasn't it school policy for problems like this to be reported to upper management, or at least the girl's housemistress?' Mallett knew the wounds and was poking at the painful areas.

'I'm not certain of school policy relating to an event like this, but I started off dealing with it myself. When I did decide to take it further I was either prevented by confrontational barriers put up by the deputy head or it occurred at a time when there were no members of the house staff or senior management available.' Margaret had warned him about giving speeches. He was saying too much.

'When you returned to school following the Easter break. You had the opportunity then, didn't you?' Mallett wasn't letting this one go.

'At that time I felt I had controlled the situation. I had sorted it out. She was leaving that term. God! There was no way of knowing all this would blow up.'

'Your classroom, Mr. Stephens, offers numerous nooks and

crannies where a couple might find a little peace and quiet, a romantic alcove, wouldn't you say?' Mallett had moved on. A different area, a sick motive, but with same intention.

'Not really. There's nowhere to canoodle in there.'

'Between the units on the wall where the door is, or was. Surely there's room there?' Mallett pressed.

'Hardly. That was crammed with units, bookcases and a computer unit. There were no breaks. A solid line of furniture.' The two men were jousting.

'Mr. Pearson has told the court that he cannot recall a computer on that wall.'

Mark seethed. 'He is wrong or mistaken. To set the record straight, he was hardly ever up there and couldn't possibly maintain that it wasn't there. I know it was. I have never kissed Susan Bennett there or anywhere else.' Mark shouldn't have said it. He couldn't control his frustration at trying to convince this court about the position of a bloody computer unit.

Mallett was encouraged. Stephens was getting rattled. He sensed his prodding was succeeding. 'So you met Susan Bennett in Wokingham. That was an extraordinarily strange thing for a teacher to do. Meet a pupil out of school. A secret assignation.'

'I met her to stop the girl harassing me. She was threatening to do some wild things. It was a last resort.'

'No, Mr. Stephens. I put it to you that this was a rendezvous of two people having a relationship. A girl of fifteen and a married, middle-aged teacher. You arranged it for the purpose of seeing her. You preyed on that girl. Isn't that true, Mr. Stephens?' Mallett snarled and broadened his chest within his tugged robe.

'I did no such thing. My daughter came with me. It was a desperate effort to prevent the girl making a fool of herself and my holiday a misery. I only spent half-an-hour or so. I thought I had it sorted out.'

Mark was arguing under heavy, smothering water or in a dream where every action is sluggish and barely mobile. Why should anyone want to drown him in these lies? He thrashed out at his thoughts.

'Only half-an-hour or so. Is that truly how long you were there?' Mallett sneered with just his eyes.

'Yes. I was playing tennis later that afternoon. Norman can vouch for that.' Mark was adding too much.

'Neatly packaged, Mr. Stephens. A daughter alongside you, but who never saw Susan Bennett, a good friend who played tennis with you when you were supposed to be engaged in acts of indecent assault and a car you couldn't use because the MOT had run out. Far too neatly packaged I feel. This is a manufactured day isn't it, Mr. Stephens? One you have contrived to cover up your sordid mission to Wokingham.'

'No way!' Mark was taking the bait. They were reading his hostility.

'Not one mention of this when you were first interviewed by the police. Why didn't you tell them there and then? Get this cleared up and save our time? Instead, just the silence of guilt.' Mallett was testing the waters.

'I could have. Could have told the police all of this. I had nothing to hide. I was given legal advice. That was to say nothing until I knew the charges against me. It would have been foolish to ignore professional guidance.'

Mallett saw no future in pursuing that. It was important to raise it just to throw some doubt on his story. 'Okay, I think we get the picture, Mr. Stephens. Now, you say my explanation is wrong. So let's consider what must be the most significant evidence this court has heard. Mr. Gidden, a forensic scientist of considerable experience, has told this court that he believes you wrote the letter to Susan Bennett. A letter cancelling yet another romantic tryst. You cannot deny that you did indeed write to Susan Bennett, can you, Mr. Mark Stephens?' His voiced was raised. This was his moment. Mallett's eyes were electric. Blazing searchlights never leaving Mark's face.

'I did not write that note. I don't care what has been said.' The denial was emphatic. But I did write the envelope! He shouted that in his head. And there was a distant recollection of doing so. What was it for? He was disturbed from further thoughts by Mallett's roar.

'Mr. Gidden said quite clearly that you did,' Mallett insisted.

'Obviously handwriting analysis is not an exact science. Thank goodness.'

'Meaning?'

'He's got it wrong of course. He's been fooled!' Mark bit back.

'I think the jury will have to decide that.' Piers Mallett smiled at the twelve riveted jurors, as if to say, you know better, don't you?

'No further questions, your honour.' Mallett fell back in his seat, still grinning victoriously to himself, but really for the greater audience.

Dave Patterson took the stand the following Monday. He would be the only teacher from Thomas Graham School to appear for the defence. Most of the others had nothing to offer. They had slunk away to bury their ostrich heads, or had already identified Mark Stephens as the unclean leper.

Dave ran through his role at Mark's interview with the headmaster, described Mark's room and the position of the computer, much to the annoyance of Judge Chalden, who was fed up with some of the minutiæ of this trial. Dave was able to confirm Mark's account of the two girls' relationship; the dominance of Susan Bennett and the weak subservience of Pauline Green. Dave Patterson knew the duties at Cairo House and supported Mark's assertion that you couldn't go missing for several hours unnoticed, and that it would be impossible to escort one or two girls up to the staff accommodation without being spotted. It was just one voice.

Mark wondered whether that would be enough. Or would they consider it a sign of minimal support. Were the majority of teachers harbouring a suspicion of his guilt?

Dave Patterson was Mark's best pal at school. Now his only one it would seem. Margaret helped him paint the best picture of Mark Stephens. Tales of how they played soccer together when he first joined the school, of Mark's sense of fun and humour. The court had lightened up. There was almost a jovial air as Dave Patterson' anecdotes brought suppressed chuckles from some of the jury, and even a smirk from the Judge - a rare occasion - when Dave complained about not getting an award for being top scorer in Mark's football team.

Mallett made an attempt to devalue Dave's evidence, but he trod cautiously. He acknowledged the man had charmed the jury and they wouldn't tolerate an assault on his character or his honesty.

Norman Munnie was a bumbling witness. You don't choose your alibi witnesses. They just happen to be there. Thank goodness. The poor man couldn't quite get to grips with the procedure. He somehow managed to take the oath clutching the wrong Bible. It was probably nerves that made him grab the Catholic one from the usher. He wasn't to know that he'd get a selection to choose from.

All he had to tell this expectant room was that he had played tennis with an old adversary. He had no notion of how these sinister allegations had been made against his friend. Such innocents were fair game for Piers Mallett. He fed off ignorance and those unprepared. As far as Norman was concerned he had started playing tennis with Mark after he had arrived at four o'clock as planned on 6th April. It wasn't a remarkable game. Mark had played well. Out of his skin actually. But in a cynical cross-examination Piers Mallett tried to introduce doubt, where there was none. Prodding for a rethink to ensure that his recollection of the events fitted in. Norman was certain of what had occurred that afternoon, but was forced to provide more than just memory to satisfy the wringing interrogation by prosecution counsel.

Norman remembered when he had left work and timings of his journey. He would have recalled if Mark had arrived late. He couldn't abide lateness and he had been upset more than once by his opponent's poor time-keeping. This was a refreshingly prompt appearance.

Despite him being an ideal candidate for the tormenting prosecutor, Norman remained resolute. He knew these things. They were of stone. He couldn't be moved, even when Piers Mallett suggested numerous reasons why he should have been mistaken or had invented ever having played tennis on that day.

Mark felt nauseous when Anna was led to the stand. Her head was bowed. The long blonde hair hiding her face. She wiped it aside to glance at him. It hurt her to smile. It hurt to see her father accused and alone.

Piers Mallett was rubbing his hands like a glutton faced with a scrumptious meal. He would relish this tasty dish once Margaret Cullen had concluded her examination. There was little for Anna to say. She explained, in a soft and trembling voice, how she had persuaded Mark to take her to her boyfriend's house and went along to Wokingham for the ride. Her father had left her in the car for about forty minutes. His mood was buoyant on his return and he drove her to Gary's house. She was able to describe the car park, sitting opposite a concrete wall listening to the radio in her mother's Mini, but not much else. But it was as much as was needed.

'Love your father, don't you?' Mallett began when he was allowed to get at her. Sickly and deceitful in his intent.

'Yes.' Anna's reply was jittery.

'Do anything for him, wouldn't you?' Piers Mallett wasn't holding back and his direction transparent. Anna was like a defenceless goldfish, Mallett a predatory cat stalking the bowl. Mark was a chained spectator at the ritual sacrifice of his child. He begged to strangle Mallett on the spot.

Even Anna in her glacial integrity was feeling threatened. 'Not anything.' She felt safer saying that, but she couldn't think of anything she wouldn't do for her Dad.

'Lie for him?' The purpose disclosed.

'No.' Anna blubbered. She couldn't hold the tears.

'What is the name of your boyfriend and his address?'

demanded Mallett, with a quick peek over his shoulder towards Jean Baxter.

Anna shrank. Gary was off the agenda. And the parting far from amicable. She didn't want him involved.

'Why?' she said between sniffs.

'Are you reluctant to let us have this information?' Mallett enquired, casting suspicion on her reason.

'He's not... my boyfriend... not now.' Anna swallowed several times. Accentuated dips of her head as she did so.

Mark was desperate to comfort her. Mallett turned to face him. Eager to register his success with a self-satisfied grin. One that Mark wished he could have removed with his swinging foot.

'Name and address please, Miss Stephens.' Mallett repeated his demands.

Anna pleaded with Mark with her despondent eyes and trembling lips. 'Gary... er... Cottee.'

'And his address?' Mallett watched as Baxter jotted it down.

'Three, Crown Drive... Shepperton.' Anna collapsed to the small seat in the box. She dreaded what her erstwhile boyfriend would say.

Baxter fled from the courtroom with a nod to Mallett and the Judge. She was hot foot to Shepperton. This story was bullshit. The little cow was lying to protect her disgusting father. Jean Baxter knew her mission.

Anna hurried from the witness box. She fell into Alison's arms outside in the corridor. It was five minutes of lusty weeping before she could speak to her mother.

Fortunately Judge Chalden concluded proceedings for the day. Otherwise Alison would have followed her daughter into the witness box, just as apprehensive and terrified. Knowing what Piers Mallett had done to Anna.

Mark, Anna and Alison sat close together in the small cafeteria on the first floor of the courthouse. Each comforting the others. Each carrying their own baggage load of pain and anxiety. Words were quietly swapped and so were warm smiles and occasional touching of hands. They were a lost threesome, so confused by the vicious onslaught for no reason. Mark Stephens hadn't committed any crime. But no one was listening. He was still shouting from inside an insulated, stainless-steel room. Living only with echoes.

Alison looked superb when she was escorted into court the next day. Her figure had hardly changed since Mark first met her when she was eighteen. Black suited her. She could look sexy, elegant and sophisticated all at once in black. The courtroom that had been Mark's environment for a long time was a new world to Alison. Frightening. Mark tried to help her from his perch in the dock with an encouraging grin. One of his roguish ones that humoured her. But that was wiped off and replaced by a face creased with anger when he saw Susan Bennett's father slip into the public gallery and squash himself into a corner seat. Luckily Alison was unaware. She faced the jury with her back to the dingy man who was attempting to blend into the panelling behind him.

George Bennett wanted to see him. He had touched his precious daughter. That was his territory. Susan had wanted Mark Stephens. But what he had with her was special. This teacher was the beast. A father's love is a tender love. A special love that she'd kept quiet about. It was obvious how she felt. George would be safer when Mark Stephens was put away. And he was there to see it happen.

Alison spoke slowly and deliberately as Margaret led her through her testimony. Telephone calls to the house from Jan Edgerley and Ann Bull alias Susan Bennett were confirmed, and a long account of how Mark's car was marooned without an MOT, and her annoyance that he was using her Mini, gently explained.

Mark recognised how fragile she was. A fine glass that if treated roughly would shatter. Margaret was guiding her with extreme caution. She too could sense Alison's brittle state and was anxious about leaving her in Mallett's clutches. Margaret dragged out the examination, hoping to build Alison's confidence. Primary in her plan was to demonstrate what a complete wife she was to Mark. Show the jury that he wouldn't forsake her for a mucky relationship with Susan Bennett. Then there was no more to ask, and she was released into the extricating hands of Prosecution counsel.

Mallett worked on confusing Alison. He didn't delve into the phone calls. He needed the jury to forget Susan Bennett's haunting voice played to the court on Mark's answer machine. He wanted to know dates when Mark's car had last been used and when the new MOT had been obtained. Alison, stricken with her own terror, afraid any slip would send her husband to prison, gave wrong dates. And with constant niggling questioning froze altogether, like a rabbit trapped in fear by the headlights of an oncoming juggernaut. It wasn't essential information. The court had as exhibits details of the old and new MOT certificates.

Mallett gave up asking any further questions and held his arms above his head. Even through his thick skin he could sense that he was antagonising the jury.

Judge Chalden allowed Alison to remain seated in the box until she had regained reasonable composure. She was quivering with apologies when she met Mark for lunch. It wasn't a frailty he had seen her display before.

'Oh, Mark, I just went to pieces. Seeing you like that, and that foul man. I couldn't remember anything. What a bloody fool!'

'Forget it. It wasn't important. You did your best. I'm not disappointed.' But he was. They hadn't seen her at her best. He wanted them to see that. It hurt to see Alison reduced to a whimpering mess. He had never seen her so defeated. He blamed himself. It was his poor judgement putting her through it. An unbelievable strain.

In the afternoon Dave Patterson arrived back at the court. This time escorting four pupils from the school. Each wore the striking blue blazer and the proud badge of Thomas Graham School. They were lost souls dragged from the rural seclusion of their boarding school and shoved through a maze of grey London streets to this austere assembly. These were the alibi witnesses Robert had dug up from numerous enquiries resulting from his visit to the school. Three boys and a solitary girl. They acknowledged their former teacher with an embarrassed nod of the head and some economic squeaky words. Their eyes were mostly hidden. Also there was a brash young man who Mark recognised as a former pupil. From Susan Bennett's year. Justin Hinton wore one of his father's suits and a badly knotted tie as thin as tagliatelli. He couldn't help being cheerful. Life was being kind, and at seventeen he was indulging himself. Only a casual and brief greeting was possible. He had been told not to fraternise until after he had given his evidence.

First on the stand was Alan Bilston, a slob of a boy at fifteen. His school tie was already tugged from his neck and his top button undone on his shirt. Dave Patterson had done his best to keep them looking smart, but as they sat waiting it was only natural for them to pull at the strangling bits.

Margaret took Alan back to March 2nd 1994. A hazardous journey for his cluttered memory and untidy recollection.

Somehow he remembered it vividly. No mistake. He had played table-tennis with Mark most of the afternoon that Mark was supposed to have spent upstairs in the staff room indecently assaulting Susan Bennett.

Mark was delighted. But his joy soon turned to excruciating frustration as Piers Mallett had Alan doubting his own name let alone the accuracy of his recall. Alan did his best to fend off the snide offensive by Mallett, but he was no match for the master of the disparaging suggestion.

Steven Hogg and a Chinese boy Ken Lo followed Alan to the stand. Both separately gave evidence that, on April 20th they had watched television with Mark in the house common room. Unfortunately it was Steven's recollection that they had watched Aston Villa in the League Cup, but according to Ken, who prided himself on an excellent memory, they had watched a basketball match. It would have been expeditious to have had only one of them to give evidence. But such was the honesty of the defence campaign that even the truth was going to be a cumbersome weapon to wield.

A television programme guide provided by Robert Manning showed that there was indeed a football match on, and a match programme brought along by the avid Villa supporter, Steven Hogg, confirmed this game took place.

Piers Mallett, looking for a likely sitting duck to shoot down, chose to pick on Ken Lo when the Chinese boy occupied the witness box. Ken's English wasn't good, encouraging Prosecution counsel to line up his sights. But Mallett had not reckoned with Ken's surprising intelligence. Mallett wanted to lever open this alibi.

Reading from the television programme guide, now another exhibit, he challenged the recent immigrant from Hong Kong to explain how he could have possibly seen a basketball game on that day.

Ken had no fear of this man. He was quick to respond. Sharp and indignant. His English clucked and coughed as his penetrating eyes targeted Mallett through thick-lens glasses. Mallett was told without ceremony that the television guide that he had been presented with did not show any of the satellite channels, and that the basketball game between Sweden and Romania had been shown on Eurosport, a channel not listed in the guide. He could even tell the nonplussed prosecutor the score. Eighty-eight, sixty-four to Sweden. He dared Mallett to check it.

Piers Mallett was not amused. The damn chink had made a fool of him. Now he wished he had chosen the Hogg boy for his inquisition.

Tara Potter, the lone girl pupil, was decidedly uncomfortable in front of all these serious people. Her bulging eyes surveyed the room, stopping to give Mark the longest look. There was no change in her expression, no blink of her dome eyes.

Tara had trouble with dates, and needed considerable assistance locating April 20th in her cluttered itinerary. Margaret, with permission from Judge Chalden, was allowed to assist. Tara had seen Susan Bennett and Pauline Green roller-blading that afternoon when Mark was supposedly propositioning the two girls up in his staff quarters in Cairo House.

Mallett turned Tara's memory to pulp, and maintained that nothing she could recall should be relied upon at all. With a retention like that she was not capable of identifying activities and associate them with accuracy. She simpered with every question. A forlorn sight.

Mark wanted to hug the girl for her brave effort. Inconceivable considering his present predicament. Her courage was immense. A timid and reticent girl ready to be humiliated in order to snatch some justice for her ex-teacher.

Slick as Brylcreem, Justin Hinton took to the boards in Court Six. His audience was exactly what he enjoyed. At school he had revelled in centre stage, no matter what role.

Robert had struck gold by accident. In a routine enquiry concerning the dates that Mark was on duty in Cairo House he had spoken to Justin about Susan Bennett. It ignited a tirade about the obnoxious old moose who had, on one occasion, claimed that he had had sex with her on a nearby common.

'I wouldn't touch her with a barge pole. The ugly bitch had some nerve. Told a few of the class, and it spread like wildfire. You know what kids are like. You should have heard the grief I got. They wouldn't let me forget it. I tried to tell them the cow was lying, but they just laughed. Said I was too embarrassed to admit it. No one in their right mind would confess they'd had it away with that dumpling. I got hold of her at break and nearly throttled her. Told her to own up and tell them she had invented it. But she wouldn't. Made her feel big. Something to boast about. She knew no one with any taste or sense would get across her monstrous body. Luckily over the next few days people dropped it, and I had it off with some of the other girls.' Justin had added with pride. 'Got me a better reputation. I think the class realised I hadn't touched her. It was just a bit of a laugh for them at the time.'

Justin told the court what had happened. Robert had cleaned up the wording for his statement, but the court was made well aware of what had happened and the significance of it. He was a good performer. Instant hit with the jurors. They needed some entertainment after such a lengthy trial. Margaret wanted to keep him there. She explored what else he could contribute. He was the last material witness. A good turn and a memorable performer.

'Mr. Hinton, take a look at exhibit one. It is supposedly Mr. Stephen's handwriting.'

An usher hurried to hand Justin the envelope and letter.

'How accessible were examples of Mr. Stephens' handwriting?' Margaret was at the lucky dip, or in the last chance saloon.

Justin Hinton smoothed his gelled hair with one hand and peered at the writing on the envelope. It brought back memories of onerous tasks and coursework assignments.

'Too accessible,' Justin blurted. 'All of Mr. Stephens' notes for our literature course were hand-written by him. A lot of the other teachers would type them out, but not him. Reams of the stuff. And then there were the exam papers. Sure he'd photocopy some of the text we were dealing with, but all the questions were in this.' Justin waved exhibit one.

Margaret cringed. Mark gulped. Mallett's lip curled in a wry smile.

Justin felt the elastic snap. The courtroom fizzed with furtive whispers. He placed exhibit one gingerly on the edge of the box as if it was now contaminated. For once he was lost for words.

'Susan Bennett was in your class and would have access to a variety of documents written by Mr. Stephens. Is that correct?' Margaret had slipped up and was doing her best to retrieve as much as she could.

'Yes,' Justin confirmed flatly. The sparkle had gone.

When Piers Mallett rose to cross examine, Justin was deflated. He knew he'd let Mark down. What a fool. Why didn't he think? He wanted to kick himself, and let others join in. But that was Mr. Stephens writing on the envelope He had recognised it immediately. Even recognised the envelope. Couldn't quite place it though.

'Bit of a lad at school were you, Mr. Hinton?' Mallett's final assault. His mission to slap this young man down. Far too inspirational to let him leave the stand unstained.

'Not really.' Justin realised he had to fend this man off. Gone was the oozing confidence he had brought with him. The bubble had burst and he only hoped there wouldn't be too much damage in the aftermath.

'Think you're a wow with the girls?' Mallett's eyes flickered. 'Eh?'

'Some,' Justin admitted.

'Bit of a trophy collector? Like to get as many conquests under your belt as you can?' Mallett had a twinkling in his eye as he urged the witness on. Encouraging him to bolster his own ego.

'No.' Justin was aware and countered with firmness.

'Susan Bennett was one of your scalps, wasn't she? You did have sex with Susan Bennett on the common, didn't you?' Aggression replaced incitement.

'No, I didn't. I wouldn't touch an ugly moose like that.' Justin wanted to stamp on that suggestion with force. A young beau has to consider his pride.

'Something you wouldn't readily admit to. So you denied it. Couldn't bear the ridicule could you?'

'You're dead right there! They took the piss as it was.' Justin was incensed.

'I suggest that Susan Bennett told the truth about what happened on the common, and you, as we have seen, were adamant to conceal this brief encounter. It damaged your reputation. And that you are in fact the one not telling the truth. Lying to the court aren't you, Mr. Hinton?'

'Certainly not!' Justin looked at Mallett through rifle sights, with enraged eyes.

It was difficult to determine what impact Justin Hinton had on the respective campaigns. Both counsels could glean some comfort from his appearance.

A whole day was devoted to character witnesses. Of which there were fifteen. They came from every facet of Mark's life, but in particular Margaret had chosen to include parents of children who Mark had taught at school or privately. She was keen to select mothers of teenage girls who had been tutored in secluded corners of their homes, often in their bedrooms. They came willingly. Once, of course, they had confirmed with their daughters that all had been well during *their* lessons.

One after another middle-aged women came to praise him or simply to dismiss any suspicion of his guilt. Mark felt awkward as they gave him such splendid references or told how ordinary he was.

Cameron Rudley from the legal fraternity represented the tennis club region of his social life, while Professor Ellery Peters was added to the list in order to impress and to applaud Mark's academic success.

Piers Mallett declined to cross examine such minnows except for the occasional cynical questioning to illustrate the irrelevance of these toadies. He did pick on one rather nervous mother and suggest her daughter's enjoyment of her private lessons with Mark may not rest solely on the educational input. Judge Chalden, ever chivalrous, was quick to admonish him for his unwarranted insinuation.

At the end of a day that saw the stream of accolades for Mark Stephens, Judge Chalden, somewhat agitated by what he considered a plethora of people singing the praises of the accused, addressed the court.

'Three days should do it Mr. Mallett, Mrs. Cullen. I'm a little tetchy, made worse by today, and I need a result. Summing up by the two of you, and then myself.' He was almost talking to himself. Loud thoughts rather than instructions. 'Two days at the most, and jury out on the third. Yes. Any comments on that?' His head swung between them. Both agreed with his assessment; they didn't dare contradict.

Piers Mallett was in his element summing up. It was a different face and a fresh language that the jury beheld. He was their friend. Helping them come to the right decision. Only considering the evidence. He wouldn't conceivably ask them to convict Mark Stephens if the case wasn't conclusively proven. On that day Piers Mallett was a saint and a nun, seeking only justice for the innocent young victims so terribly violated and then dragged through their torturous ordeal in court. Could they imagine such a horror? Seeing their children put through this ordeal?

Mark Stephens had indecently assaulted fifteen-year-old Susan Bennett. Too young to make a rational decision. This teacher had taken advantage of his position. Persuaded her to start a relationship for his own gratification. Why should she have lied about the affair? Make up all this detail? For what reason? And this teacher's lascivious appetite drove him to enrol Pauline Green into his perverted plan. Another fifteen-year-old. And assault each girl in front of the other.

'Most damning, members of the jury, and so clear cut, is the evidence supplied by Mr. Gidden, the forensic scientist. Mark Stephens wrote to Susan Bennett, telling her he couldn't make a rendezvous. Is this the action of an innocent man? Vehemently he denies that he is the author of this letter. And with that lie he condemns all his other statements, made there on that stand, to the same scrutiny. He has lied and lied and lied. Trying to squirm out of these charges. In doing so he has gone to great lengths to create a version that shows Susan Bennett as a pestering schoolgirl with a crush. An obsession.

'He has involved his family and friends in this charade. Innocent people who have intentionally lied out of loyalty, or unwittingly perjured themselves for this disgusting man.

'The proper channel to follow when dealing with the problem Mr. Stephens wants us to believe he faced, was to report such unsolicited approaches by a pupil to senior management. He didn't do this. Not because he didn't get on with his immediate superior. He didn't do it because there was nothing to report. Nothing at all.

'Mark Stephens preyed on Susan Bennett. She did not go looking for him. He set out to waylay her. She fitted the bill. A lonely, unliked girl. Eager for attention.

'Every witness from the school has been ready to swear to the ordinary nature of the girls, an unremarkable association. Certainly they got into some trouble. Which one of us didn't at school?' A crooked smile accompanied his remark. 'No one could call them angels. But, they are not the vicious liars the defence are asking you to believe they are. No, no.' Mallett tapped the woodwork in front of him and held on to his grim countenance.

'It was a brave action to come here and testify. Not something a young girl does lightly. For their sake and for justice I must implore you, from the evidence presented, there is only one verdict, and that verdict is guilty. Convict Mark Stephens.' Mallett gave a firm nod of the head and offered his grave face to the plum-eyed jurors.

Mark screwed up his eyes. Alison glowered furiously from the public gallery. She was ready to kill Mallett. Anna and Jayne gave their father comforting looks. And deep in a corner George Bennett rubbed his hands and snarled at Mark. Touch my lovely daughter would you!

Margaret Cullen knew she had to perform better than Piers Mallett. More than just upstage him. She was the favourite auntie to every juror. Standing at the door of her country cottage, welcoming. The sweet aroma of warm pastry wafting past her gingham apron. She made every man and woman on that jury feel comfortable; convinced that she was the good fairy godmother.

Mark Stephens had done nothing wrong. Sure he had managed the situation clumsily, made mistakes and acted recklessly. But he hadn't committed the crimes he stood accused of. Susan Bennett had fabricated the whole thing. Somehow, probably through her dominance in their relationship, convinced

Pauline Green to lie for her. It was an insidious falsehood that stemmed from Miss Bennett's uncompromising obsession with this teacher.

'You have heard the name Clair Hooper mentioned in passing, caught glimpses of her in testimony, but you have not heard from her. This girl is central to this case. It was her who first went to Mrs. Edgerley, the housemistress. And prompted by what Clair told her, Susan Bennett was interviewed. Susan Bennett, the defence believes, and I think you must also, invented the whole gruesome business to give herself the status she yearned. To lift her prestige at the school. She wasn't liked, verbally abused and, except for Pauline Green who she kept in tow, friendless. Mark Stephens was a hapless victim in this girl's malevolent plot. He was a generous, gregarious teacher and in spite of being the same age as Susan's father, a person who Susan developed an obsession about.'

George Bennett shrunk a little in his seat. He was uncomfortable at being mentioned.

'And when Susan Bennett confided in Mark Stephens about how she felt, he thrust her away. There was no way he wanted her. That, members of the jury, was a fatal rejection. When her fantasy affair with Mark Stephens, that she had boasted to Clair Hooper about, was reported to Mrs. Edgerley, Susan was able to reek her vengeance.

'No one witnessed Mark Stephens taking Susan Bennett or Pauline Green to these staff quarters in the boarding house. No one witnessed Mark Stephens going to Susan Bennett's home. No one witnessed the canoodling that she says went on in the classroom. Why? Because there was nothing to witness.

'You saw Susan Bennett in that box. You were spectators to her lies. I didn't phone, she stated categorically. And *hey presto* her voice bounces out of Mark Stephens' answer machine. Susan Bennett has lied throughout. Vicious, malignant lies that threaten an innocent man's liberty.' Margaret turned over a page and surveyed the first few lines. The jury didn't flinch.

Treading carefully, Margaret continued. 'The prosecution

claims a short note written, they say, by Mr. Stephens is proof enough of his implication in these obscene deeds. It is not. Mr. Gidden admitted that it was possible to copy someone's handwriting, given that they were artistic. Susan Bennett was a competent artist. And she had copious examples to copy. Justin Hinton confirmed that. All of Mr. Stephens' study notes were hand written.

'Mark Stephens told you the truth. Warts and all. He even had to suffer the pain of telling you the contents of the letter Susan Bennett had written after she had made these baseless accusations. A sickening letter she admitted sending.' Margaret paused to let them remember Mark's agonising testament.

'This is no new ploy by Susan Bennett. She has done this before. A dress rehearsal for her wicked allegations against Mr. Stephens. Mr. Hinton was then the victim of this girl's vindictive deceit. She craved notoriety. This was her only way.

'Mark Stephens is not guilty. He did not commit these sordid acts. Victim not violator. Acquit this man. That is your just duty. The only fair verdict.' Margaret encouraged them to do so with arms raised as if to embrace, from a distance, all twelve of them.

Alison and the girls nodded in agreement. Eric Thomas whispered support. A good summing up.

George Bennett grunted and slid out before he could be assaulted by Jayne's steely eyes.

Judge Chalden used the rest of that day and most of the next to wade through the evidence that had been presented by both sides.

Margaret emphasised to Mark how important the Judge's directions were. A great deal depended on his influence over the jury.

It was the first time that Chalden had spoken at length. He was a sour man who seldom smiled. With his half-glasses perched half way up his nose he was able to refer to the written text in front of him, as well as to occasionally peer menacingly over the spectacles to observe the jury. It had been a long trial and his summary would take some time, he told them. His job was to highlight the relevant evidence and point them in the apposite direction. Sometimes earlier matters are sidelined, their impact softened, or forgotten totally. His duty was to resurrect them and grade their importance.

Mark was adhered to every word. Chalden's crisp and cold words. Concern soon replaced vigilance when the Judge referred to the two girls in a fatherly manner. As if they were precious innocents. Hardly condemned Susan Bennett for lying or scrutinised closely the evidence of Pauline Green. There was meticulous reference to Susan Bennett's story and far too little emphasis on Margaret's demolition job on her. Even those staff from Thomas Graham School who stabbed Mark in the back were identified as upstanding members of the teaching profession. 'Reliable witnesses whose evidence could not be ignored.' Defence witnesses were not offered the credit so readily given to those of the Prosecution. Every detail of their evidence analysed and questioned. Chalden chose to scrutinise in microscopic detail the alibi statements, as if poking around for a fatal flaw. Mark was unsure if it was just his interpretation. That he was misreading the trend. Thinking that balance was too easily perceived as bias.

A meeting at lunch-time with Robert and Margaret soon confirmed his initial feelings. Margaret was maddened by Chalden's clear partiality, but could do nothing to counter it. Save use it in the event of an appeal. A prospect she didn't mention to Mark, for good reason.

Alison too was disquieted by the distorted version she was hearing. She couldn't stop huffing in puzzlement throughout their brief meal.

It didn't get any better with the resumption. Chalden homed in on the evidence of Arthur Gidden like a laser-guided missile. There was no doubt this was the pivotal occurrence in the trial for the austere Judge. He had been convinced by the seedy little man from the ministry. But what had made it persuasive, as he told the jury, was the obvious absence of an expert witness appearing for the Defence to challenge Mr. Gidden's findings. 'They must have been aware that exhibit one was in Mark Stephens' handwriting.' It seemed for several minutes Chalden reiterated his amazement that Mrs. Cullen hadn't called her own forensic scientist to dispute this crucial Prosecution evidence.

Mark's tongue dried. His mouth was dropped open. To make it worse the Judge was insistent that should the jury decide that Mark had written the note to Susan Bennett, his denial must throw doubt on other aspects of his statement. The Defence case was visibly cracking. Chalden was devaluing the truth with his cemented position.

Optimism was in short supply. But there was a glimmer when Chalden pondered whether the incident involving Pauline Green was corroboration or collaboration. The distinction was scrupulously explained.

When Judge Chalden tapped his papers on the desk and announced he had concluded his summing up it was three in the afternoon. Mark was abandoned, dazed. Margaret was furious, and Piers Mallett struggling to suppress a smug grin that he was sharing with Jean Baxter.

Alison, Eric Thomas and the girls waited on the steps of the court-house while Mark was in conference with Robert and Margaret.

'Shit!' Margaret Cullen was shaking with anger, and her vocabulary untypical. 'I don't believe that man. Damn judge didn't give us an inch. Sat on us. Made those bloody girls appear martyrs. Mallett's feeling pleased with himself. Bastard!'

Robert sat clutching his forehead. 'He made a meal over the handwriting. Couldn't have given it higher profile if he tried. That's all it's come down to. It's sickening.'

Mark was nursing a gnawing pain in his stomach and a singing head. 'Doesn't look good, does it?'

No one answered. No one needed to. It was exploding before their eyes.

'If only we could have called an expert witness. To give us something. Everything else was in place. I worked my butt off in there.' Margaret was a hard nut but she wasn't far short of tears.

Mark felt their accusing eyes on him. He owed them an explanation. Come clean. It didn't matter now.

'A confession.' Mark spoke to his lapel.

Margaret and Robert leaned towards him. Almost threatening.

'I... er... I think I did actually write it.' He sank lower, ducking their missile scrutiny.

Robert and Margaret stood to look down on Mark. Their hunting eyes huge and disbelieving.

'What on earth do you mean?' Robert spoke for both of them.

'On the envelope. It's my writing. Not the note inside. I didn't write that. But the envelope. I'm sorry. Can't understand it.' Mark smothered his head with his hands and leaned so far forward he was almost kissing the carpet. He smelled its dust.

'Let me understand this.' Margaret was fighting to get a grip on Mark's revelation. 'You're telling us, now, after all this time, Mark, that you have always known that the envelope was written by you?'

'Well it does look like my writing. That's all I can say. I tried to ignore it. And as you know even tried to alter my handwriting. I was a damn fool. But it really doesn't matter, does it?' Mark's head made denying movements. Dejection was total.

'Yes, you are a fool, a bloody fool. First by hiding this from us, and now by dismissing it as unimportant.' Robert was mad.

'And an idiot for considering defeat!' Margaret was scribbling on her pad. Thinking way ahead of the two men. 'It's too late to do anything here. We can't go back now.' Margaret was thinking out loud. 'But we have to work quickly. If things go against us we need to have something to use at the appeal. This sounds just right.' Margaret made more notes and then left the room. Mark headed for Alison outside as Margaret slid back into the courtroom. She had to study exhibit one in a little more detail. Just like a hound with a fresh scent.

Sent to settle his fate; they filed out hardly daring to look at him. Each juror directed to convict if they were convinced of his guilt beyond all reasonable doubt or acquit if reasonable doubt had been established. Mark tried to read their faces. Sombre, tired faces. Surely they wouldn't, couldn't, think he was guilty. That evil little girl, Susan Bennett, hadn't persuaded these people that he was the monster she had invented, had she? He urged them with his mind and his anxious face, as the single line was sucked through by the swallowing door.

Waiting. There is waiting for a train, waiting at the doctor's surgery and waiting for your wife to get ready to go out. But there's nothing as terrifying as waiting for twelve ordinary citizens to decide your destiny. Every internal organ in Mark's body was strung taut or knotted in contorted agonising twists. He could hardly breathe. Most of the first few hours that the jury were out Mark, Alison and the girls played with cups of coffee in the café and pecked at miserable pastries. There were periods when Robert and Margaret joined them, but only to wash down hurried snacks and then fly off. To the disgust of the whole family George Bennett was huddled in a far corner nursing a drink, accompanied by Jean Baxter. He too had fleeting visits from Piers Mallett sporting a ridiculous smirk, that he swung round to exhibit to Mark whenever he had the opportunity.

An usher came upstairs at midday to inform them that the jury was breaking for lunch. It gave Mark the chance to get outside and nibble at a three-tier sandwich artistically constructed from a medley of salami, lettuce and pliable cheese.

Inside his jacket pocket he fingered the note he had written the previous evening. An emotional letter to Alison. If this went sour there were things he had to tell her. He could always talk to her better on paper. That was his medium, his articulate communication. His anger and his bitterness punctuated the practical and the caring. He had never written such sadness and passion. As Alison collected her coat Mark slipped the envelope into her handbag.

When they arrived back the jury were still out. Mark only had scenes from films or out of novels to feed his imagination. A table would be strewn with exhibits, writing pads at each position, collars loosened, one or two vociferous, others twirling ball-point pens, the indecisive slumped back in their chairs, the assertive prodding the air with agitated fingers, and barking, bombastic voices.

At 2pm Judge Chalden hauled the jury back in. He was testy and not pleased with the lack of progress. The foreman could offer him success on two of the charges, but failure to agree on the others.

'Which of the four charges have you agreed on?' Chalden asked. Disappointment lingering in his impatient demeanour.

'Charges one and two, your honour,' responded the foreman. His first words in open court. The only juror who would speak. A crisp announcement.

'Do you find the defendant, Mark Terence Stephens, guilty or not guilty on charge one?' the court clerk requested.

Mark didn't breathe. His mouth remained gaping. His pulse thumping in his head.

'Not guilty.' Sharp and cleansing from the foreman.

An eraser in Mark's head scrubbed that one out. A hiss announced an intake of air. He breathed out with a puff through his nose. He hadn't touched the girl. Hadn't put his finger into her vagina. All that shit she had tried to sell was seen only too clearly as counterfeit. Stupid, but he needed them to even convince him. After all this time and all the lies he was having difficulty holding on to the truth.

'Do you find the defendant, Mark Terence Stephens, guilty or not guilty on charge two?' the court clerk asked again.

'Not guilty,' came the reply, as lucid as the previous one.

Mark banged the rail with his fist. His face alight. Margaret gleamed. Mallett growled with his eyes and his gritted teeth. Another charge of indecent assault just chalk dust.

Judge Chalden thanked the foreman and sent him back to reach a conclusion on the other two charges, wishing him success and informing him that he would now accept a majority verdict on the remaining issues, eleven to one or ten to two.

Back in the canteen Mark breathed easier. Surely it would be over now. Alison managed a smile and Jayne and Anna had begun talking excitedly. Margaret was in and out snatching slugs of coffee, but Robert stayed longer. He warned Mark that it wasn't over yet, despite the great news so far. Robert was cautious and had seen too many premature parties before.

When Robert did leave them he came back with Margaret and, to Mark's bewilderment, Justin Hinton. Justin gave Mark a huge smile as he was led away to another table equidistant from the two factions. They sat in huddled discussion. An inaudible yet intense deliberation that Margaret was obviously orchestrating and that Justin was enjoying immensely. He was back in the limelight.

'What's going on?' Mark accosted Robert as he skirted their table to reach the coffee counter. 'Why's Justin here again?'

'Just something that Margaret is following up.' Robert was not prepared to say much.

'Like what?' Mark pleaded to know.

'You'll find out soon enough,' Robert assured Mark. 'Now let me get some coffee; and don't worry she's working hard for you. A demon all right.' Mark released his grip on Robert's sleeve and plonked back down onto his plastic chair.

It was nearly four in the afternoon when the jury finally returned to deliver their verdicts on the two remaining charges. Not a paper rustled or a person breathed aloud as they shuffled in. Only the young girl in the front row looked at Mark. But her eyes were heavy and doleful. Dark and apologising eyes. Mark gulped. Surely not?

'Do you find the defendant, Mark Terence Stephens, guilty or not guilty on charge three?' the clerk barked.

The foreman stared only at the paper in his hand. Everyone leaned forward as if to meet the words earlier. Hijack them half across the room.

'Guilty.' His voice was low and defensive this time.

The word rang and banged in Mark's skull, and kicked him in the groin. It slammed into his head again and again. Down an infinite corridor it echoed and swooped with thundering concussion and came back dark and murderous, exploding with a deadly thud.

Mark was left paralysed by the word. *Guilty*. He couldn't move.

Alison clung to her mouth and gasped. The girls' lips trembled and they hunted for their father's face. Desperate to hold him.

'Guilty.' It came again. An assassin's bullet thumped into the body, already dead.

George Bennett slithered out of the courtroom. He was pleased. A smile spread across his face, extending strands of saliva like guy ropes from the corners of his mouth, as he scuttled out into the cold London street. A hunched Dickensian wretch.

Piers Mallett started tidying up. Margaret looked round to take some of the blame. Mark was a statue. The air gushing in and out of his nose. But no one could see the pressure building up. Mark didn't know such rage. An extinct volcano. Hell no, only dormant until now.

Mark's brain heaved, and he catapulted himself to the very limit of the dock rails. 'You don't know what you've done!' All the words wanted to escape together. He had to keep it in some order. 'You cannot possibly believe I have done this! It's a sick joke. It's not real. Tell me it's a bloody nightmare.'

The jury cringed and cowered. There was nowhere to hide.

'The fucking little bitch lied to you. You saw her. I've done nothing. Nothing at all!' Mark parcelled his face in his shuddering hands and fought some leaking tears.

'Mr. Stephens.' For the first time Judge Chalden looked at him. Glared at him. 'That will do.'

Margaret shook her head at Mark, but he had already fallen

back into a seat, and his security guard was towering over him.

The jurors were dismissed and hurried from the scene of betrayal. They felt the guilt now.

'We will recess for thirty minutes Mrs. Cullen. Your client will require a break. I will hear from you and Mr. Mallett after that.' Chalden was going to keep them there until it was over. Not another day. He had a new case to preside over in the morning.

Mark was eased to his feet and accompanied to a room behind the dock. Margaret and Robert followed him there.

Alison, Jayne and Anna were escorted into the corridor by Eric Thomas. He couldn't console them, but he could rescue them from their cruel abandonment in the public gallery. They held each other and sobbed.

'When we go back in there you will get a chance to explain your actions. Let them know what prompted you to do it. Show some remorse. To produce evidence in mitigation.' Robert outlined the next stage in stumbling jumble. He knew he was wasting his time.

'The better news first.' Margaret offered some hope where there was only despair.

Mark looked through his fingers at his barrister. 'What news?' Grasping at threads.

'That damn envelope. You did write it. That's your handwriting all right.' Margaret was motherly.

'How do you know?'

'You wrote between five and ten of them. Must have been the year before last. With a little prompting Justin recalled them. On your desk. A pile within the pile. Apparently you weren't the tidiest of teachers. But there amongst other papers was this stack of brown envelopes that you intended to send out some theatre programmes in. To some kids who couldn't get them on the night. Well, it will take a little more enquiry, but I expect we'll find that the brown envelope that you have feared for so long was one of those, and somehow Susan Bennett took it from there.' Margaret raised her eyebrows and questioned Mark with twinkling eyes. 'Remember?'

Mark tugged at his chin. 'I can't picture them on my desk. They could easily have been swamped by a tide of other papers. It was a shambles. But... I can remember something. Yes. It was *Twelfth Night*. Yes. We went to the theatre. The Roundhouse at Cricklewood. I can remember now; some pupils needing the programmes, and... the envelopes. I wrote them out for the holidays. I never sent them. I didn't send anything to Susan Bennett.' Mark's eyes jabbed at Margaret.

'Listening skills, Mark! I said she most likely took it off the pile on your road accident of a desk.' Margaret wanted him to focus on it.

'What a bloody fool. Fancy not considering that.' Mark arced his head with a broad and despairing sweep and produced a fizzing sigh of disappointment.

'Unfortunately,' Margaret began again, 'it won't help us that much now. When we go back through there,' Margaret pointed to the door that led back to the courtroom, 'Judge Chalden is going to decide your sentence.'

'Can't we ask him to consider this? Get a retrial? Quash the conviction? Let's go in there and tell them.' Mark waved and hailed. But it was a train that had left the station.

'No. We've done all we can in there. The envelope will be the war-head; our missile for the appeal. Until then we keep it under wraps. But what we need to do is to prevent Chalden sending you down. We have to secure bail ahead of the appeal. I will request the need for reports, which should give us four weeks. But there are factors, that Mallett will highlight, that make a custodial sentence a popular option for Mr. Justice Chalden.' Margaret was thinking quickly and trying to determine how Mallett and Chalden would play it. 'Normally you would go in and apologise to your victims and to the court, give an explanation in mitigation, and I would stick a halo above your head and paint you brilliant white. You have no record and are of good character. That's important now. Christ! We had the world in there telling them what an angel you are.'

In no time at all they were called back to the courtroom. There was no jury now. The lawyers were to make the decisions from here on.

'Mr. Mallett?' Judge Chalden prompted.

Mallett held on to his gown and tugged hard. 'There are two important factors that I feel need to be considered, your honour. I will be brief.' A sickly smile was launched towards the bench. 'The sentence must be custodial. Of that there is no doubt. Here was a man in a position of responsibility who seduced a girl of fifteen and performed lewd acts with her and her friend. He abused his status. This was a sexual offence and of such a serious nature that there can be no consideration of anything less than imprisonment. I believe Regina versus Garnett (1989) is a good guide on this.' Mallett had lost his viciousness. With the victory under his belt he was anxious to tidy up these tiresome loose ends. He was willing to co-operate for the sake of a quick conclusion.

'Mr. Stephens, in insisting on a plea of not guilty, forced these two girls to come here and give evidence. A difficult and painful experience. This must be taken into account. If he had saved them this ordeal and been totally honest, they would not have had to endure such a traumatic episode. The court must not forget this when determining sentence.' Mallett lowered himself to his seat. He had nothing else to say. Triumph was his and that was all he needed.

Margaret held the answer. Knew the truth. But it had not been presented to this court, to the jury. She couldn't mention it.

'My client is not going to apologise to the court, excuse his behaviour, beg for forgiveness. There are no mitigating factors. He did not do this, and will not be coerced into changing anything that he has already told you. We have new evidence, which unfortunately comes too late to influence this court, but which will form a substantial foundation for an appeal hearing. He is an innocent man.' Margaret hovered on these words. She wanted them to sit awhile in the dusty-attic heads of Piers

Mallett and Bernard Chalden.

'It is the statutory duty of this court to obtain and consider a pre-sentence report. I ask for an adjournment of four weeks to enable enquiries to be made. In the meantime may I also request my client is released on bail during this period. The court has heard from numerous character witnesses supporting Mr. Stephens, and the prosecution will concur that there are no previous convictions.' Margaret left it there.

Mark wasn't going to give them an inch. He held the truth like a limpet, and no one was going to jemmy him from his resolve.

Judge Chalden craned his neck and screwed his eyes into his half-glasses. 'What is the use of considering a pre-sentence report Mrs. Cullen? Your client denies all knowledge of this crime. Has no remorse. No probation officer or social worker can offer any guidance under these circumstances. I would welcome some help here. How could these agencies assist me in my consideration of a custodial sentence? I accept that Mr. Stephens is a man of exemplary previous behaviour. But he is a man who has given in to temptation. And it only takes the once.' A shaking of the wig and a pointing of the pen emphasised his implication.

'In denying this crime he dragged these young girls to this courtroom. It can be a frightening affair for an adult. But for a child? I cannot excuse this. The two girls bravely gave evidence against Mr. Stephens, and were subjected to a hostile cross-examination by you, Mrs. Cullen. It is unforgivable that his insistence on pleading not guilty put these fragile young ladies through that appalling experience.

'No mitigation, no statement to this court explaining his actions. It is, in my mind, a grave mistake on his part. I am willing to listen. To hear what drove him to it. Perhaps understand the weaknesses of the moment. A mid-life crisis. A middle-age cry for help. But, no, we have nothing. I have nothing.

'Persons in positions of responsibility, as Mr. Stephens was, must bear, however onerous, a greater burden. They are entrusted to care and protect, not use and abuse those in their charge. He took advantage of his role at the school. Massaged what was perhaps a schoolgirl crush for his own perverse satisfaction.'

Chalden stopped to examine papers in front of him. His cheeks were flushed and his finger rapid in its path down the sheet he was studying.

'I am inclined to be guided by Regina versus Seaman (1982) and Regina versus Tozer (1991), Mrs. Cullen. This must be custodial. Had he admitted the offences, saved us the torment of this trial, it may be a different matter. But there is no alternative.' Chalden raised his head. Nodded in short sharp movements at Mark and shook his head at Margaret.

'Eighteen months,' he snapped.

Margaret took a deep breath. 'Leave to appeal, your honour?'

'On what grounds, Mrs. Cullen?' Chalden was stacking his papers. It was a request he failed to appreciate.

'New evidence, as I stated, that has only just reached me, your honour.'

'Tut, tut, Mrs. Cullen. Next time get it neatly packaged. Too much court time has been used up in this case. What is this new evidence?'

'May I approach the bench, your honour?' Margaret entreated.

'If you feel that is necessary, Mrs. Cullen.' There was a stilted formality to the conversation. Chalden knew Margaret was annoyed by his refusal to accept pre-sentence reports and amazed at the arbitrary nature of the sentencing.

Margaret spoke in whispers to the Judge. She informed him of her success in locating the origin of the envelope.

'Pity we didn't hear all this a day ago. I'm not sure I like what's happened here.' Chalden was backtracking, but he couldn't reverse far.

Margaret backed away from the bench. Chalden was bristling. He hated being wrong. There was currency in the new evidence and he knew a great deal he had said and directed would explode in his face at the Court of Appeal.

'Leave granted, Mrs. Cullen.' Reluctantly Chalden allowed it. And left the courtroom an even grumpier man than usual.

Mark could only stare across at Alison's weeping eyes and the scared faces of his daughters as they huddled together, almost in reach, yet miles from his touch. A tap on his shoulder announced his removal from the dock. An apologetic security officer summoned Mark into the back room. Now he was frightened. It hadn't gone to plan. What was to happen now was unknown; not at all in the blueprint he had been given. He sat waiting to be processed. He wasn't conscious of any of the procedure that had clicked in, or his role. In fact he didn't care. His world had been left outside. His family scrambled away to be comforted and protected from all the foul gossip that would filter or smash into their lives. Stolen were his friends and his books, his horizon and his aspirations, his spontaneous humour and his choices. Sat in a barren room cheated of all this.

Robert came in through another door.

'What happens now?' Mark's voice came from deep in his throat. A scared, swallowed little voice.

'They'll probably take you to a London prison to start with and once you've been assessed send you down to a less frightening open establishment near the coast. Maybe Ford, that seems favourite. But what you have to do is to remember that Margaret has more than reasonable grounds for appeal, and she is already planning to get you out in the meantime. Chalden was well out of order sending you down without reports. But I think he's regretting it already.' Robert was trying to buoy him up. The next few hours were going to be tough. He knew that but he wasn't ready to enlighten Mark too much.

Even Mark's stomach was rebelling. There were distant gurgling urges that threatened to explode as heartburn or reverberating belches.

'Your family want to see you. Will you be okay?' Robert

added.

'No. I don't want them to see me in here. I don't ever want them to picture me in here.'

Robert left to explain to Alison and the girls. As he slipped out the guard slid back in, hiding the handcuffs behind his back. Mark looked up into his apologetic eyes. With a nervous shrug of his shoulders he produced them. 'Sorry mate.' Two limp wrists were shackled together. And into those marble hands, now stuck together resembling ones used in prayer, a tear slithered and soaked the corner of the return rail ticket he clutched.

꧁꧂

Marissa Caldwell heard the news that evening. Jean Baxter, excited by the conviction, had phoned all the people involved in the case to offer congratulations for their sterling efforts. The beast had been sent to prison. Another pervert off the streets. Oh! How it pleased the malicious policewoman. She even contemplated having a drink with some of the men from the station after such a rewarding day. That would surprise them.

Marissa was not so euphoric.

Progress in the trial had been fed down to her by Baxter and other members of the social services. In particular details of Susan Bennett's evidence was graphically described. From then on Marissa had been seriously uncomfortable. From day one she had been told categorically that Mark Stephens had committed these acts against two, maybe three, innocent girls. Now she was shielding vital information, gathered during her confidential sessions at the school. What Susan Bennett had confided in her in no way resembled her testimony in court. Marissa couldn't forget Susan's explicit account of how Mark Stephens had, on several occasions, forced himself on her. The vivid picture of him using her body when and how he wanted. A piece of meat ready to be penetrated when the urge came.

Marissa Caldwell hated Mark for what he had done to this young girl; convinced he was an evil abuser.

But now Marissa was forced to re-examine all she had taken as gospel truth, and lay out all she had now and rebuild from there, otherwise she wouldn't have the clarity she needed. Susan Bennett had told the court an entirely different story to the dreadful account she sat back and listened to in Octavia House office. And Pauline had urged Susan to see sense. Mark Stephens had been convicted in the Crown Court of indecent assault following Susan Bennett's allegations. It didn't take too much soul searching to realise that she had to act, and act now.

She wouldn't approach Jean Baxter, or anyone in the department. This was crucial to Mark Stephens and she was well aware of the possibility of someone intercepting her critical evidence. It should be simple to find out Stephens' solicitor and contact him direct. A phone call to Dave Patterson would be her first move.

Chapter 11

He still held on tightly to the useless rail ticket as he was led into the bare, vaulted interior of a white van at the back of the Crown Court building. There were two other men already seated on the long wooden benches. Young men with growling faces and dangerous eyes. They hardly looked at Mark as he climbed in. Too concerned with their own incarceration. Something they had witnessed before by the look of them.

'About fucking time. Been in 'ere fucking two hours.' One of them spoke; tattooed and shaven-headed. He didn't look at Mark, only at his own handcuffed wrists and at the side of the van.

Mark wanted to explain about the delay. Even to apologise. Then thought better of it. This was a different world. One that he would have to learn. It was best to keep a low profile until he understood how to survive it. Now he was well out of his depth and aware a wrong move could lead to a very uncertain future. He would be dumb and stupid for as long as it took.

It was Wandsworth; sinister Victorian from the outside but illuminated in every corner once inside the garden-brick walls. Now he was just part of the herd. Cattle delivered to be interned. The others knew the routine and were quick to scamper out of the van as soon as it halted and the doors flung open. Ready to obey; avoid any confrontation with the screws who closely examined the new intake.

Mark crept out, unsure of what awaited him; not unlike a pit pony taken to the surface after a decade underground. The nature of the crime he had been convicted of was not a secret kept from the master race in charge of the prison, and there was little ceremony in his induction at this penitentiary. Every face bland and dispassionate to all the yobs and fraudsters ahead of him, was lit with knife-edge contempt.

'Stephens 426897.' He was last to be called on a list of eight. Others had come from a variety of courts and were seated in the cutely named Processing Room. It was alphabetical. He was used to being on the end of such exercises.

Thrust into his supporting arms was a selection of clothing that he would need in the prison workshop and around the establishment generally. A swaying pile of second-hand, labelled garments, dark blue cotton and striped shirts that smelled of the damp laundry and the pervading odour of stale farts. That stench was everywhere. It was an aroma close to the reek of the kitchens. Too close to be distinguished at times.

An officer beneath a tightly fitting cap, delegated to interview new prisoners, greeted him with a display of teeth posing as a smile.

'I don't have to tell you that what you're in here for isn't highly regarded by the staff or the run-of-the-mill inmate. We have accommodation for sex offenders under our segregation policy and you could be housed along with our other oddities in this particularly treasured section of the jail.' This screw wasn't keeping it secret how he felt about convicts who had been sent down for fucking about with children. 'I strongly advise you to spend your time with our selection of pretty boys and pædophiles, you'll be safer there. Sure some are wearing dresses and you'll get your arse pinched, but such novelties might be up your street, arsehole!' The prison officer enjoyed his own joke and stamped down forcefully one of his shiny black boots to demonstrate his feelings towards the slime-ball teacher, tottering behind the leaning tower of clothes.

Mark was taking sides already. This man wasn't going to listen to his hard luck story about being convicted of something he had never done. 'Just a cell. It's a short stay. So no big deal, please.' He wasn't going to be intimidated. But he was immediately aware that even a brief period of accommodation was destined to be tough. From inmates and staff alike he was certain he'd run the gauntlet.

'Have it your own way,' smirked the officer. 'Now if you'll stick that pile on the floor, there are a few formalities to go through.'

Mark lowered the uniform and the scratchy towels and endured a series of personal questions about his health and interests, and then was lectured about the rules he had to obey and the routine he would need to follow.

'Governor runs a tight ship. Likes it to go smoothly.' He pushed his open hand forward to demonstrate the uniform progress of life in Wandsworth Prison. 'Gets bloody agitated if there's a problem. Makes your life a fucking misery if you let him down and upset the pleasant balance that he reckons he's achieved. So keep your cell clean and tidy, get to meals on the run, don't arrive late for workshop sessions and look fucking happy whatever you're doing. He likes that. Thrives on his contented lags he does.' He chuckled at his last comment. It was clear that this smarmy young officer thought the governor was a right tosser.

Mark could imagine this cocky warder wanting to kick the shit out of all the prisoners if he was allowed to, and Mark was sure he would be one of the first on this list.

'I'm putting you in with a couple of charmers to start with. Some right likely lads, in for habitual housebreaking. Not exactly their first night like you.' His head quivered as he completed some paperwork on his clipboard, and there was a smile askew on his mischievous face. He knew these men were from a very different tribe to Mark.

By the time Mark was shown his cell the rest of the prison was silent, save for the ripple of purring cat burglars and the heavy snorting of obese armed robbers. His footsteps clanged on the metal stair rungs and echoed through the central auditorium. Only the strategically placed warders observed his progress through the girder interior of the prison to the rabbit hutch cells on the first floor.

Leo Hooper and Danny Legg were asleep when their cellmate was ushered through the heavily riveted door, and could only manage a feeble grumble as Mark shuffled around in the darkness attempting to make as little noise as possible as he made up his bed. Loose springs tinkled as he wrapped a thread-bare sheet round the marshmallow foam mattress. Mark was fastidious about preparing for bed, from cleaning his teeth thoroughly to folding his clothes. Such precise preparation wouldn't last long.

Springs continued to adjust and twang throughout a night that he didn't sleep. Mark listened to the puffing sounds of his fellow inmates and their occasional grunts and episodes of frantic scratching. But occupying him was the escape plan. Not an over the wall or through the tunnel under the stove passage to freedom. No, it was how to explode this ridiculous convic-tion. Now there was the envelope. He had been a fucking idiot and could have pummelled himself for his stupidity. Mark held on tightly to that lifeline. And along with the vivid avenue to liberation was the retribution scenario. Susan Bennett was dead. Murdered in so many gruesome yet pleasurable ways. Accompanying her to a foul slaughter were Pauline Green and half the teaching staff at Thomas Graham School. Mark per-fected his plans all through that long night. Flashing blades, snapping pistol fire and thunderous blasts of highly unstable explosive mixtures. He danced on their treacherous bodies and prodded their dead, plastic frowns.

Normality whacked him hard in the face at six o'clock the next morning. A quacking voice ordered him to get out of his nest and to grab his towel, to move at the double to the freez-ing washroom. To shit, and shave, and shower. And in the frenzy that was the blurred form of scurrying shadows of his cellmates and of others joining from tributaries at the double around him, he did. Not in the order he preferred or at the pace he deserved.

And he followed the same stream tracking the steaming stench of breakfast, and onto flannel-smelling Formica tables where they competed to eat.

A humming cathedral of nodding diners. A school hall feel

except for the caged eaters, separated off from the main scrum, at the far end, near to the serving area. Section 43 prisoners nibbling and peering, nervous at the exposure. Frightened birds. It was the only time they were seen by the other inmates. There were times when hostile elements rained hot tea and offensive desserts in their direction, through the mesh. But mostly they were ignored. Unclean and rejected. Stateless refugees of the system. Contemptible outcasts.

No one on Mark's table spoke until they had wiped the porridge from their lips and stepped back from the heat of their mugs of tea. Till then they had all been unconscious and blind to the scuffling others about them. So, then they looked. Gave the guests at their table the stinging inspection. Mark had arrived at a potpourri of criminal incompetence. A hapless kidnapper, three gloveless house-breakers and a grimy character who had set light to his wife's lifeless body and left his initialled lighter at the scene. They knew each other from months of splattering breakfast. Mark was a new boy and of great interest.

'What you in for?' It was what they all wanted to know. It determined status. Damian Foster had stolen since he was five, been inside, on and off, for twenty-two years. Habitual rather than hardened. 'What you gotta do?' Another factor in deciding rank in this incestuous community.

It was short-sighted not to have thought this through. Mark grappled with some exotic ideas, yet was careful not to alienate the righteous criminal ethos of this establishment. 'TDA.' Mark announced. He had seen a pub theatrical group put on some tosh about prison life and remembered what car theft was called. Perhaps the technical term would convince them.

'What they give you for that? Not your first time, obviously.' Damian was losing interest in the new boy. He had been hoping for a notorious thug, or even a murderer. They were few and far between in the canteen these days.

'Eighteen months.' Mark was able to tell them the truth there.

'Three and a half years, me.' Damian thumped his chest and stuck it out proud, like a strutting partridge.

'Aint nothing,' declared the grinning wife killer. 'Ten for manslaughter, me.' He held his chin in the air. 'Getting rid of the fucking bitch was worth it,' he added with a bursting chuckle. Mark detected something less than stable; volatile. He would keep clear of this individual.

A throbbing buzzer dragged every prisoner upright. A snake of shambling legs delivered trays of spent crockery and it rained cutlery at the exit, where every knife or dangerously jagged fork was accounted for.

'Stephens?' A screw shouted his name as the flood of prisoners left the canteen.

'Yes?' Mark returned the enquiry. Around him mocking laughter greeted his compliance. He was already standing out.

'Deputy Governor's office, now!' It was an order. Mark wasn't used to obeying the demands of doughnuts like that. But he would do many alien things while he was in there.

'Where's that?' Mark cringed at his own greenness, and wished he could sound as hard and as hardened as the rest of the grisly inmates, who appeared to bellow and bark at each other, even in casual conversation.

In the Deputy Governor's office he was seated in an outer room with some of the other recent arrivals. His stomach ached just like it did when he was hauled to hear Tom Pearson admonish him for his poor punctuality. From the mutterings of the men leaving the inner office it was clear that they were being allocated jobs. 'Sweeping up the fucking workshop. Why do I get the shit jobs?' groaned one of passengers from the prison van the previous evening as he loped through the door. Now his tattoo was displayed below the tightly rolled sleeves of his striped shirt. An enormous cross surrounded by entwining roses, faded red. The word *Mum* was clearly visible where Jesus should have hung, and there was other scribbling near the base of the cross. But the main thing was it was a tattoo, it had currency there. You thought twice about crossing a bloke with a real tattoo. Mark half wished he had one. Perhaps something evil, a vicious serpent maybe. That would have warned off a few hardnuts.

Mark was hailed into the office. The Deputy Governor, Clive Wilkins, looked a like a deputy governor of a prison. It seemed even in the street you would have guessed his occupation. Hair shaved to his temples and little left on top to style. Maybe it could be placed in the morning in an attractive position but the slightest breeze would have sent it swaying out and over his ear. His suit wasn't a uniform, and yet it was. Silver grey and striped. And a stiff shirt chaffing his neck where folded skin caught the cutting collar. He didn't speak. On his desk a matrix matching up the complex series of tasks designed to keep prisoners from thinking about their cages and the available manpower, absorbed his thoughts.

'Ah, Stephens.' Clive Wilkins looked over his glasses. 'Do sit. I see that you were a teacher.'

'Were? I am a teacher.' Mark had to hold on to that. No one was going to snatch that from him.

'On the outside you were a teacher. In here you are Prisoner...' He ran his fingers across the page. 'Prisoner 426897 to be exact.' Clive Wilkins enjoyed bringing the pretentious schoolmaster down to earth. 'And I can make your stay as easy as you want it. That is as long as you understand who I am, and who you are not. Do I make myself clear?' Wilkins was a nasty little man with the charisma of a pea. But inside HMP Wandsworth he could be a huge man, and he wanted people like Mark Stephens to understand that. 'Now, it would be wasteful to have you assembling the aerosols that they are doing on the belt in the workshop. What we need to do with you is to second you to the library. Brian Smithson runs it. Excellent fellow. Shame about the missing thousands from the Carnegie Library Funds that he was in charge of.' Wilkins smiled out of the side of his mouth. 'Sorting out the returns, and getting them back on the shelves. Probably that sort of thing. Brian has been waiting for some other brainbox to arrive. We always get a few of you intelligent guys. Always a few to go astray.' Clive Wilkins looked across at Stephens; something resembling a twinkle in his eye. 'Like the young girls, eh?'

Mark wanted to dive over the desk and flatten the horrible git. Fortunately he simply looked straight through the depraved smirk.

'Well, that will keep you out of mischief during the day. And in the evenings I hope you will agree to take some of the lads for English lessons. Keep your hand in, eh?'

Mark liked that idea. 'Okay.' It had been a year since he had taken a class. Admittedly the pupils would be different, but it would be good to get in front of an audience again. Might be an alternative avenue to achieve some prestige.

'Good! I enjoy it when I can source these things with people on the ground. That will save getting someone in from outside. I'll run you along to the library if you wait outside until I finish with the others.' Clive Wilkins was pleased with himself.

Brian Smithson was every bit a librarian. Reading glasses on string, pens in his shirt pocket and a complete disregard for anything other than his beloved books. Even this miserable library was a godsend to him. He wasn't fat but his body had sort of slumped, so that most of his torso seemed to be crammed into his trousers and was slowly creeping into his podgy legs. If he hadn't taken a liking to using expensive prostitutes and delved into the library funds to support his hobby he would still have been rummaging through some weighty tomes in an elegant provincial library.

Clive Wilkins stood between Brian perched on the second rung of a step-ladder and some shelves. It was the only way to distract him. 'I've someone to give you a hand, Brian.'

Brian grunted. 'Not another airhead who doesn't know a Dickens' novel from a comic. They're no help to me.' Brian tried to extend an arm around the Deputy Governor to reach the bookshelf. He never looked Clive Wilkins in the eye.

Wilkins grabbed the librarian's lunging hand. 'No Brian.

This time I have got you somebody useful. An English teacher. Very well qualified. He'll be a great assistant. And he will take some lessons during the education period. Probably promote the library then. How about that?'

Brian pulled back his hand and searched for Mark's. 'Hello there. Brian Smithson at your service. Welcome aboard.' It was refreshing to have someone with intellect alongside him. There was a suffocating loneliness, even in a crowded prison, without erudite repartee.

Mark introduced himself. Clive Wilkins departed, hailed by his beeping pager. 'Some decent books, I see.' Mark tried to break the ice.

'Not as many as I would like,' bemoaned Brian. 'Still it's something to build on.'

For the rest of the day, except for a brief lunch break, Mark obeyed Brian's instructions. He stacked and he classified. He dusted and he labelled. He read some pages, and best of all, he smuggled, for his own enjoyment, a few classics that he always promised himself he would read again.

When he returned to his cell his fellow lodgers were changing out of greasy overalls. He hadn't really met them. He'd heard their sleeping noises and caught their shadows as they escaped to breakfast. Now he was face to face with them. They looked him up and down. Assessing the new face. Like a dog sniffing another's arse, unsure if he was friend or foe.

'The name's Leo, and this is Danny.' Stripped down to his underpants Leo swaggered around the bunk bed. Again there was a plethora of tattoos. Both men had them. Villains in their twenties or early thirties. Solidly built and street-hardened.

'Mark,' he clumsily announced, and held out a hand. Neither attempted to shake it. It wasn't what they did.

'So you've got a cushy number in the library, Mark?' Danny emphasised his name. 'Us blockheads are stuck in the fucking workshop. No comfy little job for us.' A general complaint, but no envy and very little animosity.

'Not many rules in here, Mark, except territory, if you get

my drift. You know where yer bed is, but you may not understand the layout of the sitting-room, so to speak.' Leo made a circular movement with his hand to demonstrate the area of the cell not covered by the bunk bed and the small cot. 'That chair is mine. Danny has the stool. You'll have to do with squatting on the bottom bunk.

'And this is my picture gallery. Nice, eh?' Leo smiled at the haphazard array of pin-ups that smiled back at him. Danny's are those over there. And this bit of wall, sorry about the size, is yours.' To the left of a distorting mirror was a small flaky patch littered with flapping Sellotape that had obviously been used previously for display purposes.

Mark panicked. He hadn't anything to paste up. It was essential he conformed to this practice. Be one of the lads.

Leo detected Mark's discomfort. 'Get 'em from the papers and some mags the visitors bring in. You'll soon get a collection.' As a gesture he pulled a loosely adhered blond with enormous tits from his gallery and handed her to Mark. 'Here, this will do for a start.'

'Thanks.' Nothing remarkable, but it meant a lot. Mark was warming to the half-naked man.

'TDA, eh? What's a teacher doing nicking cars?' All the decoy information had reached Danny already.

Mark tried to duck it. 'We're talking expensive motors, and in great numbers. It was international.' He wanted to make it sound like a massive criminal operation.

'What, Rollers and the like?' Leo enquired.

'Yeah, and Mercs and Italian sports.' Mark did his best to sound like the mastermind, or at least more than just a dodgy dealer.

'I'd like one of them Maserati's they're...' Danny was stopped short by the sound of the meal buzzer. Almost instantly a near stampede was initiated on the landing outside.

Mark had smelled the lamb casserole all afternoon. The sweet stench of boiled mutton gravitated from the kitchens and permeated every corner of the old part of the prison. Dinner had announced its appearance later that evening by the sickly smell drifting through the many open doors on all landings.

It was an orderly queue of hungry criminals. Trays held out level in front with a plate ready to be filled, alongside a large stone mug awaiting the same fate. For some inmates it was their only chance to catch up with news from other areas of the prison. In particular those with inside knowledge or those who had welded a close relationship with one of the screws. A low hum of secrets shared and information broadcast stuck like clinging poison air to the curving line. Unlike the rowdy banter spilling from the scrummage tables. Once the meal had been collected and recognised groups had rendez-voused, there was a frantic exchange of harmless gossip. And when all were seated the dining area was an insane zoo. The only time that Mark felt the power of a mob. In other circumstances poised for revolution. Dark and threatening insurrection.

Any hope that the lamb would taste better than it smelled was quickly dispelled when Mark took his first mouthful. It was an awful sludge of sticky sauce that held it paste-like, the meat in suspension, and every scrap of vegetable cooked pale and mushy. He managed two spoonfuls and gave up. His plate was snatched by Leo, who had, along with Danny and some pals, joined the new boy on a table on the periphery, away from the hub. It would take some time for Mark to acquire the taste for prison food. He sat upright watching the stooping shoulders engineering scooping thrusts, and listening to the slurping swallow of the others at the table. You soon learned to eat anything and everything in this prison.

Cutlery was beginning to scratch at the last coating of sauce and plates were being tilted to suck what remained. It had been a good meal by usual standards. Mark dreaded what would be served up the next day. Quite abruptly there was a pause and prisoners eager to pursue the final dribble were held poised but inert; their eyes on a beefy character sat in the very middle of the paralysed dining area. Mark was baffled by the sudden calm.

'What's wrong?' he whispered to Danny.

Danny replied with a quiver of his head and buttoned lips. No one spoke or moved for a couple of minutes. As swiftly as it had begun the silence ended. But even the coagulating gel on the plates was scoffed according to the diners' original plans.

'What was that all about?' quizzed Mark again.

'A warning. Someone's been targeted. Bruce Martin, the big fucker with the shiny head, runs the place. He aint 'appy with a fellow in here. We'll soon learn more. It 'appens now and again. You know, some slimeball messing about with kids or a pensioner mugged by some druggy. Bruce runs a clean ship. A good honest burglar or even a heavy duty merchant who's done someone in; they're favourites. But 'e can't stand them perverts.' Leo explained to Mark's moon face.

The Governor heard about the silence session at dinner and made sure there was no socialising after classes in the evening. He could sense trouble and was determined to prevent it in his establishment. Mark read on his own while Leo and Danny went to art classes, where they played cards for cigarettes. And on their return there was only a matter of minutes before lights out.

Mark was uneasy about the business at dinner and hoped it had nothing to do with him. The TDA story was weak. But was it falling apart already? There was a lot of chatter in the darkness. And many more questions. Were they grilling him?

Mark lay awake for several hours replaying the last year, and fathoming out how to play it from now on. He stayed alert through Leo's furtive wanking and Danny's ranting in his sleep.

And in the grey light he choked on mental pictures of Alison and the girls at home, of his mother fussing round her tiny flat filled with photographic memories and his brother babbling about his beautiful Jesus with such energy and faith. He wanted them to snatch him up and take him with them. The darkness and the images conspired to embellish his loneliness.

Uncomfortably early Mark sat down to breakfast with

Damian, Danny, Leo and the wife killer. It wasn't a meal where discussion was high on the agenda. The table they occupied was nearer to the centre of the canteen. A conspicuous site. Bruce Martin was holding court not far away. Mark couldn't hear him, but he spoke with skulking actions to two of the warders, waving his heavy forearms with their blue and crimson tattoos. They reciprocated with shrugging shoulders and apologetic hands. And as Mark watched he saw Martin nod towards his table. He froze. Danny collected his half-eaten breakfast and scurried to another table, like a sinking man dashing for a life raft. Further nods and aiming glares saw the rest of the table tottering off to a refuge with their swaying trays. Mark looked at his food and ate, and when he drank he watched the horizon of his coffee and nothing else. Although he didn't look around he knew what he would have seen. Every face was turned towards him and every eye burrowed into his head. And in the eerie silence, that replicated that of the previous evening, a lone tormentor tapped a teaspoon. A frightening slow rapping to torture him. A sad and abandoned leper, and dreadfully alone. Soon every diner picked up the rhythm. Like the stroke-drummer on a Roman galley, the initiator beat faster. And then louder. Mark ate. Chewing his food aggressively for his audience. He was petrified, but he wouldn't show it. An unbearable fanfare smashed at his head. Mark drank through gritted teeth. The symphony played on.

Then nothing. A wave of a conducting hand halted the din. Prisoners talked at their tables and trays were carried to be emptied. And the focused, drilling eyes turned elsewhere. Mark didn't exist. At his table, still shipwrecked, he dared to breathe, dared to look around at all those who had set their sights, made him their target. He hadn't stolen cars. They knew that now. Knew why he was inside. Mark swallowed as shallowly as he could.

Nobody spoke to him. Even Brian only gave him tedious tasks in the library. He was desperate to talk, but knew the consequences. Mark was not given further attention at the

remaining meals that day. But he ate alone. And in the cell
Danny and Leo spoke about him but not to him. They talked of
liars who tried to sell them a camouflage story about stealing
motors, and how you didn't lie to cellmates, about an unwrit-
ten code that all rated criminals observed and how there was
always one fucker who tried it on, some fucker who needed to
cover his tracks, who needed to paint his shit white.

Mark had never felt so vulnerable.

'Right. Now, you'll have to take your class in here.' Clive
Wilkins pushed open the door of a small square room, the
walls barely twenty feet long. A table and chair at one end
indicated where the teacher ought to stand, and some randomly distributed chairs where the students should sit. 'I've selected
twelve lads for you to take. Some have an interest and others
are bloody dim; almost illiterate a few. Do what you can.' He
was almost encouraging.

Mark felt like shit. He couldn't believe he would get
through a lesson with the obvious animosity towards him. But
he wasn't going to bleat to Wilkins. They'd crucify him on the
spot.

Mark stood behind the table and watched his class shuffle
in. A few looked at his face. Most preferred to watch their own
dragging feet.

'Welcome.' It was a futile attempt to turn them around.
Canute against the North Sea. 'I'm Mark Stephens. An inmate
like you. Going to do some English of sorts.' There was a sneer
on every face. Mark bounced on. 'For some reason I've become
public enemy number one. I can't do much about that. Only
ask you not to judge me on what you've been told. That isn't
me.' He wasn't denting their armour. Sultry and silent they listened. To his voice, but not his words. Mark sighed. 'Let's get
on then.' None of them had a pen or paper. Clive Wilkins had
left without leaving anything, and the warder outside the door
merely shrugged off his enquiry with a lost and unhelpful face.

'Nothing to write on, or with. So let's talk. English is a lot
of talking at times. It's something you normally love to do, I'm

sure. Except now, in here, with me.' Mark begged them with his body language to melt, but they had him fixed in their glare. His words were meeting solidly erected barriers. Barricades he couldn't break down. 'What do you lot read, other than The Sun?' Not a flicker. He wanted to break the ice. Some humour. 'Now I've been told that some of you are quite proficient in the language, read widely, and, I was told, were looking forward to these sessions.' Mark leaned against the table. A relaxed pose, but he was far from composed. 'And others need a little help; didn't spend enough time in lessons when they were at school. Don't blame you really, they can be pretty boring.' Mark smiled.

They didn't.

As if on cue a voice from the back struck up. Nobody flinched with surprise, or turned to wonder who dared break the silence. A set-up. 'So, you were a teacher outside, that right?' A cold and deliberate enquiry.

Mark welcomed the sound of someone else speaking, but he didn't welcome the question. 'Yes. I am qualified, if that's what you want to know.' Mark turned it his way. But not for long.

'Taught children didn't you?' The man was talking from a sunken, slouched position, with his feet spread so far forward that they extended way under the chair in front of him, and his head rested on the hard back of his own chair.

Mark identified the path that the questioner was taking. There was no way he could deflect it, but he tried. 'I did. But that doesn't mean I can't help you.'

'How old were these kids that you taught?' No change in tone or intimation.

'They ranged from eleven year olds in Year Seven to sixteen year olds in Year Eleven.' Mark needed to exhibit some professionalism.

'Mixed school was it? Boys and girls like?' The laser-guided rocket was homing in.

'Yes, it was a mixed Grant Maintained school. Probably similar to the one you went to, except it had boarders as well.'

'Boarders eh? Slept there did they? That was handy wasn't it?' A few faces recognised the corner Mark was in and smirked.

'Enjoyed teaching the girls, eh? With their sexy uniforms eh?'

'Not really.' Mark was tightly fixed in the confines of the trap.

'Couldn't leave them alone could you? Interfered with them we hear.' It was a threatening voice now.

'You hear wrong.' Mark shook his head, gritted his teeth. Any denial was useless, but he wasn't going to let them think he was ready to admit guilt.

'What you in here for then, teacher? Don't reckon it's for nicking exercise books, eh?' Some chuckles now.

'Listen to me. I know it sounds old-hat and everyone claims it, but I did not do it. The girl made it up. It's an awfully long story. You have got to believe me.' Mark hated crawling, but he was in the lions' lair.

'I didn't do it.' The questioner parodied Mark to the amusement of the class.

'Course you fucking did. Fucked about with a young girl. We don't like arseholes that do that. Do you understand, teacher? And we don't want arseholes like you trying to tell us what to do. So fuck your lessons.' His inquisitor lifted his chair and banged it against the wooden floor. This was immediately followed by the rest of the room. A sound of thunder that shook the building.

Mark held his hands to his ears and shut his eyes. He was going through hell.

Alerted in the hallway outside, the somnolent warder rushed at the door. When it was flung open every chair had landed and stayed. And another decoy was in the middle of asking what appeared to be an intelligent question. It was incredible timing, and a move that had obviously been used more than once. Dazed and perplexed the screw surveyed the class and the distraught teacher. 'Cut it out, or you go back and get locked in. Okay?' He was a dim, lard of a man so easily manipulated by the organised force of the prison network. Each inmate nodded and smiled. He couldn't touch them. He managed a tough stare and a warning grimace and he was gone. Back to a small-screen television and some peace and quiet.

An icy and menacing silence remained. There wouldn't be a lesson. Mark Stephens had nothing to teach them and they were forbidden to share his knowledge. To them he was the fucking pervert who had assaulted young girls. He was shit, unspeakable scum.

So no one sat with him and no one dared speak to him, and he was forced to inhabit a vacuum world. Persona non grata; lonely and tainted.

There were visits. Alison and the girls came as soon as they were allowed. They were bubbling with the news of the fresh evidence and the optimism that Robert was sowing. Despite the setting Mark was relieved to simply talk. But he tried not to cry. He spent a long time fighting his tears in front of Alison. When they touched it was public; watched closely by the prison officers overseeing the family visits. At the other tables set equidistant apart the squabbling children were made to look over at Mark, and the scowling prisoner husbands whispered to warn their washed-out wives of the pædophile in their midst. And in turn their faces condemned him. They looked at Alison and the girls and tutted their sympathy.

'How are they treating you?' Alison was unsure what would sound best. It was a beginning.

'I'm coping. They know why I'm in here. I tried to lie about it but they found out. There are ways. I suppose I am still learning the ropes. Perhaps I can convince them of my innocence.' He spoke erratically, attempting to keep Alison from worrying. He knew there was little chance of changing their perception of him. Public enemy number one.

'What's the food like?' Anna enquired naïvely, as if he was in hospital.

'Breakfast isn't too bad, but it's the dinner that is worst. It seems to taste the same every day, despite being supposedly different. I think it sits in the same sort of gel, a standard background that boiled-out meat languishes in, devoid of its own flavour. But worst of all your wind smells exactly the same as the food being prepared. And everyone farts, all the time.'

'Can we bring you something in?' Jayne asked; desperate to help her father endure his stay.

'A few goodies are allowed, but you don't have to bother. Hopefully I will be hauled out of this place soon. What's the latest from Robert?' Mark searched Alison's face for a positive response.

'He phoned last evening. Knew we were coming to see you. He expects to get here tomorrow. Margaret is apparently making a request for your release pending the appeal. And she's hopeful.' Alison's countenance sparkled. 'Something about some amazing new lead from a woman in social services who contacted Dave Patterson initially and then telephoned him. Name of Caldwell. Apparently she has important information.'

'Caldwell? Never heard of her.' Mark strained hard. He often forgot people's names.

'Sounds promising doesn't it Dad?' Jayne was enthusiastic. She touched her father's cheek with the back of her hand. He held it and squeezed.

'If only I could go home with you lot.' Mark sighed.

Alison felt for his hand. 'We'll smuggle you out in my bag.' She smiled an *if only* smile.

'Everything all right at home, Alison? People been asking how I am? Any problems?'

There had been a bawl across the street in the village, about four phone callers who withheld their numbers and shouted obscenities, several embarrassing encounters with friends who just didn't know what to say and an ominous silence from those who should have contacted her. But she wouldn't tell him. All he needed to know was that things were normal, extremely normal.

'No, we're managing fine. Don't you worry. Now, tell us about what happens in here.' Any question would do to stifle Mark's concern. Alison had to protect him.

'I'm in the library, as you might have guessed. There's a chap running it, in for fiddling the accounts where he worked. Odd bod but harmless. And also I have the honour of taking a class in the evenings. I've taken one so far. It was a bloody disaster. They didn't want to learn.'

'You're a good teacher, surely you can make a success there. You'll win them over. It will take your mind off things.' Alison encouraged him. 'Remember you're going back to work; soon. Once this is all over Charles Cornwall has said the Union will thump the school at the Industrial Tribunal. This will be just a bad dream, quicker than you might think now.'

'I hope so.' Mark was feeling a little better. The hateful eyes around the room were leaving him alone. They were huddled and protective. It was back home at the breakfast room table. A family time.

His dream was shattered by a droning bell that signalled the end of visiting. Screeching chairs and the flap of coats filled the insipid room. Boisterous farewells echoed. Mark held on to Alison for a long time. He needed to show those scowling faces that this was him. Not what they were being told to believe about him. Anna and Jayne held both their parents as if adding an extra bond. No eye was dry. Waving groups watched the entwined bundle of people as they meandered through the tables to the door.

Mark only let go when most of them had gone. And only moved when Alison and the girls had disappeared through the double doors. Then he had to line up with those who despised him. No prisoner left the visiting room without a body search. Too much contraband entered Wandsworth that way. Second only to the stores brought in by bent screws.

Danny and Leo were persisting with the silent treatment back in the cell. The pin-up that Mark had been given was back on Leo's section of the wall. He expected his was now bare. Not so. In his absence they had been busy. The flaky patch of wall was now covered in a collage of photographs from mail order catalogues and other magazines. A wall full of young children. He got the message. Mark's stomach hardened. He didn't say the things that were bursting to escape. Just threw himself on his bed and sobbed silently until he slept.

Robert Manning could visit at any time with permission from the Governor. So when Mark was hailed from the library the following morning he wasn't surprised to be met by his solicitor. Alison had prepared him for the meeting.

Robert was cheerful. It was his rule. You mustn't let them see you at all uncertain and apprehensive. 'How are you?' The usual question.

Mark could have screamed. He was far from all right. The plan was to lie low, be swallowed up by the prison, not stand out, blend in. But now he was a loud siren and a flashing red light. There was no one who didn't know him or the crime he had been convicted of. 'No, Robert. They've been told. Everyone knows what I'm in here for. All fingers point at me. A diseased carbuncle infecting their precious, criminal world.'

'They were bound to find out. You can't keep it quiet. Prison officers are told. It only takes one to blab. They enjoy that. Stirring things up. And, of course, there were the papers. You obviously didn't see them. The conviction was in most of the tabloids and the heavies. Not headlines or front page, but enough for people with nothing better to do to observe.

'It's a deliberate ploy to divert attention. Making one of the inmates the target rather than the prison or the system.' Robert was blunt. 'Were you offered segregation?'

'Yes, but I am not giving in to these animals. I am innocent. They'll learn that. I'm determined.'

'Now, take it easy. That's a tall order. There's no need to be a bloody martyr. Make it simple. Move in with those undesirables. Curl up and hibernate for the time being. It won't be for long. You don't need this trauma. Personally I'd be in there tomorrow. There are some real maniacs in this place.'

'I won't let them win. I can't.'

Robert gripped his lips together and shook his head. 'Have it your own way, but do tread carefully.' He pulled out some papers from his briefcase and spread them in front of him. 'This is a copy of Margaret's submission to the court. I can't leave it with you in here. So read it after I précis it for you. She is applying for your immediate release at a hearing next week. We have discovered other envelopes bearing your writing and intended for pupils, just like the one used by Susan Bennett, and we have at least three pupils who remember you preparing them or seeing them on your desk. The jury convicted you because they believed the expert witness, and combined with your denial concluded that they could not take your word for the incident supported by Pauline Green.

'Henry Brolin has taken another look at the writing on the envelope and that on the note and is strongly of the opinion that they were written by different people. It's there, Mark. All you need. Margaret is confident. She says they must free you without delay. Plus a surprising piece of fresh evidence has been offered by a counsellor with the social services. A Marissa Caldwell spoke to me about a meeting she had with Susan Bennett last year. She was providing support for your supposed victims and interviewed all the girls back in June I think. Seeing how she could help. You get the picture? Well it appears what Susan Bennett told this Caldwell woman was nothing like the statement she made to the police. Totally different. All kinds of sexual violations were committed by you in the account she gave this counsellor. But now she has heard the evidence that Bennett gave the court she has come forward, and is ready to testify on your behalf. To expose the discrepancies. Brilliant isn't it?' Excitement lit Robert's eyes.

It was infectious. Mark grabbed Robert's forearms across the table and shook them. He showed his teeth and grinned. Thrilled at the news.

'Now read the details and let me know if there's anything missing or there are any other stones we haven't looked under.'

Mark studied the papers for approximately twenty minutes, occasionally looking up at Robert but not speaking. It was a sound document. The team had done well. They had kept faith. So many had kept faith. Mark paused to think of the list. For once he was looking to praise and not condemn. Susan Bennett and the ostriches at the school weren't being mutilated now. 'It's good. I wouldn't have the audacity to tell you your job. And, really, I can't add to it. Thank Margaret for me.' Mark wanted to read it again and again. Keep Robert there. Keep talking about success and release, of freedom and innocence. The longer he stayed the less time Mark had to face the hatred.

'I'll talk to you soon. We should have the exact date by the end of the week. Remember what I said. Play it safe. Don't be so damn proud. I'm concerned about your safety in here. We are so near, Mark.' Robert was almost emotional. Pleading for common sense from a client wasn't his style. Usually he was detached; not unconcerned but not woven into the drama like now. He was more involved than he had ever been in previous cases.

Mark's English class that evening was empty. He waited for the menacing faces. They didn't arrive. Other classes were boisterous along the hallway, but his was silent. Not the silence of the previous lesson, the threatening silence of brooding resentment. It was the silence of an empty stadium holding a postponed concert.

Clive Wilkins strode in and broke it. 'Ah! Stephens. I'm afraid this isn't going to work. Our little community appears unhappy with your CV. Don't like child molesters you see. Disappointing isn't it? You with all those qualifications and no one wanting to benefit from your wisdom.' Wilkins was enjoying breaking the news. 'I have tried to persuade them. He's paying his debt to society. Just a one off mistake. Try and understand the temptations. A human weakness. But no, they insist you aren't going to get their custom. So your teaching stint is cancelled until further notice. And to make it even more untidy I can't offer you a place in any of the other classes to keep your mind off your unpopularity. Boys won't attend them if you're in there. Back to the cell I'm afraid.' Wilkins gesticulated with shooing hands. 'Silverman, escort Mr. Stephens back to his accommodation, will you.'

He waited on his bed until Danny and Leo arrived back from their class. Nothing had changed. There was further reference to abusing children and how good Mark's gallery was looking. It was a sinister mixture of sarcasm and contempt. All directed before and beyond Mark. He was the invisible germ that they wished to cleanse.

Mark heeded Robert's warning and locked himself in the same soundproof protection that had been administered to him. A reciprocation of Coventry with Coventry. A cocoon of silence. There was some safety for him there.

Leo and Danny spat him goodnight and then left him alone.

Morning sent them all scurrying to the washroom. Clouds of condensation filled the cool shower room like a thickening fog. It was a jungle of bodies frothing beneath the pelting water. Mark found a corner away from the bulk of the bathers, cloudy and anonymous. Prison soap came in bricks and stunk of toilet cleanser. Mark scraped it round his body hoping to conjure up some lather before rinsing it out of the clinging hair under his arms. Spray from the shower head plunged down in distinctly separate streams as he turned his face up at it. He watched them like steel rods smacking into his face. If only he could purge the hate with the same gushing flow.

With his head under the surging water he heard nothing else except the thundering of his waterfall. The steamy atmosphere also camouflaged the activity around him. When he came out from the spilling water he was alone. All the other naked bodies had slid out of the shower room. They had deserted him. In the distance, some two sections or so away it seemed, there was a violent argument taking place. Whistles were blown to alert other guards to what appeared to be an altercation of some sort. Mark dried his hair and then rubbed at an extended leg, and he listened.

A voice close by alerted him.

'Stephens isn't it?' A gruff and dangerous voice. 'Child molester I believe?' Bruce Martin's thick, bullet head came through the mist. He wasn't unaccompanied. Four of the ugliest brutes in the prison were at his side. Naked, Mark felt more than just insecure. He bent forward and held the towel to cover his genitals and simply peered at the gang of men in disbelief. Frozen in fear. A petrified mouse caught in a clearing by a swooping owl. 'We don't approve of you fucking perverts in 'ere mate. Do you fucking understand? And what we do to them is what you are about to find out. We fucking 'alf kill 'em.'

Martin hammered Mark's left cheek with a swinging punch that splintered two teeth, and sent him sprawling to the ground. He pushed up on an elbow, but was immediately met by Martin's arcing arm again. A blow to Mark's temple that laid him out in the suds and swirling water of the draining floor. What appeared to be an assisting hand pulled him upright. But it was only to reinstate the target. Two more crunching thumps thrust Mark's head backwards and into the brick wall. His skull cracked audibly as it thudded against the resistant brickwork.

Mark didn't have time to explain; to tell these creatures their mistake. Then one doesn't tell a charging rhino the error of his ways to prevent mindless violence in the Savannah. These animals didn't speak either. Savagery was the only language they knew.

And as Mark's unconscious body slid down the slimy wall it was met by the lashing feet of all five men. They jabbed and stamped. Every pound of their weight was behind the vicious impact, kicking all the air from his lungs and turning his creamy flesh an angry red.

He was left with blood dribbling from the corner of bloated lips, eyes closed and purple and the fresh bruises turning a maturing shade of violet. He gargled a cry for help as the last drips from his shower splashed cynically on his grotesque face.

'Christ Almighty!' exclaimed the bumbling prison officer when he found missing Prisoner 426897. He scooped up Mark's head which had nearly turned over, face down into the shallow pool of scummy water. He held it, yelling. A posse of warders came skating through the slurping flood of the shower room and, stalling for a moment at the sight of Mark's flaccid body, hurried to bundle up the twisted carcass. They had seen the same battered head, plum-coloured bruising and bleached skin on too many victims, some of whom never fully recovered. Someone was going to get done for not preventing it. They weren't that concerned about Mark Stephens. There were their own hides to consider.

'Who the fuck was on shower duty?' Shouted out a senior officer directing proceedings.

'Robbie and Tugs; it's their day.' A treacherous voice announced. Ready to clear his name.

'Dealing with that row in the bogs, weren't they?' An officer hanging on to Mark's feet suggested.

'Why is it we fall for that trick every fucking time?' The senior officer was frustrated.

'It was Martin I bet, and there was more than just that argument in the toilets to persuade them to ignore the rest of the prisoners.' A young officer nursing Mark's head said what so many of them were afraid to acknowledge.

'Shut it! Robbie and Tugs don't do favours. You're out of order, mate.' An old hand slapped the newcomer's wrists.

Not much of the wrapped towel remained in position when they arrived at the prison hospital with Mark's elastic body. He was not in a position to care. Doctor Pradeep Bandari expelled the air in his lungs in exasperation. Another prisoner beaten senseless. Another body to rebuild. His lancing eyes sought every warder in turn. A look that condemned them for their inexcusable lapses or blind eyes.

'In there!' Pradeep ordered.

The slinking men dropped Mark onto a trolley in a curtained-off cubicle, then scarpered smartly, save for the senior man whose duty it was to provide background to the injuries received by the inmate and to complete the necessary paperwork.

As he worked Pradeep lectured. 'I am sick and tired of treating victims of vicious assaults in this damn prison. It isn't necessary. Come on, we all know that brute Martin runs the place. When is the Governor going to have the bottle to sort him out? Smacks of the nineteenth century. This isn't bloody Newgate, bloody prison! Hold that swab there will you.' Doctor Bandari was fed up with trying to mend broken limbs, relocate off-set jaws, place black, grapefruit-sized testicles on surgical cushions, sew up scalps and reduce dislocated joints.

Mark moaned and jerked. Pradeep sprung at a hypodermic and sent him crashing into a hurtling slumber.

Three hours later Pradeep peeled off his gossamer gloves and tipped them into a dish along with blood-covered gauze and off-cuts of bandages. A competent radiologist imported from nearby Roehampton Hospital confirmed there were no broken bones, except for a hairline crack to the skull. Doctor Bandari was relying on a great deal of instinct and a morsel of medical intuition with regard to internal injuries and hæmatomas. Time would tell; he was sure. Mark Stephens had avoided some of the fatal wounds inflicted on several of his former patients, but only fistfuls of painkillers would prevent him writhing in pain when he regained consciousness.

Chapter 12

Mark's face was stuck to the pillow when he woke. Congealed blood and saliva glued his mouth to the cotton bedding. Even so he found it difficult to move his leaden head; only his blinkered eyes followed the contraptions that were posted round his bed. Dangling plastic packs of transparent fluid and some flickering monitors attached by tangled wires. A full bladder nagged. A cumbersome body that felt as if it had been crudely forged out of wrought iron kept the right hand side of Mark's face breathing into the starched sheets. He was sore. Every violent blow had left its memory; as a deepening colour and a Braille-examined tenderness.

'How are we feeling this morning? I'm sorry, a silly question. You look like shit and I bet you feel like it.' Pradeep Bandari bounced into the room, cheered by a rest and no queue of other half-murdered inmates.

Mark tried to reply. Only snorts and groans gurgled from his bloated, crusty lips.

'Take it easy. You don't have to talk. I have a bad habit of chatting to all my patients. One-sided conversations. Even with the ones in coma, and dare I say it, ones that are dead, on occasions.'

Pradeep pulled open a drooping eyelid and uncovered an area of bruising around Mark's abdomen. 'Well the good news is, you haven't really broken anything, or should I say *they* haven't broken anything, and there doesn't appear to be internal damage, otherwise you would have probably croaked in the night. There's a fracture at the back of your skull but it isn't too much to worry about. All in all you came out of it lucky.' Pradeep nearly went anecdotal and described the fatalities and brain damage cases that had been in the same bed. Fortunately he was aware of Mark's consciousness otherwise he would have willingly given an unsuspecting body a gruesome account of his battles to save lives after a prison beating. 'Should be able to shift you to an open ward tomorrow, as long as you keep down the meal this evening and have a dump in the morning.'

Mark could have told him that the latter was more on the cards than the former, even without the injuries. He tried again to communicate. This time the words that slipped through the strands of saliva came out in a muffled but recognisable form. As a deaf person speaks. 'Make sure they don't tread on me in the night.' Mark was still in danger in the prison hospital and he wanted to make certain this crazy doctor was alert to the perils he faced.

'Good. The breath is rancid but the sense, clear and relevant.' Pradeep Bandari's face was level with the straining utterance coming from the squashed mouth and the desperate eyes. 'I'll keep you somewhere safe.' Pradeep left the room. There was only one path to follow. Mark couldn't be allowed back into the mainstream of the prison.

The trolley that trundled Mark out of the intensive observation unit and along the uneven corridor to a small side ward in the main hospital building took him to a refuge. One he wouldn't like but that he would reluctantly accept. Even here there was the torpedo mesh to separate sexual offenders from the heavyweight criminals. Mark was one of three patients whose nursing included extra security measures to keep them from the violent backlash that their crimes attracted. Even the orderlies were separately recruited.

Within a couple of days the crippling pain in Mark's chest and at the base of his spine became annoying dull pangs, and even the torturing headaches were bearable with robust painkillers. His face had returned to approximately original proportions.

Alison was allowed a visit. She came with Robert. It was both business and nearly pleasure. She kissed his forehead and gripped his shoulder. Robert shook his hand with a *we are almost there* double grasp. There were questions about the attack, and words to tuck him in with and stroke his confidence. It was how Margaret wanted it. Mark needed to be on form for his appearance in court. Sure the bruises actually helped, but if he was a dejected specimen it wouldn't assist the process. An innocent man required an energy the judges related to, a vigour that they recognised. Lame and grieving appellants prospered badly.

'I did say.' Robert approached it as delicately as he could. 'It's a jungle in here. You should have taken my advice. Now look at you.'

'Not an improvement. I can vouch for that,' added Alison. 'Do you know, Robert, this man was so handsome when we first met. I worshipped the ground he walked on. Would have done anything for him.'

'You saying I'm ugly now?' Mark enquired, with only the hint of a lisp.

'No, darling, I just wanted to say what a shame it is that your beautiful face has had to be battered so.' Alison smiled. She was sad to see him puffed and beaten, but happy that from now on he would be away from those who perpetrated the crime. Happy Robert was there to bolster him further. She was convinced that the appeal would be successful. And when they spoke closely as Robert waited discreetly at the door she whispered gushing enthusiasm in his blood-clot ear and into the scythed patches in his hair.

Mark stayed in the safety of his hospital bed for two more days. His only visitor besides Alison and Robert was the Governor of Wandsworth, Brian Collinson. A real honour.

'So sorry to hear of the problem,' Collinson began. 'Can't think what came over the lads.'

No wonder they thought he was a tosser, Mark thought.

'This is an isolated incident, Stephens, and I trust you aren't making a big thing of it. Don't want a lot of silly chatter outside about brutality and that sort of thing, do we?' Collinson was a real wet. Brought in because of his administration skills, but with very little idea about the reality of prison sub-cultures and the power struggles that ensued. Or about the casualties and the decaying ideals of those committed to reform of the penal system. All he saw was a sex offender who had been beaten up, and he was there to make sure that's how it stayed and that there wasn't a great hullabaloo centred around this trivial incident.

'I have had a word with my deputy, and the only safe passage for you is to be housed with our other special guests, out of harm's way.' Brian Collinson walked round the bed as he spoke. Visiting prisoners in the hospital was a bloody nuisance. He wouldn't stay there longer than necessary. 'I'm pleased to see you making a good recovery. And I am sure you will understand that what happened to you, although awful, was something we could not have prevented. You chose to go through the normal channels and not take advantage of a facility deliberately initiated to avoid this sort of incident.' Collinson began to sound threatening. 'Now, you get better, Stephens, and spend the rest of your time here in a safe environment.' Collinson slipped out of the door waving a commanding finger. Mark hadn't spoken. Collinson was good at monopolising a conversation. It was often essential or diplomatic not to let an inmate reply.

Although Mark welcomed being discharged from the hospital he dreaded what awaited him when he was installed in the Sectioned area of the prison. There was a picture, perhaps distorted, that he had developed during those tranquillised periods between medication and visits.

His imagination didn't let him down. If mainstream Wandsworth was a zoo then this portion was a circus. It was with great amusement that the guard at the studded metal door ushered Mark in, dismissing his escort with a chuckle. 'Welcome to Crazy Land.'

Mark followed the swinging chain of the officer who led him to his accommodation. 'You're going to like this. Only two to a cell in Wonderland.' Mark could see that it was one big joke for this warder. 'And Colin is right up your street.' The goon nearly doubled up with laughter. 'In here.'

It was the same size as his previous cell. There were two single beds and no bunk. Colin's bed was already made and was further from the door. Mark's was just the springs with the mattress leaning against the wall. A pile of bedding was still swaying on the sagging coils, a heap of the same threadbare sheets and blankets. Colin was elsewhere, but he had left his life behind him. And what Mark saw confirmed his worst fears.

'Right, make yourself comfortable. Your cellmate, I use the term loosely I trust, is in the kitchens. He's one of the cooks. Prepares that delicious grub they serve you in the canteen.' It was a huge laugh for him. So amusing. 'Good luck. You'll meet Colin, or Colleen as he prefers, this afternoon.' The warder disappeared, but his chortling continued for at least a minute as he made his way back to his post at the entrance to Santa's Grotto.

Colin's long, pink quilted dressing gown hung from a hook on the wall, and looped over the collar was a pale blue chiffon scarf. In a corner of the immaculately spruce cell Colin had skilfully crafted himself a makeshift dressing table from food boxes he had obviously smuggled from the kitchen. An old beige curtain was draped over it as a final aesthetic touch. Not quite the colour Colin wanted, but until he could steal or borrow something more in keeping it would have to do. Neatly arranged in front of a fragment of broken mirror were bottles of lotions and jars of creams, and a frightening array of cosmetics that would look more at home in a theatrical make-up department. Everywhere there was a woman's touch. Strategically placed rugs, polished ornaments on narrow shelves and a collection of cleaning materials tidily stacked. Mark wasn't looking forward to meeting his room-mate.

He didn't have long to wait. Mark was making his bed when Colin minced in. A lull in dinner preparations gave him the opportunity to smuggle back a small jar that he planned to use as a vase for a ghastly plastic carnation he had been given by another prisoner.

'My goodness, am I in luck.' He stood sideways at the doorway, one hand on the frame and the knee of one leg bent. 'They're delivering scrumptious men for my delight now.' Colin ventured in, slowly approaching Mark.

'Hey, the name's Mark.' He wasn't aggressive, but it was deliberately confrontational. He wanted to halt Colin's progress towards him. Build a barrier immediately. Homosexuality wasn't a team he played for but he was no queer-basher. It was okay as long as it wasn't in his face. But now he felt threatened.

'Mark? Um... quaint.' Colin stroked his chin. 'Never give me another guy who wants to be in here do they?' He sounded bitter. 'Got it in for me. Other queens get their companions. They leave me to fester.' Colin was a menopausal woman now.

Mark didn't like the mood swings. 'I'm sure we can get on.' He was eager to keep on the right side of this man, placate him without having to get near his arse. 'You keep this place spick and span. A lot better than my last place.'

'Yes. Takes all my time. I hope you aren't messy. Can't stand mess. Look at my hands. Working in those kitchens and then cleaning this place.' Colin sat at the broken mirror and spoke to his reflection. 'My skin is so dry and my nails forever breaking. I'm a disaster. No wonder no one wants me.'

Mark was almost feeling sorry for the faggot. 'You had better tell me what's mine. I don't want to tread on your toes, cross any lines.'

Colin rose to point out his greater possession of the humble cell, and Mark's squashed fraction of the floor space. He studied Mark's face as he swept a dainty hand across the territory. 'Done you up good and proper, didn't they. Look at the swelling. Such a pretty face. Some people have no respect.' Colin reached out to stroke Mark's puffed cheek.

Instinctively Mark pulled back. Lurched away at the clawing, feminine fingers.

'It's all right luvvy I wasn't going to infect you with anything.'

'Sorry, I'm just not back to form. A little nervy. Understandable don't you think?' Mark hadn't meant to react to offend Colin. He placed a hand gingerly on Colin's turned back. A reassurance of sorts.

Colin's bizarre behaviour was nothing. The whole place was a collection of weirdos. Some quite unassuming at first sight, but later to display odd, even disgusting mannerisms. They had committed every despicable crime you could imagine. And now he was included in their ranks. No threat was posed by this mongrel collection of sexual offenders, and security significantly relaxed. With Colin dressed to kill and busy tarting up his face, Mark felt happier outside the cell, venturing to the communal area where there were equally outrageous dressers and furtive little men cock-tugging in shadowy corners. He dreaded the washroom scenario. There wouldn't be the violence. At least there was that.

Mark slipped into a common room where only a few oddities spoke with exaggerated gestures or held hands.

'Hello there.' A crisp voice behind him turned Mark spinning around. A man peeked nonchalantly from above the flapping wings of a newspaper. 'Took a hammering I see. Happened to me. Still can't get this leg to behave properly.' He tapped his left kneecap. 'I'd like to say you're better off here, but you aren't. It's just different.'

Cautiously Mark edged towards the newspaper now held flatter for him to see the speaker. A quick inspection detected nothing dangerous. No sexual bushwhacker or flaming old queen.

'I'm the nearest you'll get to normal.' He lowered the paper to the floor. 'Neil Symmonds.' A hand was offered.

'Mark Stephens,' Mark reciprocated.

'I know. Followed the case in the papers.' Neil was quick to inform him. 'I hope you did it.'

Mark shot back. 'What do you mean?'

'Sorry. What I meant was, they did you for it. It would be a bloody shame if you had been fitted up.'

Mark wasn't sure he understood the logic. Neil did.

'Well I didn't. Not that anyone in here is interested or believes me.'

'They don't give a toss. Why should they. We all have our own crosses to bear. Someone wailing their innocence cuts no ice in here.' Honest information from Neil. 'Yell the injustice of it all hanging and rotating from a ceiling fan with your dick alight and you'll still go unnoticed.'

The image almost had Mark smiling. Neil was a refreshing new buddy. 'That's enough about me. What are you in for that you didn't do?'

A low and painful blow. Neil took a while to answer. 'I did it. Paying my due and all that.' No explanation given. It hurt too much. She was his brother's daughter. His niece. Only ten. Just the once. So lonely after his wife had left. Oh, how filthy he felt.

Mark wished he hadn't asked. The question had knocked the wind out of him. No sharp banter, only a stooped head and mumbled words. A diversion was needed. 'Hope to be out in a matter of days. Appeal coming up. My barrister is applying for an early release. New evidence.'

'Another innocent man who is going to scamper free on appeal. Heard it before. Just a pound for every one and I'd be a fucking millionaire.' Neil was brightening up.

Colin collected Mark from the common room. It was time for lights out. No frantic buzzer; just a word in the ear and a sauntering back of mostly couples.

It was no easy sleep. Colin cried often during the night, but he didn't leave his bed and Mark's worst fears were not realised.

Even the morning washroom held few dangers, but there were some horrific sights; scars from rampant infections caused by elaborate body piercing, mainly to the genitalia, and the ludicrous mutilation that sex-change surgery had left. But at least no one was lashing at him with their boots or trying to crack his head open like an egg. Of course there were the searching eyes on his body, and for some, quizzing his face for a come on. The loners trapped in their own miserable fantasies or fetishes faced the walls and tugged at their cocks, or spoke to imaginary child partners or ambushed victims. It was an asylum rather than a prison and Mark hoped he could survive the madhouse.

Breakfast in the mesh cage was an ordeal. Outside were the faces of thunder with armour-piercing gazes, that ate their food like competing puppies and barked at each other in trivial exchanges. Mark wondered whether he was looking in or looking out. On his table, that Colin had wiped over several times with a damp cloth and dried with an absorbent paper towel, they nibbled their food in accordance with their status in the aviary.

A hungry convict dreams of very little besides food, even the pigswill dished up as an excuse for a meal. It keeps him from having other desires and contemplating menacing notions. But often a satiated gaolbird poses the greater threat. So, when the bulk of the canteen had topped up with stodge they were ready to target the freaks behind the wire. Especially now there was a new boy that they had just expelled from their club.

In the middle of the canteen Bruce Martin raised an arm and the clockwork warders turned their backs or spoke to prisoners lined against the wall. They wouldn't watch. He pulled his obese form from the table and approached the chicken-wire. Four of his goons tagged along.

'How are we this morning, gentlemen?' A general, and mocking greeting. 'Sent you another pervert as you see. He eyeballed Mark.' His mouth smiled at the edges. 'Breakfast wasn't much was it?' The frightened faces nodded in agreement. 'I just don't know what things are coming to. I'll have a word with the chef on your behalf. In the meantime let me supplement your meagre diet. I feel responsible.' Martin beckoned one of his toadies forward.

A gormless disciple, sleeves rolled up high, strained to carry a large bucket. An accomplice hurried to help him by sharing the weight. They charged at the mesh, lifted the pail shoulder high and ejected the contents onto and through the netting. Luckily the filtering mesh held on to the larger, plastic lumps of shit. But a vile mixture of watery excrement and urine showered through and onto the panicking diners. The stench was hideous. Crouched and coughing the heaving patsies wiped the khaki liquid from their eyes and the corners of their mouths.

'Bon appetit!' Bruce Martin stood close to the mesh to get a good view of the spluttering men and bellowed with laughter. His henchmen followed suit. It was more than their lives were worth not to greet this prank with less than a hearty joviality.

Mark wasn't quite in range and was only hit by a few stray spots. Martin recognised the anger in his lancing eyes and blew a kiss. And was gone.

And with his going came a posse of prison officers in high dudgeon, alarmed and confrontational. The cavalry arriving at The Alamo only to find Custer and the other heroes just bricks in a monumental pile of stiffs.

'Okay what's been going on here?' Such a daft question.

Mark couldn't control himself. His blood slammed hot and kicking in his head. 'Going on? You fucking idiots! Crooked fucking dicks!' He stamped his foot and surveyed the stinking men and dripping curtain of filth, and the slithering path of descending turds slumping to the floor from the inadequate wire defence.

'Watch yourself, Stephens.'

'You all fucking disappeared. At the click of that arsehole's finger you hightailed it, or curled up with your eyes tightly shut like hibernating squirrels. You should all be locked up in here. Yellow bastards!' Mark tried to control his wrath with rapid shallow breathing.

'Get him out of here!' ordered a senior officer who had

heard enough. No prisoner who wasn't paying was allowed to talk to the staff like that. 'And let's organise some of these mutts to clean the place up. Smells like a sewer in here.'

Neil Symmonds caught up with Mark that evening. He had escaped the full force of the hurtled fæces and received a similar spattering to Mark. In his mood of atonement he would have welcomed a smothering of crap.

'You calmed down now? They'll have it in for you from here on. Keep down. Low profile. Ride it out. Does no good to draw a target on your face.'

It was wise advice. Mark knew that. 'I know. Blew up. Strain of the appeal and being beaten senseless.'

'You're right. This place has been sold out to the highest bidder. Saw a ton of dope and cash going to the screws when I was that side of the fence. There's no one who can't be bought.'

'If I had the time and commitment I'd help. Got my own crusade I'm afraid.' Mark was apologetic. He fancied getting involved. His pulverised body wanted revenge. To hit not only the hooligans who did it, but the system and its treacherous confederates that had snatched the pieces of silver.

'Martin's a real bastard. Inside and out. They'll get you if you cross him. Take a back seat. I'm even beginning to believe you are innocent. No guilty man would have the gall to stand up to that turkey.'

Mark slept between Colin's raving and desperate weeping. A fitful sleep that threw up a fresco of contemporary horrors to torment him. If he didn't get out soon he was sure he would go crazy.

The whole of the segregated community greeted each meal with trepidation after the attack the previous day. Lunch and dinner had been served to them in their cells, away from the aping sniggers of the offenders. Untouched and unrepentant. But breakfast was a new day, and Clive Wilkins was determined to restore normality. Business as usual.

Behind their protective wire, which still carried the odour of blocked drains, the scared birds hurried to eat. But those they feared on the main floor seemed preoccupied. Not an insult or a putty face pushed up to the mesh to taunt the men they had covered in a particularly nasty combination of piss and shit. Mark observed the frequent expeditions of runners from Bruce Martin's table and scrums of men in conspiratorial mode. He feared a further attack. Generals were briefing their men and lining up for another offensive.

He was wrong.

What was orchestrated from a smashed plate and stamped feet would be more sinister and further ranging than even Mark appreciated.

Every corner of the canteen fell silent. In their cage Mark and the sex offenders followed suit, expecting another outrage; sitting ducks. Guarding officers looked nervously at each other and at the daddy of the prison, Bruce Martin. In the deadly hush they clucked around like disorientated birds.

Chosen to begin the riot, a violent young inmate made the most of his role. He stood on his table and hurled the plate to the floor and stood like a colossus daring anyone to admonish him. Neighbouring inmates put up defensive hands to protect themselves from scudding fragments that ricocheted from the site of impact. Then the drumming of the heavy boots. Every boot. A thunderclap din that sent the warders scurrying for safety or assistance. A few feeble sex offenders joined in from inside their sanctuary. It was a shallow effort at conformity. A sad attempt to win friends or stall retribution.

Bruce Martin had it well planned. There was no escape for the scattering screws. At each exit three or more large prisoners blocked their way and bundled them to the floor. There was no resistance when their long key chains were confiscated, and they sat on the floor where they had been unceremoniously dumped. Those who were on the payroll felt better about the situation than those who had remained uncorrupted, honest fellows. Apparently not the best policy, they were now thinking. Gangs of hurrying men were charging down corridors securing as much of the prison as possible. From a low squeak the siren wound up to a high-pitched shriek. It was a brief battle for territory before the lines were established. Bruce Martin knew the areas that were easier to defend and where he could hold out for longer. He had hostages. Eight prison officers. That was currency.

A beckoning hand guided Mark and the rest of the caged prisoners back to their quarters, where they were locked in for their own protection. Two officers, fortunately not crooked ones, stayed to guard the low-life community. To their dismay they were sandwiched between two citadels of revolting prisoners and not adjacent to an escape route. They would have to sit this out.

Brian Collinson and Clive Wilkins ran into each other. The siren had sent them racing from their offices like headless chickens. Their first prison protest. A procedure had been practised after the Strangeways riots five years earlier. Those sectors occupied by the prisoners were being isolated, the police had been hailed and the Home Secretary informed. Brian Collinson and his deputy discussed the situation in a frenzied exchange where they met on the landing between their bases. Most of all it was the publicity that they feared more than anything else. Heads could roll for this, and there was no better way of ensuring dismissal than by being vilified in a tabloid newspaper.

Communications with the rioters wasn't organised until the middle of the afternoon. Bruce Martin had captured several locations where there were phones. But refused to talk until he was able to assess his capability to withstand a siege.

'Now take it easy. Let's not let anyone get hurt on either side.' Clive Wilkins had been on the hostage negotiation course run by HM Prison Service and with no one else properly trained the police and Brian Collinson had reluctantly let him talk to the rioters. 'Just tell us what you want. The purpose of your action. We'll see what we can do. If you wish you can call me Clive.' Boy, that really hurt. He wanted the inmates to fear him, and now he was their bloody friend on first name terms.

'Who am I speaking to?'

'Come on Wilkins, you fucking know who I am!' Bruce
Martin was in a strong position. He knew the damage his little
rebellion could do to Wandsworth and the management. 'Let's
cut the crap. Listen carefully.' Clive Wilkins could hear the
rustling of paper. Martin had his demands written down. 'The
place is overcrowded, there are no proper facilities, the food's
shit and the regime is led by the fucking Gestapo. And that
includes you. This is a unanimous uprising. I speak for all the
lads in here. We demand a maximum of two to a cell, sports
facilities, including a gym and time to use them. No more than
four hours a day working in the bloody workshop and some
decent grub. Got it? Oh, and get these fucking freaks out of
here. This doesn't include them.' It wasn't on his list but thrown
in as an afterthought. The phone was slammed down. 'That'll
give 'em something to think about.' He beamed as he confronted his lieutenants.

The Deputy Governor passed on the demands. 'Fuck it!'
Brian Collinson stormed. 'Fuck that arsehole Martin! Nothing
moves without him shoving it.' It was the first time he had
admitted Martin's status in *his* prison. It hurt.

'We stall them until we can establish the extent of their
occupation, Brian. Give me the plans of the prison.'
Superintendent Guy Phillips of the Met was deciding on strategy for the moment. It was an old map of the buildings.
Probably from the sixties. It overlapped the table and had to be
lifted at the edges to see some of the compound. 'It would
appear they have kept this area here and sacrificed some of
their own cells that stray into a difficult sector to defend.'
Phillips tugged and twisted the map. Waved his hand across
and narrowed down sites with a stabbing finger. He wasn't bad
at interpreting an opponent's game plan.

'The crucial aspect is the human one.' Brian Collinson
broke in. 'If I lose an officer here then I'm history. Hostages
limit any action. We must not sacrifice a single man. Whatever
we do, promise the damn earth if we have to, but we must not

jeopardise any of the staff that are being held in there.'

Mark and Colin, from their bunker, listened to the hollering that rose and fell; cascading echoes of the rampant insurrectionists as they sprang from room to room destroying as much as they could. Anything that smelled of repression and was a flag for incarceration. Martin had been forced to give them their head. To blow off steam. They needed that.

'They're destroying the place!' A senior officer announced returning from the front line. 'There are toilet bowls and cisterns being thrown down stairs and out of doors, and the water is just pumping out from the broken pipes. We'll have to get the supply switched off.'

'While you're doing that get the power cut as well. We probably can't starve them out as they are holed up in the kitchens, but we can make it tough for them without light and heat. Their nights will be long and cold.' Guy Phillips was quick to pick up on a ploy.

'Don't make them do something stupid. My men are in there.' Brian Collinson had an interest. He didn't want the police to take knee-jerk decisions that could blow this up and transform misfortune into chaos.

All through the day each side consolidated. Where there were no real barriers the prisoners erected makeshift barricades from furniture and furnishings along hallways and at low level windows. Clive Wilkins secured areas that were perilously close to the rioters' stronghold and could provide shelter for a mass escape. Wandsworth was cordoned off, houses nearby evacuated and a ring of armed police officers installed beyond the outer walls. Neither side spoke, well aware of the housework that had to be done. Once the confrontation was clearly demarcated and battle lines drawn a period of busy and serious mediation would ensue.

'We can see a little from the helicopter and from some of our rooftop surveillance but it's patchy, and with the old part of the prison there aren't any large windows to use. It would seem they have kept the officers together and assembled them in a cell on the third level,' an eager police sergeant gushed as he confronted his superintendent.

'It's their prize. They'll be protecting their jewels all right.' Brian Collinson ordered another coffee and shrugged his shoulders. 'What happens now? Do we break the silence? Phone them? Tell me Clive.'

'There appears to be no real danger for the hostages at the moment. We let them stew for a while. Let them wonder what we are up to. They'll soon make contact when we have stayed quiet. It should make them nervy.'

Brian Collinson pulled his mouth open to speak but stopped short of an utterance. A singing noise like a bamboo cane being thrashed through the air cut him off. It was followed almost immediately by a splintering smash. And from high above their operations centre the maniac cackle of Brian Martin lacerated the night air.

'They're on the fucking roof!' roared Wilkins.

Chapter 13

Susan Bennett was holding herself together. Mark Stephens was pushed well back into a compartment of her past that she had locked. He was in prison. Not for long. Served him right for rejecting her. There was a certain satisfaction in getting away with it. Fooling all those people. Some tight corners, but exciting on the whole. Now she had faded back to obscurity. Baxter had finished with her. And being no further use there were no visits by the truckling policewoman.

She was supposed to be attending a further education college, some vague course to do with office routine; and working part-time in the Spar grocery store a hundred yards up the road. Pauline Green was in North London and didn't phone much. Loneliness haunted Susan. During her infrequent visits to college and during her time at the shop she met few people and made no friends.

Susan's mother was wrapped up in her own misery, pined for her youth and chased her sanity, which the menopause perilously toyed with; and shopped to dislodge the tedium that sat heavily on her. George Bennett moped round the house blaming the world for his sour life. Susan avoided him. Moving from room to room to escape any chance of that predatory stare and the dreadful phantoms she saw in his face. And when her mother went out she made certain she left the house as well.

It was inevitable, sod's law, that there would come a time when such arrangements didn't go to plan. A Saturday evening. Susan had nowhere to go; not unusual. Her mother announced a sudden departure to meet a friend. Spur of the moment decisions were more exciting. A friend that George found hostile. There were plenty of them in that category. It was easy for him to refuse any invitation to join her.

Susan watched her mother from the darkness at the top of the stairs; in the brightly lit well below. An upturned face smiled a goodbye to her daughter's grimace. Susan saw her eagerness to climb into the long coat that took her away from her brooding husband; an escape from his hanging face and dour eyes. And when the door clicked shut the air in the house turned thick and threatening.

Susan occupied her territory upstairs and George Bennett prowled around the living room downstairs. A stand off. She would lock her door, play some music and go to sleep early. He wouldn't dare come near her. She was older now. Too old for him to continue. It was all right when she was younger. An easy target. And Susan was adamant she wouldn't be a victim any more.

The television was blaring downstairs. Susan made a last sortie to the kitchen. Some supplies to last out the evening. She grabbed an elderly apple, some crisps and a can of Coke. A frenetic movement as if she was a contestant in a televised shopping game where you were timed to collect a list of items. And as she scuttled round the brown melamine units with a swaying tray, scooping up her snack, she spotted the glinting blade of a sharp kitchen knife that was lying on the stainless-steel draining board. Instinctively she grabbed that as well. The shrunken skin on the Golden Delicious needed paring. And she carried it, along with her scant victuals, past the jabbering TV; and climbed the stairs with eluding, double-flight bounds.

George Bennett heard her and watched from the slit of the door her leaping escape back to the bedroom. And when she had disappeared he stood in the hallway and stared up into the blackness that had swallowed her ducking form.

Knowing she was there; vulnerable, stirred that old urge. He slipped back into the living room and faced the television. He didn't watch it. His eyes were on the wall ahead. Not that the message to his brain carried that distinct image. It was background to scenes more vivid. He watched the home movies in his head. And he drank. With successive drinks the pictures became more demanding. He stroked himself and filled his trousers with a hungry erection.

Susan didn't hear him creep up to her door, or see the handle turn slowly. But she heard the sudden release and a muffled curse when it wouldn't budge. He rested his head on the painted door and breathed heavily. Beyond that blockade was her precious body. He wasn't going to let a flimsy door separate him from that prize.

Susan retreated to the head of her bed holding her knees tightly against her chest. She knew he was still lurking. As much as she wished she knew he wasn't prepared to go away.

The doors on that landing were only hardboard on a shoddy frame and the locks hardly a deterrent to an incensed and desperate man. He shoved with his shoulder knowing something was going to give. It was a rhythmic rocking, leaning back and then releasing the full weight of his body on the doomed door.

George Bennett fell into Susan's room. She heard the snap of the breaking lock and the thrump of his toppled body. In the furthest corner of her bed she cowered, under as much bedding as she could gather. Useless armour.

From the floor he drooled. He could smell her now. With a shaking arm he pulled himself upright. Her body shook from beneath a firmly wrapped duvet. His hand slipped beneath it. Searching for some bare flesh to start from. She would submit if she felt his wandering hand seeking her pleasure zones. Of that he was certain.

Susan tugged the quilt, to squeeze her body with the strangulating material, an outer skin to separate her from his flaccid flesh.

A strong grip on the quilt with both hands, a whip-like flick and she spun out of the duvet like a yo-yo, and was still twisting when she tumbled back onto the bed. He was rough. It had been a long time. Almost like pulling a wishbone he opened her legs wide apart and immediately thrust his fingers inside her pants. Forcing them into her dry vagina. Susan screamed with pain and shame. She pushed up on her elbows and grabbed at his lunging arm. He threw her hand away and burrowed deeper. Then, reaching back, he tugged at his trousers until they fell below his knees. There was movement enough, he didn't need to remove them totally. Susan had to look straight into his face as he moved his body up and directed his penis with a gripping hand. With a thrust that began at his flabby arse he forced himself into her. A satisfied sigh signalled the beginning of a violent jamming. His head rolled, and he spluttered the incomprehensible guttural sounds of his own enjoyment.

Susan was thrown, limp and flapping with his every slamming jolt. She provided no encouragement as her whiplash head was tossed and banged like a dummy. Her arms did not repel him or hold him. They hung over the sides of the bed and flopped up and down with his urgent rhythm. On occasions her open palm rattled the tray where her half-eaten supper wasted and where the sharp kitchen knife clattered.

Searching fingers felt for the handle the next time her hand collided with the tray. An unconscious reaction. It was wooden and fitted neatly into her grip. Clasped firmly and positioned like a dagger, in stabbing mode. And when he next pushed into her, invaded her body, stole more of her self-esteem, violated her, dared to treat her like a disposable doll; then she raised that weapon and buried the shining blade, with all the force her pulverised body could muster, deep into him. Deep into his milky thigh. A shudder ran up her arm as the knife hit the femur and the end of the blade broke off. A reciprocal penetration.

God! It felt good to stop that machine. To halt his locomotive drive.

Shrunken and torpid he fell out of her. He didn't scream. Escaping air whistled from his lips followed by a subdued groaning. He didn't know what had hit him. No idea he had been pierced by his darling daughter.

She sensed his bulky form roll off the bed and crash onto the floor; and stay there. His body rocked and moaned on the floor. Susan didn't move. There was no remorse. She didn't care. Only about the blood on her carpet. She glanced to where the spilling crimson should have been. There was only a small pool. She had missed the artery. He lay clutching at the handle as if to pull it out. His eyelids flickering and his eyes barely open. It stuck out of his leg like a toy; but it was in solid. Excaliber cemented in the sinew of his bald leg.

For the first time she confronted him. Stuck her yelling face into his. 'That's for all you've done to me, Daddy. Fuck me! Fuck me and fuck me. Is that what fathers do to their loving children? Of course it fucking isn't!' Susan howled and bawled. Tears for every time he had done it.

George Bennett shuffled on his naked arse as far as the door, where he sat leaning on one elbow. The blood trickled down his ivory leg. He watched its progress. He could move no further. Susan glared at his clumsy progress and stabbed him again and again with her stiletto stare. And then she slunk back to the headrest of her nightmare bed, and clasping as much of her body with arms that had suddenly grown, dragged her fleshy form as small as she could, like a traumatised ape, and rocked herself... and rocked herself... and rocked herself.

Tiles rained down all night like terracotta hail. And with every crashing shower the triumphant rioters began a chorus of abuse. Picked out by police spotlights it was pure theatre. The rebellious inmates were thoroughly enjoying their notoriety and the blatant vandalism. It was what you had to do in any worthwhile prison riot. Destruction was high on the agenda along with prolonged vigils in appalling weather and the raucous demands yelled to media ears behind the besieging forces.

Not that Bruce Martin was going to spend too long outside. He'd show his face. Show the country who he was. The face of the mistreated convict. Seen on television tying the inevitable banner calling for prison reform, but then sloping off for a cold meal and a fag and letting other lackeys hold the fort.

'They're tearing my prison apart.' Collinson was tired and pissed off. 'There won't be anything left at this rate. They are in two blocks and most of the tiles have gone from there. God knows what the place is like inside. My staff tell me there are fires everywhere, either for warmth or simply part of the demolition process.' He gave Guy Phillips a despairing look.

The policeman tried to be positive. 'We've had Martin back on the line. He's reiterated his demands. Wilkins is reading him a letter from the Home Secretary. He's considering the reforms that have been mentioned. It's basically another stalling tactic, but we need all we can get. They'll come down when they're cold and the novelty wears off. You've just got to be patient in a situation like this, Brian.' The two men raised their cups of coffee and slurped the hot liquid simultaneously.

Most of the rioting prisoners were resting after a day well spent. They had smashed every toilet bowl and basin with legs taken off tables or sections of pipe they carried as weapons. Accompanying scornful laughter there was the systematic tearing down of showers, burning furniture and papers, hurling anything that could be thrown with force and effect and running round the prison building shouting all manner of tribal anthems. It just needed some alcohol and the party would have been in full swing. There were some drugs but not enough to share. Those in possession were jealously guarding their stash. It would be one other reason for them to start fighting among themselves over the next few days. What they needed was a new incentive. Take their minds off the cold and the darkness.

Margaret Cullen sat on one of the long wooden benches in the musty corridor of the High Court. She felt good. On her lap she rested some of the papers that she was going to use when she was called. But for now she refreshed her memory. They would want her to be quick. So getting things in their right order was essential. Hit them with the most powerful arguments first and then support them with solid but less relevant addenda.

It wasn't the appeal proper, but they needed to know what was in store so that there was justification for letting this convicted sex offender out of jail and onto the streets.

'Morning, Margaret.' Robert Manning trotted up to the barrister, her head buried in the wings of a file. 'Sorry I'm late. Last minute phone calls, bloody traffic; you name it.' He too was bouncy.

'I think we have a wait on our hands here. There's no knowing when they'll get time to see us. I've told my chambers not to expect me back today. My clerk will deal with the mundane. But I do have a delicious brief to work on this evening.' It was another indecent assault case. Her speciality.

'My current files have formed a mountain on my desk. Let's not talk about it.' Robert had devoted so much time to Mark's case that he had badly ignored some of his other clients. 'Let's hope this goes smoothly from now on, otherwise the partners at my firm are going to get on my back.'

'Have you got the Hinton statement with you?' Margaret enquired.

'Certainly have.' Robert was as thorough as usual.

'And the one from the Caldwell woman?'

'Of course.'

Margaret smiled. 'Sorry to check on you so, but you know what a worrier I am. I don't think we will need them, but you never know. Don't say I said this; but some of these judges are well past it and you have to remind them what is relevant. Even then they can be cantankerous and demand some innocuous document just to prove they are still on the ball. You can understand my paranoia after what we've been through?'

'Mrs. Cullen?' A quaking voice rattled down the otherwise deserted passageway.

'Come on Robert we're on.' Margaret was crisply on her feet and collecting up her papers. 'Let's go. Fingers crossed. Mark Stephens should be a free man when we come out of here.' She completed the sentence as she strode towards the usher at the double oak doors. Robert, dragging his coat, and juggling with his briefcase, scampered behind her.

Linda Bennett jangled her keys at the front door. The door of a chamber of horrors. Television blabbering came muffled through the living room door ajar, and she walked past what she thought would be her husband sat gawking at some inane programme. He would be no fun to talk to. Susan would probably be asleep so she rustled up a tea and some biscuits and sat at the kitchen table. She detected no movement in the house. Only a heavy silence beyond the jabbering box. Her nails were a mess. Chipped varnish on three and a broken one that needed a reshape with her emery board. She peered through the gap of the living room door as she passed. There was only the flickering picture. She climbed the stairs to retrieve the nail file from her dressing table. He had most likely nodded off on the sofa.

Mrs. Bennett held the stair rail to begin her descent to her cup of tea half drunk and biscuit half eaten. Not knowing that her life was about to be ambushed by a sickening revelation. Barely detectable above the droning television downstairs, a faint clucking noise like that of a choking animal. She moved closer to Susan's door. The lock was damaged and some splintered wood. What had she been doing? Mrs. Bennett's first thought. She pushed at the door ready to wake and quiz her daughter. It only gave slightly and then slid back. Another push with more force and still the resistance. What had she put in the way? She wouldn't be thwarted by her daughter's games. It was too late in the evening to fool about.

'Susan! Open this door.' She shouted loudly so that her dozing husband in front of the television would be alerted as well. Perhaps it would send him stumbling up. She stood back, hands on her hips. Annoyed. 'Come on, Susan!'

There was no reaction. And no response from downstairs. Only the persistent low crowing from inside. She shoved the door with both hands and a foot. The obstacle was dislodged and the door swung open. A darkened room, a clinging odour.

Light from the landing intruded. On Susan's bed simpering and quivering was a bundle of bedclothes, and struggling to squirm out of sight, her husband. His trousers lashed round his ankles and the tails of his shirt rolled up around his podgy stomach as he shuffled for cover. And sticking from his marble leg one of her kitchen knives. The blood ponding beneath him. Thick and black, like bitumen in the feeble light. Gone was the urgency to open the door. Struck dumb and immobile Mrs. Bennett fought to piece it together.

Susan sensed her mother's presence and eased her turtle head from her duvet lair. Her eyes spoke for her. The gears started turning in Linda Bennett's head, but she wrestled to fend off a frightening scenario. Susan unwrapped her invaded body for her mother to see. Linda Bennett's eyes darted back and forth. From her dribbling daughter to her gurgling husband.

'Susan?' Her head shook. 'Susan?' she squeaked again.

'Mum.' The years were shredded away. Susan was a little girl frightened by a bad dream. She held out her arms. 'Mum. Mum, help me.' A seven-year-old pleaded.

Linda Bennett jumped out of her nightmare and rushed to meet her daughter halfway down the bed. She held her baby. It had been so long since she had been able. She had worked it out now. They wet each other with their tears. They needed to cry. Crying for the shadow years. One wept for a lost mother found and the other for a daughter so terribly abandoned. In their huddle they looked down on the pathetic ogre whimpering below them, clutching at his pierced leg.

'For how long?'

'Years and years. For so long.' Susan rested her head against her mother's shoulder. It was over now. They would talk more in the months ahead. She wouldn't blame her mother. Susan knew her mother would have to live with that herself.

They left George Bennett pinned to the sticky carpet. An ambulance was called. Two inquisitive paramedics parcelled him up but never asked questions of the women who remained behind shut doors as he was hauled downstairs and trucked to the hospital. A loosely laid blanket covered the jutting handle of the knife Susan had left in him.

With her glacial coating cracked she was melting. Susan Bennett could not hold on to the biggest secret. And in the assurance of her mother's cradling arms she started, amidst new and streaming tears, to tell the true and painful story of her dreadful lie.

It had gone too quiet for Mark's liking. They had listened to the showering missiles and the echoes along the pipe work as the plumbing was wrecked. From the small windows there was the trashing of other prison furniture. Desks and cabinets smashed and burned. And through the lingering smoke the rallying holler of the crazy horde. Now it was night. There was no electricity and those who dared to or cared to cuddled up for warmth.

They hugged even tighter when the pregnant silence was broken by a loud impact against the outer door. The investigating prison officer was met by the face of one of his colleagues pressed forcibly against the barred window. His throat neatly decorated with an underlining carving knife.

'Open the fucking door.' A coarse voice demanded. One hand held the officer's hair and the other scraped the blade across his neck. Behind the gruesome captor a small army of rioters salivated. A new game was beginning.

'Can't do that.' The guard responded. He had to defy them at least once.

Spurts of blood started to escape from small nicks on the captive's neck as the blade was run across it slowly. 'Next time he gets the full treatment. It'll only take him seconds to die. Now, open the fucking door. Don't try and be a fucking martyr. Don't want to blame yourself for your mate's fucking death.'

The second guard joined the confrontation. 'What do you want in here?' A stupid question, but he was desperate to display a defence. Couldn't capitulate without at least seeming to be honourable.

'You fucking twats. Open the fucking door or you're looking at a dead man.' The knife was pressed harder, and trickles
of blood ran down to the prison officer's white collar and
soaked in.

There were screams from the crouching prisoners inside the
'no-go zone' as the lock was turned and the scrambling yobs
entered.

'Nothing I could do. You saw what he would have done.' It
was a weak explanation that was soon lost beneath the cries of
the charging warriors.

At first the cowering group of pædophiles, rampant homo-
sexuals and non-aligned and specialist sex offenders were surveyed with caution and suspicion by the henchmen of Bruce
Martin. Hunched oddities that they despised. Behind the sepa-
rating mesh fence they were a different species to be abused
whenever they had a need to queer-bash or divert grievances.
Clubbing their open palms with their hurriedly devised
weaponry changing gangs policed them until word filtered
through that Bruce Martin wanted them brought nearer to his
headquarters that had been established beneath the roof top
theatricals.

Systematically, usually in pairs, these pathetic men were
taken to a cell where their screams were audible to both the
boys on the roof and the indecisive men manning the operations centre. Most were beaten senseless. Limbs were broken,
ribs cracked and skin left a blend of the darker end of the red
and blue sections on the Dulux paint colour chart. Mark was
beaten harder and more viciously than the rest. He shouldn't
have come off so lightly after his first licking. Neil shared the
honour of being pounded senseless by the pipe wielding apes.
Slumped in a corner Mark's closed eyes, swollen and blinded
resembled blue-veined eggs. He slipped in and out of consciousness.

And his attackers chatted for hours about the beatings
and how brave they had been to beat the crap out of the

sick teacher.

Margaret tripped down the steps outside the Court of Appeal. She was Julie Andrews skipping over the Alps from the *Sound of Music*. Robert still followed in her wake. Success had taken only a matter of forty-five minutes. It was the walkover she expected but could not guarantee. She couldn't remember being so pleased about a decision going her way.

'Great!' Margaret turned to Robert and squeezed him tightly with her plump arms. His eyes widened. Usually a woman so matter of fact, he was taken by surprise. 'They will contact Wandsworth. You get word to Alison Stephens and I'll get the appeal papers finalised. He's out. Marvellous isn't it?' She was floating well above The Strand pavement.

'It is good Margaret. You've done well. But, can I throw a medium sized spanner into the works?'

'What is it?' Margaret didn't like the build up.

'I didn't want to alarm you before we went in, but, there's been a riot at the prison. I'm not sure how this affects Mark, but I know they're there in force. Seems to be a well orchestrated demonstration. I've had reports of fires in the complex and a roof top occupation.' Robert hated putting a damper on Margaret's bumper day.

'Sod it! Let's hope it's an isolated disturbance and that Mark has kept clear of the rioters. He's been separated so the chances are he has not been touched by the uprising.' Margaret had plummeted down to earth again.

When Susan Bennett, still held firmly by her mother, finished flushing out every compartment of her despicable fabrication it was getting light outside. Linda Bennett couldn't shut her eyes. They were opened wide by her daughter's first word of confession and never closed again. And now she looked out of the window; a steady gaze above her daughter's sunken head, and attempted to take it all in. Susan was still sniffing and she pulled her even closer. Only hours earlier her life was ordinary.

Definitely dull, but uncomplicated. Now she was having to reorganise it all. In her arms was a child who was the instigator of an abhorrent falsehood that had sent an innocent man to prison. A man she had hated. Wished was dead. How do you take that all back and make it better? Her head was cluttered with so many crazy tributaries and confused directions. And added to this was the realisation that her husband had been abusing their daughter for years under her very nose. A loathsome monster that she had once loved, married and stood by for too many years to dare thinking about. It was an insane mess. And she was a mess.

For once she didn't seek the mirror to check on her appearance. She left Susan sleeping. She showered and dressed. That morning wasn't one for taking a pride in herself. There was, however, a purpose to that day. Something she couldn't have said about all the other typical days in her life.

Susan was drowsy when her mother pulled at her arm to urge her to dress. 'Why do I have to get up?' she asked. 'I feel like hell.'

'We have a lot to do Susan.' A gentle voice for a victim.

'What?' Susan felt like shit and was reluctant to leave the softness of her bed. He was gone and she didn't have to worry about lying there in fear. Dreading him appearing unshaven at the door with that stupid grin.

'You know where we have to go.' Linda's voice was a little sterner.

'Where?' Susan was almost complaining.

'Police station, silly.' Linda smiled encouragingly. She knew this would be difficult.

'You mean I've got to tell them?' Susan sat up and launched a rapier stare in her mother's direction. 'I can't!' She threw herself back at the pillow.

'Mr. Stephens is in prison. You lied and put him there. Surely you can't expect to allow him to continue suffering for something he hasn't done? What you did was awful.' Linda was stroking her daughter's shoulder and talking quietly in her ear.

Advocating reason in a firm and positive way. Still pulling at her gently.

Leopards and spots. Susan Bennett wasn't going to change over night. Mark Stephens had spurned her. It wasn't easy to forget. She had spent months holding on to that resentment. To become the honest little miss before you could say Jack Robinson was a little too much to ask. 'I wish I hadn't told you.' She was quite sincere.

'Well you have. You needed to. They'll understand why. There will be counselling. I know it's not going to be easy for you, dear. I'll be there.' Linda Bennett could see Susan was slipping back. It was safer for her hiding behind that lie. Now it was important to get her to speak to someone. Imperative for Mark Stephens. And there would most likely be a question of wounding, and a destructive account of systematic incest to survive. She wouldn't worry Susan with that now. 'Come on, let's get dressed.'

Reluctantly Susan crawled out of bed. So many people she'd fooled and now they were going to know the terrible thing she had done. How would she face them? 'It's not possible. I can't. I can't.'

Linda Bennett found strength of purpose she didn't realise she had. 'You will! And I will back you all the way. It wasn't your fault. You have to remember that.' Linda wouldn't mention her monster of a husband. In fact he would rarely be mentioned again.

'Hello there, Susan.' A homely desk sergeant greeted mother and daughter. Susan Bennett was well known at Wokingham Police Station. Throughout the investigation she had been a frequent visitor along with Jean Baxter. Handled like a maltreated child. Given the tour and several sweets. Poor little darling so vilely abused by her teacher.

Susan didn't reply to the sergeant. Her mother stepped in. 'Is WPC Baxter here?'

'Let me see.' The policeman referred to a list on his desk. 'Nope, looks like she's in court today.'

'Oh.' Baxter was the only one they had had contact with.

'Can anyone else help? Do you want to tell me what it's about?' The desk sergeant was eager to assist.

'I'm not sure.' Linda had to think. Susan only studied the floor and avoided the sergeant's gaze. 'Is there anyone that dealt with Susan's case?'

'Bernard Mills is head of the unit and worked closely with Jean Baxter. I'm sure he's around.' A quick phone call confirmed that Mills was in the building, and Susan and Linda sat in the waiting room until he came down to see them.

'Hi, there.' Sergeant Bernard Mills strolled in to greet an edgy Mrs. Bennett and the lolling head of her daughter Susan. He sat down next to Susan, head bent, trying to look into her eyes. 'We haven't seen Susan for a long time. How are things?'

Susan didn't respond. Linda Bennett opened her mouth to begin, but closed it firmly. She wasn't sure how to broach the subject.

Sergeant Mills looked at both of them in turn. 'Well? What's the purpose of the visit?' It was clear that George Bennett's injury hadn't yet been reported to the police, or at least news of it hadn't reached Mills.

'Susan has to tell you something.' Mrs. Bennett left it at that.

'I see. What is it, Susan?' Fatherly he could be for a while, but Bernard Mills was getting impatient.

Susan's sagging head didn't lift up. She sniffed and shrugged her shoulders. 'I lied.'

'Lied? When?' Mills hadn't fallen in. It didn't register that she was referring to the evidence that put Mark Stephens in prison.

'He did nothing. Wouldn't do anything.' Still she spoke with her head nearly on her knees. 'It was him that did it all.'

Now she was definitely confusing Bernard Mills. He was just twigging, almost on board. 'Who did nothing? And who did it all?' He could see this wasn't a casual visit.

'What she's saying is that she made it all up about her

teacher. None of it was true.' Linda Bennett stepped in to clear up the shambles.

'You mean she was lying all the time?' Sergeant Mills jumped to his feet. This was messy. Heads would roll. 'Are you sure?' Of course she was sure. It was a ridiculous question, but one instinctively thrown. 'So what did she mean by someone doing it all?'

'That's another story that you'll have to deal with later. Let's get that poor man out of prison first. You are going to be sick and tired of this family when we're through.' Linda Bennett sighed and waggled her head.

'Look I'm going to have to get Jean Baxter in before we go any further. This was her case. I couldn't possibly make any decision without her say so.' Mills was edgy. It was a hot potato that he was eager to drop. 'I'll see if I can get hold of her right away.'

Bernard Mills rushed from the room and grabbed a young constable sauntering by, nearly spilling the papers he was carrying. 'What's up sarge?' He was shocked by the sudden assault.

'Get on the blower to the magistrates' court. WPC Baxter's there. Tell her it's urgent she gets back to the station now. This minute!' Mills struggled to work out how to alert her without the accompanying heart failure. 'Susan Bennett's here. Just mention that.'

They waited together. Mills wasn't keen to hear anything else. This was one big, fucking cock up and he was handing it over to that bitch Baxter as soon as she returned. A hot potato that was going straight in her lap.

When she arrived it was like the Wicked Witch of the North landing on her magic broomstick. A frightening voice bellowed before her physical presence. 'Hello Susan. Hello Mrs. Bennett.' She greeted them at the same time she removed her coat. 'What drags you in here?' Her eyes pierced through the slumping form of Susan Bennett and fried the lame smile of her mother.

Sergeant Mills pulled her aside and primed her. Any sign of

a grin turned into a snarl.

'So, Susan. Some family problems I hear.' News had obviously come through about the stabbing. 'You're upset. Understandable. Now I understand that your father is going to be all right. Sometimes these arguments get out of hand. I'm sure we can smooth this over for you. Make certain there are no charges.' It wasn't even subtle.

'She lied. Miss Baxter. Forget all that other business.' Linda didn't know how that was going to hurt the WPC. 'My daughter sent a man to prison for something he didn't do.'

'Take it easy. Let's keep calm here.' Jean Baxter grabbed the high explosive and looked at the fuse. It was flaring. 'You are saying that Susan made her story up. That we spent months investigating, prosecuting and securing this man's detention on a pack of lies? Now does that really seem possible?' She trod on the fizzing end. 'Susan is distressed. Saying many things. Confused and bewildered. Let's look at this in twenty-four hours.' Under water in a bucket. That would do. 'I won't enquire into the injury to Mr. Bennett, but it would appear Susan is perhaps feeling the effects of the court case, and not coping well. I will contact the social services. I'm sure counselling of some type would suppress this anxiety.' There, it was dismantled. Not a bomb after all.

Susan lifted her head. Looked at the policewoman through her stained eyes. If the fuse ever went out then Susan had snatched a flaming torch and was furiously re-igniting it. 'He never did it, bitch! You kept me going. I might have told someone earlier if it hadn't been for you. Mr. Stephens never laid a finger on me. Oh, I wished he had! Oh, I do.' She covered her face with slapping hands. 'But, you didn't get the bastard that fucked up my life did you?' Susan could only shake her head wildly. 'But I did!'

Her mother grabbed her and held on.

Baxter reacted. A last ditch ploy. Mad and desperate. 'Perjury is a very serious crime, Susan. If you have lied then you can be prosecuted. Wasting police time as well. Think again, Susan.' She thrust her sorceress face as if to collide with Susan's and she breathed out fuming air to emphasise the threat.

Susan didn't bother to reply. Linda bared her teeth at the frenetic woman. 'She lied. Why she lied will come out. But for now get the man out. Save him any more suffering. You don't come out of this without egg on your face, do you?'

Bernard Mills summoned Jean Baxter from the room. Stared straight into her face from only a few inches. 'This is fucking serious. I'm not getting any of this shit thrown in my direction. And if it does come flying I'm making sure it won't stick. Get it? Sort it out! Now!' He didn't pull rank often. This was an exception. Justifiably so.

Baxter returned, tail between her legs. 'Right, Susan. Let's have the real story.' It was a complete fuck up. Jean Baxter knew her chances of promotion were in the toilet now.

Mark Stephens didn't know where he was going. Bruce Martin had sent for him. He stumbled over stray timber, tile chippings and other debris as he was pushed in front of two of Martin's sidekicks accompanying him. He had only blurred sight out of the right eye. The left was just a dull ache and a pulpy globe when he felt with his trembling fingers.

'Have a word with these cunts can you, teacher.' Martin was sitting in the only armchair, sucking on a huge joint. 'Can't get 'em to realise that I mean business. Got ten of their fucking screws and still they aren't fucking moving themselves. They know what I want and what I'm prepared to do.' Martin was raving. 'Now I aint waiting no more. I fucking am not! That arsehead Wilkins is on the other end. You tell him that I'm going to give you, and the other fucking shirt-lifters and kid fuckers flying lessons if he doesn't come up with a deal today.' He flung the handset to Mark, who only held on to it because it struck him in the stomach and he was able to clutch at the cord.

'Flying lessons?' Mark enquired through split and swollen

lips.

'Yeah.' Martin looked around at his henchmen. 'You and the other fucking arseholes are going off the plank if need be. But, I forgot to tell you, there aint no fucking water. Only thin, fucking air. Get it? You're skydiving off the roof if they don't pull their finger out.'

Mark found his ear with the cool plastic of the receiver. Wilkins had heard a lot from the loud bawling of Bruce Martin. 'I don't know how much you have understood,' Mark spluttered through his throbbing lips, 'but if I can sum it up succinctly. Mr. Martin is threatening to chuck us off the roof if you don't agree to his demands.' Mark made every effort to sound in control. He hid his fear well.

'Now, Stephens, hold on. Tell him we have the Home Office minister with responsibility for prisons arriving shortly. He'll be the one to make the promises. We can't do anything here. Keep him calm if you can.' Mark could detect the prevarication. Martin wouldn't be fooled.

'Don't try and fob these men off with your clichés and jargon. They can recognise bullshit.'

'That's right! Don't give us no crap Wilkins. Get it fixed!' Bruce Martin snatched the phone from Mark and barked down it at the Deputy Governor. He slammed down the handset and fumed. 'I aint joking. You lot are dispensable. No one's going to cry over you lot snuffing it.'

Mark stood in what he perceived as the centre of the room. It was difficult to focus on the walls, and the people around him were indistinct splotches or distorted shapes. Martin was close to boiling point. It wasn't going to plan. Not that he had thought this part through very well. Mark was too vulnerable there. Unstable and frustrated, Martin could do anything. A quaking sex offender rocking on the spot, already looking like death was as easy to dump as a sack of garbage. The piggy in the middle licked some blood that slid down his cheek from a head gash. He had never been so scared.

'That's great news, Robert. I'm so pleased. In fact I'm ecstatic!' Alison shouted to the world once she had finished hearing that Mark was to be released pending the appeal. She knew that with Justin Hinton's testimony and other pupils from the school, plus Marissa Caldwell's evidence, her husband would be cleared. And if she had been at Wokingham Police Station she would have been witness to the most compelling exoneration of him possible.

There were things to undo. She had put the house on the market when Mark was convicted. Exchange of contracts was imminent. She would pull the plug on that. They could stay. Half the contents of their home were in tea chests and cardboard boxes piled up in all the rooms. She would unpack those before he came home. Clean it spotless. She even thought about some yellow ribbons. But dropped the idea. Keep it low key. A homecoming not a carnival.

'I pestered him at school and I phoned him at his home.' Susan was releasing it all. Gushing from her. A purging. 'Even got him to meet me in Wokingham town centre. He was angry. It hurt when he told me to keep away.'

'Fucking bastards are playing tricks with me. Think they can treat me like a fucking idiot!' Martin thumped the table and got to his feet. 'Who do they think they are dealing with? I mean fucking business.' He strode round the room, circumnavigating Mark. 'I'll show them!' His circles were spiralling towards Mark until he met him face to face. He wasn't such a big man. No taller than the teacher he stood with his nose almost pecking. Martin had a pig face with orange peel skin and the breath of a camel. 'Get him onto the roof!' The stale spit sprayed in a stinging shower. Point blank rage.

Mark was grabbed from behind and led up a rickety ladder. An icy wind cut at his wounds. He could feel the vastness of the sky that he couldn't see. Bundled forms, blanket wrapped, were perched randomly in what was left of the loft.

'A pilot without a plane,' announced the man whose hands shoved Mark along a beam.

'Martin's fucking mad if he does it. We'll all be done for murder.' A huddled form spoke from the eaves.

'You go and tell him then!' The dissenting voice was rebuked by Mark's guide. 'You dickshit. Think you can cross him? He'll stick you out here instead.'

Back into his shelter slid the protester. A tortoise head retracted.

In the crows-nest of a galleon tossed by the Atlantic swell Mark listened to his own loud breathing and the shuffling of nearby heavily-clad rioters. He felt the up-rush of cold air, from the damp tarmac three storeys below. Abandoned four feet from the edge. Only his feet were faintly visible. Feet that he kept perfectly still. The beam his shuffling form had been marooned on was only as wide as his shoes stuck together. He was cold. Never felt the cold normally. So alone. Deserted. And a million miles from Alison and his girls. He cried for them. Gushing rivulets of salt tears that burned his face and ran into his terrified mouth.

'It was just to make them think I wasn't just the ugly duckling at school. They called me Moose. And when the girls were talking about boys. That's what they always talked about. Then I told them. Made it real for me. Never been so popular. Even believed it myself some of the time.' Susan smiled to herself. She remembered what it was like to imagine being in Mark's arms. 'I wouldn't have kept it going if he hadn't gone with that Hooper slag. That's what really bugged me. Made me want to stitch him up. Made me write that letter to him. It was just as disgusting as he said. I don't know what got into me. Didn't know love could turn so easily to hate.' She spread a dirty tear across her face that had stopped and tickled her cheek. 'And then the school started asking questions, and then you came along and made me hate him even more. Kept it on the boil all the time. I might have come clean long ago. I made Pauline lie.

Don't blame her. And then there was what he did to me. My fucking Dad I mean. All the time. Blamed Mr. Stephens for it somehow. Not sure why.'

Baxter cringed. What a bloody mess. She would pass on that investigation to someone else. Not that she could stay in Child Protection any longer.

'Nice out here isn't it?' Bruce Martin stood behind him.

Mark stopped breathing, closed his bloated eyes and made fists with cracked hands. If only it was worth praying. This would be the best test yet.

'Nobody's listening to me, teacher. Nobody cares. And they don't care a toss about you. I've warned 'em. Time and time again. Bruce Martin don't take it kindly when he's ignored.'

Below Mark there was the murmur of people. Way down they were. As if in the belly of a gorge.

'So now we have an audience. Let's see what they think of this demonstration. Treat me like shit would they.'

Mark recognised the low hissing of a Roman crowd when a gladiator was poised to impale an opponent with the trident. His disciples had not believed he would do it. There was only their gasps. It was the last thing he heard.

Raising his scuffed and blood-stained boot to the height of Mark Stephens' lower back, Bruce Martin struck viciously, to send Mark sprawling out beyond the roof. And clutching at the air that refused to support him. Loose clothing opened out in the racing blast as he swam in the gushing stream of his descent.

'Mark Stephens was a good teacher. He never touched me. I lied and I lied and I lied.' Susan Bennett hit the table with her collapsing body, and thrashed with her fists on the hard surface to beat out the demons.

His skull crushed on impact. Blood spurted out and speckled the onlookers. Mark Stephens was a broken egg, curdled yolk remains in a crimson lake. And his puppet limbs lay humorously contorted as if he were mocking his own ridiculous, lifeless body.

Alison sang as she skipped past the boxes of books that had been stripped from Mark's study. An insistent phone was hailing her from her refurnishing chores. She couldn't erase the smile from her face. It was all falling back into place. That which had been torn apart was being magically repaired. Now he was on his way home.

'Hello.' A friendly greeting. It didn't matter who it was. She was splendid. Undaunted.

'Mrs. Stephens? Mrs. Alison Stephens?'

'Yes.' It was the call. Mark was coming home.

'This is Brian Collinson, Governor of Wandsworth Prison.' His stomach tightened and he held his breath.

'Yes?' Alison's cheeks puckered; sucking back a bubbling smile.